'BREA
THE 4ᵗ
DIMENSION'
by
Terry Cavender

(Story One)
'THE MYSTERY OF
LE CHÂTEAU
DE WALINCOURT'
And
(Story Two)
'FIND
THE FÜHRER'S
GOLD!'

Acknowledgements:

This book is dedicated to my beautiful and brave wife Maggie who has always given me her support (above and beyond the call of marriage), daughter Sara and son-in-law Ian and Richard and Renate.

My sincere thanks also go to Nicky and Harry Clacy, Simon Delaney, Michelle Leach, my venerabley friend Major Peter Todd (Foto-Todd), and Professor Elizabeth Howell

3

Also by this <u>Author</u>:

'A Boy From Nowhere'
'Three Tall Tales'
'Three More Tall Tales'
'Even More Tall Tales'
'Another Three Tall Tales'

(Co-authored with Brian (Harry) Clacy)
'Tell It Like It Wasn't (Part 1)'
'Tell It Like It Wasn't (Part 2)'

'BREAKING THE 4TH DIMENSION'

'Two Tales of Time-Travel, Hidden Treasure, Treachery, Royalty and Skullduggery'

CONTENTS

An Introduction to Time-Travel

A very brief history of Royal Visits to
Leconfield, East Yorkshire

The Gem that is Beverley Minster

Paris – 'City of Lights'

Amsterdam – 'City of Diamonds'

'BREAKING THE 4TH DIMENSION'

'An Introduction to Time-Travel'

I'm reliably informed that Time-Travel is the concept of movement between certain points in time, analogous to moving between different points in space by an object or a person, typically using a hypothetical device known as a Time Machine. Time-Travel is a widely-recognized concept in philosophy and fiction. The idea of a Time Machine was made popular by the esteemed author H. G. Wells' in his novel '*The Time Machine.*' At the moment we don't know if Time-Travel to the past, or to the future, is physically possible. The great seer 'Nostradamus' predicted time-travel, so perhaps someone went back to see him and tell him all about it?

'Michel de Nostradamus'

My wife was saying only the other day that, "forward time travel, outside the usual sense of the perception of time, is an extensively-observed phenomenon and well-understood within the framework of special relativity and general relativity. However, making one body advance or delay more than a few milliseconds compared to another body is not feasible with current technology. As for backward Time-Travel, it is possible to find solutions in general relativity that allow for it, but the solutions require conditions that may not be physically possible. Travelling to an arbitrary point in spacetime has very limited support in theoretical physics, and usually only connected with quantum mechanics or wormholes, (also known as Einstein-Rosen bridges) and temporal paradoxes."   All perfectly straightforward then - (I nodded sagely, pretending that I understood what she was on about, then asked her what we were having for dinner on the 3rd of December 2099).

Now, just to assure you that *'I'm down with the kids*," here's my 'Narrative Arc' for:

'BREAKING THE 4TH DIMENSION'

a mixture of 'Fact' and 'Fiction.'

The stories are, essentially, about Time-Travel – (if such a thing really exists). I've often thought about Time-Travel; is it happening now or do we have to wait until a specific moment in time when some genius lurking in a hidden laboratory actually discovers how it's done? So, will it be then, and only then that Time-Travel can begin from that precise point? Or, conversely, are Time-Travellers already lurking amongst us as I write this? I saw a strange looking man with his head wrapped in what looked suspiciously like a tinfoil Beanie hat in Beverley's Wednesday Market last week. Go figure.

One only has to delve into a popular search engine like 'Google' to read the myriad apparently 'Loony Tune' stories that have been lodged there about Time-Travellers, some of them which, admittedly, seem quite feasible.   It would be truly mind-blowing if Time-Travel did exist. Just imagine if, for example, you could hurtle back through time back to the Holy Land and meet Jesus and His Disciples or see all four Beatles performing in their last live concert at the Candlestick Park Stadium in San Francisco - or even better, travel back in time to your childhood when you were surrounded by all of your loved ones. Wouldn't that be lovely!

Hang on though, what would the pitfalls be meeting up with your younger self for example? Could you warn yourself that you were about to have an accident or would that be changing the future – or had you already travelled back in time and warned yourself about an impending disaster? "*Don't get on the aircraft*!" - so you wouldn't be having an accident anyway? Ey up! - a headache coming on - and I haven't given a great deal of thought to travelling forwards in time! Would you really want to know what's waiting for you around the next corner, it might be a bus! Would the National Lottery numbers ever be safe again, would there be lots of skint bookies if you somehow knew the name of the horse that won the 3.30 at Epsom for the following week?

As you can no doubt imagine, there are many complex theories about Time-Travel. For example, here's a couple of quotes from a comprehensive, interesting and informative article written by the Canadian journalist, Professor Elizabeth Howell, from which I paraphrase:

'It is generally understood that traveling forward or back in time would require a device — a time machine. To accomplish this, time machines often are thought to need an exotic form of matter with so-called "negative energy density." Such exotic matter has bizarre properties, including moving in the opposite direction of normal matter when pushed. Such matter could theoretically exist, but if it did, it might be present only in quantities too small for the construction of a time machine.
(Elizabeth Howell)

The complete article written by Elizabeth can be read in the publication ***Space.com*** dated the 14th of November 2017, entitled '*Time Travel: Theories, Paradoxes & Possibilities*).

To be honest, I'm going to have to give that a bit more thought, Elizabeth, (possibly assisted by the consumption of a couple of bottles of Timothy Taylor's 'Bolt Makers' Ale to act as brain relaxant) before I come up with my own solution, which I will then have forgotten come the morn.

'BREAKING THE 4th DIMENSION'

encompasses the use of Time-Travel, so I hope that you enjoy flitting around a couple of historical time-zones with me - (or have you already read this next week)?

Now – please bear with me whilst I do a bit of scene setting:

'A very brief history of Royal Visits to Leconfield, East Yorkshire'

Leconfield is a small but perfectly formed village, situated just three miles outside of the delightfully quaint market town of Beverley, East Yorkshire. Leconfield has been graced by the presence of Royalty on many occasions, starting off, apparently, with Queen Boudica - who is reputed to have been thrashing around the area in her chariot during the 1st Century (thrashing around because the roads were probably in much better condition back then than they are now).

King Henry the Eighth, a legend in his own lunchtime, was a much-revered Monarch (and known as the best-dressed Sovereign of the era) but one who is largely remembered as having been a bit of a mean-machine who oversaw the destruction of religious buildings and works of art and was famously instrumental in having a couple of his wives beheaded. A gruesome 'factoid' - King Henry the Eighth had over 72,000 people executed during his reign.

King Henry also made boiling in oil/tar or acid a legal punishment (that's boiling people – not food). Apparently, his Inquisitors and Henchmen had a great deal of sport lowering victims slowly on ropes towards the containers of boiling liquid and then raising them back up again at the last minute - before eventually lowering them again and immersing them fully in the fearsome liquid - (could that be classed as a suspended sentence)? There were other 'choices' available to those responsible for punishing miscreants – they could be pressed, hanged, drawn and quartered, burned to death, or beheaded. Very civilised people, the Tudors, not.

It is believed that King Henry visited the moated Leconfield Castle several times in 1541, on his many 'Progresses' around England. His Majesty, it would appear, particularly relished the hunting and hawking around Leconfield.

'All that is remains of Leconfield Castle is the Moat'
(which can still be seen surrounding what was
the perimeter of the Castle grounds)
(Foto-Todd)

Someone obviously said something untoward that filtered back to the Royal lug-holes, causing Leconfield to fall into Royal disfavour because, as far as I can ascertain, it wasn't until much later on in time when an RAF base had been constructed there, (cunningly named RAF Leconfield to confuse enemies of the state), that on the 4th of November 1940 the by then substantial air base was graced by the presence of Air Marshal Princess Alice The Duchess of Gloucester.

The Princess liked the place so much that she returned there 38 years later on the 31st of May 1978 to what was then Normandy Barracks, it having been invaded by squaddies and renamed the Army School of Mechanical Transport (ASMT), which in turn became the Defence School of

Transport (DST). Princess Alice was the widow of the late Duke of Gloucester, third son of King George the Fifth and mother to the current Duke of Gloucester, His Royal Highness Prince Richard.

After that, things livened up with further Royal visits to Leconfield, (not all at the same time I hasten to add). There was Her Majesty Queen Elizabeth the Queen Mother who flew in there to see, amongst others, the actress Dawn French (who was living on-site in married quarters with her family, her Dad being an RAF Flight Sergeant), His Royal Highness Prince Charles The Prince of Wales, His Royal Highness Prince Andrew, Her Royal Highness Princess Anne The Princess Royal, Her Majesty The Queen accompanied by His Royal Highness Prince Philip the Duke of Edinburgh on a couple of occasions and last, but not least, the heir to the throne, His Royal Highness Prince William, Duke of Cambridge who, alongside other brave RAF 'Search and Rescue' crews, frequently flew in and out of E Flight 202 Squadron RAF, which was by then tucked away in a purpose built corner of Normandy Barracks, proudly retaining its designation as 'RAF Leconfield,' until, quite disgracefully, being disbanded.

Many's the time in my role as SO2 Media Ops for DST, (you'll need to look that title up), I had occasion to call into E Flight (usually because of my involvement with Royal and other such VIP visits) and stood there in the busy Operations Room would be a tall familiar figure, smiling, chatting and drinking coffee, 'twas the handsome and dashing Prince William, (a special person doing a very special job). Strange place Leconfield. It must, I suppose, have been something in the air. Over the years there has been a lot of 'bowing and scraping' going on there.

'The Gem that is Beverley Minster'

When visiting Beverley, or even driving past there from a distance, one can hardly fail to be impressed by the eye-catching gem that is Beverley Minster. This most impressive and beautiful building has a long and colourful history, starting when it was constructed way back in the 14th Century. There has been a Christian community on the site of Beverley Minster for over 1300 years, the first community being founded by John, Bishop of York – the future Saint John of Beverley. A Norman church was built on the site followed by the present Gothic church. The Minster was reduced to the status of a parish church after 1548 and ceased to be a Roman Catholic church. In its early days, the Minster attracted many hundreds of Pilgrims and much-needed coin of the realm from those who came to view the shrine of Saint John of Beverley. St John's bones were supposedly interred in a Crypt there and were considered by many to work miracles.

One of the local wealthy families, the Percy's, owners of both Leconfield Castle and a large estate at Leconfield, lived just up t'road from Beverley. The Head of the Percy family, the Earl of Alnwick, occupied the castle in the 15th century and was visited there by King Henry the Eighth on several occasions. As well as being loyal monarchists, the Percy's were great supporters of Beverley Minster, generously providing much-needed finance to assist with its maintenance.

On one particular occasion, in 1541, whilst King Henry was en route to Bonny Scotland, to meet up with a few kilted troublemakers, that is when the Beverley segment of this story takes place.

There are many excellent books available for those who wish to 'read in' to the construction, history and ongoing activities at Beverley Minster, a few that I thoroughly recommend to you are:

'Beverley Minster an Illustrated History' - by Rosemary Horrox.
'Who Built Beverley Minster?' - by P S Barnwell and Arnold Pacey.
'Beverley Through Time' - by Patricia Deans and Margaret Sumner.
'Of A Fair Uniforme Making' 'The Building History of Beverley Minster 1188 – 1736' - by John Phillips.

'Paris – City of Light'

Like London, Paris is steeped in history and is definitely a city that you must try to visit at least once during your lifetime. I've been fortunate enough to have been there several times and loved every second of it. I mean, what young lad or ladette hasn't pretended to be one of the 'Three Musketeers? Personally, I always favoured 'Dartagnan' but didn't learn to spell it properly until I was in my early 20's! I'll never forget the excitement of seeing the Eiffel Tower for the very first time, and also the beautiful Notre Dame Cathedral. I spent hours looking for Victor Hugo's character Quasimodo in the Notre Dame. I was convinced that I'd spotted him in the bell tower sat astride a swinging bell and called out his name loudly several times, but he never replied. Then someone pointed out that he wouldn't have been able to hear me as the bells had made him deaf. Moving on.

During the Middle Ages, Paris was the largest city in Europe, it was an important religious and commercial centre and the birthplace of the Gothic style of Architecture. The University of Paris on the Left Bank, founded in the mid-13th century, was one of the first in Europe. Paris suffered from the Bubonic Plague in the 14th century and the Hundred Years War in the 15th century. Between 1418 and 1436, the city was occupied by the Burgundians and English soldiers. In the 16th century, Paris became the book-publishing capital of Europe, though it was shaken by the French Wars of Religion between Catholics and Protestants. Then in the 18th century, it became the centre of the intellectual ferment known as the 'Enlightenment,' and the main stage of the French Revolution from 1789, remembered in France every year on the 14th of July with a military parade.

'Gay Paris,' the capital city of France. Since the 17th century, it has been one of Europe's major centres of finance, commerce, fashion, science, music, and painting. Paris is the second-most expensive city in the world - as you'll know if you've ever bought a bowl of 'French Onion Soup' there. The City of Paris's administrative limits form an East-West oval, centred on the island at its historical heart, the Île de la Cité; this island is near the top of an arc of the river Seine that divides the city into southern Rive Gauche (Left Bank) and northern Rive Droite regions.

Paris is renowned for its museums and Surveyorural landmarks: the Louvre is one of the most visited art museums in the world. The Musée d'Orsay and Musée de l'Orangerie are noted for their collections of French Impressionist art, and the Pompidou Centre Musée National d'Art Moderne has the largest collection of modern and contemporary art in Europe. The historical district along the Seine in the city centre is classified as a UNESCO Heritage Site.

Popular landmarks in the centre of the city include the Cathedral of Notre Dame de Paris and the Gothic Royal Chapel of Sainte-Chapelle, both on the Île de la Cité; the Eiffel Tower, constructed for the Paris Universal Exposition of 1889; the Grand Palais and Petit Palais, built for the Paris Universal Exposition of 1900; the Arc de Triomphe on the Champs-Élysées, and the Basilica of Sacré-Coeur on the hill of Montmartre. All in all, Paris is a city not to be missed out of your travel itinerary and is quite rightly named the 'City of Light.' Again, a segment of the story centres around Paris during the French Revolution era.

'Amsterdam – City of Diamonds'

Amsterdam is the capital of the Netherlands, although conversely, it is not the seat of the government, 'The Hague' is. Amsterdam city is located in the province of North Holland in the west of the country. Originating as a small fishing village in the late 12th century, Amsterdam became one of the most important ports in the world during the Dutch Golden Age (17th century). During that time, the city became the leading centre for finance and diamonds. The commercial capital of the Netherlands and one of the top financial centres in Europe, Amsterdam is also the cultural capital of the Netherlands.

Many large Dutch institutions have their headquarters there, and currently, seven of the world's 500 largest companies are based in the city. The Port of Amsterdam to this day remains the second largest in the country, and the fifth largest seaport in Europe.

Amsterdam's main attractions, including its historic canals, the Rijksmuseum, the Van Gogh Museum, the Stedelijk Museum, Hermitage Amsterdam, the Anne Frank House, the Amsterdam Museum, its popular red-light district, and its many cannabis coffee shops draw more than 5 million international visitors annually, many of them wandering around puffing on wacky-baccy and singing songs like the Beatles 'All you need is love.'

The city is also well known for its nightlife and festival activity; several of its nightclubs are among the world's most famous. It is also one of the world's most multicultural cities, with at least 177 nationalities represented there. Having visited Amsterdam on more than one occasion, I can highly recommend it as not only being the 'City of Diamonds' but the 'City of Mischief.' The excitement there is palpable.

So, there you have it, Paris, Amsterdam, Beverley – and we even pop into Berlin. They're the skeletons upon which the flesh of this story is loosely hung. I have allowed my occasionally febrile imagination to run riot and written a story based around 'Time-Travel' and blended it in with actual historical events, including those leading up to the execution of King Louis the Sixteenth of France in Paris back in 1793, a seemingly nice fellow, but who was in reality an iron hand in a velvet glove sort of chap, and the visit of King Henry the Eighth to Leconfield Castle, East Yorkshire in 1541 and we also pay a visit to the Führer of Germany, Adolf Hitler as he sits in his bunker with the Third Reich crumbling around his ears..

Writing this story has been a bit of a carefully balanced exercise between historical fact and fiction. In doing so, I have exercised a fair degree of 'artistic license.' Thanks for showing an interest in my latest offering and I hope that you enjoy reading:

'BREAKING THE 4ᵗʰ DIMENSION'

as much as I've enjoyed writing it.

My wife Maggie has accused me of being a 'Mouse Potato' i.e. someone who spends far too much time working on the computer, but I'm willing to: 'Risk the name to achieve the aim.' So, without further ado, I'll let you crack on.

"It was a dark and stormy night.

Terry Cavender

STORY ONE

'THE MYSTERY OF LE CHÂTEAU DE WALINCOURT'

CHAPTER 1
Present Time Zone

CHAPTER 2
The Time-Traveller's Store at Kingswood, Kingston-Upon-Hull

CHAPTER 3

The Place De La Revolution, Paris – 1793

CHAPTER 4
After the Execution of
King Louis the Sixteenth of France

CHAPTER 5
A Night in Confinement

CHAPTER 6
The Secret of La Conciergerie

CHAPTER 7
Back in Kingston-Upon-Hull

CHAPTER 8
King Henry the Eighth's
'Yorkshire Progression' - 1541

CHAPTER 9
The Plot Thickens at Leconfield Castle

CHAPTER 10
Ye Sun Inn, Beverley in 1541

CHAPTER 11
Strange happenings
inside Beverley Minster

CHAPTER 12
The Crypt of Saint John of Beverley

CHAPTER 13
Return to the current Time-Zone

CHAPTER 14
A Royal Visit to Beverley Minster

CHAPTER 15
A New Adventure Begins

CHAPTER 16
Return to La Conciergerie, Paris

CHAPTER 17
Le Château De Walincourt

CHAPTER 18
Amsterdam – 'City of Diamonds'

* * * * * *

'THE MYSTERY OF LE CHÂTEAU DE WALINCOURT'

'Background'

Graham St Anier, a retired policeman and resident of Beverley, East Yorkshire, had recently returned from a hair-raising 'Time-Travel' trip to Paris, France during the French Revolution in 1793. Whilst there he had been falsely accused of spying and fallen into the clutches of the evil Citizen Maximilien Robespierre, escaping only by the skin of his teeth.

After returning to the current time-zone from Paris and when things had calmed down a bit, Graham was ferreting around 'The Beverley Old Book Shop' in Dyer Lane, Beverley when he came across an ancient leather-bound tome containing an equally ancient parchment that had been rolled up tightly and secreted away inside the spine of the book. Being an ex-

copper, an intrigued Graham purchased the book and took it home for further investigation.

After carefully extracting the parchment from its hiding place and figuring out its contents, he found, to his utter amazement, that it revealed the story of how the tyrannical King Henry the Eighth, who it was known had visited Leconfield near Beverley several times during 1541 on one of his many 'Progresses.' was instrumental in having something of great value hidden away somewhere inside Beverley Minster during one of those visits.

Precisely what that 'something' was, wasn't made particularly clear in the parchment, but its writer had indicated that something of great value, secreted in a wooden chest, had definitely been hidden inside the Minster. The information whetted both Graham's policeman's instincts and investigative appetite sufficiently enough for him to want to delve deeper.

Intrigued, he decided to travel back in time, once again using the Time-Machine, the "T2 Time-Transporter,' back to medieval Beverley in 1541 to see if could discover where and precisely what had been hidden away in Beverley Minster by the devious King Henry. The plot definitely thickens and takes Graham off into unimagined, dangerous and exciting adventures.

'CHAPTER 1'

'Present Time-Zone'

Graham St Anier stood outside the quaint 'Beverley Old Book Shop' in Dyer Lane. He glanced at his watch, now working properly, the battery recently having been replaced by a charming lady staff member working in the Dickensian looking Prescott's 'Watchmakers and Jewellers' shop, tucked away in a corner of Saturday Market, Beverley for as long as anyone could remember and was comfortingly familiar. An absolute joy to look around there, Graham often spent time chatting with the ever-helpful staff, just looking at and discussing the contents of the twinkling and imaginative displays. Similarly, the 'Beverley Old Book Shop' was another delight not to be missed and Graham also took every opportunity to pop in there, spending as much time as he could just browsing and even making the occasional purchase. He always found it to be an excellent way of disregarding the woes and pressures of the world for a couple of relaxing and interesting hours.

'The Beverley Old Book Shop in Dyer Lane, Beverley'

The sky was grey and guess what, it was raining again, well, it was more of a miserable Yorkshire drizzle actually. Graham yawned and thought, *"Is that all it ever does in Beverley at this time of year, tipple down?"* He pulled the collar of his ancient Gannex raincoat up and peered at what was on offer in the window of the old bookshop. There were all sorts of interesting books cleverly displayed in the window by the shop owner, so as to catch the eye of passers-by and entice them inside and hopefully part with some cash.

Inside the bookshop there was always a large selection of books on multifarious subjects, ranging from dusty, ancient tomes right through to children's colourful annual manuals such as the 'Beano' the 'Dandy' and the 'Eagle' displayed alongside faded, curled up patterns for knitting cardigans and jumpers, and the ever-handy Fanny Craddock Cookery Books offering newly-weds sage guidance on how to prepare exotic dishes for the delectation of visiting Royalty and other lesser mortals. There was always a surfeit of the usual '*When I am old I will wear purple,*' or '*When I am Seventy*' type of books, presumably obtained from relatives of those who had gotten old, worn purple or simply passed over the great divide.

The shelves behind the whirly glassed cob-webby window at the front of the bookshop and the little display table outside its doorway were inevitably jam-packed with enticing and interesting books and colourful curly-eared magazines, some nearly new and others fairly old. "*Might as well have a mooch around here whilst Stephanie's having her nails done. She'll be ages,*" thought Graham. He pushed the creaking shop door open and stepped inside. The old-fashioned bell hanging above the door jangled, doing its job and making enough noise to awaken the dead.

It was lovely and warm inside the cozy little shop; there was always a faint smell of lavender polish hanging in the air there, as if someone had just finished dusting and polishing the old, solid wooden bookshelves. It was all a touch Dickensian. Graham loved popping in there for a good ferret around and, other than the content of the bookshelves and displays, it hardly ever seemed to change. The familiarity of the place was oddly comforting. Graham had discovered many interesting books there and as a true Yorkshireman, he took great delight in knowing that they hadn't cost him an arm and a leg to buy.

The proprietor of 'The Beverley Old Book Shop,' David Brown, a professorial-looking man of indeterminate years, was sat at the desk by the cash register reading one of his books. He looked up at Graham and smiled, "*Ah, as I live and breathe, Mr. St Anier. Morning - nice to see you again!*"

29

Graham smiled, *"Yes, I can't keep out of here, it's one of life's little pleasures."* The 'Keeper of Books' smiled and nodded, *"Well, you've arrived at the right time. I've just taken delivery of a couple of boxes of dusty old tomes that I bought from a clearance sale at a local manor house. The old lass that lived there died, so her son and daughter wanted everything disposed of as soon as possible. Quite sad really. Either the old lady or her dearly departed was an avid reader because there were tons of quality books in the library, most of 'em leather bound."*

Graham said, *"Oh, that's tickled my fancy."* A smiling David continued, *"Anyway, I put in a reasonable bid for them and fortunately it was accepted. I didn't cop for them all, but I did manage to get my sticky mitts on quite a few of them. Cost me an arm and a leg though. It'll take me ages to recoup some brass!"* Graham smiled as David continued, *"I haven't had the opportunity to examine them thoroughly yet, but you're welcome to have a look through them yourself and see if there's anything there that you'd like. They're in boxes in the upstairs room, just to the left of the detective novels. I won't be bringing them downstairs for a few days yet."* Graham nodded and replied, *"OK, thanks David, I'll nip up there and do a bit of 'book surfing' then."*

Graham was panting for breath by the time he reached the top of the steep, curving tiny stairs, *"I'm going to have to give that pork crackling a miss,"* he thought. Over in the far corner of the room were stacked several cardboard boxes, their lids open, revealing a large amount of leather bound books stashed inside. *"Wow, plenty of choices there,"* thought Graham.

He gingerly eased several of them out, assuming that because of their age they'd be quite frail. Much to his delight, they proved to be in extremely good condition, the covers were made of quality leather with finely tooled gold lettering on the front of the books, which was repeated on their spines. Riffling through a couple of them it was quite apparent to Graham that they would have been quite expensive when new. Riffling through one of them he saw several beautifully drawn hand-coloured sketches, mostly depicting hunting scenes, each picture separated by leaves of delicate protective tissue paper, placed there to preserve them from ink seepage off the printed pages. Clearly quality productions, designed to last.

One of the book titles that particularly attracted Graham's attention was:

'𝔄 𝔥istory of 𝔏econfield 𝔠astle'

"*Mmm, that's interesting*," thought Graham, "*I didn't know that there'd been a castle at Leconfield. It's certainly not there now.*" He knew that there was an old RAF Base just outside of the village and that it was now a Ministry of Defence Driving School, but that was all. He walked across to a comfortable padded seat by the bow-window, sat down and started to flick through the pages of the book.

As he was examining the book's contents, he ran his hand down the spine of it and felt a slight bulge towards its centre. Thinking that it might be damaged, he examined it more closely. Closing the book, he held it up to the light, looked along the spine – and saw what looked like a rolled-up piece of parchment tucked away tightly, halfway down. "*Hello, that looks interesting, wonder what it is?*" He heard a wall clock chiming downstairs and looked at his wristwatch; seeing that time was getting short and remembering that he had to collect his wife Stephanie from the Nail Salon, Graham decided to purchase the book and take it home for a more leisurely and thorough examination. He was particularly intrigued by the rolled-up parchment. *"It's probably just an old invoice or a shopping list, but you never know, might be something more interesting. Anyway, I'm having it!"* he thought.

Tidying up the other books back inside the carton, he made his way back downstairs clutching the book containing the hidden parchment. He said to Mr. Brown, *"This one looks interesting, David, I think I'll have it. How much do you want for it?"* Mr. Brown smiled and replied, *"Oh, just give me a tenner. I haven't had a chance to have a proper look at any of the books yet but I'm sure you'll find something of interest in that one."* Graham nodded, *"Once I've had a good read of it, if I do find anything of note, I'll pop back here and let you know. Might even buy some of the others."* Graham paid Mr. Brown the princely sum of £10 before leaving the shop to go and collect his wife Stephanie. She didn't take too kindly to being kept waiting and there was always a chance that she'd do a quick body-swerve into one of the many shoe-shops or dress shops in Beverley, the thought of which made Graham's wallet and stomach constrict.

He couldn't wait to get back home and closely examine his purchase. He'd felt a bit uncomfortable about not telling Mr. Brown of the parchment find, but in all probability, it would come to nothing, so where was the harm? He convinced himself that if the rolled-up document proved to be anything of value or particular interest, he'd return to the bookshop and square things away with Mr. Brown.

Later that evening, after dinner, Graham was sat in his 'man cave' and well away from his wife Stephanie's prying eyes.

Taking his time, he gently and very carefully eased the piece of rolled up parchment along the book's spine, poking at it using the rubber end of a long lead pencil, then completing the operation by using Stephanie's eye-brow tweezers to gently extract it from its hiding place. The parchment had been rolled up tightly and was secured by a small piece of faded red silk ribbon. Graham carefully slid the ribbon along the parchment, freeing it, then gently unrolled it and carefully placed it on his desk, flattening it down with paperweights at each corner.

The title at the head of the document had been written out in beautiful old-fashioned script, it stated:

'Ye Secrete of Saint John's Crypt'

What he then read caused Graham to take a sharp intake of breath and his blood to race. He was excited, *"Wow! I can't believe it,"* he rubbed his hands together and thought, *"I'm definitely having some of this! 'Ye Secret of St john's Crypt.' Mmmm, I've just got to decide if I should tell Mr. Brown about it or not."* He thought for a moment then decided that Mr. Brown would have to wait.

The yellowing parchment had been signed and dated in a spidery but legible, blotchy inky script at the bottom by a Sir Simon Delaney of Molescoft. Graham thought, *"Interesting. I'll have to look his details up on t'internet."* He carefully placed the parchment and silk ribbon inside his desk drawer before locking it. He then picked up the heavy book and opened it. *"Might as well have a leaf through this, seeing as how I coughed up a tenner for it. There might be some more information about Saint John's Crypt in here."* he thought, leafing through the first few pages.

❈ ❈ ❈ ❈ ❈ ❈

'CHAPTER 2'

'The Time-Travellers Store at Kingswood, Kingston-upon-Hull'

Graham was visiting the 'Time-Traveller's' Holiday Store **'T.T.H.S.'** at Kingswood, near Hull where he'd booked an appointment to meet up with the Manager, a cheerful Scotsman, Mike Fraser, so that they could both have a chat about organising Graham's next holiday. Mike smiled and leaned back in his creaky faux leather chair, "*Well Graham, I hope you've recovered from your last hectic adventure in Paris in when was it, er 1793?*" he asked. Graham nodded, "*Oh yes, I was well over that a few days after getting back here. It's amazing what a good bath, a few pints, and some decent scoff can do to restore flagging spirits.*"

Mike smiled, "*Have you had the FLI (French Language Implant) and GLI (Geographic Locator Implant) removed from your larynx?*" Graham smiled, "*Yes, and I didn't feel a thing this time.*" Mike nodded, "*Och, those Implants are wee but they still take a bit of getting used to. We could leave them in situ, but they're very expensive and you'd have to sit there whilst the technicians went through the lengthy and time-consuming process of re-booting them for different languages and time-zone every time you scooted off on holiday. It's easier for us just to remove them and reboot them in slow time.*" Graham, rubbing his throat, nodded in agreement.

"*Anyway,*" continued Mike, "w*hat can we do for you today then – you're nae going back to 'La Conciergerie Prison' in Paris I take it?*" Graham smiled and shook his head, "*Wild horses wouldn't drag me back to that hell-hole, well certainly not during that particular time-zone. I might just pop back there at some stage in this time-zone to have a look around the specific cell where I was held prisoner, just to see what, if anything's changed.*"

Mike laughed, "*You never did say what really happened to you whilst you were back there. I read the PHR (Post Holiday Report) on your holiday file but that just gives the bare bones of it. I'm sure there was much more to it than that.*" Mike sighed and shook his head, "*Ye ken, it's not often we have to mount an ERP (Emergency Rescue Package) to pluck our customers out of a sticky situation and return them back home to safety. Luckily for you, we had a ''T2 Time-Transporter' available that had just returned from the Battle of Trafalgar or you might have had to spend a few more days in the hoosegow. *"

"*Yeah, sorry about all that kerfuffle, things just got a bit out of hand,*" said Graham. Mike grinned, "*No prob, Graham, it's what we at '**T.T.H.S.**' do best. We had to mount an ERP last Christmas when one of our regular Time-Travellers got* *into a spot of difficulty whilst observing 'Custer's Last Stand! The Native American Indians had captured him and were going to remove his scalp until they took his hat off and saw that he was as bald as a badger's bum! We got him out of there by offering Big Chief Sitting Bull and his lads a couple of crates of 'Red Eye' whiskey and some shot glasses. It was a very close call; the tomahawks and skinning knives were being sharpened when the 'T2' de-materialised just outside the Big Chief's teepee! Great cries of 'Manitou!' as we whizzed him away during the confusion."*

"*Yes,*" said Graham, *"well I can't begin to tell you just how relieved I was when your "T2 Time-Transporter" de-materialised in Paris. I honestly thought I'd had my chips that day. A not very amenable git called Citizen Armande Parmentier was coming to take me for an interview, without coffee with a miserable piece of work, a professional torturer called the 'Fang Farrier,' who, amongst other things, was an expert at removing teeth and eyes - 'sans' anaesthetic. He'd already had a good go at my cell-mate."*

Mike smiled, *"I once had a School Dentist just like him, sounds a right charmer It's a good job we got you out when we did then. Under our STG (Safe Teleportation Guarantee) we're duty bound to get you back to this time-zone, no matter what it takes. That's why the travel insurance cover costs you just that little bit extra. We always point out to our Time-Travellers that it's worth the extra expense to take out ERP Travel Insurance."* Graham grinned, *"Well it was worth every penny. I was puzzled though when your rep asked me for my EHIC Travel Document when he arrived in Paris. I didn't have it, my captors did, and I didn't want to hang about there, particularly as the Frogs were snapping at my heels."*

36

Mike nodded and said, *"We just use the EHIC as a quick form of ID. We hide a wee microchip inside it. Actually, we had to make a couple of attempts at coming to get you because of a few technical problems. That's the joy of Time-Travel, if we can't manage to get to you the first time around, we just reschedule, re-set the TSS (Time Sequence Starter) and begin all over again. The only thing we can't change is, unfortunately, death. That's totally out of our hands. Once you've docked your clogs, that's it."* Graham nodded.

Mike continued, *"Having said that, we've only lost two Time-Travellers since we opened five years ago."* *"Oh, what happened to them?"* asked Graham. *"Unfortunately, they went down with the Titanic. Some technical problems between our Cosmic Portal and Quantum Mechanics Entanglement. All terribly sad and it caused a bit of a shit-storm with the authorities, but there was nothing we could do about it. It's so complex working with different dimensions because occasionally they get distorted. It's all to do with energy fields, magnetic fields, and the atmosphere. Our Technical Director, Professor Grant Carney, an absolute wizard with physics, is currently working alongside the Americans right at the very forefront of 'Time-Transporter' development. The Prof was one of the first men involved in breaking the 4th Dimension and helping to conquer the complexities of quantum entanglement, dark energy, time crystals, and wormhole technology. He's just resolved the troublesome technological elements of the cosmic portal, so now we're all good to go with our new, improved 'T3 Time-Transporter.' You've probably read something about it in the newspapers?"*

Graham nodded sagely, not really having much of a clue what Mike was talking about. Mike continued, *"Just between us two, we're hoping to be bringing the 'T3 Time-*

Transporter' into service earlier than we expected. It's been designed to hold a lot more passengers, which means we'll be able to Time-Transport wedding groups and things like that. The Prof's just been ironing out the last few wrinkles relating to the absorption of gamma rays and negative radiation. We think he's got it well cracked now. It's all quite fascinating."

Graham said, *"Well, to be perfectly honest, Mike, I had read about it, but not a lot of it sank in. It's all technobabble to me. I think I understand how we can travel back in time, but I get brain freeze when I try to work out how you can travel forward in time to have a look at something that hasn't happened yet. I mean, I'm not a duck-egg, but I just couldn't get my head around it all."* Mike laughed, *"Let's leave the complexities of it to the Professor and his American Astro-Physicist mates to wrestle with. Anyway, sorry, I've bounced off at a complete tangent. You were going to tell me all about your time in Paris."*

Graham settled back in his chair, took a deep breath and said, *"If you've got fifteen minutes or so to spare I'll give you the full tale."* *"OK, but just hang on a wee sec,"* said Mike, *"and I'll get a couple of mugs of coffee organised. Yours is regular if memory serves?"* An impressed Graham nodded. About ten minutes later when Mike returned, he smiled apologetically, *"Sorry I took so long, there was a humongous queue at the coffee machine. I managed to scrounge a couple of 'Hob Nob' biscuits for us whilst I was waiting."* he said, passing Graham his coffee and biscuits.

Mike heaved himself into his chair then dipped his biscuit into his coffee, quickly munching half a 'Hob Nob' before it fell off and landed in his mug. He tutted, then said, *"Shite, that always happens tae me! I have ruined more shirts than soft Mick. Right Graham, come on then, let's have both barrels.*" Graham took a sip of his coffee, grimaced then said, "*Well, it all started to go pear-shaped shortly after I'd arrived in Paris, back in 1793.*"

'CHAPTER 3'

'The Place de la Rèvolution, Paris - 1793'

It was the 21st of January 1793. The large, smelly and belligerent crowd assembled in the Place de la Rèvolution were waiting for the arrival of King Louis the Sixteenth. They weren't there to pay their respects. The King had been condemned to death by the National Convention and the 21st was the fateful day that their sentence would be carried out. No-one had really believed that King Louis would be executed, after all - who would dare to execute a King? Surely, the citizen's had thought, he would just be reprieved and banished from the realm? No, it had been confirmed that the King's head was to be parted from his shoulders and the date had been set. There would be no going back.

The jostling, grumbling crowd waiting impatiently in the very heart of Paris, quietening down as the humble little tumbril carrying the King, surrounded by an unenthusiastic and totally disinterested mounted escort, made its way slowly through the mob, trundling to a halt at the foot of the scaffold, on which stood the blood-stained Guillotine. A fearful sight guaranteed to turn its victim's bowels ice.

The crowd fell deathly silent until suddenly a wag shouted, "*Make way for the King! He's come for a short back and sides!*" which led to uproarious and mocking laughter. Stood in the rear of the tumbril, King Louis the Sixteenth, gazed sadly at the faces of the baying crowd, To Louis, this was all like a very bad dream. He let his sad eyes sweep once more across the heads of those that had come to witness his execution. A lone female voice from the back of the huge crowd called out "*Vive le Roi!*" The King smiled and nodded in the direction of the friendly voice. At least he had one loyal supporter in the hostile mob. Louis sighed and thought, "*And after all I have done for these ingrates.*"

The King was putting on a brave face, but when he covertly glanced across at the scaffold and saw the Guillotine at its centre and the Public Executioner, Charles-Henri Sanson, with his two gormless looking assistants peering down at him, it was all he could do to stop his legs from shaking. He thought, "*Surely this is some terrible nightmare from which I will soon awaken?*" but in his heart of hearts, he knew that it wasn't a nightmare, it was for real. He could not, would not escape this horror by the simple expediency of wakening himself up.

A reedy voice called out from the crowd, "*Huh, look at the state of 'im, fellow Citizens! He's not in the least like 'is fancy portraits. Look at the size of his conk!*" everyone laughed and jeered. The King arched an eyebrow, thinking, "*That hare-brained dullard would not have had the temerity to even think that, never mind express it, but a few months ago.*"

41

'King Louis the Sixteenth of France'
(Guillotined on the 21ˢᵗ of January 1793)

The soldier in charge of the mounted escort urged the King to step down from his 'carriage.' *"Come along, Citizen, make haste!"* he ordered, adding cruelly, *"We haven't got all day! Well, you haven't anyway!"* Louis couldn't believe the indignity of being expected to struggle down from the back of the rough old tumbril without being offered any assistance. *"I have fallen amongst thieves."* he thought. The unkempt tumbril, stinking of horse manure and death, had obviously originally been used on a farm but had then been commandeered by the authorities to transport hundreds of despised Aristocrats and their families on their final journey to the Guillotine. Lesser beings were made to walk.

The King had known many of the Guillotine's victims, plenty of whom had been courtiers, friends, and some of them close confidants. He considered it to be truly shocking and unbearable, that all of those innocent men, women, and children had been so cruelly and unnecessarily put to death purely because of their social position in French society.

***'Aristocrats arriving in a Tumbril at
the Place de la Révolution'***

The manky old straw on the floor of the tumbril was sticky with large gobbets of congealed blood, left there from its continued use assisting with the transportation and the disposal of the remains of previous victims of Madame Guillotine. *"How disrespectful and demeaning."* thought the King, *"They could at least have done me the courtesy of providing me with fresh straw for my final journey. I am, was, their King."* He turned to the driver of the tumbril and in a firm and confident voice said, *"Monsieur, I presume that we have arrived at our final destination?"* The driver nodded, *"Aye, indeed you have, Citizen."* Louis' voice softened, *"Merci Monsieur. I have greatly enjoyed travelling in your tumbril."* The King looked up at the sky, *" Bracing weather for this time of year, n-est-ce pas?"* The Driver nodded, impressed by the King's display of courage in adversity. Jumping unsteadily down from the old tumbril, with as much dignity as he could muster, Louis waved away the soldier escorts who had finally stepped forward to assist him. Someone wag in the crowd shouted, *"Here Louis, give us yer fancy shoes mate, you won't be needing 'em where you're going!"* The crowd laughed and jeered again. Louis just smiled.

As Louis stood by the rear of the tumbril, one of the guards, clutching a short length of rope, moved behind him and made to tie his hands behind his back, whilst the other two none too gently pinioned the King's arms to his side. Louis attempted to shrug them away, *"Monsieur's, how ridiculous is this!"* said Louis, *"Do you really expect me to run away?"* struggling with them as he tried to free his hands. It was no good, they held him firmly, *"Non!"* he cried, *" I shall never consent to this indignity. Do whatever else you have been ordered to do, but you shall not bind me!"* *"Oh, we'll see about that, Citizen!"* replied one of the soldiers as he gripped the King's hands and bound them tightly together, the length of rough hemp biting fiercely into his wrists and making him wince with pain.

The soldier said, *"Listen mate, we've 'ad strict orders to bind your 'ands, so stop being difficult and don't let's be having any more nonsense from you. Your sort's not giving the orders anymore - we are!"* he gloated, leering and thrilled that he was able to address his King in such a derogatory fashion and without fear of retribution. *"So, you would bind me like some common criminal, eh?"* said Louis. *"Yes, that's right, mate,"* said the soldier, *"I just explained why! Anyway, we don't want your clean little hands getting in the way when that sharp blade comes sliding down the well-greased tracks of the Guillotine to meet up with your neck, do we, eh, Citizen Capet?"* then sniggered. The King had been stripped of all his titles and renamed 'Citizen Louis Capet' by order of the Revolutionary Committee.

Another of the other guards turned towards the King's tormentor and said, "*Oy Marcel, let's have a bit more respect, eh! No matter what this man's said and done, he's about to meet 'is Maker, so there's no need to make things any worse for him, is there! Let's just get the job done, eh!*" The Guard, Marcel Camargue, had the good grace to look embarrassed. "*I was just doing my job,*" he said. The guard who had spoken up for the King said quietly, "*My apologies, Sire, he's as thick as two short planks. We've had our orders and you have my word that we'll be as quick as we can.*" The King smiled at him and nodded graciously, "*Merci, Monsieur.*"

His tormentor, the oafish and now sulking Marcel, continued to bind Louis wrists, ensuring that the rope was pulled as tight as he could make it, taking great delight when the King winced as the skin on his wrists was nipped. Marcel grinned, "*There we are 'Citizen Capet, job's done. Now, if you'd do us the honour of making your way over to the scaffold, I would be most grateful. Sorry that there isn't a red carpet, Citizen Capet.*" he said, bowing mockingly, and then forcefully nudged the King towards the bottom step of the scaffold.

As he walked towards the scaffold steps, Louis paused momentarily and glanced up at the dreaded Guillotine, an infernal machine that had been painted, somewhat ironically, a dull blood red, its gleaming sharpened blade perched on top of the cross-beam like an impatient vulture eagerly awaiting its next victim. A rough old blood-stained basket had been placed at the base of the Guillotine, waiting to catch the heads of victims. Louis' mouth had gone dry and his tongue was sticking to the roof of his mouth. No matter what happened though, he was determined to get through the next few minutes with as much dignity as he could muster.

Louis placed his foot on the first step of the scaffold and as he did so, a stunned silence descended over the crowd. They could hardly believe that this man who had previously been their King, King Louis the Sixteenth of France, after all the talk, rumours and tittle-tattle, was about to be decapitated. The sheer finality of it all shocked even them. Louis took his time, gracefully ascending the steps, not wanting to stumble. As he reached the top, he paused and gazed across at the group of 'persons of consequence,' stood in a half circle at the side of the Guillotine, positioned there to act as witnesses to this gruesome, monumentally historic event.

At their fore was a white-faced Irish-born Priest, Father Henry Essex Edgeworth, whom Louis had asked to be present. As he walked towards the Guillotine, the King paused momentarily at the Priest's side, nodded and smiled at him. The Priest bowed his trembling head, "*Sir*e," said an emotional and tearful Edgeworth, "*I see in this last outrage only one more resemblance between Your Majesty and the God who is about to be your recompense.*"

As the Priest was speaking to Louis, a uniformed soldier stepped out from behind the group, rudely elbowing the Priest out of the way, saying to the King, "*Right, brace yourself, Citizen Capet!*" before spinning the King around and unceremoniously grabbing a handful of the Kings hair at the back of his head and then sawed at it with a knife in such an over-enthusiastic manner that in a very short time he had lopped off a great chunk, ensuring that the King's neck was now completely exposed for a clean cut of the Guillotine's blade. The crowd gave a collective gasp. "*Bloody hell, they're actually going to do it!*" someone shouted. Louis smiled gently at the soldier, saying, "*If I might be permitted to say, Monsieur, may I respectfully remind you that you are not trimming the mane of a horse. Your hairdressing technique leaves much to be desired."*

The soldier, Etienne d'Avron, normally such an insensitive dullard, had the good grace to look embarrassed before sniffing dismissively then hurriedly stuffing the large wad of the King's hair into his pocket. Etienne knew that there were those in Paris who would pay good money for a lock of the King's hair. Now that Etienne had completed his allocated task, the Public Executioner, Charles-Henri Sanson, nodded at him and then waved his hand imperiously towards the scaffold steps. Etienne, taking the hint, hurried across to and down the steps then scuttled off through the crowd, his small part in the unfolding tragic, historic events overed with. As he elbowed and shoved his way through the crowd, he was thinking to himself, *"If I could get my hands on some of Queen Marie-Antoinette's hair then there's really good money to be made. I'll have to make sure that I'm on duty when she's brought here."*

Whilst all the execution preparations, procedures, and pantomimery were taking place on the scaffold, stood at the back of the crowd, within sight of the Guillotine, was Time-Traveller, Graham St Anier, watching the proceedings with a sense of trepidation and awe. He'd been looking forward to his Time-Travel holiday for ages, but now that he'd travelled back in time to Paris in January 1793 he wasn't really sure that he'd made the right decision to come and witness this gruesome execution. This was no Madame Tussaud's exhibition, it was the real thing.

When originally planning his holiday, he'd been offered the only two remaining Time-Travel vacancies left available. He could also have witnessed the trial and execution of Marie Antoinette later on that year in October 1793 but thought that

that would be a beheading too far, so decided to visit Paris and witness the effects of the Revolution instead, which included the opportunity for him to watch the execution of King Louis the Sixteenth. Yes, he'd thought, it would be gruesome but it had happened, so he might as well have a look whilst he was there. After all, "*It's not real, it's already happened.*" was how Graham justified it to himself.

The huge crowd that only a few moments before had been howling for the King's blood had fallen silent when he'd arrived in the rear of the small, insignificant tumbril and were watching the proceedings with great interest. They were kept back from the scaffold by the military. "*I'll watch what happens next then make my way back to the Pension Sainte Marie,*" thought Graham. He was beginning to feel a bit uncomfortable, surrounded by the bloodthirsty and belligerent French mob, but it had been his choice to travel to Paris and witness these events, so he might as well get his money's worth. After all, he couldn't alter the course of events, it was strictly forbidden for Time-Travellers to interfere in any way, they weren't even supposed to swat flies. Notwithstanding that, 'La Belle France' was definitely off Graham's bucket list for any future Time-Travel holidays.

The King, with great serenity, was obviously determined to meet his Maker in as dignified a manner as possible and would not to allow his former subjects see that he was afraid, which in truth he was. In the background, a squad of 15 to 20 military drummers tapped away persistently and dramatically on their side-drums. Tap, tap, tap, like the second hand of some nightmarish clock. Up on the scaffold, the King glanced across at the lead drummer and gave him a slight nod. The man turned, held his hand up and ordered his companions to stop tapping on their drums. As one, the drums fell silent.

The King gazed around the crowd, took a deep breath then began to address them, in a clear, authoritative voice, saying, "*I forgive those who are guilty of my death, and I pray God that the blood which you are about to shed may never be required of France. I only sanctioned upon compulsion the Civil Constitution of the Clergy.*" As Louis tried to continue, an officer with a drawn sword, bustled his way forward through the drummers and bellowed at them to continue beating their drums - so as to drown out anything else that the King had to say. The last thing that those in positions of authority wanted was for the mob to be swayed by the King's hypnotising rhetoric, causing them to change their minds and call for Louis to be reprieved.

'Play On – Mes Amis!'

Had they chosen to do so, nothing could have stopped the crowd from surging forward and rescuing the King, there were just too many of them. Much to the officer's relief, that didn't appear to be even a remote possibility. The drummers resumed their relentless and mesmerising tapping. Realising that he had been deliberately silenced, a defeated Louis gave up trying to communicate with the crowd. He knew that for him, it was the bitter end.

The Public Executioner, Sanson, loving every moment of this high theatre, stepped forward and glancing up dramatically towards the release mechanism of the Guillotine, nodded smugly to his two assistants, indicating that he was satisfied that all was in readiness for the execution to begin. Sanson, a sallow-faced and miserable individual was not known for his sense of humour, although it was rumoured that one day when some Marquis or other was seconds away from being beheaded, a messenger clambered up onto the scaffold, shouting and waving a rolled up parchment, probably a reprieve. Sanson had sneered and pointed towards the basket that would shortly receive the victims severed head, saying, "*Place the communication in there, Monsieur, he can read it later!*" then proceeded to release the Guillotine's blade to chop the victim's head off.

Louis recognised that his time had finally come. Sanson and his two eager assistants guided the King over to the bloodstained planking, (called the Bascale), at the base of the Guillotine. The old bloodstains around the base of the Guillotine had been sprinkled with sand and sawdust, but even that was lumpy with coagulated blood and needed changing. There had quite obviously been several other executions either that or the previous day. The blood-stained basket, waiting to receive his head, was placed just beneath where the Guillotine's blade would finish its terrible journey.

The King turned to Sanson and said, "*Ah, Monsieur Sanson, how thoughtful of you - there is even a place carved into this rough planking so that I can rest my chin there comfortably. Merci.*" Sanson shook his head, "*You are mistaken, Citizen.*

That niche is for your forehead to rest upon, not your chin. A mere technicality, but let me assure you that the end result will be the same."

An unusually twitchy Sanson, the grey sweat now clinging to his face like a second skin, arrogantly waved towards the bed of rough planks on the Guillotine, indicating that the King should lay himself upon them, instructing him to "*Lay face downwards, if you please, Citizen Louis Capet,*" using the King's 'new' name and then added, voice dripping with sarcasm, "*Make yourself comfortable, Citizen, this will take but a moment.*" His bound hands causing him some difficulty, the King eventually managed to position himself on the planks with as much dignity as he could until finally, he lay face down, his forehead on the wooden support. None too gently pulling the King's collar back, Sanson made sure that the King's neck was fully exposed. "*So, my time has finally come. There is to be no reprieve.*" thought Louis and began muttering a prayer.

The drummers, overcome by the moment, had faltered and their instruments were now silent. Not a sound came from the crowd who were now watching the proceedings with undisguised awe. The two Executioners Assistants stood at each side of the King, holding his arms tightly so that he was unable to move, then Sanson reached out and gripped the rope that would release the Guillotine's blade, saying, "*Citizen Louis Capet, you are to be executed for crimes against the people!*"

There was a collective intake of breath as, with a flourish, Sanson tugged on the rope, attached to the spring release mechanism, freeing the sharp, heavy 45 degrees angled blade which then began to slide noisily down the heavily greased and tallowed metal-lined grooves of the upright stanchions. Time stood still and the heavy blade seemed to take forever, sliding in apparent slow-motion down towards the Kings exposed neck. Louis tensed as he heard the ominous rumbling noise made by the heavy blade as it slid down the Guillotine's runnels towards his neck. He just had sufficient time left to think, "*I wonder if…*" before the blade slammed into his neck but, horror of horrors, it failed to completely decapitate him, leaving his head dangling obscenely, hanging on by a large piece of flesh. The crowd gasped with shock at the horrendous spectacle.

The mortally wounded King gave a blood-curdling scream, then gasped with shock and his body trembled. Executioner Sanson shouted to Cléry, one of his gormless assistants, "*His head has not fallen at the first stroke, his neck is too fat!*" Someone in the crowd screamed out, "*Merde, what senseless cruelty is this! Sanson, you are a useless, inefficient shite-hawk!*" Someone else called out, *"Huh, what a dèbâcle - it should be the imbecile Sanson whose head is on the block, not the Kings!*"

The heavy blade, dripping with royal blood and gore was quickly drawn back to the top of the Guillotine by the now panicky assistant, Cléry, who quickly released it, once again sending it hurtling down the runnels of the Guillotine, this time to do its job properly. With a sickening thud, it finally severed the King's head from his body, which fell into the waiting basket. There was a stunned silence, then came a half-hearted, unenthusiastic cheer from the crowd. The executioner's assistant, Cléry, stepped forward, lifted the gruesome severed head out of the basket by its hair then walked around the scaffold, displaying it to the crowd, dripping blood everywhere. The King's lips were still moving but uttered no sound. Cléry then carelessly threw it between the Kings stilled legs, mumbling *"There you are Citizen Capet, you can kiss your own arse for a change!"*

'Madame Guillotine'
(Place de la Rèvolution, Central Paris, now the Place de la Concorde)

The crowd remained silent, shocked by the enormity of what had just occurred. Unbelievably, the King had been 'topped.' The unenforced silence was quite spooky and you could quite literally have heard a pin drop. The only sound was of coughing, sniffing and feet being shuffled. Then suddenly, breaking the spell, there came a cry from a grinning, blood-spattered, toothless old harridan who had been stood gawping near the foot of the scaffold, *"Le Roi est Mort! Vive le France! Vive le France!"* she cackled and then did a silly little jig.

Encouraged by the old woman, the crowd then began to shout *"Vive la Nation!"* *"Vive la Republique Française!"* throwing their hats into the air, waving their arms and cheering to celebrate the death of the despised King Louis the Sixteenth. They were finally free of him. Many of them rushed forward, roughly shoving the soldiers to one side, in order to dip their grubby handkerchiefs and pieces of paper into the copious amounts of glutinous royal blood that had gushed onto the floor of the scaffold. The citizens wanted a souvenir of the occasion – and who knew, there might be some money to be made from selling souvenirs of the gruesome spillage?

The two Public Executioner's assistants hurriedly lifted the King's decapitated body off the Bascale, then in a most undignified manner bundled it into the roughly constructed container placed at the side of the Guillotine. The King's head fell off the Bascale and onto the rough wooden floor, rolling to a halt at the feet of the mortified witnesses. Cléry, the one who had been displaying the King's head to the crowd, picked it up off the floor and disrespectfully threw it into the wooden container on top of the King's body, before slamming the lid shut and then wiping his bloodied hands on his already stained pantaloons.

So, that was it then, after all the fuss and drama, the dirty deed had been done. An ignominious end for the King of France. Meat in a butchers shop would have received better treatment on the block than he had. Before being hustled off the scaffold, the priest crossed over to the wooden box containing the King's remains, made the sign of the cross and gave the King a final blessing. Assistant Executioner Cléry, elbowed his colleague in the ribs, "*That blessing won't do 'is Royal Majesty any good, not where he's gone,*" he snickered, before receiving a sound smack on the back of his head from Sanson, "*Get on with your duties, you ignorant oaf!*" ordered Sanson, "*Can you not see that there are many more 'customers' arriving by the tumbril load!*"

The two assistants dragged the box containing the King's remains noisily across the floor of the scaffold then bounced it down the steps before swinging it, as the crowd encouraged them by shouting, "*Un, Deux, Trois!*" and heaving it unceremoniously onto the back of the little tumbril. Some of the more belligerent members of the crowd pushed forward towards the side of the tumbril then spat spitefully on the lid of the makeshift coffin and cursed the King. *"Bon Voyage, Louis!"* *"Rot in hell, you swine!"* *"We can eat as much cake as we like now!"* they jeered. The container was secured in place with rope, then the tumbril trundled slowly off through the crowd, accompanied by its small military escort.

Arrangements had been made for Louis' body to be hauled off to the nearby cemetery at the Church of the Madeleine, where it would be hurtled unceremoniously into a large pit and then covered in quick-lime, joining the many others there who had suffered a similar fate. The precise location of the King's remains would be unmarked, the authorities not wanting a focal point for those Royalists that remained to grieve, plot and scheme.

The man driving the tumbril, Jean Wilés, took a hefty swig from the bottle of cheap rough wine tucked in a bag at his side, belched, sniffed, wiped his nose on the back of his shiny sleeve and thought, *"Think it's time to change the straw, this bloody tumbril's starting to whiff and it's full of accursed horse-flies!"* then he had another thought, *"Once I get away from this mob I'm going to have a quick look in that box. There might be something of value that I can have from off the body, maybe a ring or something. These Aristo's, they all try and hide precious jewels in their vestments and Louis won't be any different. If there is something tucked away there, I might as well have it. He won't be needing any of it."* Jean grinned as he tapped the rump of the old nag pulling the tumbril with the end of his whip, *"Every cloud has a silver lining. Gee up, Bonaparte!"* and started whistling as his horse clip-clopped slowly through the jeering, spitting throng.

A similar gruesome fate awaited the King's wife, Queen Marie Antoinette, and many of her Aristocratic cohorts, but it was her destiny to remain incarcerated inside the Conciergerie Prison in central Paris for many more months until the 16th of October that same year, before keeping her own appointment with Madame Guillotine, after which she would then join her dearly departed husband, Louis, in the pit at the Church of the Madeleine.

'Queen Marie Antoinette of France'

Preparing for her execution, the Queen had put on a plain white dress, her hair was shorn, her hands bound painfully behind her back and, in addition, she was put on a rope leash. There was to be no escape. Like Louis, she was placed in an open tumbril for the hour it took to convey her to the Guillotine sited in the Place de la Révolution. Those of lesser importance were conveyed to other Guillotines at the Place St Antoine or Barriere Rauverse.

Marie Antoinette was guillotined at precisely 12:15 p.m. on the 16th of October 1793. Her last words were, *"Pardon me, sir, I meant not to do it."* to Citizen Sanson, the State Executioner, whose foot she had accidentally trodden on after climbing the steps up onto the scaffold. After being Guillotined, like her husband King Louis, her remains were transported to the Madelaine Cemetery where they were then hurtled unceremoniously into an unmarked grave near that of her husband.

'The Guillotining of Queen-Marie Antoinette of France'
'At the Place de la Revolution on the 16th of October 1793'

Both Marie Antoinette's and Louis the Sixteenth's bodies were exhumed on the 18th of January 1815, during the Bourbon Restoration, when the Comte de Provence ascended the newly re-established throne as Louis the Eighteenth, King of France and of Navarre. Louis the Seventeenth, born Louis-Charles, was the younger son of King Louis the Sixteenth of France and Queen Marie Antoinette. Since France was by then a Republic, until his death from illness in 1795 at the age of 10, Louis the Seventeenth never actually governed.

The Christian burial of the exhumed royal remains was carried out three days later, on the 21st of January 1815, in the Necropolis of French Kings at the Basilica of St Denis.

'CHAPTER 4'

'After the Execution of King Louis the Sixteenth of France'

"*My God,*" thought Graham, his face strained and tense, as he trudged through the maze of rubbish strewn alleyways and slippery cobbled streets of Paris, his mind whirring at the appalling scene he'd just witnessed, "*how gruesome was that. There's a lot to be said for the introduction of Community Service! I'd better get back to the Pension Sainte Marie as fast as I can, I've got an appointment with the 'T2 Time-Transporter' and I definitely don't want to miss that. It's high time I got back home.*" He pushed his way through the swelling crowds, making his way back to the Pension Sainte Marie where he'd taken rooms for the duration of his stay in Paris. Although relatively busy, the streets were much quieter than normal, the majority of the population, like him, having gone to witness the King's execution, many of them remaining at the Place de la Revolution to continue watching and jeering at the seemingly never-ending line of fearful

Aristocrats being carted there for execution. It was a new form of entertainment that cost them nothing.

When Graham eventually arrived at the Pension Sainte Marie, he twisted the heavy metal door handle, pushing the creaking door open, then stepped inside. As he waited for his eyes to adjust to the Pension's gloomy interior, the door was slammed shut behind him. Before he knew what was happening, several rough hands had grabbed hold of him, pinioning his arms to his sides and holding him so forcefully that he was unable to move. *"That's him, Citizen Captain!"* cried a voice, *"The little rat's been behaving suspiciously since he arrived here!"*

Graham recognised the voice as being that of the bellicose Innkeeper of the Pension Sainte Marie, a shabbily dressed, grubby and totally uncouth, Citizen Martin Lalouche.

'Citizen Martin Lalouche'
'Proprietor of the Pension Sainte Marie, Paris'

Lalouche turned and, with a show of hand-wringing respect, addressed Citizen Captain Armande Parmentier, to whom he'd sent a message earlier that day asking him to come and investigate Graham's activities. *"He's a bloody English spy*

I tell you, Citizen Captain! My daughter, Josephine, discovered several important looking documents hidden under the bed in his room. I can't read what they says 'cos they's written in English, but Josephine took them to the Priest and got the gist of their contents from him." Parmentier nodded, *"And the Priests name?"* he asked. *"Father Moulin. He confirmed that they're written in English. Here Citizen Captain, have a look at them!"*

Lalouche passed the documents over to the self-important Citizen Captain Armande Parmentier, who scrutinised them carefully. Parmentier may have been considered a blundering idiot by many, but he was, nevertheless, very dangerous and had connections at the highest levels. He had to be treated with great respect.

'Citizen Captain Armande Parmentier'
'Captain of the Citizens Guard, Central Paris'

After examining the documents for a few moments Parmentier held up a small white card, *"Very interesting,"* he said pompously, *"I can read a little English but cannot understand this, anyway I do not have my pince-nez with me."* Parmentier was lying through his teeth in order to cover

61

up for his intellectual shortcomings. His parents had been too poor to send him to school, so he was barely able to read and often bluffed his way out of difficult situations when required to read official documents and notices.

He turned to Josephine and said, *"Mademoiselle Josephine, read this card for me, if you will, and tell me what this writing says."* Josephine curtseyed. "*Certainly, Citizen Captain.*" Parmentier smiled at her in what he considered to be a winsome manner but in fact oozed with lechery, *"Now, now, there is no need for any of that sort of subservience anymore, Mademoiselle, we are all equals here."* "*Huh,*" thought Josephine, *"some more than others, you greasy swine."* Parmentier continued, *"Just tell me what is written on this piece of card if you please."*

Josephine was nervous and very afraid of Parmentier. He made her skin crawl but she did her best not to show it, *"To be honest, I could not understand what was written on the papers, Citizen Captain, but I thought that they might be important so, as Papa said, I took them all to the Priest, Father Moulin. and he explained their contents to me."* She pointed to the white card, *"This strange little document, Citizen, is called an E.H.I.C."* Parmentier shrugged, *"An E.H.I.C. you say. Mmmm, what is an E.H.I.C?"* Josephine continued, *"It's something called a European Health Insurance Card."* Parmentier nodded sagely, *"Hmmm! It is more than likely some sort of English coded document."* He sniffed, *"Huh, E.H.I.C. indeed. The Englishman must think that we are idiots."*

He addressed the men holding Graham, *" What say we clap some manacles on the 'Roast Beef,' my lads! Then we'll escort him to La Conciergerie where a certain acquaintance of mine, who is most adept at extracting information from the unwilling, can have a little chat with him about these papers and perhaps persuade him to explain precisely what he is up to whilst here in Paris"* He looked at Graham and said, silkily, *"You may have heard of my venerable friend, Monsieur Pontonier?"* at the mention of the torturer Pontonier's name there was a sharp intake of breath from those stood in the Pension. Graham shook his head. Parmentier continued, *"Ah, then it will be a treat for you to meet him, English. Monsieur Pontonier has his hands full at the moment, so you will have to wait in a cell alongside one of the disgusting Aristos. You can cool your heels and ponder on the delights that await you."* Everyone laughed, dutifully. The mere mention of the torturer Monsieur Pontonier filled them with spine-tingling dread. He was the stuff of nightmares.

A confused and now fearful Graham asked, *"Gentlemen, may I ask just what is going on here? This is all a misunderstanding, I'm not a spy, I'm an innocent English traveller…"* as he was trying to explain, he was struck a heavy, glancing blow on the side of his head, causing him to gasp and sink down onto the floor, dazed. Rubbing his clenched, meaty fist, the deliverer of the blow, Citizen Captain Parmentier, said, *"Mmmm, that was most satisfying."* He turned to his men and said, *"Mes Amis, pick that son of a prostitute up from off the floor and take him outside to the tumbril. Tie his hands to the back of it. He can walk to the prison. Make sure that he does not escape, or make no bones about it, you will be the ones answering to Citizen Robespierre, not I!"*

Citizen Captain Parmentier, a lout, and bully of the first order grinned wolfishly, displaying what remained of his few remaining yellowing, rotten teeth, looked down and said to Graham, who was sprawled on the floor, *"Gentlemen indeed!*

Haha – let me assure you, English, we are no gentlemen, as you are soon to discover!" Graham visibly blanched as he got a full blast of Parmentier's rancid, garlic-ridden breath full in his face, "*Phew*" he thought, rather irrationally considering his current dire circumstances, "*Dog's breath! He needs to get some of those cavities sorted.*" Parmentier ordered, "*Get the handcuffs on the spy's hands and then rope him to the tumbril,*" waving dismissively.

Graham was not given the opportunity to get back onto his feet, instead, he was dragged by his heels through the straw-covered floor towards the door of the Pension, his head bouncing painfully along the flagged floor. As he was dragged past the Innkeeper Lalouche, Lalouche stepped forward and kicked Graham savagely in the stomach, making him gasp out loud and double up with pain. Parmentier laughed and said, "*Ah, my dear English, there is plenty more like that waiting for you where you are going!*"

Parmentier then turned to the servile, Lalouche, saying, "*You have done remarkably well today, Lalouche. Citizen Robespierre will be informed of your loyalty to the cause and your initiative in helping us apprehend this English spy. Now, this has been very thirsty work, so perhaps a complimentary drink might be in order, eh?*" A preening Lalouche nodded, "*Of course, Citizen, your wish is my command!*" He turned to his daughter and clicked his fingers, "*Come on girl, don't stand there looking gormless, stir your bones! - fetch the Citizen Captain some wine*" then whispered to her, "*The good stuff, not the usual shite that we dish out to the guests!*" Parmentier smiled, "*I would imagine that this has been one of your more successful days, Lalouche! It is not every day that a foreign spy is apprehended. Let me assure you that we will all benefit from this.*"

The repulsive Lalouche nearly swooned with pleasure. "*I was only doing my duty, Citizen Captain,*" he said, wringing his hands, then, ever the opportunist, enquired, "*Er, just as a matter of interest, Citizen Captain Parmentier, do you think that, er, there might some sort of a reward for the English spy's capture?*" Glaring at the Innkeeper through rheumy eyes, Citizen Parmentier stepped towards a fearful Lalouche, causing him to slither backward, then replied, "*Citizen Lalouche, you and your daughter, the pretty little Josephine, have done your duty admirably and in so doing have served France well by capturing an enemy of the Republic. That alone should be sufficient reward for you. Now, be about your business!*" Lalouche smiled ingratiatingly, "*Just thought I'd ask, Citizen. You never know,*" then gave a low bow.

Lalouche knew full well that Parmentier considered himself to be 'Le Grand Fromage' (*The Big Cheese*) around this neck of the 'arrondissement' and was definitely not a man to fall out of favour with. His reputation for being an overbearing, bad-tempered and brutal man preceded him. What Martin Lalouche didn't know was that a very substantial reward was paid out by the authorities for the capture of spies, but on this occasion, the reward would be nestling safely in Parmentier's purse before the day was out.

Josephine poured the Captain a large glass of rich, ruby red wine and passed it to her father, who polished the rim of the glass with his apron then passed it to Parmentier. Josephine said, "*Pardonez-moi, Papa. Am I given to understand that the English spy will not be returning here?*" Lalouche replied, "*I doubt that very much, my dear.*" Josephine continued, "*Should I, therefore, remove his things from his accommodation and prepare it for the next occupant?*" Lalouche shook his head, "*Not today, Josephine,*" he said, "*better to leave everything exactly as it is in there. The Citizen Captain here may wish to carry out an examination of the accommodation himself – and if that is his desire, then I'm sure that you can show him around.*"

Parmentier nodded his approval then took a slurp of his wine before winking slyly at Josephine. His reptilian tongue flicked across his wet lips, nearly causing Josephine to have a fit of the vapours, so she scuttled out of the room as fast as her feet could carry her. "*I'd rather gouge my eyes out with a rusty spoon than spend a moment in a room alone with that filthy lecherer.*" she thought.

Placing his drink on the table, Parmentier stood up, stretched, belched loudly then said to Lalouche, "*That is an excellent suggestion of yours, Citizen. I will indeed carry out a thorough search of the Englishman's room – and yes, your pretty young daughter may assist me. Thank you for the offer of her services.*" Lalouche bowed his head, "*Ça me fait plaisir, Citizen Captain, I will summon her immediately.*" Lalouche bawled, "*Josephine, get your idle body in here, now!*"

Outside in the road, roped to the rear of the smelly, straw-filled tumbril, a bruised and dazed Graham looked at his red and chafed hands, and wondered just how he was going to make good his escape and reach the 'T2 Travelator' in time to return home "*What a cock-up!*" he thought. As the citizens of Paris walked past him they lowered their eyes, not wishing to become involved.

'CHAPTER 5'

'A Night in Confinement'

During the French Revolution, La Conciergerie became the main prison in Paris, housing some 2,700 prisoners, most of whom were eventually Guillotined. In the main, Prisoners were crammed into the ancient, stinking and rat-infested cells, their suffering added to by the horrendous and unhygienic conditions. Only 'celebrity' prisoners were assigned cells to themselves, other unfortunates either had to double-up or were just crammed into cells built to contain one person. So, even in adversity, rank, status and wealth had its privileges. Queen Marie-Antoinette herself was held prisoner at La Conciergerie. Jailers lurked near the cell doors, determining whether visitors would be allowed inside to see their friends or relatives, often bringing them food and something to drink. 'Bribery and Corruption' was the order of the day.

Trials followed by executions was the norm, so the turnover of occupants was faster than a busy 'Travelodge.' Prisoners could be tried one day and then executed before the following morning. An appeals procedure was non-existent.

67

Straw-filled tumbrils were queuing up in the 'May Courtyard' of La Conciergerie on a daily basis to be loaded up with those unfortunates who had been sentenced to death and who were then transported past jeering crowds to the various Guillotines sited throughout Paris.

'La Conciergerie, Paris'
(Once a Royal Palace and home to the Revolutionary Tribunal)

Deep down in the rat-infested bowels of La Conciergerie Prison, a heavy wooden iron-bound cell door swung open and Graham, hands now freed from the handcuffs, was hurtled unceremoniously inside, skidding across the filth-ridden floor. Several startled rats, their feral, beady red eyes glittering in the feeble candle-light, scuttled to the safety of their homes in the dank, moisture ridden corners of the cell. With an air of finality, the cell door was then slammed shut, the lock clicking ominously. The stench in the miserable cell made Graham gag, instantly reminding him of a visit he'd once made to the 'Black Hole of Calcutta.'

A fellow-prisoner, secured by heavy ring-bolted chains embedded in the cell wall, glanced up at Graham and smiled at him sympathetically then, in a reedy, trembling voice said, *"Ah, welcome to my humble abode, Monsieur. My apologies for the smell – but you'll soon get used to it. It's known here as 'Eau de la Conciergerie.' Permit me to introduce myself, I am François III Maximilien de la Woestyne, 3rd Marquess of Becelaere, Grande of Spain and Lord of Walincourt. Forgive me, I would offer you my hand, but as they have removed my fingernails and crushed the ends of my fingers, that would pose me great difficulty."*

Graham stood up and brushed the manky straw and filth off himself. Glancing at the man's badly damaged fingers, he was mortified by the shocking state of them, *"My God, you mean that they actually pulled your fingernails out – how barbaric is that! You must be in absolute agony!"* François nodded, *"Oui Monsieur, it is most unpleasant."* Graham asked *him, "How did it happen?"* François smiled, *"Of late I have spent many memorable moments with our Public Interrogator, Monsieur Albert Pontonier, a miserable and perverted creature. Alas, his cruel and inhumane behaviour is symptomatic of our times. Unfortunately, there are many more like him who have risen to the surface of the swamp since the Revolution."*

Citizen Albert Pontonier'
(French Public Interrogator)

François continued, *"Monsieur, Pontonier thinks little of employing the use of thumb-screws and similar disgusting implements of torture in order to elicit confessions from his often innocent victims. Ice runs through his veins. He takes an unnatural delight in inflicting pain on helpless Prisoners and I believe that under normal circumstances he would have been placed in an asylum and never heard from again. Naturally, one confesses to anything just to get the pain of his perverted ministrations to cease. I cannot fathom how a reptile like that could become an elevated servant of our newly formed Republic. And you know what is so amusing, my friend? I have done absolutely nothing wrong - other than being an Aristocrat, that is – which is an accident of birth of course. God help me had I done anything more serious!"* he sighed, *"Still, they can only chop your head off once. Are you facing similar difficulties, my friend? I suppose that you must be if you are a 'guest' here in this miserable establishment!"* Graham nodded and replied, *"Well, yes and no. I mean, I haven't actually done anything wrong. You see, the French authorities think that I'm a spy because I'm English, but of course, I'm not." "Then why are you here?"* asked François. *"Well,"* replied Graham, " *What I actually am is a Time-Traveller."*

François raised a quizzical eyebrow as Graham continued, *"Yes, I know that you probably find that hard to believe. I'll explain, but first, let me introduce myself, I'm Graham St Anier. I'm from Kingston Upon Hull in England."* François smiled gently and nodded, *"Yes, I have heard of the place. They do say that, like London, it is a place best avoided. You are a 'Time-Traveller' you say?"* Graham nodded again. François smiled, *"Well, that is a first for me, Monsieur Graham! I must say that if you do have the means to travel in time, you have chosen most unwisely to come here. A 'Time-Traveller' eh. I wonder what the probing Citizen Robespierre will make of that, forgive me, outlandish statement, once he hears it!"* Graham said, *"Well when I tried to explain it to that brutish Citizen Captain bloke, Parmentier, he just laughed in my face. I'm sure he thought that I was making it all up."* François gave a sympathetic nod, *"Oh, that buffoon. He probably didn't understand a word you were saying. He finds it difficult to string a sentence together. He makes a good officer of the Republic. Pardon me, my friend, I am being a little sardonic."*

François patted the straw beside him, *"Come and sit here next to me, it will be good to indulge myself with some intelligent conversation. There is much for us to discuss, and as for your claim to be a 'Time-Traveller' - do not despair, after all, no-one believed that great sage Nostradamus when he described many and various matters beyond our perceived wisdom. One has to keep a very open mind on such subjects as 'Time-Travel.' Regrettably, I doubt that the Captain Citizen to whom you refer, or even Monsieur Robespierre, possesses the intellectual capacity to do so.*

Huh, and as for Robespierre - anyone who is a lawyer by profession is half-way to be being an unprincipled rogue."

Mike said, *"Robespierre, I've read all about him, a bit of a toe-rag apparently?"* François smiled again, *"I assume that the term 'toe-rag' is derogatory and means that he is something along the lines of being a miserable wastrel?"* Graham nodded as François continued, *"Oui, Graham, you are correct. Citizen Robespierre is now known to us lesser beings as the 'Incorruptible Lawyer and Politician.' Huh, it was he who outrageously and rather coldly stated that "Louis must die so that France may live."* Mike replied, *"Well, he's certainly had his wish fulfilled today!"*

François paled and gasped, *"You don't mean to tell me that His Majesty is no more?"* Graham nodded, *"I'm sorry to be the bearer of grim tidings, but I'm afraid so, François. Your King Louis was Guillotined just a few hours ago. I was there at the Place de la Rèvolution, watching the proceedings. It was all very gruesome. He was a very brave man."* François was mortified, *"Mother of God, if His Majesty has been executed, then what hope is there left for us lesser mortals. It is truly the bitter end, we are all doomed,"* said a very shocked François, glancing despairingly at Graham before making the sign of the cross, his badly torn fingers dripping blood onto what had obviously been a very expensive and once pristine shirt.

His shoulders sagged and he made a helpless gesture of resignation. Graham placed a comforting arm around François trembling shoulders, looking with great sympathy at his torn and crushed fingers, *"My God, you have been through the mill haven't you, old lad!"* A tearful François, wiping his eyes with the back of his hand, nodded, *"Oui. Forgive my tears of self-pity, Monsieur Graham, I am but a carapace of the man I once was. Time spent in La Conciergerie has a detrimental effect upon one, as I'm afraid you are soon to discover. Alas, unless you are a member of the new privileged elite, there is but one way to escape from La Conciergerie and that is via a trip to Madame Guillotine!"*

Glancing across at the solid cell door and checking that no-one was listening at the small grilled window in its centre, Graham said, *"Just between us two, François, I won't be lingering in here for too long."* François, smiled, *"Ah, you have managed to arrange for a rescue to be carried out, Monsieur Graham?"* Graham nodded, *"Yes, all I've got to do is get myself out of this hell-hole and make my way to a pre-arranged place on the outskirts of Paris, jump into what we call a 'Travellator' then I'll be off back to my own time-zone."* *"You seem very confident of doing that, my friend."* said François, shaking his head, *"Alas, escaping from here is much easier said than done, We are well guarded and closely monitored day and night. Not only that – I am sure that the Jailers will eventually come and chain you to the wall, like me."* he said, rattling his chains. *"To be honest, I'm not too concerned about it,"* said Graham, *"it's written into my Travel Insurance that I can be 'recovered' if I get into trouble and need extracting, so the gang at T.T.H.S. will definitely come up with something."*

François shook his head, *"Listen, my friend, I know not of whom or what you speak, but you exude an air of confidence which convinces me that you may well have a chance to be rescued. It is common knowledge that an Englishman is as good as his word, so perhaps you could help me in some small way if you do manage to escape?* Graham smiled, *"If I can, then I will, naturally,"* he replied, *"but before you ask,*

I have to tell you that I won't be able to take you with me when I do escape. I can only go by myself."

François' face fell and he looked crushed, *"That is such a disappointment,"* he sighed. An embarrassed Graham replied, *"I'm sorry, but those are Time-Travel rules you see. I'm totally sympathetic to your plight, but Time-Travellers are forbidden to do anything that would affect people's involvement in the course of historical events. It's non-negotiable."* François sighed again, his hope of rescue dashed, *"Ah well, what will be, will be. Je ne regrette rien."*

After a pause, he continued, *"Well, Graham, I doubt very much that I will survive the Revolution with my head still attached to my shoulders, especially if the vial of poison I have secreted about my person is discovered."* After a few more moments of silence, Francois said, *"You have an honest face, Graham, so with your permission, I would like to entrust you with my little secret?"* *"Please do,"* replied an intrigued Graham. *"I have made specific plans so that at least my three wonderful sons will not finish up in the gutter once everything in France has returned to normal and the Royal family are restored to their rightful place if they ever are."*

François bent down and eased his shoe off, wincing as he did so, his torn fingers causing him a great deal of pain. With the cup of his hand, he carefully pressed and twisted the heel of the shoe, revealing inside it a cleverly constructed compartment into which was lodged a small, ornate silver box. He smiled, *"Not too long ago, this little box contained a quantity of fine snuff. It was a present to me from my beloved wife, who is also held prisoner here in La Conciergerie. The heartless prison authorities will not allow me to spend even a few moments with her. God preserve us both from their wicked ministrations.*"

With great difficulty, François eased the little snuff-box out of the shoe-heel, then prised the box lid open, removing a small square of folded silk from inside it, which he then carefully spread out across his knees, "*Just prior to my arrest, Graham, I managed to hide the family gold, silver, and several other precious artifacts away but did not have the opportunity to pass the information on to my three sons. By that time they had left France for the safety of Spain. Fortunately, I was able to send them there in order to prevent them from being denounced and taken prisoner, like their parents. Had they been detained, they would only have suffered from this sort of unpleasantness,*" he waved his torn hands in the air, "*and I can only guess at how it would have ended for them. My wife refused to accompany them to Spain and chose to remain with me at the Château Walincourt – a wrong move as it transpired because here we both are. Anyway, I digress. On this small piece of silk, I have written the instructions and a map indicating precisely where in my Château a considerable fortune has been hidden away in order to keep it out of the hands of those thieving and conniving French revolutionaries. God rot them.*" François sat back, exhausted by his little rant. Even in the poor light provided by the stub of a small, guttering candle, on a sconce fixed to the cell wall, Graham could see that the small square of silk lain across François' knees was covered in neat writing with a complex diagram at the bottom of the notes.

Graham nodded and said, "*Oh yes, our fighter pilots used to have something like that hidden away in their uniforms to help them escape from the Germans in case they were shot down and captured during the Second World War.*" François looked puzzled, "*You are speaking in tongues, Monsieur!*"

Graham smiled at him, "*Don't worry, François! If we get time, I'll explain it all to you later.*"

With difficulty, François very carefully folded the delicate square of silk material back into a neat square before tucking it inside the snuff-box and snapping the lid firmly shut. Replacing it in the secret compartment of his shoe he then clicked the shoe-heel back into place. François sighed, "*Well, my friend, it does not take the intelligence of an Archbishop to work out that I am destined to follow in King Louis footsteps, although I may yet deny them the pleasure. In case you are wondering how I intend to do that - the other heel of my shoes contains a small vial of quick acting and very potent poison. I will swallow it, if and when I feel that I am unable to stand any more of their cruel and inhumane treatment or that all hope is gone. I am determined that I will not be dragged through the streets of Paris like some common thief being taken to the Guillotine to be unjustly executed for the entertainment of the masses. My wife has a similar measure of poison secreted away in her footwear, although I pray fervently every day that the authorities will recognise that she is completely innocent of any of the fallacious charges brought against her and will release her. I fear, though, that it will not be. Alas, we have both fallen amongst thieves!* "

François beckoned to Graham, who leaned across to listen to what he had to say. Lowering his voice, François whispered, "*Monsieur Graham, if and when you do escape from here, would you consider somehow getting the snuff-box containing the silken map to my sons? They would be most appreciative and you would be handsomely rewarded for your efforts.*" Graham put his arm around François' shoulder, "*Listen, mate, as I've already said, I'd love to help you, but in my time-zone, there are very strict rules about*

'Time-Travellers' interfering with the course of historical events. I shouldn't even have mentioned the Second World War to you, a bit of a slip of the tongue there. It's an absolute no-no, so, much as I'd love to help you, I just can't."

A disappointed François shook his head and sighed, "*Well, Monsieur Graham, I don't really understand any of this 'Time-Travel' business, however, I respect your commitment to not behaving in an ungentlemanly manner. A man is only as good as his word. I will just have to revert to my other plan.*" "*Which is?*" asked Graham. François checked to see that no-one else was listening or watching through the small window in the cell door then turned and reached behind himself to the cell wall, first selecting then with difficulty carefully sliding out a smallish square of blackened stone, grimacing as he did so because of the pain from his damaged fingers.

Behind the stone, a hole had been hollowed out in the crumbling masonry. He muttered, "*This hiding place was carved out over many months by a previous companion who was here sharing this cell with me for a while. You may be familiar with his name – the author Jacques Cazotte?*" Graham shook his head, "*Afraid not. I'm an avid reader of John Le Carré's novels myself.*"

François continued, "*I am not familiar with Monsieur Le Carré's writing, however, I digress, Poor Jacques, he has now crossed the great divide and gone on to better things. They treated him and his family very badly, you know, taking an indecent delight in what they were doing. The so-called Liberals bring great shame to our beloved French nation.*" He shook his head, "*I will hide my snuff-box in this small compartment here in the wall and, if I am allowed to linger, I will try and get someone else to assist me either to escape or deliver the snuff-box to my family. If I cannot, then both it and the silk map will probably stay hidden in there for all eternity. At least those shameless and cowardly revolutionary swine will not get their thieving paws on it. That they will eventually have the coat off my back and sell the remainder of my apparel to the peasants I have little doubt.*"

An exhausted François paused as he heard footsteps heading along the passage leading towards the cell, accompanied by the ominous jangling of keys. "*Ah, alas, my friend, time for more fun and games with the torturer, Monsieur Pontonier, methinks.*" said a trembling François as he quickly removed the snuff-box from the heel of his shoe and tucked it into the cavity in the wall, then slid the stone back into place. He brushed the few bits of dust and crumbled masonry out of sight so that no clue to the hiding place would be given. The cell door was noisily unlocked and swung open, revealing Citizen Captain Parmentier with an evil grin on his face.

The two prisoners looked at Parmentier, both of them filled with trepidation. He leered at them and said, "*Ah, gentlemen, I trust that you are both comfortable in your cushy billet?*" then, pointing his forefinger, said, "*You must come with me.*" François replied, "*Ah, Monsieur, which one of us is to have the privilege of spending some quality time with Monsieur Pontonier being dazzled by his quicksilver wit?*" he asked. "*Not you, you little runt.*" came the sneering reply, "*The English spy is about to have the great honour of meeting Citizen Maximilien Robespierre. As for you, François, you must wait for a few more hours to meet Monsieur Pontonier. He is busy entertaining a new batch of Aristos. Did you not hear them begging for mercy? You could hear them all around the prison, like little girls they were!*" he said before throwing his head back and laughing. He waved imperiously at Graham, *"Come, English, up off your fat rump!"*

'Citizen Maximilien Robespierre'
(Guillotined in the Place de la Revolution
on the 28th of July 1794)

French lawyer and politician, Maximilien François Marie Isidore de Robespierre was one of the best known and most influential figures associated with the French Revolution and the 'Reign of Terror.' A member of the Estates-General, the Constituent Assembly and the Jacobin Club, he was, conversely, an outspoken advocate for the poor and for democratic institutions. Robespierre also campaigned for universal male suffrage in France, price controls on basic food commodities and the abolition of slavery in the French colonies. A keen opponent of the death penalty, nevertheless he still played a key role in arranging the execution of King Louis the Sixteenth. Robespierre was eventually arrested himself and after a show trial, like many of his victims, was Guillotined. 'Time-Traveller' Graham St Anier, was destined to make Robespierre's acquaintance long before Robespierre went to keep his appointment with a bloodthirsty Madame Guillotine.

The 'èminence grise' Robespierre, affecting a sophisticated indifference, sat with his feet up on the desk, gave a lengthy yawn then spoke languidly to a nervous Citizen Parmentier, *"So, Parmentier, you say that this wretch, St Anier, is an English spy. What evidence do you have of his spying activities"* A blustering and tremulous Parmentier replied, *"Well, I er, you see, it, er,"* An impatient Robespierre rapped the desk with his hand, *"Come along man, don't dither, speak up, time flies, let me hear your report!"* Parmentier standing directly in front of Robespierre, cap in hand and blushing like a naughty schoolboy, was desperately trying to stop his knees from knocking. Robespierre had the power of life or death over lesser mortals, so it didn't do to show him any sign of weakness, inefficiency or indeed cause him the slightest offence - as those that had done so had found out to their detriment.

In a wheedling voice, Parmentier said, *"Citizen, the maid, Josephine Lalouche, who resides with her father, Citizen Martin Lalouche, at the Pension Sainte Marie, was cleaning the Englishman's room when she discovered those very documents that you have on your desk. They were hidden underneath the spy's mattress and fell out onto the floor when Josephine reached under the bed to get his piss-pot."* he said, pointing at the bundle of documents on Robespierre's desk. *"This pile of papers is the only evidence that you have, Parmentier? These few piffling and inconsequential documents that may, or may not belong to the prisoner?"*

Parmentier nodded, *"Yes sir, that is correct. The prisoner has confirmed with me that they are indeed his property. They look important and contain many strange phrases, perhaps a code?"* Robespierre gave the documents a dismissive glance, *"I take it that you do not have any English, Parmentier?"* Parmentier shook his head, *"No Citizen, I do not, nor does the young lady who found them, but she had the good sense to take them to a local priest, who kindly translated the contents for her."* Robespierre nodded, *"And are you able to tell me what the priest said?"* A miserable Parmentier looked at the floor, shook his head and mumbled, *"The girl did explain the contents of the papers to me, Citizen, but I couldn't really understand what she was talking about."* Robespierre sighed, *No matter, I will plough through the papers myself. Have the girl Josephine and the priest brought here, I wish to speak to them both. I have a distinct feeling that there is more to this business than meets the eye."* Parmentier replied, *"I have them both downstairs, Citizen."* Robespierre replied, *"Ah, a spark of initiative, so you can do something right, Parmentier. Well done. Now, let me speak with the Englishman, then I will speak to the other two."*

This wasn't going as well as Parmenter had thought that it would. What he'd really expected was a hero's welcome from his master. Robespierre unexpectedly smiled at Parmentier, who was so unnerved by Robespierre's rictus grin that he lost control of a key bodily function and broke wind. He glanced apologetically at Robespierre and said, *"Pardonner mâï péter, Citizen."* Robespierre raised an eyebrow and wrinkled his nose in disgust before waving a perfumed lace handkerchief, pilfered from an Aristocrat, in front of his face, *"Has the Englishman been interrogated since his arrival here in La Conciergerie?"* he queried. Parmentier shook his head, *"Not yet sir, it was my intention to take him for a short session with the 'Fang Farrier' er, Monsieur Pontonier, to soften him up a little. Monsieur St*

Anier will soon confess to any misdemeanours, particularly after he's had a few teeth removed with the heated pincers."

Robespierre shook his head and tutted, "*My dear fellow, there are occasions when even I, Robespierre, sink into the depths of despond. We must learn to use more subtle methods than heated pincers - although I admit that they usually have the desired effect. I'm informed that Citizen Pontonier, the 'Fang Farrier' the soubriquet you have so disrespectfully accorded him*" Parmentier wriggled with discomfort, "*is currently perfecting the art of removing the eyeballs of his victims, usually those with aristocratic leanings, using a small, curved and very sharp scalpel. It is quite astounding the amount of information he extricates from his 'guests' without even having to draw a drop of blood. It conjures up a terrible picture, does it not. You should go and watch him in action, Parmentier, it is quite an informative and salutary experience. I'll tell him that you're coming, he can keep an eye out for you!*"

Parmentier visibly paled. Robespierre gave a faint smile and said, "*Come, Citizen, I am teasing you!*" he sighed then continued, "*Have the prisoner St Anier brought before me. if you please. I am intrigued by these documents and wish to interrogate him at the earliest opportunity.*" Parmentier gave a half-hearted bow and with great relief scuttled out of the room to collect the prisoner from the cells, in accordance with his master's wishes. It would not do to keep a busy man like Robespierre waiting.

Graham was eventually brought before Robespierre, where he stood with his head bowed; he was filthy, exhausted, and aching all over from when he'd been roughed up by Parmentier and his men. He was also very thirsty. The water in the filthy bucket in the corner of the cell looked undrinkable and he'd thought it wiser to give it a wide berth. He sighed, this was definitely not turning out to be the holiday that he'd imagined it would be.

As he stood there, Graham eyed the carafe of clean sparkling clear water on Robespierre's desk with lip-smacking envy. Robespierre, who was affecting to read the pile of documents on his desk, slowly lifted his head and stared at Graham with a laser-like intensity that Graham found to be more than a little disconcerting. In addition, the added threat of Parmentier standing behind him out of his line of sight was nerve-wracking - not knowing if and when a stinging blow would be delivered by the ever-obliging bully. "*It's going to* be the '*Good cop, bad cop. routine,*'" thought Graham.

Robespierre smiled and gestured towards a chair at the front of the desk. Sounding benevolent, he said, "*My dear fellow, do take the weight off your feet. Would you care for a drink of refreshing water?*" Graham nodded and with great relief sank down onto the plush velvet padding of the richly decorated gilt chair, "*Thank you, sir.*" Perhaps he'd misjudged the man and this wasn't going to be as bad as he'd imagined. Parmentier slid behind the back of the chair, hovering over Graham.

A seemingly solicitous Robespierre enquired of Graham, "*Is the chair comfortable, Monsieur St Anier?*" Graham nodded. Robespierre continued, "*It should be, it came from the Kings apartments at the Palace of Versailles. Of course, he won't be requiring it anymore!*" Robespierre picked up the carafe then slowly and tantalisingly poured some sparkling water from it into a fine crystal glass, then held it up to the window, "*Mmmm, this looks most refreshing.*" he said, then proceeded to drink it all himself, before dabbing his wet lips, in a somewhat fey manner, with his lace handkerchief, then placed the empty glass back onto his desk right in front of Graham. Robespierre nodded at Parmentier, who then stepped swiftly forward and pulled the chair from under Graham, sending him sprawling onto the floor in an undignified heap. He laid there floundering, winded by the fall.

"On your feet, you misbegotten poltroon!" shouted Robespierre. Graham struggled to his feet, fighting to regain his breath. Robespierre continued, *"I warn you, this is not some sort of social gathering for idle English gentry. Now, I would like you to explain to me, English swine, precisely what you are doing here in Paris during these troubled times. If your explanation is believable, which I doubt very much that it will be, then I might consider letting you have a sip of this refreshing water, Monsieur"* he hissed. Graham replied plaintively, *"There's nothing to tell you, sir. I'm not a spy, I'm just a visitor to these parts, a tourist."* Robespierre sneered, *"You English are such consummate schemers and liars. Who in their right mind would want to visit Paris during 'difficult' times such as these, eh? Come now, I am a very busy man, I will give you one more chance. What is the true purpose of you being here? Speak up!"*

Graham paused, sighed, then said, *"Sir, it's true that everything is not as straightforward as it seems."* Robespierre nodded, *"As I thought, continue!"* Graham replied, *" You may find this difficult to believe, but I am, in fact, what is known as a 'Time-Traveller' from the 20th Century."* Robespierre's jaw dropped and he shot Graham a look of pure astonishment, the gold pince-nez clipped onto the bridge of his beaky nose slipping off and dangled in front of his fancy waistcoat. After a moment he threw his head back and whinnied, *"Zut Alors! You hear that Citizen*

Parmentier? Our Monsieur St Anier is a 'Time-Traveller,' no less!"

Parmentier scratched his head and looking embarrassed said, *"I am truly sorry Citizen, but I don't know what that phrase means."* Robespierre, suppressing a smile, sighed and said to Graham, *"Ah, you see, Mister St Anier, you can't educate pork - you can only try to cure it!"* Robespierre nodded imperceptibly at Parmentier who then stepped forward and gave Graham a stinging slap on the back of his head. Robespierre sniggered, *"I warn you, Monsieur, our brave and loyal Citizen Captain Parmentier is a master of basic interrogation techniques, so you'd better tell me the truth!"* Graham, rubbing the back of his head, replied, pleadingly, *"But what I am telling you is the truth, sir, I am a 'Time-Traveller.'"*

"That is patent nonsense!" roared Robespierre, *"Do you take me for a fool, Englishman!"* He turned to Parmentier and with a contemptuous wave of his hand, in an icy voice commanded, *"I lose patience! Take this raving lunatic back down to the cells. I will deal with him later. My presence is required at the National Convention for a meeting that will undoubtedly drag on for some time. It would seem, Parmentier, that another nest of Aristocratic vipers has been discovered cringing in a Château on the outskirts of Paris. They will all need to appear before the Convention before being found guilty and deposited here for a while. A mere formality, but a necessity. Whilst I am away, Monsieur Parmentier, let our English guest enjoy an hour or two with Citizen Pontonier, the 'Fang Farrier' as you refer to him - nothing too radical mind you!"* Parmentier nodded and smiled.

Robespierre continued, *"It will undoubtedly prove to be a salutary and memorable experience for the spy. Once he regains his senses, Parmentier, have him brought back here and we will continue our conversation where we left off. Er, not too many of his teeth to be extracted, Citizen, or he will be unable to converse sensibly with me. It is difficult enough trying to understand his fractured French as it is!"* Parmentier nodded and replied, *"As you command, Citizen."* Parmentier grabbed hold of Graham's shoulder and said, *"Come with me, spy!"* then dragged Graham out of the chair and pushed him through the doorway.

Robespierre shook his head as Graham was dragged out of the room, loudly protesting his innocence, *"Time-Traveller indeed, that's a new one on me. The English think that we French are uneducated fools!"* He stood up, stretched languidly and thought to himself, *"Ah Maximilien Robespierre, tell me, where did it all go so right?"* then, looking out of the window, noted that the weather had taken a turn for the worse. Snatching up his cloak, he threw it around his shoulders then cursed roundly, *"Merde – il pleut!"* before stomping off to his all-important meeting.

'CHAPTER 6'

'The Secret of La Conciergerie'

The heavy ancient cell door swung open, it's ungreased hinges squealing like a stuck pig, then Graham was hurtled unceremoniously into the cell, sprawling onto the urine stained, evil-smelling straw that covered most of the well-worn flagstones. A leering Parmentier followed him in, *"Well, Monsieur 'Time-Traveller,' Citizen Robespierre was highly amused by your foolish explanation. It was quite obvious to him that some English village is missing its idiot!"* He stepped forward and cuffed Graham on the back of his head, *"Let us see if you are quite as amusing when you meet up with Monsieur Pontonier who, as you now know, specialises in administering to fingers, teeth, and eyeballs, although I think that your fingers, eyeballs, and teeth are safe – just for the moment."*

Graham gulped as Parmentier continued, *"Old Citizen Pontonier, the 'Fang Farrier,' is a little busy just now,*

administering certain encouragements to the Duc d'
Orleans, he is the one you heard begging for mercy when we
came in here just now. But do not be disappointed for I will
ensure that you meet up with Pontonier once he has finished
dealing with that howling pomaded poltroon. Monsieur
Pontonier takes a great degree of pleasure in softening
prisoners up for Citizen Robespierre, he has it down to a fine
art, as you will undoubtedly soon discover." Despair was
written all over Graham's face. Parmentier laughed, turned
and stomped out of the cell, slamming the door behind him
and bellowing at the grubby Jailer who was lurking in the
background to lock it.

Graham sat on the cell floor in the candle-lit gloom,
wondering how he was going to get himself out of the mess
he was in. He mumbled unconvincingly, "*Where there's life,
there's hope.*" Sharing the cell with Graham was an
Aristocrat called François, who said to him, "*Monsieur, for
you, for all of us, all hope is lost. If you have anything to
confess I would advise that you should do so before you go
to see that instrument of the devil, Monsieur Pontonier. He
is relentless in his pursuit of the truth. Let me assure you that
even if you are innocent you will plead guilty to anything
after his most indelicate ministration. No part of the body is
sacrosanct!*" Graham replied, "*Yes, but I haven't done
anything wrong!*"

François smiled sympathetically, "*I myself have committed
no wrongdoing whatsoever, but confessed to being a traitor
just to stop him inflicting further agonies upon my person.
He still removed my fingernails with a hot needle and then
crushed my finger ends with finger screws. Where is the
justice in that, eh? These Revolutionaries are madmen!*"

A frustrated Graham said, *"But there's nothing for me to confess! I tried to explain everything to your Citizen Robespierre. I told him that I'm a 'Time-Traveller' and that I'm due to be transported back to my own time zone this very evening. What more could I tell him?"* François sighed, *"Alas, Monsieur, that fanciful tale will not satisfy Robespierre. It is quite apparent to me that you are not some sort of lunatic, which would also have been evident to Robespierre, an expert in investigatory matters. He would have recognised that your explanation was pure fabrication, undoubtedly formulated in desperation. But be warned, my friend, if you do not tell him the truth then you will suffer the direst of consequences."*

An exasperated Graham replied, *"Well, what I told him was the copper-bottomed truth. I am a 'Time-Traveller.'"* François smiled gently, *"I don't wish to give you cause for further concern, but let me assure you that all of us held prisoner here in this dreadful place are doomed, despite any explanations that we care to offer Robespierre. Our early demise is a given, there is no escape. Many have tried and all have failed. The Guillotine is the only way out,"* he lowered his voice, *"unless, that is, you are fortunate enough to be in possession of that which is hidden in my footwear."*

There was the sound of approaching footsteps shuffling down the passage until they stopped outside the cell door. The key was inserted into the lock and slowly turned. Graham's heart sank, *"Oh no, here we go!"* he thought. As the cell door swung open, the Jailer, a rotund Pierre Marchant, entered the cell, holding up a lantern inside of which a small candle stub flickered. He whispered to Graham, *"Monsieur English, you must come quickly, follow me. Your escape from here has been arranged, I will explain more as we make our way out of La Conciergerie. We must move with great haste, I have been warned that Citizen Captain Parmentier is on his way here to collect you, so we have very little time! Viste! Viste!*" Graham struggled to his feet and made his way to the door of the cell.

François called out to Marchant, "*Please Monsieur, take me too, I beg of you*! *I will see that you are well rewarded.*" The Jailer shook his head, *"I cannot help you, Aristo. Alas, there is insufficient time, nor do I have the required implements with which to remove your shackles, otherwise I might consider it, as I am already risking my neck for the Englishman here! No, you must remain. Anyway, I have received payment for the Englishman so I do not need a sou from the likes of you."* The Jailer glared at François, hissing, *"Dare to whisper one word of what you have seen, Monsieur, and I will make sure that whatever remains of your miserable life will be made very uncomfortable!"* then spat on the floor.

Marchant turned to Graham, "*Come now, Monsieur, let us beat a hasty retreat before we are discovered!*" Graham moved quickly, saying to his rescuer, "*Don't worry, mate, I can't wait to get out of this place and back home!*" then turning François said, "*Good luck buddy, I'm so sorry that I couldn't take you with me. As I explained, I'm not allowed to do anything that would change the course of history. It's 'Time-Travel' rules!*" before legging it out of the cell as fast as he could, following closely behind a sweating Pierre Marchant.

"*À bientôt, Graham,*" François called after him, his quivering voice oozing with desperation and defeat. He noticed that in his haste to leave, the Jailer Marchant had left the cell door unlocked and ajar. "*That is a foolish mistake that even Captain Parmentier cannot fail to notice. He will quickly deduce that there has been mischief afoot. There will be hell to pay,*" he thought.

The once powerful and influential sophisticated Aristocrat, François III Maximilien de la Woestyne, 3rd Marquess of Becelaere, Grande of Spain and Lord of Walincourt slowly stood up and on trembling legs tried to move towards the open door to slam it shut, until suddenly remembering that he was chained to the wall and could move no further forward than a few feet, "*Merde! So near, yet so far away!*" he said, returning dejectedly to his corner of the cell. Sitting down, he made himself as comfortable as he could on the pissy straw.

He was in the depths of despond and realised that for him there would be no escape from his hell-hole. He would have to remain there in the stinking cells of La Conciergerie Prison until such time as Citizen Maximilien Robespierre or one of his cohorts had decided what his fate would be. It didn't take the brains of an Archbishop to deduce that an appointment had already been pencilled in for him to meet up with Madame Guillotine. It was just a matter of when - the 'where' was inconsequential.

François well remembered the day when he'd appeared before the Citizen's Court, the 'Citizen in Charge' shouting, "*Bring the guilty Aristo swine before the Committee!*" Shockingly, and most unfairly, he hadn't even been given the opportunity to present any sort of defence and had realised that his fate had already been decided as he was found guilty and condemned to death with indecent haste. François leaned back against the cell's slimy wall and gave a wry shake of his head as he contemplated his future or distinct lack of it.

'François III Maximilien de la Woestyne'
(The 3rd Marquess of Becelaere,
Grande of Spain and Lord of Walincourt)

Virtually every day, including Sundays, François heard the fearful shouts of protest and howls of anguish as his fellow Aristocrats, both male and female, young and old, were dragged from their cells in La Conciergerie, loudly protesting their innocence, before being led off to the Guillotine. He gazed down at his ruined fingers, fingers that had often drawn gasps of admiration as they had swept expertly across the keyboard of the Clavesin (*harpsichord*) producing heavenly music whenever he'd played. Such was his musical expertise he had once been invited to play before the King and Queen at Versailles, where their Majesties had thanked him personally after the performance. What heady days those had been. Who could have guessed then just what unspeakable horrors lay ahead for all of them, from His Majesty downwards?

Overcome with grief, François' head sagged and he wept bitterly, knowing full well that for him and his beloved wife there would be no escape from their current dire circumstances. He was surrounded by unavoidable death. Somehow the Englishman, Graham, had managed to arrange his escape, but because of the 'Time-Travel' rules nonsense, either couldn't or wouldn't take François with him. That was a particularly bitter pill for François to swallow, especially when he could see freedom beckoning through the open cell door. So near, yet so far away. He wondered why it was that the English always seemed to escape things by the skin of their teeth?

The only positive thing that he could do was to tuck the small silver snuff-box away in the little hidey-hole behind the stone. It was a small triumph if nothing else. He turned and slid the loose stone out of the cell wall, removed the snuff-box from the heel of his shoe, kissed it tenderly then placed it in the hollowed out cavity. Pushing it right to the back of the cavity, he then slid the stone back into place, before spitting on his fingers and collecting some filth up off the floor to put around the edges of the stonework, patting it in so that it wouldn't look as if it had been tampered with. He viewed his finished work and was pleased with the effect. If by any faint chance he survived or could bribe a Jailer to get a message to his sons, they could recover the snuff-box. He made himself comfortable, as best he could, on the manky, stinking straw and drifted off into a troubled sleep.

He was rudely awakened by a sudden noise at the door of the cell and looked up to see a sour-faced Parmentier glaring down at him. "*Where is the Duty Jailer and more importantly, where is the English spy?*" a furious Parmentier roared. François shrugged his shoulders and smiled, "*I do not know Citizen, as you can see, I have been sleeping.*" Parmentier walked across the cell and punched François brutally in the face, breaking his nose, "*Lying Aristo swine!*

Huh, no matter, I will find the English spy and bring him back here where he belongs. He will be punished and you will be dealt with severely for withholding information, you scum."

A dazed and badly injured François thought, *"Huh, you pox-ridden cochon, let's see you explain the disappearance of my English friend to that fils de salope, Citizen Robespierre."* Parmentier spitefully back-handed François across the face, saying, *"I will be back to sort you out late!."* he said, before storming out of the cell, calling loudly for the guards. As he wiped the blood from his face, François managed a grim smile, *"Huh, with a bit of luck Parmentier will be too late to catch my English friend and then he might get some of his own medicine as a reward. I just pray that they don't put him in here with me."*

It was the afternoon of Monday the 28th of July 1794 and Citizen Maximilien Robespierre lay trembling, face down on the Guillotine, hands tied firmly behind his back, fearfully waiting for the newly sharpened blade to fall. He shrieked, *"You fools, you do not understand what you are doing! I am innocent! I have done nothing wrong!"* The Public Executioner, Charles-Henri Sanson, smiled and said to him, *"There, there, Citizen, if I had a gold coin for every time I'd heard that then I wouldn't be doing this for a living, would I! Having said that, I do owe you a vote of thanks though, for all the 'customers' you sent to me."* He sighed and looked at his fob-watch, *"Well, all good things must come to an end. I will now do my sworn duty and release the blade. Adieu and Bon Voyage, Citizen."*

Robespierre screamed with fear, *"Noooooo, please, I beg you!"* Sanson pulled a grubby handkerchief out of his pocket and stuffed it roughly into Robespierre's mouth to silence him, saying *"Please Citizen, you are demeaning yourself with your pathetic mewling!"* then said, *"Oh, before I do release the blade, I have one last request for you Monsieur Robespierre. Could you please do your best to exercise a bit of control and try not to fill your pantaloons, it is so unbecoming for an ex-member of the National Convention would you not agree?"* A gagging Robespierre, face puce, shook his head furiously and tried to spit the handkerchief out of his mouth.

Sanson turned to his assistants, sniggered and said, *"Huh, they can dish it out these lads, but they can't take it. Hold his arms firmly lads and let us proceed, there's a queue of customers forming up that must be dealt with."* He reached out and gave the rope hanging at the side of the Guillotine a sharp tug, releasing the finely honed blade. With a thud, a few seconds later it was all over and Maximilien Robespierre was no more. The crowd cheered and jeered. One of Sanson's assistants picked up Robespierre's head, and removed the now blood-stained handkerchief from its mouth, a set of false teeth firmly clamped to the cloth, then handed the gruesome package to Sanson.

Sanson unclamped the teeth then stuffed both the teeth and the handkerchief into his pocket. *"Huh,"* he said, *"I'm not wasting a good snot-rag on that piece of dog meat, it is made of the finest Cambric, presented to me by a member of the discredited aristocracy as a 'farewell' gift. I'll be able to get a good price for these teeth, they are of the finest quality"* He pointed at the decapitated body *"Into the box with his remains!"* he ordered. His assistants unceremoniously dumped the body and head of the late Citizen Maximilien Robespierre into the box.

A slightly shocked assistant stepped back. *"What's the matter now?"* asked Sanson. *"Look at his face, he is still blinking, Monsieur Sanson!"* Sanson smiled, *"It is of no consequence, that happens occasionally. Have I not explained to you before that victims remain conscious for at least four seconds after they are decapitated? Now tuck him neatly into the box,"* said Sanson, *"He's only small, there's room for another one in there,"* he rubbed his hands together, *"so, let's have our next 'guest' up here. There is much left to do today!"* Sanson turned to the other Assistant Executioner, *"Huh, so much blood pumping from such a puny body. Sprinkle some more sand around the base of the Guillotine, we don't want anyone slipping and having a nasty accident, do we!"* They all laughed.

'CHAPTER 7'

'Back in Kingston-upon-Hull'

Mike Fraser, 'Senior Time Travel Adviser' at the Hull-based 'Locators Time-Travel Agency' smiled as he listened to Graham St Anier describing his Parisienne escapades. *"So, once me and the Jailer got outside La Conciergerie nick, there was your Time-Marshall sat on a horse waiting for me. He also had a horse there for me, so I vaulted onto it like 'Clint Eastwood' did when he was escaping from the Apaches and then we galloped off through the streets of Paris to get to the de-materialisation zone as fast as we could. It was all a bit hairy."* said Graham.

"What happened to the Jailer chappie who got you out of there?" asked Mike. *"Oh him, well he'd copped for a bag of gold coins and arranged to go with his family to somewhere outside Marseilles. The money he'd been given by the Time-Marshall was enough to enable him to start a new life there under an assumed name, so he was as happy as a pig rolling in shit, which was appropriate because he smelled like one. Anyway, he legged it and so did we. We knew that Citizen Parmentier and his band of thugs would be coming after us, so we'd galloped off into the night as fast as we could. The*

Jailer had his own nag and headed off in the opposite direction to collect his family. Anyway, thanks to you and your team's fantastic recovery arrangements, we were able to rendezvous with the Travellator in good time and before you could say 'Jacques Robinson' we got back here all in one piece. It was such a bloody relief to get out of Paris, I can tell you. Those were dark days."

Mike smiled, *"Och, you were quite lucky really. It's only quite recently that we've been able to monitor Time-Traveller's whereabouts and activities with any degree of accuracy. Our 'T2 Time-Transporters' have only recently been fitted with the latest monitoring equipment, so along with that and your body implant, it allowed us to plot exactly where you were. We always knew what you're doing at any given time. That information was then filtered through to our Operations Room where they logged it in and monitored it on a 24 hours a day basis. We knew that you were in trouble when we saw that you were slung in a cell in La Conciergerie Prison, so we sent a Time-Marshall back to Paris with instructions to wangle his way into the prison, find out which cell you were in and bribe a willing Jailer to release you, then get you straight back to the de-materialisation zone in time to meet up with our 'T2 Time-Transporter."*

Graham smiled, *"I'm glad that you did. I've never been as relieved as I was when I saw the Time-Marshall and then the 'T2,'"* he said. *"I'll bet you were. I would have been ma self,"* replied Mike, as he slid an invoice across the desk to Graham. *"Well, I hate to be the spectre at the feast, Graham, but the cost of all that additional security work has been added to your bill. Worth every penny I should have thought?"* Graham sighed and nodded, *"Certainly was, Mike. It was a great holiday, but it got a bit hairy and scary at times. That Citizen Robespierre certainly wasn't someone to be tinkered with - and that git Parmentier was a right piece of work."*

Mike nodded and asked, *"I wonder what happened to your cell-mate, François. Did you ever find anything out about him?"* Graham nodded his head, *"A bit. I went to the Treasure House in Beverley and looked that up. François III Maximilien de la Woestyne, 3rd Marquess of Becelaere, Grande of Spain and Lord of Walincourt remained in La Conciergerie Prison for several more months then was Guillotined, the poor sod. He mustn't have been able to use the poison he had hidden in the heel of his shoe. They probably stole his shoes from him. Shame that, he was such a nice bloke. I'll bet it was that toe-rag Parmentier that saw him off."*

"Fascinating stuff." said Mike Fraser, *"Anyway, you're here now, so what can we do for you today then?"* Graham smiled, *"Well, I was out in Beverley last week with the Memsahib and called into the Beverley Old Bookshop."* Mike nodded, *"The one in Dyer Lane?" "Yes, that's right,"* said Graham, *"Do you know it?" "Och aye,"* said Mike, *"I often pop in there, usually when me and t'wife go to the Beverley Saturday Market. Brilliant place. I spend many happy hours leafing through the books whilst my better half is out and about decimating the shops and market stalls."*

Graham continued, *"Well, to cut a long story short, when I was in there one day, I discovered an old book about Henry the Eighth. I never realised that he'd visited Leconfield, just outside Beverley, on several occasions in 1541. Something else I didn't know was that there used to be a castle in Leconfield, but it's long gone now. I went up to have a look at where it once stood, but it's just a field covered in horse dung now, although there's still the signs of a moat surrounding the site. It gives you an idea of the large area that the castle covered. Must have been very impressive in its time. Anyway, after thinking about it, I thought I'd travel back in time and then go and have a look at the castle when it was in its full working splendour. Who knows, I might even get the chance to see Henry himself if I get the date right!"*

Mike smiled, *"Och, that sounds really interesting. I have nae done a Tudor trip ma self yet, but I fully intend to."* *"Yes, you should,"* said Graham, *"I'll be travelling alone again. My wife wants to travel back in time to Jerusalem to see what all the fuss was about, so whilst she's away doing that I'll have a look around closer to home."* *"OK,"* said Mike, *"Let's fire up my computer and see what we've got available for, what did you say the year was?"*

"The Spring of 1541," replied Graham.

'CHAPTER 8'

'King Henry the Eighth's 'Yorkshire Progress' in 1541'

'King Henry the VIIIth,
To six wives he was wedded.
One died, one survived,
Two divorced. Two beheaded'

'King Henry the Eighth of England'

'Queen Catherine of England'

It was a late Spring day in 1541 and the weather had been unexpectedly glorious – Yorkshire at its finest. There was a great deal of activity in and around Leconfield Castle, situated just outside of Beverley in East Yorkshire. Although termed a Castle, it was, in reality, a fortified and substantial 84 roomed manor house surrounded by a moat. Nevertheless, it was classed as being a noble house of the first order. King Henry, accompanied by his entourage, clattered into Leconfield Castle's cobbled courtyard after having spent most of the day out hunting. The King was in fine fettle that day, having chased and killed a stag.

Meeting the King, and in order to offer him the required and expected salutations, standing on the steps leading to the entrance of Leconfield Castle's impressive main hall, was the head of the Percy family, William de Percy, the Earl of Alnwick, who bowed his head and sank down onto one knee, warily asking Henry, *"How went it today, Your Grace?"* Henry smiled, *"Ah William, come sir, up off thy knee. The devil fetch me, it hath been a truly splendid day's hunting and we have also had a fine day's hawking. As you can see, we have killed ourselves a magnificent beast and wish to make a gift of it to the Percy household.*" The Earl was genuinely pleased. "*Your Majesty is, as ever, far too generous. I offer thee my humble thanks, sire,*" he said. "*Pah,*" replied Henry, "*'Tis naught. 'Tis we who should be thanking thy good self for thy fine and generous hospitality during our visit here.*"

William de Percy was relieved that he was copping for some fresh meat. Little did King Henry know, but there was currently a distinct lack of fresh food to be had in and around the Beverley area as the majority of it had already been commandeered and cooked in order to fill the faces of the King, his accompanying nobles, courtiers and substantial military escort, (although admittedly the military only received the poorest cuts of meat and whatever else the gentry had chosen to discard). Then, of course, there was the cost of providing the extra heating, stabling of the horses and payment for the ever-present Blacksmith. All in all, the Earl's finances were taking a bit of a hammering. The Earl was well known for being parsimonious and a bit of a nipscrew. He was a man who hated parting with anything and could, in the local vernacular, 'peel an apple in his pocket.' but where royal visits were concerned, there was no other choice other than to 'cough up.' It would not do to ruffle the King's feathers.

"Thank God that the King and his entourage are leaving for York within the next few days." thought the Earl, "*My coffers and supplies are sorely depleted. My pockets are as empty as those of a soldier returning from leave."* Royal visits inevitably placed a huge strain on household budgets and the Earl's was no exception. The King's stay could be anything from a few days up to a couple of weeks – depending upon the hunting, the political situation or merely as the fancy took him. Nevertheless, the honour and prestige of having the

King and Queen visiting him at Leconfield Castle was beyond measure and had the added bonus of placing the Earl at the very top of the local social ladder, so he just had to grin and bear it.

"Come, your Majesty, let us celebrate your hunting success." said the Earl, *"We have had a fine repast prepared, which awaits thy pleasure."* Henry, a renown trencherman, smiled, *"We shall enjoy that greatly, for we art truly clemmed. If you could hear how my belly rumbles. Thy victuals are delicious and without comparison and in truth, we are also parched! Come, we would dismount, prithee attend us!"*

The excruciating and elongated pantomime of getting King Henry dismounted from his horse without hurting his gouty leg, and whilst his retaining a modicum of dignity and decorum, began. Get it wrong and heads would be cuffed, irrelevant of status. *"Curse this troublesome leg of ours, William,"* said the King, *"how the constant ache from it easily takes the shine off our day if we allow it to. 'Tis strange that we can dispose of our enemies with speed and impunity but this damned leg of ours is a constant rub, despite the best ministrations of our alleged finest Physicians. Huh, charlatans to a man!"* he complained.

Eventually, and much to everyone's relief, the King successfully dismounted and then hobbled his way up the steps leading into the castle. Once at the top of the steps he turned to the Earl and called out, *"Come, my Lord, stir thy bones, let us not tarry further – there is good company and fine food aplenty to be had, with a flagon or two of heady wine to be imbibed, I'll be bound!"*

After copious quantities of food had been consumed and startling amounts of drink guzzled, later on in the evening and after everyone had repaired to their rooms, Henry's Queen Catherine had dismissed her Ladies in Waiting, Elizabeth Lady Fitzwalter, Anne, Lady Hastings, Lady Maud Parr, and Lady Elizabeth Howard. Their constant inane clucking and twittering had begun to grate on the Queen's nerves, all she wanted was a few moments of tranquillity for herself. What with those four chirruping Ladies-in-Waiting and her Maids of Honour, Catherine hardly ever had a moment's peace or privacy.

Much to Catherine's delight, the King had invited her to attend his private chamber, with only the two of them present. His attendants had been dismissed for the remainder of the evening. She could read Henry like a book and knew just what he had in mind for her. Still, it was a rarity that the King and Queen had such moments to themselves, undoubtedly it would be a memorable occasion, greatly enjoyed by the pair of them. She would bathe, change, dab a spot of French perfume about her person then probably just, 'Lay back and think of England.'

In the King's candle-lit chamber, with a log fire crackling noisily in the background and spitting red-hot embers into the hearth, Henry and Catherine were sprawled out on a comfortable tufted 'love seat.' Henry said, "*My lady, we would have you harken unto this*," as he unfurled a parchment, "*Tis a little something that we hath composed and have been waiting for the appropriate occasion to read it to thee. In truth, Catherine, this hath been a most perfect day and we thought that now would be the right moment for us to read it out to thee, my sweet. Prithee, harken.*" Henry took a sip of wine, cleared his throat noisily, took a deep breath then began reading:

105

"As the holly groweth green
And never changeth hue
So I am, e'er hath been
Unto my lady true."

Overcome with emotion at what he considered to be the exquisite brilliance of his composition, Henry dabbed at his tearful eyes with a perfumed lace handkerchief. It was a surprisingly emotional response from a man who had had thousands of his subjects imprisoned and cruelly executed, without so much as a blink of an eyelid. *"My lady, harken unto this most familiar composition. Tis entitled, 'Pastime with Good Company.'"* Henry sang:

"For my pastance,
Hunt, sing and dance,
My heart is set,
All goodly sport
For my comfort
Who shall me let?"

Queen Catherine smiled demurely and then kissed the palm of Henry's meaty hand tenderly, *"My husband, my Henry,"* she said, *"*s*uch beauteous words. Thou art truly a gifted and talented poet and thy voice sendeth a chill down my spine."* An unusually coy looking Henry blushed and replied, *"Tish, think naught of it my lady; the first little couplet is as fresh as a daisy and 'tis one we cobbled together for thy delectation whilst on the tedious journey here from Lincoln. There are several more such couplets for thy delectation, but we will ration them and read but one to you each day as a token of our undying affection."* The Queen said, *"I can hardly contain my impatience, my Sovereign."* whilst thinking to herself, *"Praise heaven that I will not have to* *suffer the crippling boredom of listening to some of the many other endless dirges that he hath penned.*" She fluttered her eyelids at Henry and gave him a coquettish smile.

Henry's poetic demeanour changed in a flash and he smiled lasciviously whilst placing a bejewelled paw on Catherine's thigh, "*Come now Catherine, 'tis a while since we hath made merry, let us off to the bedchamber for a spot of regal swiving. Hey up, lass - I am informed by Sir Percy that swiving is all the rage in Yorkshire, indeed 'tis second only in popularity to jousting.*" The Queen looked at him and, arching an eyebrow, said, "*Your Grace, do you take me to be one of your steeds, to be ridden at a whim.*" she replied.

The King looked at her, momentarily confused, then realising that he was being teased. With a wicked glint in his eyes, he said, "*Thy Sovereign King warns thee, sweet lady, withhold thy favours at thine own peril! We mean to have our wicked way with thee this night. 'Tis high time for a spot of mischief making!*" "*Sire,*" she replied, "*I came to thee as a true maid, are you now to sully me? I am but an innocent lady, not some common serving wench.*" Catherine stood up and walked to the rear of the love seat.

Henry laughed uproariously, "*By God, but you try my patience, Catherine! How my heart pounds!*" he said as he struggled to his feet then did his best to chase the Queen around the seat, waddling in a most undignified manner because of his gouty leg. Catherine though was pretending to love the thrill of the chase and was shrieking with theatrical delight. The King cried out, "*Slow down my sweet so that we might have a fair chance of apprehending thee! You will break my wind if we continue the chase at this pace.*" "*Oh well,* " thought Catherine, "*I'd better do my duty and let him catch me.*" slowing down perceptibly in order to let the lusting King reach her.

As Henry held her tightly, Catherine feigned a maidenly swoon, "*Unhand me sire or I will summon the Yeomen of the Guard to protect my honour!*" she said. The King roared with laughter as he reached for his glass of wine, shouting, "*God preserve us, not the Yeoman of the Guard! See how we tremble at the very mention of their name, my lady!*" He raised his wine glass, "*Hah, here's to life's pleasures! Now, my Lady, let's be having a peep at those pretty duckies of yours. Tis a while since they have had an airing! What say you, eh?*" The Queen smiled and shook her head, "*Nay Sire, that will not do! Unhand me this instant!*" feigning a virginal reluctance which only succeeded in testing the King's limited patience. He was used to having his wicked and salacious way with whomsoever, wherever and whenever he chose.

"*Come Madam, 'tis time for us both to disrobe and take a tumble in the hay!*" said a leering Henry. Pretending to be outraged, Catherine replied, "*Sire, thou art naught but a carpet-knight!*" Once again Henry roared with laughter, "*Madam, get thee hence to my bedchamber, we must tarry no longer. Come, indulge us our whims and thy rewards shall be great! Mayhap we will gift thee Yorkshire, once our frolickings are at an end and we are replete!*"

Outside of the solid doors of the King's chambers, listening to the regal racket emanating from inside, two thoroughly bored Yeomen of the Guard, Yeomen James Jenkin and John Powell, looking very smart in their green and white livery, were on duty fire-watch. They glanced sideways at one another and sniggered. "*Here we go again, John, such a palaver, eh. Cor, he's a bit of an old goat is that Henry,*" whispered James. His mate John smiled and winked, saying quietly, *"Aye, well they do tell that Queen Catherine is a bit on the racy side when the fancy takes her – the talk around the barrack room is that she's got ants in her pants. He's a lucky old sod is 'H.' Wait 'til the lads hear about this!"* James replied, *"I should be very careful about repeating that sort of tittle-tattle if I were you, John. It could easily cost thee thy noddle should one of the h'officers overhear any of thine idle prattle. Failing that, you could end up as a gong-scourer, shovelling royal shite for the rest of thy career!"*

They heard the King's booming voice followed by a high pitched shriek from the Queen, *"Oh Henry, you mustn't!"* The Yeoman sniggered and James whispered, *"Oooooh Henry – you did! Cor, I'll tell you what, that Henry's a fast worker*!" Much to their relief, the two Yeomen would soon be handing over their duties to the incoming fire-watch who would then remain there outside door duty throughout the rest of the night, their prime concern being to maintain a constant vigil to protect their Monarch and his Queen, listening for suspicious noises or the smell of burning from the ever-present risk of fire.

'CHAPTER 9'

'The Plot Thickens at Leconfield Castle'

The following day, the King, who was in remarkably good humour, had commanded a member of his extensive entourage to seek out the appointed Surveyor of Beverley Minister, Sir Simon Delaney of Molescroft, and have him brought before him for an audience. A puzzled and very concerned Sir Simon had been informed by the Captain of the King's Escort that his presence was required by the King, and was immediately charged to leave his residence at the rear of Beverley Minster and travel to nearby Leconfield. As he rode away on the magnificent but frisky steed brought by the Escort for his use, Simon's fearful wife, the Lady Susan, stood in the doorway of their residence in floods of tears, waving to him as he rode off along the cobbled street, heading for Leconfield. Sir Simon clung to the horse, hanging on for grim death. He was not a particularly competent horseman, in addition to which, it had been several years since he had been out riding.

Shortly after his arrival at Leconfield Castle, Sir Simon was stood in the cavernous main ante-room of the castle, nervously fiddled with his nether garments. He was filled with apprehension and his heart was fluttering, as he waited impatiently for the doors of the King's chambers to swing open. He had heard that the notoriously short-tempered King Henry, depending upon his demeanour on any given day, could be either brutal or extremely generous, however the fancy took him. Sir Simon had no idea what to expect, nor had he been given any inkling as to why His Majesty wanted to speak to him. As far as Sir Simon was concerned he had done nothing wrong.

He was puzzled as to why he hadn't been given the slightest hint as to why he'd been summoned to the royal presence, so it could go either way for him. He'd tried to elicit an explanation from the large, fearsome Captain of the King's Escort, Captain Sir David Kiernan, but his query had fallen on deaf ears. The ride through Beverley and up to Leconfield had been carried out in virtual silence, other than the clattering of horses hooves and shouted orders to pedestrians to *"Make way for the King's men!"* Eventually, they'd arrived at the Castle and clattered across the wooden drawbridge that had been lowered to allow them to cross the deep moat and gain access to the main courtyard.

Once halted, Simon slid from the saddle, not particularly impressively, then had handed his bridle to an obsequious groom, with great relief. Following Captain Kiernan up the steps leading into the castle, Simon ached all over, for he was no horseman and had used muscles that he'd long forgotten were there. He prayed that he wouldn't get a cramp. Simon planned to walk back to Beverley after his audience with the King.

**'King Henry- awaiting the arrival of
Sir Simon Delaney of Molescroft
at Leconfield Castle'**

The Gentleman Usher coughed, politely. "*Sir Simon Delaney
of Molescroft is without, Your Majesty.*" The King, who was
reading, looked up, frowned and removed his gazings
(spectacles). "*Excellent, bring him before us, then leave us
be,*" he commanded. The Gentleman Usher gave a sweeping
bow, his forehead nearly brushing the floor, "*As you wish,
Sire,*' then backed expertly out of the chamber, before
beckoning Sir Simon, who was lurking just outside the door.
Simon had intended taking a sneaky peep into the King's
Chamber but decided against it. The Gentleman Usher said
quietly, "*I will present you to His Majesty, you are then
required to bow and wait until he speaks to you. Say nothing
until then – and under no circumstances are you to lay a
hand on his royal person. That is, as you know is treasonable
and punishable by death.*"

With ill-grace, Sir Simon nodded, and replied, "*Yes, I am
well   aware of the required niceties, but thank you for
reminding me. For your future reference, I am a Knight of
the Realm - in case that fact had escaped your attention –
and am well versed in these matters.*" Ignoring Sir Simon's

waspish comment, the rather fey Gentleman Usher continued, *"Very well then, but be aware, Sir Simon, elegance, politeness, good manners and decorum are required at all times and please remember the rigid code of etiquette that I have previously outlined, then all should be well"*

Sir Simon nodded, as the Gentleman Usher droned on, *"If I might, you should also bear in mind that His Majesty possesses a sharp eye for detail and has a prolific memory. Be sure of your facts, and last, but not least, have a care for His Majesty is very easily vexed."* Simon nodded. *"Now, follow me if you please."* Sir Simon followed the Gentleman Usher as he minced into the King's chamber, Simon skipping uncomfortably to try and stay in step with him. His nerves were on edge and his mouth was so dry that he could feel his top lip sticking to his teeth.

The Gentleman Usher slid to a halt then coughed, politely. *"Your Majesty, might I present Sir Simon Delaney of Molescroft."* The King waved his hand impatiently, *"Let him approach us then!"* The Gentleman Usher stepped to one side and Simon, doffing his cap, sank down onto one knee before his Sovereign. With some effort, Henry struggled to his feet and smiled, *"Greetings, Sir Simon, welcome, 'tis good to finally meet thee. Come now, sir, up off your knee, a courtly bow is more than sufficient. You mustn't spoil us. Pray, come sit you down here next to us. We have certain, er, delicate matters that we wish to discuss with thee, in private,"* said the King waving the obsequious Gentleman Usher away, ordering, *"Get thee hence my good fellow!"* The Gentleman Usher bowed and exited the chamber, closing the double doors quietly behind him.

Without realising it, Sir Simon's jaw had dropped as he took in the splendour of the King's luxurious apparel and accommodation, their magnificence reflecting his undoubted importance. Simon was also astounded by the rich, thick carpeting, and the colourful fixtures and fittings that festooned the Kings chamber, many of them emphasising the Tudor King's favoured colours of Green and White. Simon had rarely witnessed the like. The heavy, silk curtains and tapestries simply took his breath away.

King Henry smiled as he saw Sir Simon gawping, *"We note that thou art admiring our fixtures and fittings, Sir Simon?"* Sir Simon replied, *"Er, er, yes my Liege. Forgive me, I do not mean to cause you any offence. They are of such outstanding beauty and I have not seen their like before. Truly splendid."* Henry nodded, *"Yes, our Knight Harbinger does an excellent job of work. We have a particular liking for those two wall-hangings over there,"* The King pointed at two huge, colourful tapestries, *"That one there is called 'The Labour of Hercules' and the other 'The Triumph of Baccus.' We favour them both greatly and insist that they always accompany us where 'ere we go on our travels."*

Glancing slyly at the King as he was speaking to him about the tapestries, Sir Simon, himself a rather slight individual, was astounded at the statuesque physicality of Henry. He must, he guessed, weigh something in the region of 200 pounds and stood at least six feet two inches tall. His bristling ginger beard made him look truly fearsome. Simon had heard through the grapevine that Henry was something of a trencherman and that he was so fat that *'three of the biggest men that could be found could fit inside his doublet.'* That was certainly an exaggeration, but Sir Simon hadn't realised just what a man mountain the King really was. *"By Saint George, he's a big bugger."* he thought.

Simon had also heard that King Henry had become increasingly incapacitated, paranoid and bad-tempered, primarily as a result of being in constant pain from his jousting injury, the painful open wounds on one of his legs festering and refusing to heal. The cells in the Tower of London were cram-packed with those that had fallen foul of him on one of his bad days, often some for a very minor misdemeanour or perceived slight. The King was definitely not a man to be tampered with. Sir Simon had to fight hard to stop his knees from knocking, in fact, he was so weak with fear that he could hardly stand, such was the effect that King Henry had on lesser mortals.

The King heaved himself back into his luxurious chair, the physical effort of doing so causing him to break ferocious wind, which he affected not to notice. *"Well, Sir Simon, we are sure that you are wondering why we have summoned thee to our presence?"* Sir Simon nodded, *"Aye, Your Majesty, I pondered why a humble person such as missen might be of service to thy royal personage?"* Henry replied, *"In truth, we are of a mind to ask that you indulge in a spot of 'connivance' with us if thou art game and spirited enough to do so. What sayest thou?"* Sir Simon replied, *"I am yours to command, my Liege."*

The King patted a chair at the side of him, *"Come along now, let us not stand on ceremony, place thyself down here beside us, Sir Simon. A glass of refreshing wine, mayhap?"* A surprised Sir Simon nodded and said, *"That would be a most generous and welcome gesture, Sire."* he'd heard that the King could be parsimonious, someone had once been sent to the Tower for a few months after being overheard saying that the King had been known to peel a pineapple in his pocket - but here he was not only offering him a glass of wine but was actually going to pour it for him. A singular honour indeed.

Sir Simon took his place at the side of the King, being very careful not to make physical contact with him, especially the swollen and gouty leg that Henry had just heaved onto a purpose-built padded 'Gout Stool' placed in front of him, grimacing fiercely as he did so.

Once comfortable, the King took a deep breath then smiled. Leaning forward he poured a glass of rich red wine for both himself and Sir Simon. Henry laughed and said, *"You can beat an egg, you can beat a drum, but you can't beat a good drop of robust wine, eh! Our Doctor, Sir William Butts, would be greatly displeased were he here to see us imbibing at this hour of the day, so let us keep this minor transgression between ourselves, eh! What Billy Boy doesn't know won't harm him! The Doctor has the demeanour of an old fishwife on occasion."* Simon sat back and held his wine glass in a vice-like grip in an attempt to disguise the fact that his hands were trembling, *"Not a word of it shall pass my lips, Sire,"* he said before taking a welcome sip. Henry winked at him, *"We would hope not, Sir Simon, for it could easily cost thee thy noddle!"* then laughed uproariously. Simon gave a somewhat timid titter, praying that it was the correct response and that the King was only jesting. One could never be certain.

The wine tasted better than Simon could ever have imagined. *"So, this is how the other half lives,"* he thought. Henry enquired solicitously, *"Doth the beverage meet with thy approval, Sir Simon?"* Simon nodded, *"Aye thank you, Sire, 'tis just t'job."* Henry smiled, *"What's that phrase you Yorkshire lads use – 'A reyt grand drop of stuff, sither!'"* Simon smiled and nodded, gradually relaxing.

Henry continued, *"You know Sir Simon, we speak and read both Latin and French and understand Italian and Spanish but the Devil fetch us, the strange Yorkshire dialect and phrasing never fail to defeat us! It is oft as difficult as Greek!"* Henry threw his head back and laughed loudly. He was obviously in a very expansive mood. *"We shall have to pay more heed to the use of Yorkshire vernacular, after all, we have been the Duke of York since the tender age of Three!"* he said. They both laughed heartily. Simon thought, *"Things are going too well. This must be the calm before the storm."*

"Now, Sir Simon, undoubtedly thou art wondering how you may be of service to your Monarch?" Simon nodded. *"In truth, your Majesty, the thought had flitted across my mind, though I am happy to serve thee in whatever capacity thou doth require,"* The King nodded then heaved open a large leather-bound tome that was laid on the desk in front of him. It was heavily inscribed with tooled gold lettering on both its cover and spine. Sir Simon just managed to stop himself from gasping out loud when he saw up close the several beautiful and sparkling rings adorning King Henry's porky fingers, just one of which would allow him to live in the lap of luxury for the rest of his days.

Henry opened the book and leafed through it until finding the page he was seeking, then continued, *"Now, let us get down to the business of the day, shall we? We have read here in these listings that thou holdeth the appointment of Surveyor of Beverley Minster. Is that information still of pertinence?"* Sir Simon nodded, *"Indeed it is, Sire. I assumed the post several years ago and retain it to this very day. I am well rewarded with a small stipend for my efforts, entirely sufficient for my needs I hasten to add."*

"*Excellent*," replied Henry, "*We are of a mind to visit Beverley Minster come the morrow. We require you to meet up with us there and escort us around its glorious interior. It is our desire to seek out every nook and cranny. Wilt thou attend me there?*" "*Yes, of course, Your Majesty, t'would be an honour for me to do so*," replied Simon. "*Then speak you to my Gentleman Usher regarding the time and means of our arrival at the Minster door, which will be twixt five and six o' the clock, nigh to twilight. He will apprise you of the precise details. We have commanded that the streets and alleyways surrounding the Minster be cleared of the civilian populace by my faithful Yeomen and that the Minster itself will likewise be vacated by anyone else other than the two of us and our military escorts. We do not wish to see any other hangers-on, gawpers or lurkers thereabouts. You are to meet us at the side entrance to the Minster.*" Sir Simon nodded, "*As you desire, Your Majesty.*" Sir Simon was puzzled as to the reason why the King would want to visit the Minster at such a relatively late hour, and also as to why he wouldn't be using the main entrance, but dare not ask the King to explain.

Henry leaned across to Sir Simon, "*We have a particular desire to seek out the 'Shrine of Saint John.' Knowest thou of what we speak?*" " Sir Simon nodded, "*Indeed I do, Your Majesty. The Shrine stands in the retrochoir, to the rear of the high altar of the Minster.*" Henry nodded, Sir Simon continued, "*The Shrine is in very good condition, the townspeople and parishioners having contributed generously towards its upkeep. Many Pilgrims have made, and continue to make, donations at the Shrine because Saint John's relics contained therein are believed by them to work miracles.*"

Sir Simon was in full flow, "*The large tomb was built using dolomitic magnesian limestone, traditionally sourced from*

118

the quarries at Tadcaster and Cadeb, names of which I'm sure your Majesty is no doubt familiar." The King placed his hand over his mouth, not quite smothering a yawn. His attention span was beginning to falter and in truth, he cared not a jot about Tadcaster or Cadeb. Failing to take the hint that His Majesty was becoming a tad bored by the subject, Sir Simon ploughed on regardless.

"*As you are no doubt aware, sire, Beverley is a sanctuary town with rights granted to the Minster by King Athelstan in 937, and is one of only two towns in the North of England with that particular status.*" The Kings eyes were beginning to glaze over, Sir Simon, with the bit between his teeth, continued, "*Those fleeing persecution or who had been accused of wrongdoing travelled here from all over the country to seek protection and also get a fair hearing. They were permitted to remain there for up to 30 days. The Sanctuary Chair in the Minster is a survivor of the era of Bishop John, or as we know of him, Saint John of Beverley, who set up a Monastery on the site of this current Minster prior to his death in the year of our Lord, 721.*"

With great enthusiasm, Sir Simon continued, "*The Minster is also, sire, England's largest parish church.*' Sir Simon had failed to notice that the King's attention had wandered and that his eyes were half closed. The King was thinking, "*This interminable discourse is about as interesting as watching a coffin lid warp.*" The King, who was experiencing difficulty maintaining focus, suddenly yawned and rudely interrupted Simon, "*Enough of all that fiddle-faddle, for now, Sir Simon! You may speak to us further on the subject once we are inside the Minster. A picture is worth a thousand words, is that not so?*" Sir Simon nodded in agreement. He was surprised at the Kings mercurial change of temperament. One minute he was sat there, exuding bonhomie, the next he was huffing and puffing his displeasure. This was indeed an exercise in tiptoeing on gilded splinters for Sir Simon.

As Simon's explanation faltered to a halt, the King noted the look of concern on his face, Henry patted Simon's knee, smiled and said, *"Forgive me, Sir Simon, thou need not concern thyself with my brusqueness. We have much to do in our life and must ration our time accordingly. We will reveal all to you once inside the confines of Beverley Minster."* Simon nodded, *"Very well, Sire, and I will ensure that there will only be those present there as per your instructions."* Henry's eyes glinted and his jovial face turned to stone, *"You better had, Sir Simon! Walls have ears and what we will have to say to thee at the Minster is for thine ears and thine ears alone!"*

The dark cloud that had crossed Henry's face disappeared as quickly as it had arrived. *"Now then, enough of that, let us tempt you to another glass of this most excellent wine? 'Tis provided for us by the good offices of the Earl of Alnwick, William de Percy, the Master of this fine fortress."* Without waiting for a reply, the King poured them both another generous glass of wine, filling the glasses to the brim then said cheerily, *"Your good health, Sir Simon!"*

They sat sipping the rich, red wine whilst the King graciously continued to make small talk with his visitor. *"Do you ride, Sir Simon?"* *"Only when I must, Sire, for in truth I have a habit of falling off my own ancient steed,"* he replied. The King smiled and nodded, *"We greatly admire the gentlemanly skills of riding, jousting, tennis, archery, and hunting, but, alas, because of our present physical 'difficulties' must now cut our cloth accordingly. It is a cause of great sadness to me."* he said, rubbing his bandaged leg, alluding to the limitations caused by his serious jousting accident on the 24th of January 1536, the results of which had severely curbed his physical activities, leading to the massive increase in his weight.

It was said that because of the constant pain caused by the suppurating ulcers on the King's legs, it greatly affected his behaviour – often to the detriment of those in close proximity to him. Catch him on a bad day and it was rumoured that your head would be parted from your body before you could say 'Boo to a Goose' - or even worse, he had heard that the King if the fancy took him, could order that you be boiled alive! As the years passed his temperament had become increasingly more difficult to gauge. Immaterial of their rank or status, courtiers trod lightly each day until the King's frame of mind had been ascertained. Fortunately for Simon, today appeared to be one of the King's better days.

Once the King had emptied his wine glass, he yawned, belched loudly and said, *"Time flies like an arrow, now be off home to thy lady, Sir Simon. What is her name?"* *"Tis Susan, Sire."* Henry nodded and smiled, *"Kindly pass on our respects to Lady Susan. Now, we are sure that, like us, you have much else to do. We will see thee anon, fare thee well."*

Sir Simon placed his half-empty wine glass on the table, stood up, then, as if by magic, the double doors to the chamber swung open and the Gentleman Usher reappeared. *"Sir Simon is departing. Be so kind as to inform him of the arrangements that have been made for our visit to Beverley Minster tomorrow."* said the King, waving his bejewelled hand imperiously. The Gentleman Usher nodded, *"As you wish, Sire."* then both he and Sir Simon bowed deeply before exiting backward out of the chamber, the Gentleman Usher expertly pulling the doors quietly closed behind him.

Once the doors had closed, the King poured himself another glass of wine, scowled, rubbed his aching leg and mumbled, "*A pox on this accursed trotter of mine!*" He eased himself out of the chair and stood up with difficulty, "*Methinks 'tis time for me to pay a visit to the privies and ease my bowels. Let us hope that they hath warmed the seat.*"

'CHAPTER 10'

'Ye Sun Inn, Beverley in 1541'

It was a chilly evening and all was deathly quiet in the large, uncultivated field at the rear of the Sun Inn, Beverley. Suddenly, in a small wooded area at the far corner of the field, the air was disturbed and out of nowhere, with a gentle humming sound, the 'T2 Travellator'' de-materialised. After a few moments the door in the side of the 'T2' hissed open and Time-Traveller Graham St Anier stepped out into the year 1541. He was dressed in the appropriate clothing for the period, cloak, doublet, and hose, and slung over his shoulder was a leather satchel containing a few of his 'necessaries' such as a toothbrush and tube of toothpaste, a roll of toilet paper and a small sachet of aspirins. He felt faintly ridiculous in the medieval clothing but obviously wanted to blend in with the crowd.

He had a quick look around to see that no one was in the vicinity to witness his arrival, then reached across to the alphabetical key-pad at the side of the T2's door and tapped 'RTB' (*Return to Base*) on it. He then took a swift pace backward as the 'T2's' door closed and sealed itself with a hiss. After a few moments, the 'T2' materialised and vanished into thin air, leaving no trace whatsoever of it ever having been there. Even the blades of long grass in the field showed no indication of the 'T2' having landed there.

Graham smiled and thought, "*Right, well here I am, back in Beverley in the year 1541.*" He sniffed appreciatively at the crisp, fresh air that carried just a hint of wood-smoke, "*Mmmm, that smells nice, makes a change from the usual niff of petrol fumes. I'd better go and book into my accommodation.*" The 'Time-Travellers' office had organised a room for him at the Sun Inn as part of the 'Time-Travel' package deal. He was quite excited at the prospect of seeing the Sun Inn as it was in 1541, as back in his own time-zone he was a regular there, often eating one of their splendid traditional Sunday roasts and knocking back several of the many different varieties of beer available at the bar. Pulling his cloak around his shoulders to help ward off the chill, he strode briskly across the field to find the front entrance of the Sun Inn, keeping a watchful eye out for cow pats.

'Ye Sun Inn, Beverley'

On arrival at the Sun Inn, Graham eased the door open, took a deep breath then confidently stepped inside. To his relief, it was lovely and warm in there and he was greeted by the portly and cheerful Landlord, a rosy-faced William (Billy) Elvidge, who said, *"Good evening, Pilgrim. My name is William Elvidge, although everyone addresses me as Billy. I am the Landlord of this fine establishment."* Graham replied, *"Evening. I believe that a room has been reserved here for my use over the next few days. I am Graham St Anier."* Billy smiled at Graham and said, *"Indeed it has, sir. Welcome to Ye Sun Inn, the finest establishment this side of Lincoln, if I might be so bold. I am glad to make your acquaintance, Pilgrim, and am honoured that thou hast chosen to lodge here and share our facilities."* Graham nodded and shook hands with Billy, *"It's a pleasure to be in such a fine establishment, Landlord."* replied Graham, removing his cloak.

Billy took Graham's cloak and placed it on a nearby wall hook. *"Better let thy cloak air off, we don't want it getting covered with mildew."* Graham nodded his thanks. Billy continued, *"We are pleased to welcome another friendly face in here. It has been a tad quiet since the last Pilgrims departed here but a few days ago, so quiet in fact that I was able to offer your agent preferential rates. You are here to visit the Minster, I take it?"* queried Billy. Graham nodded, *"Aye, that's correct, Master Elvidge."* Elvidge interrupted him, *"Oh no need to be quite so formal, sir, 'tis Billy, if you please."* Graham nodded, *"Well, Billy, I have travelled here from Lincoln in order to offer up a few prayers and to pay my respects at the Crypt of Saint John of Beverley. I would also like to have a good look around the Minster and the town of Beverley if there is time to fit it all in."* Billy nodded, *"Very well, sir, now if you would care to follow me, I'll show you to your accommodation. Er, I note that you have very little baggage with you?"* commented a puzzled Billy.

Graham smiled, "*That is correct. I am travelling light, the majority of my luggage remains at Lincoln, to where I will be returning at the conclusion of this short Pilgrimage. I have sufficient items with me to last me until then. I am happy to pay for my room in advance if that troubles you*?" The Landlord smiled, "*Nay sir, not necessary. Payment hath been made in advance by your agent, so, fear not, Mrs. Elvidge, my Elizabeth, and missen will ensure that thou art well catered for and that thy needs are fully met during thy stay here with us. Now, this way if you please.*"

Graham followed Billy as he waddled off through the Inn towards the living accommodation. Graham smiled as he walked past the kitchen, where there was a large notice nailed to the wall, stating:

'PISSING IN YE COOKING HEARTH IS STRICTLY FORBIDDEN.'

That's a bit of a relief," thought Graham.

Later on, that evening after he had been well fed, Graham was sat, legs outstretched, contentedly toasting his toes before a blazing log fire in the cozy bar room of the Sun Inn. The thick wax candles placed in several wall alcoves around the Inn to light the place were spluttering as the gobbets of rich yellow fat were ignited by the wicks, causing a fair degree of guttering, but still providing a warm, welcoming glow.

Graham smiled as he recalled Billy Elvidge's invitation to "*Come, Pilgrim, sit you down alongside the hearth and warm thy hocks, 'tis as cold as a witches tit this night, if you'll pardon the vulgarity.*" Graham had eaten a very wholesome dinner, Mrs. Elvidge was an excellent Cook and was not ungenerous with the portions that she served him. Graham's boilers were well and truly filled. He sat back enjoying listening to the badinage of the other patrons, lulled into a sense of contentment by the soporific crackling of burning logs in the fireplace and started to drift off.

The Landlord startled Graham from his reveries when he called out, "*Prithee Pilgrim, might I tempt thee to a flagon of our fine traditional Yorkshire ale? 'Tis said by many of our visitors to be akin to 'Nectar of the Gods' and cannot be bettered*!'" Graham smiled and nodded, "*Madness not to, Mr. Elvidge, er Billy.*" Billy smiled, "*I'll pour thee a flagon and fetch it ower in a moment, sir.*" delighted to have made a sale on such a relatively quiet evening. Even the passing trade had been miserably poor over the last few days. "*If I may say so, Billy, Mrs. Elvidge provided me with an excellent repast this evening, thy victuals are beyond comparison,*" said Graham, entering into the spirit of things and using the Tudor vernacular that he had been briefed to try by the advisors at 'Time-Travellers.' The Landlord was delighted, "*Why, I must thank you, Pilgrim, 'tis most Christian of thee to say thus. I will relay thy kind comments to my wife Elizabeth. She would have been much distressed had it not been so.*"

Billy reached across the bar and twisted the squeaking spigot on a firkin of beer that was resting on a wooden cross-frame and poured a quantity of richly coloured frothing ale into a jug, then took both it and a pewter tankard across to Graham's table. "*I've had my Elizabeth place a fire-pan in thi bed, sir, just to warm t'bedding up a little, although the fire in the room hath removed the chill from out of the air. 'Tis uncommonly cold for this time of year and we would not have thee nithered.*" Graham nodded in agreement as he poured himself a tankard of ale, then took a hefty swig.

He smacked his lips, and sighed, "*Ah, 'tis a reyt grand drop of stuff. This is the life,*" he said to Billy, "*and tomorrow I'm going to start the day off on the right foot by having a hearty breakfast followed by a good mooch around the Minster.*" Billy asked him, "*Regarding breaking thy fast come the morn, sir. As thou may have noticed, my Elizabeth is a cook of the first water and her food is much sought after around these parts. She will be delighted to provide you with a fine repast with which to start thy day off on the right foot.*" "*Yes, well I look forward to that. You can't beat a 'Full English' breakfast,*" replied Graham, "*then it is my intention to nip across to the Minster and pay my respects to Saint John and examine the beautiful stained glass windows.*"

Billy nodded, "*A 'Full English' breakfast. I like the term, we will use that in the future. A hearty 'Full English' breakfast will be available to thee from seven of the clock onwards. It will be available in the same room as where your evening meal was presented.*" "*I will try and do it full justice,*" replied Simon, topping up his tankard from the jug. "*This is a cracking drop of ale, Billy.*" he said. Billy smiled and rubbed his hands together, "*'Tis indeed. Mayhap I will join thee in a drop - if thou hast no objection?*" Simon smiled, "*None at all. There's plenty of ale left in this jug. Grab a tankard and come sit beside me. I'd like to know a bit more about the history of the Sun Inn, perhaps you can tell me something about the place?*" Billy smiled, "*I wouldst not take ale from thy jug, Pilgrim, t'would not be improper for me to do so. I'll pour a fresh one for missen then appraise thee of the Inn's history thus far.*"

As they sat by the fireside, Billy explained the history of the Sun Inn, saying to Graham, "*And that's how I came to be the Landlord here. Now, regarding the morn, If you desire it be so, I will instruct my son to rap on thy door when he is on his way to collect a supply of fresh milk and eggs from the local farm>*" "*That would be just the job, Billy,*" said Graham, "*I want to be up and about fairly early so that, as I said, I can have a good look around Beverley Minster and then, of course, the town itself.*"

Mr. Elvidge placed a warning hand on Graham's shoulder, "*If I might be so bold, a word of caution, sir. 'Tis rumoured that there is a very important visitor in the area and that the Minster and its surrounding streets are to be closed off to the likes of we, come the morn. T'would appear that the 'figure of importance' will also be visiting the Minster sometime late tomorrow evening. When such silliness occurs it's usually because there is Royalty passing through here on the way to York. There hath been much military activity in this area throughout the day and you know what buggers, forgive me, those soldiers are. Rogues to a man! Why they think naught of cracking you across the head with their heavy gloves for some imagined slight! I myself have been offered violence on more than one occasion whilst being about my lawful business! Tis shameful.*" Graham nodded, "*Thank you, Billy, that's good to know, I'll have to be alert and keep my wits about me. Any idea who the Royal personage might be?*"

The Landlord dropped his voice, "*Just between the two of us, Pilgrim, 'tis rumoured that King Henry himself is up here on one of his many 'Progresses.' T'would would seem that both he and Queen Catherine are tarrying awhile at Leconfield Castle. This will be something like his fourth visit here this year. It would appear that His Majesty loves the hunting and hawking up in that neck of the woods and is also a great friend of the Earl.*" Billy tutted, "*There's hardly a beast, wild or otherwise, to be purchased locally since he came here on his last visit, which was nobbut a few months ago. Everything of quality is usually commandeered for the King and his party. Fortunately, I have an arrangement with a farmer at Tickton village who keeps me supplied with fresh meat and vegetables. He has managed to avoid the swingeing forays of Sir Percy's agents so far, but I'm sure that they'll seek him out afore long."*

Graham said, *"Well, I'll take a walk across to the Minster anyway and see if I can gain entrance, then if I've got time afterwards I'll have a slow meander about the town."* *"Merry wind to thee, sir, but have a care."* replied a laughing Mr. Elvidge, *"Wouldst mind if I tarry a while here at the table with thee to share a drop of ale and perhaps indulge in a spot more blather?"* Graham grinned, *"T'would be an honour and a pleasure, Billy Elvidge. Now, you promised to tell me something about the strangely named 'Monks Walk,' across the way?"* *"No sooner said than done, Pilgrim, but before I do, let me top up our tankards before I continue with my historical discourse,"* said Billy, reaching for Graham's tankard. *"Mmm, it's going to be a late night,"* thought Graham.

The following morning, after partaking of a hearty breakfast, the best part of which was the pile of toasted pikelets that had been smothered with freshly churned butter by a beaming Mrs Elvidge, Graham was handed a hefty wedge of cheese and a cob of freshly baked bread, wrapped neatly in a clean cloth, accompanied by a corked flagon of ale to wash it down with. *"I have to say, Mrs. Elvidge, that that was the finest breakfast I have had for many a year!"* A blushing Mrs. Elvidge curtseyed and said, *"Why thank you, sir, most kind of you to say so."* She passed Graham a fairly large bundle, *"Here you are, sir, that'll save thee 'avin to reach into thi purse to purchase refreshment throughout the course of the day. 'Tis all fresh and should last thee 'til this evening when, if I'm spared, I'll have a fine repast readied for thy delectation."* Graham smiled, *"Why thank you, Mrs. Elvidge, that is most considerate of you. I shall look forward to eating the food you have so thoughtfully provided and look forward to this evening's meal with great relish."* Mrs. Elvidge smiled mischievously, *"T'will not be great relish sir, but the finest Yorkshire Relish!"* They laughed.

Stood at her side, a solicitous and unusually serious looking Billy said, *"By the cringe, Pilgrim, enjoy thy day but take heed of that which I warned thee yesterday. Be cautious whilst thou art out and about, the King's men are not to be vexed and there will be many of them about the Kings business on the streets of Beverley this very day. I have seen several of them already perambulating around the streets this very morning as if they own the place. They are without conscience. Why, tis said that if thou so much as fart out of tune they will undoubtedly use that as an excuse to haul thee into custody."*

At the mention of the word fart, Mrs. Elvidge blushed and scuttled off back to her kitchen. Graham gave a wolfish grin and nodded, *"Fear not, Billy, I'll keep my wits about me and where 'ere I will be, no wind shall blow free - if I can avoid it."* Billy sighed, *"Tis shameful how closely our lives are monitored. Huh, my late father used to say – "Where 'ere thee be, let thy wind blow free. In church or chapel, let it rattle!"* They both laughed.

"Right, I'd best be on my way then," said Graham, tucking the substantial bundle of vittles into his leather satchel, then stepped out of the front door of the Sun Inn only to pause, impressed by the view of the breathtakingly beautiful medieval Gothic architecture and majesty of Beverley Minster, towering over the Sun Inn. It was astounding to think that work had started on the Minster back in the year

1220 and had then taken a further two hundred years to complete. It also seemed strange to Graham not to have regiments of cars and lorries thundering down the road past the Sun Inn, belching out fumes, their impatient drivers tooting on their horns. All that could be heard now was the occasional chirruping of the birds. Graham drew his cloak around him to help ward off the early morning chill and continued to gaze admiringly at the Minster. The morning sun was just breaking through the clouds and it was promising to be a nice day.

As he was admiring the Minster, Graham considered how best to get himself inside there without being stopped and questioned by the military. Billy Elvidge had informed him of a side door that was reserved purely for the use of the Bishop, whose palace was within spitting distance of the Minster.

'The 'Bishop's Door' at the side of Beverley Minster'

The 'Bishop's' door was always left unlocked in order for him to gain easy and informal access whenever he felt it the need to do so. Graham decided that he would give the door a try himself. Nothing ventured, nothing gained. Knowing that King Henry would be arriving there that evening, Graham wanted to witness his arrival and see if he could discover what mischief was afoot. so he'd have to slip inside the Minster without being seen and find a suitable hiding place from where he could then monitor the proceedings. He would just have to be patient.

Graham knew, from the information contained in the parchment that he'd discovered in the Beverley Old bookshop, that today was definitely the day that King Henry would be paying a visit to the Minster in order to hide some sort of wooden chest, containing valuables, somewhere inside. In addition, the information that Billy Elvidge ferreted out indicated that the royal visit was scheduled to take place later that afternoon. Whilst wandering around the marketplace with Elizabeth, a 'nebby' Billy had overheard a group of soldiers whinging about having to be up early the following morning to empty the streets surrounding the Minster and also clear the Minster itself of any visitors or Pilgrims, then having to stand guard at the entrance to the Minster throughout the day. So, just to be on the safe side, Graham had decided to make a start bright and early and find somewhere inside the Minster where he could tuck himself away out of sight, well before the soldiers turned up. It might prove to be a long day for Graham, but he was convinced that it would be well worth the wait.

Prior to travelling back in time, Graham had searched high and low in several local libraries and bookshops and had also spent many hours in Beverley Treasure House, ploughing through dusty old books and eyeballing every website available to him. There was absolutely no mention of or reference to any hidden treasure ever being recovered from the Minster, neither was there any mention of the precise date of the King's visit there. The only details of the royal visit to the Minster were written on the little piece of parchment discovered by Graham, hidden in the spine of his book.

Graham was utterly convinced that there was a high probability that the chest was still there, hidden away somewhere inside the Minster. He was determined to seek it out and then, if he could, recover its contents. His imagination ran riot when he thought about what the contents of the chest might be. He couldn't wait to get started.

'CHAPTER 11'

'Strange happenings inside Beverley Minster'

By using the 'Bishop's' door situated directly opposite the Bishop's Palace, Graham had managed to manoeuvre his way into Beverley Minster without being detected. To his delight, he'd found it to be unlocked and unattended, so he'd slid inside the Minster then quickly sought out a dark, secluded corner where there was a conveniently placed confessional box in which he could lurk and easily monitor the goings-on without being discovered.

He'd made himself as comfortable as he could in the confessional box, having 'borrowed' a couple of 'kneelers' from the pews to sit on and of course he had the cheese, bread, and ale provided by a thoughtful Mrs. Elvidge to help sustain him throughout his wait. All he had to do was stay awake, avoid discovery and take note of the goings-on. Frustratingly, the one thing that he didn't know was the precise time that the King was due to arrive at the Minster,

135

so he had got there early and would just have to sit there in the gloom and be patient. His first clue would be when things started to liven up, which would indicate that the King was due to put in an appearance. No-one knew if the King would change his mind and arrive earlier than expected, which he had been known to do, so it was safer to be prepared for that eventuality. If they had to wait there all day, then so be it. They had nothing better to do.

It was unusually quiet inside the Minster, the entire place having been cleared of visitors, protesting members of the clergy, beggars and any other lurkers, by order of the King. What Graham took a particular interest in was the four sturdy Yeomen of the Guard who had arrived shortly after he had and who were stood dutifully at the side of the transept, closely guarding a large wooden chest. Fortunately, the Yeomen were busy chatting amongst themselves and hadn't spotted Graham. So, at that precise moment, other than himself, all Graham had to contend with was the four Yeomen, and a twitchy Sir Simon Delaney, who had arrived just after the Yeomen and who was pacing backwards and forwards along the strip of carpet placed in front of the high altar.

"It all looks very promising. I'll bet my last shilling that that's the treasure chest they're guarding," thought Graham, *"If I just sit here quietly and wait for the arrival of the main man, then all should be revealed."* In the event that he was discovered in his little hidey-hole, Graham had decided that he'd pretend to be deep in prayer. Not much of a plan but one that just might work. Hopefully, he would then just be hoofed out of the Minster without any further repercussions. He'd just have to wait and see.

The day dragged on interminably and despite trying his utmost to remain alert, Graham, wrapped in his cloak, managed to drift off to sleep a number of times. On the last occasion, he woke himself up with a particularly loud snort. Fortunately, no-one else heard him. Looking out of the confessional box at the beautiful stained glass of the Minster windows he saw that at last, it was starting to get dark outside. His mouth was dry, and he felt decidedly peckish, having finished the last of the delicious cheese and bread off during the course of a very long and boring day. He wished now that he'd saved some.

The ale that he'd brought with him, although tepid, had been used to slake his considerable thirst and, bonus, the empty flagon had come in very useful as a temporary urinal - needs must when the bladder drives. He would just have to remain patient and was sure that it wouldn't be too long before something happened. His stomach was rumbling, complaining bitterly about the lack of food. Graham was further tormented by the knowledge that Mrs. Elvidge would at that moment be preparing a delicious evening meal for him. He could almost taste the thick slices of succulent roast beef, smothered with rich gravy, and had tormenting visions of the dining table at the Sun Inn creaking with food.

Hearing a voice calling from the Minster's side entrance, Graham immediately went into the alert mode, "*Here we go, at last something's happening,*" he thought. Sir Simon was being beckoned by a Yeoman of the Guard, "*If it please you, Sir Knight, come quickly, His Majesty approacheth. With respect, you should make haste sir, the King doth not take kindly to being kept waiting!*"

Sir Simon, who had been sat on a pew in front of the altar chewing his nails, stood up and rushed across to the door, stumbling as he did so and striking his shin heavily on the plinth of a marble statue. He cursed out loud, "*By Christ's fingernails!*" then remembering where he was, glanced back at the altar and mentally apologised for blaspheming, "*Forgive me, Lord*" One of the Yeomen who'd seen him trip, sniggered, "*See that lads, what a plank! Typical gentry, they can't walk and think at one and the same time!*" he whispered.

Through the rapidly descending gloom of the evening came the sound of the clatter of horses hooves as they clip-clopped along the cold, shiny cobblestones of Highgate past Monks Walk, leading up to the front of the Minster, the jingling of tack and neighing of horses echoing around the empty streets. The King and his gallant train of attendants, (known as his 'Riding Retinue') - on this occasion consisting of The Lord Chamberlain, the Lord Steward, the Master of the Horse and several heavily armed Yeomen of the Guard led by their Captain, Captain Sir David Kiernan, by-passed the main entrance of the Minster then turned into St. John Street, arriving at the open side door of the Minster, before drawing to a halt. Despite the royal directive to have the streets immediately surrounding the Minster cleared of the populace, there were still a few onlookers stood at the side of the road gawping at the King and his relatively small retinue.

'Beverley Minster – Side Entrance (the Bishop's Door)'

The King turned to Captain Sir David Kiernan and said, rather peevishly, "*Huh, Kiernan, there are too many of the common herd here, all that's missing is the Master of the King's Puddings! We expressed an explicit desire that we did not wish to attract any unnecessary attention during our visit to the Minster!*" The sour-faced- Henry was obviously in one of his more 'difficult' moods. Those around him recognising the symptoms trod very warily. If the thin royal veneer of pleasantness was shattered, then there inevitably emerged a mean and vindictive man who would not hesitate to order that heads be lopped off then probably rammed onto pike-staffs for displaying in prominent areas, as an example to others not to transgress.

Puffing, panting, and with great difficulty, Henry struggled to dismount from his horse, assisted by the Captain of the Guard. As he cocked his leg over the saddle he broke ferocious wind. The Captain of the Guard, who was directly in the firing line, visibly blanched whilst the remainder of the King's select retinue averted their eyes, not wanting to be seen witnessing the King's struggles.

Once dismounted, Henry, hobbled across to the cobbled forecourt adjacent to the Minster's open side door, paused momentarily, then pointed at his entourage with a bejewelled gloved hand and snorted at the Captain, "*With the exception of you, Captain Kiernan, all others are to remain by their steeds, outside this entrance to the Minster! Place two guards at the door, facing outwards. No-one else is to be given entrance!*" He then turned to a nervous Sir Simon, who had been waiting at the side door to receive him, "*Ah, Sir Simon, 'tis good to see thee.*"

Sir Simon gave a deep bow. "*Your Majesty, I am much honoured to be once more in thy gracious presence.*" The

King waved his hand dismissively, *"Tish! Enough of thy feather-bedding, sir, let us proceed inside the Minster without further ado. We have no wish to stand out here inviting a chill."* Simon thought, *"Oh no, t'would appear that the King is in a poor frame of mind."*

The King was impatient and wanted to crack on, *"Sir Simon, take heed, we have no desire to tarry within the confines of the Minster for any longer than is strictly necessary. You may forget all previous notions of revealing the myriad dusty nooks and crannies of the Minster, we are not some wandering Pilgrim who wishes to gawp at fripperies and artifacts. Prithee, guide us directly to the Crypt of Saint John of Beverley without further delay."* The King then stomped off into the gloom of the Minster, closely followed by Captain Kiernan and an attentive, tremulous Sir Simon. *"If I cock this up, I'm for the chop,"* thought Simon.

This was definitely not the cheerful and outgoing Monarch that Sir Simon had met up with at Leconfield Castle the previous day. Simon called out, *"Sire, with respect, the Crypt is just over there to thy right, near the high altar and to the left of those large brass candlesticks - straight in front of the Yeomen. Pray note if you would, sire, the large slab of polished marble on the floor before you, for 'tis that which covers the entrance to the Crypt of Saint John of Beverley."*

'The entrance to the Crypt of Saint John of Beverley'

Henry and Sir Simon arrived at the slab of marble, where stood rigidly to attention like true English oaks and hands firmly clutching their Partizans, were four sturdy members of the Kings Yeomen of the Guard, Senior Yeoman Arthur Lukins, Yeomen George Hepworth, Anthony Culpepper, and Edward Whittaker, awaiting further orders. The large, highly polished ornate brass candle holders that were fitted with chunky white waxy candles had been commandeered by Sir Simon in order to cast a modicum of light on the entrance to the Crypt. The light from the candles threw ghostly, flickering shadows over the scene, giving it an air of ghostly unreality and menace.

Graham still tucked away in the confessional box, had an excellent view of the King and Sir Simon from his hiding place and could also hear quite clearly what was being said. The acoustics in the Minster couldn't be bettered. He was delighted that he'd chosen his location so well, perhaps now he might get some answers regarding the contents of the mysterious chest.

The King, pointed at the marble slab, saying, *"And this is it, you say?"* Sir Simon nodded and replied, *"Indeed it is, sire."*

"Huh, not at all impressive for so important a Saint, is it! We expected something a little more ornate and grand!" Henry nodded towards the solid oak chest laid on the floor of the transept, next to the Yeomen, *"Anyway, to business. Earlier this morning we had yonder chest carted here by those four rogues, it was covered with cloth so as to disguise it from prying eyes."* he said. A look of puzzlement crossed Sir Simon's face and he was about to ask about the chest when the King continued, *"I prithee, Sir Simon, do not strain thy brain, for all will be revealed very shortly and everything will, hopefully, be clarified in your mind."*

Henry beckoned Sir Simon, indicating for him to draw closer, then, speaking to him in conspiratorial tones, said, *"If thou art wondering what yonder hefty chest contains, sir, then know thee that at our direction, the 'Treasury of the Chamber' hath had it filled with gold coins and valuables. Thus, sir, thou now hast thy first intimation as to its contents."* Sir Simon nodded, putting on what he hoped was his 'intelligent face' and doing his utmost to look as if he understood precisely what the King was talking about, which he didn't.

Henry continued, *"That is undoubtedly a part of what thou art wondering about. Yonder chest contains funds to be used for secret Royal enterprises, let us refer to it as a 'war chest.' Yes, that would be a good description. We are having similar chests secreted away in key places outside of London in the event that there is an emergency there and our treasury cannot be accessed. Chests such as that one will be tucked away out of sight waiting to be recovered when we give the express order to do so."*

The King's voice dropping even lower and hissing with menace, he said, *"We need hardly impress upon thee what will happen to thy good self, Sir Simon, and to every single*

142

one of thy relatives, if one single word of this covert enterprise ever leaks out!" The blood drained from Sir Simon's face and he replied, "*I can assure you, Sire, that my lips are sealed.*" The King raised an eyebrow and said, silkily, "*Let us assure you that your lips will be sealed for all eternity, Sir Simon, should'st thou ever fail us!*"

They both looked across at the sturdy oak chest that had the initials 'H R' branded onto the lid. It had been fitted with four chunky, solid metal handles and then bound by several heavy metal straps, it also had a substantial bolt and hasp fitted into its lid, which in turn was secured with a strong lock. Even a simpleton could see that it was a quality item that had been made to last.

"*Now then, Sir Simon,*" instructed the King, "*have my lads open up the Crypt if you please!*" A shocked Sir Simon's jaw dropped and he sank to his knees, gasping, "*Open the Crypt, Sire? But, but, I have not had authority from the Bishop to do so. Sire, I beseech thee ....*"

The King, unused to having his orders questioned, turned puce, then trembling with fury, eyes bulging bellowed at Sir Simon, "*You dribbling, impertinent nincompoop! You seem to forget, sir, to whom thou art speaking! My will be done! Now, enough of this fiddle-faddle, our patience wears thin! We give you our Royal dispensation to break open the seal of the Crypt! The only one you are answerable to is your King, not some meddlesome prissy Bishop! You have naught else to fear other than thy Sovereign's wrath!*" He struck Sir Simon a fearsome blow on the side of his head with his meaty, bejewelled clenched fist, causing him to fall sideways and bang his head on a pew, "*Dost thou need reminding that we are the ultimate authority here, sir, not some addle-pated ninny-cock of a Bishop! Pah, Bishops, they are more trouble*

143

than they are worth! Now, sir, up on your feet and do as we bid! Our Yeomen of the Guard and their Captain will assist thee. Let us proceed without further delay." Sir Simon stood up, still dazed from hitting his head on the pew. How swiftly his fortunes had changed.

The four Yeomen were looking as apprehensive as Sir Simon, *"God's bones!"* roared Henry, *"There is naught but a few mouldering rags lurking in yonder Crypt. No harm will come to you, my lads. Pah! We are surrounded by superstitious simpletons and incompetents!"* The Yeomen of the Guard stood to attention, gazing straight ahead of them. It didn't do to get involved when h'officers and gentry were shouting at each other. They'd seen similar incidents many times whilst attending the King. Henry stared at Sir Simon, *"Well sir?!"* Sir Simon licked his lips and bowed, *"As you command, sire, but I would caution you that there are several very precious and holy artifacts laid within the Crypt. It is hallowed ground."*

The King had worked himself up into a raging fury, *"Damn your blood! We are not going to vandalise or purloin the contents of the Crypt! It may please you to know, Sir Simon, that we had given explicit instructions previously that this tomb and others like it were to be emptied of their contents and anything of value was to be confiscated. Any unnecessary images and sculptures inside of shrines were to be disposed of. There should be nothing in the Crypt other than a few old bones. 'Tis only the space of the Crypt that we require, we do not desire to have the Saints remains disturbed!"*

Pausing momentarily to regain his breath, Henry gazed malevolently at the marble slab covering the entrance to the Crypt and then took a deep breath and continued haranguing

Sir Simon, *"Art thou intimating, Sir Knight, that the clear-out of this Crypt has yet to be done?"* he asked. Sir Simon nodded. The King roared, *"Saints preserve us! Be no-one here of any doubt that the laggardly Bishop, whom we are informed hath all the presence of the lowest Gong Scourer, will be summoned to appear before me to explain why he hath chosen to boldly disregard my instructions!"* Henry stamped his foot angrily, hurting himself in the process, sending him into a further bout of apoplectic fury, He howled, *"Who will rid us of these meddlesome priests and their loudmouthed belchings!"* He shook his fist under Sir Simon's nose, *"Now get on and do not test our patience further, you dull-headed mumblecrust!"* he roared, gobbets of spittle dripping down his trembling ginger beard.

Henry turned to Captain Kiernan and said, *"Captain, thou art to keep a watchful eye on this whittle-whattle of a knight and on those of our escort remaining outside the Minster! We imagined that this would be a simple and straightforward task, but nay, t'would be easier to saddle a goose!"* The Captain bowed and nodded, *"Yes Sire."* Henry turned back to Sir Simon and nodded towards the Crypt, *"We will not instruct thee again! Now get thee hence, Sir Simon of Molescroft and do as thou art bid!"*

A shocked and trembling Sir Simon gulped, nodded and said, *"I serve to please, your Majesty,"* then beckoned the four Yeomen, *"Come lads, lower your Partizans and ease the points of their blades into the small gaps at each end of yon marble slab covering the entrance to the Crypt. Let us prise it open - and have a care that you lever in concert to ensure that the fine marble edging remains undamaged."* Henry, tapping his foot impatiently, gave a loud sigh, *"Make haste my lads, we, the Royal we, have much of import left to achieve this day."*

'Yeoman of the Guard'
(Carrying his Partizan, a 2-metre long
wooden spear with a steel blade)

The Yeomen lowered their Partizans as instructed, easing the pointed tips of their weapon's blades carefully into the small gaps at the end of the marble slab covering the entrance to the Crypt, then, after a count of three from Senior Yeoman Lukins, leant on the shafts of their Partizans, straining to lever the cover free, whilst at the same time taking great care not to cause any chipping or gouging to the marble. After a fair amount of pushing, grunting and groaning, and tutting from their impatient Monarch, they succeeded in raising the slab and carefully eased it from its resting place before sliding it across to the side of the transept floor. The flickering candlelight revealed the gloomy, cob-webbed ridden steps leading down into the depths of the Crypt.

Sir Simon looked across at the King, *"The Crypt entrance is revealed, Your Majesty."* The King sighed and replied, *"We see that thou hast a talent for stating the blindingly obvious, Sir Simon."* Simon had the good grace to look sheepish, *"Forgive me, Sire."* he replied. Captain Kernan addressed the Yeomen, *"Now, my hearty fellows, pick up yonder chest and carry it gently down ye Crypt stairs, then place it out of sight in ye farthest corner of the Crypt."* Henry nodded and said, *"Sir Simon will lead the way."* Sir Simon reached out and eased a candle from one of the nearby candlestick holders with which to light their way, being careful not to let the hot wax drip onto his trembling fingers.

The Yeomen laid their Partizans on an adjacent pew then, gripping a chest handle each, puffing and panting, manoeuvered the very heavy chest across to the Crypt entrance and began sliding it slowly down the stone steps. Eventually, after reaching the floor of the Crypt, they paused momentarily to get their breath back, then dragged the chest across to the farthest corner of the Crypt, as instructed by the King.

"Bloody 'ell," whispered one of them, *"What's he got in here, the crown jewels!"* The Yeoman opposite him replied, *"Shut up you tit, voices can carry from down here. If himself hears you, you'll be for it – nay, we all will!"* The King called out, *"Have a care that the chest is not damaged or we will have your guts for garters!"* Senior Yeoman of the Guard, Arthur Lukins called out, *"All is well, Sire."* then, whispered to his mates, *"There's no need to ask who got out of the wrong side of the bed this morning! I'll wager 'tis the King's gout that's playing 'im up. Come on, let's get cracking."* Sir Simon lit the way.

Once they'd completed their task the Yeomen rushed to clamber back to the top of the Crypt steps, they were a superstitious bunch and no-one wanted to be last out of there. It was decidedly scary in the gloomy Crypt, down in the cold and echoing bowels of the Minster where there was just the one dusty coffin laid on top of a plain stone catafalque, surrounded by statuettes and other religious artifacts, their shadows thrown onto the Crypt walls from the light of the flickering candle. Despite the King's policy of having all valuables and artifacts removed, the Crypt was still richly furnished. Had Henry made the effort to descend the stairs and enter the Crypt and seen what remained there, he would have been most displeased and heads would almost certainly roll.

The spooky atmosphere of the Crypt had put the wind up the twitchy and superstitious Yeomen. They wanted to get out of there at the earliest opportunity. Having scampered to the top of the steps, jostling each other, discipline returned as they picked up their Partizans then stood at the side of the Crypt entrance in a straight line, at attention, in front of the King, waiting for further instructions.

The King, who had by then calmed down somewhat, nodded, *"Well done lads, now report to Captain Kiernan who awaits you outside."* As they started to move off the King said, *" Ho, a word, Senior Yeoman Lukins!"* Lukins bowed his head, *"Your Majesty?"* Henry ordered, *"Instruct the good Captain that we require his presence here this instant. Oh, and incidentally, we have made the necessary arrangements for the four of you be rewarded for your valiant efforts here this day. Let it not be said that your Sovereign is ungenerous."* Lukins bowed again and replied respectfully, *"May I be so bold as to offer a gracious thanks to your Majesty on behalf of me and the lads, Sire."* Henry nodded then said, grandly, "*Think naught of it, Lukins. Now, go and summon Captain Kiernan if you will?*" Senior Yeoman Lukins nodded, "*Thy message will be passed immediately, Sire.*" Lukins turned to the other three Yeomen, and ordered, "*Come, lads, let us make haste and comply with His Majesty's h'instructions!*"

The Yeomen bowed their heads then marched off out of the Minster as fast as their legs could decently carry them. They were all uncomfortable at having committed what they'd considered as being a sinful task, disturbing Saint John of Beverley's final resting place. They'd only done it out of blind military obedience, that and their inbred fear of King Henry. They were fully aware of the types of horrendous punishments that he could and would dish out to those whom he deigned to be disobedient, disloyal or of no further use to him. They also knew what he'd had done to two of his unfortunate royal wives, so members of the common herd such as themselves stood no chance. Notwithstanding that, they were convinced that they would burn in hell for what they had done that day, breaching the sanctity of a Saint's final resting place was, in their eyes, simply unforgivable. The King, of course, cared not a jot, as far as he was concerned, he was the ultimate authority.

Senior Yeoman Lukins informed Captain Kiernan that his presence was required by the King so the Captain immediately made his way back inside the Minster. Henry beckoned the Captain of the Guard, waving him forward. Captain Kiernan drew to a halt before him and bowed his head, "*You sent for me, Your Majesty?*" The King lowered his voice, "*Captain Kiernan, as you are aware, secrecy is essential to preserve the whereabouts of yonder war chest.*" he said, pointing towards the Crypt, "*Those four Yeomen that were with us here inside the Minster today,*" The Captain nodded, *"What of them, Sire?"* Henry, a cunning, almost feral look appearing on his face, replied, *"They are to be allowed to speak to no-one about what hath occurred here today, indeed, they are not even to return to Leconfield Castle with the main party. We desire that they be 'disposed' of before this day is concluded. Do you take our meaning*?" he growled. Kiernan nodded, *"Perfectly Sire. I shall have them escorted to Fort Paull forthwith, under armed escort, where they will then be detained, incommunicado, in the cells of the fort until I can make the, er, necessary arrangements to dispose of them in accordance with your Majesty's wishes."*

The King nodded, *"Mark me, Sir David, there is to be no trace left of them."* A nodding Captain Kiernan thought, *"Hell's teeth! We won't have any Yeomen left at this rate. Four topped in Lincoln, now four in Fort Paull and presumably another four in York. They're dropping like flies"* The King smiled, *"Fear naught, Sir David, there's plenty more where they came from!"*

A compliant Captain Kiernan continued, *"It will be as if they never existed, Sire. Your Majesty will not have sight of any of them again, nor will anyone else, unless you count the fish of the Humber."* Henry smiled, *"Mayhap we will see them just one more time?"* he said. *"Sire?"* queried Kiernan, *"In their haste to leave, they have forgotten to replace the slab covering the Crypt entrance,"* he said. Captain Kiernan bowed and replied, *"I will have them return here forthwith to carry out the task, your Grace, and then I will set matters in train to ensure that they are taken away to Fort Paull."*

The King nodded, *"Good fellow. We will leave that rather distasteful but necessary task in thy more than capable hands. We know that thou art a truly reliable fellow"*

Pointing at the Crypt's inscribed marble slab, Henry said, *"Now then, let us finish this menial task with haste, we wish to return to Leconfield Castle, where Her Majesty awaits us."*

Kiernan nodded, *"Your steed is tethered by the side of the Minster door, Sire, away from prying eyes."* The King nodded, *"Excellent. We would wish our departure to be as clandestine as our arrival here should have been. Now then Captain, to more mundane matters. We trust that thou hast ensured the presence of a sturdy Yeoman at the side of our nag? We will use his broad back as a mounting block."* The Captain nodded, *"Yes, of course, Sire. Now, if thou wilt excuse me momentarily, I wouldst hasten about thy business."*

The King peremptorily waved him away, Kiernan bowed and then marched off towards the exit door of the Minster to double-check that the necessary arrangements had in fact been made to enable the King to mount his steed with the requisite amount of regal dignity.

"A man well worth his salt is Kiernan," thought the King, *"alas, once we have deposited the final war chest in York Minster, he may also have to be disposed of. 'Tis a damned shame but, alas, he knows far too much for his own good."* Henry called out, *"You can come up from the Crypt now, Sir Simon."* Sir Simon's head appeared at the top of the Crypt steps, *"I was just ensuring that all is in accordance with your wishes, Your Majesty."* he said. *"Did you pass on our respects to Saint John of Beverley?"* asked Henry. Simon nodded, unsure if the King was indulging himself in a little 'graveside' humour, but deciding to play it safe he nodded and replied, *"Indeed I did, Sire and I placed a coin at the*

side of his coffin." "*Pah, superstitious nonsense,*" replied an ungrateful Henry.

Outside, on the steps of the Minster, Captain Kiernan summoned the four Yeoman who had been responsible for moving the chest down into the Crypt. "*Ho there, you four Yeomen, you are required to return inside the Minster. The King hath one further task for thee. Follow me, quickly now, lads!*" The Captain turned and swept off back into the Minster. Senior Yeoman Lukins turned to his three mates and whispered, "*God's blood! On the Cart, off the Cart. I wish these bleedin' h'officers would make their fookin' minds up!*"

After a moment or two, Captain Kiernan and the four Yeomen reappeared at the King's side. Kiernan informed the King that all outside was in readiness for his departure. King Henry turned to Sir Simon, saying, "*So, Sir Simon, we have one final task for thee. It is our desire that you return to the Crypt and check that our Yeomen have placed the chest precisely as we instructed.*" Sir Simon nodded, "*But your Majesty, I have already done…*" then remembering the last royal explosion, thought better of it, and decided to say nothing else.

He turned and started to make his way back down the Crypt steps. The King nudged Captain Kiernan and nodded imperceptibly. The Captain quickly and silently drew his sword from its scabbard then raising it above his head struck Sir Simon a ferocious blow on his head, using the swords heavy and decorous hilt as a bludgeon. A shocked and dazed Sir Simon gasped, fell forward, sank to his knees then tumbled down the Crypt steps, until landing semi-conscious at the bottom in an ungainly heap the candle-holder and extinguished candle at his side. The four Yeomen just stood to attention, awaiting further instructions.

Henry smiled, *"The devil fetch me, that was truly a fearsome blow, Kiernan. Sir Simon is well fettled, methinks!"* he said. Captain Kiernan nodded, *"Yes, Your Majesty and a much-practiced blow it is. I have had the opportunity to use it on several occasions. Tis a blow from which I have no doubt that he will have difficulty recovering from."* The King nodded, *"Aye, t'will certainly make his pate throb if and when he recovers his senses!"* said Henry, *"Now, stay your sword, sir!"* An unsmiling Captain bowed then slid his sword back into its scabbard. The King asked him, *"Something troubles thee, Sir David?"* Kiernan nodded, *"Aye Sire, I have a faint tinge of regret at dealing with a fellow knight in such an untoward manner. 'Twould have been more proper and gentlemanly for me to have fought with him face to face."* The King arched an eyebrow, *"Well, my hearty fellow, it is what it is. And that which thou hast done should cause thee little concern nor should you have any scruple of conscience, for thou hast done thy duty in the service of thy King. Therefore, we prithee, retain thy good humour!"* Kiernan nodded and bowed, *"Your Majesty."*

The four Yeomen of the Guard had remained at attention, gazing straight ahead of them throughout the entire episode, totally unfazed by the drama had taken place. They were like four wise monkeys. *"See naught, say naught, hear naught – and, more importantly, do naught unless ordered!"* that way they would stay out of trouble – or so they believed.

The King nudged Sir David and said, *"Now, Captain, let us have yonder marble slab replaced by the lads and the Crypt re-sealed. There must be no indication of it ever having been disturbed or interfered with. We do not wish any of the others in our escort to take note of the skull-duggery that hath occurred here this day.* Captain Kiernan nodded, *"And what of Sir Simon, my Liege?"* *"There can be no quarter given, leave him down there to molder alongside his precious Saint John, for all eternity. Alas, there can be no escape for Sir Simon, so he must, therefore, rest in peace, happy in the knowledge that he hath served his King and country well!"* Sir David nodded then said to the Yeomen, "Ho there lads, you heard His Majesty, let us have yon marble slab placed back over the Crypt entrance. I will lend thee a hand. Jump to it now!"

Captain Kiernan and the four Yeomen carefully slid the marble slab back into its designated place. Once re-sited, it fitted snugly and gave the appearance of not having been moved for many years. Captain Kiernan addressed Senior Yeoman Lukins, *"Lukins, you and others return those remaining candles and their brass holders to the front of the main altar from whence they came, then wait outside for further instructions from me. Now get thee hence!"* The Yeomen bowed and went to comply with Kiernan's order.

Once the task had been completed, the sweating members of the King's Yeomen turned and gave exaggerated bows to their Sovereign, each of them trying to out-bow the other, then marched out of the Minster to rejoin their place in the Kings 'Riding Retinue.' Shortly afterward they were followed by the King himself, who stomped out of the Minster doors, greatly pleased at the evening's success and was now in a much better frame of mind.

In the fast fading light inside the Minster, Captain Kiernan turned to the slab that covered St John's Crypt, tapping the toe of his leather boot on the marble and calling out, *"My sincere regrets, Sir Simon. Mayest thou resteth in peace."*

Grinning evilly he meandered over to the altar towards the still spluttering candles, then wetting his fingers in the font reached up to snuff each of them out before striding off purposefully to rejoin the King.

All the time that the drama has been unfolding, Graham had been closely monitoring events from the safety of his hiding place in the confessional, "*My God, what a conniving and heartless sod the King is,*" he thought, "*I'd hate to bump into him on a bad day!*" He waited patiently for several minutes until he was certain that everyone had left the Minster, then started to make his way towards the Bishop's door, which he intended to slide out of then make his way the short distance back to the Sun Inn.

He glanced at his pocket watch, noting that he only had a few hours left before the 'T2 Travellator' de-materialised in the field at the rear of the Inn to collect him and return him to his own time-zone. Whatever happened, he mustn't miss that.

He'd been fortunate enough to see all that he needed to, so it had been well worth the journey. He now knew the exact location of the so-called war chest and had a good idea of what it contained. It was a great shame about Sir Simon, who seemed to have been rather an affable sort of chap, but there was nothing he could do about that and anyway, "*I wouldn't be able to lift that heavy marble slab by myself,*" he reasoned. Not only that, he couldn't attempt to rescue Sir Simon because the Time-Traveller SOP's (Standard Operating Procedures) were quite specific in that the natural course of events must never be tampered with, so, unfortunately, Sir Simon would have to take his chances down in the Crypt. Such was life in the strange world of Time-Travel.

Graham smiled and smacked his lips as he remembered Mrs. Elvidge's promise to prepare a magnificent repast for his delectation, and was eager to get stuck in, so after he'd exited the Minster via the Bishop's door, he strode quickly across the graveyard, pausing only to tip the contents of his urine filled flagon behind a gravestone, apologizing profusely to the occupant of the grave before toddling off happily into the cold night.

'CHAPTER 12'

'The Crypt
of
Saint John of Beverley'

After slowly regaining consciousness, Sir Simon laid there, wondering if he was dead, unable to see a thing in the gloom of the sealed Crypt. His head was spinning in such a devilish fashion that he thought it would never stop. Pausing momentarily to let his head clear, he was greatly relieved when his eyes began adjusting to the darkness. *"Surely I cannot be dead, not with my head pounding in this cruel manner,"* he thought. He gradually recalled what had happened to him. *"That pox-ridden Captain Kiernan is an unprincipled knave. Huh, no Officer and Gentleman be he. T'was that wretch who struck me a cowardly blow whilst my back was turned, albeit undoubtedly on the orders of the King."* He gently rubbed the back of his head where a lump the size of a duck's egg had risen. *"I now realise the depths to which His Majesty will sink in order to protect the secrecy of the whereabouts of his precious war chests. Hells, teeth, I would not have revealed that information to anyone - I gave*

him my solemn oath,' *h*e sighed, *"and precisely how will my disappearance be explained to my dear wife Susan who is expecting me home in time for Supper?"*

Sir Simon heaved himself up onto his feet. A sudden thought flitted across his mind, *"The devil take me, King Henry will undoubtedly direct Kiernan to tidy up any loose ends and arrange for Susan and my beloved daughters Katy and Emily to disappear. I cannot allow that to happen, I must stir my bones and make good my escape from this Crypt to see to their rescue."*

Sir Simon stiffened as he heard the sound of rats pitter-pattering and snuffling around in the Crypt. He'd seen rats as big as cats running around the grounds of the Minster and had always hated the thought of the disease-ridden rodents crawling about the place and urinating everywhere. Even the Minster cats had lost the battle of the rats. The impertinent 'Minster' rats had even been known to steal Pilgrims food and didn't appear to think twice about spitefully turning and nipping when being shooed away. Simon licked his lips, *"I am parched, t'would not do for me to linger here overlong,"* he thought, *"huh, I will soon put paid to Henry's dastardly plot. Tis fortunate that I have a means of escape from this place."*

He froze as he heard a faint tapping above his head and heard a distant voice calling, *"My sincere regrets, Sir Simon. Mayest thou resteth in peace."* Sir Simon shook his fist at the roof of the Crypt, *"Tis that swine Kiernan; a curse on both him and Henry - damn their immortal souls!"* he thought, *"Well, it may displease Kiernan to know, but I do not intend 'Resting in Peace,' not just yet anyway. If I am spared I will make good my escape, collect Susan and my two beloved daughters and we will hasten to depart Beverley for pastures anew. I would not leave them here to face the wrath of the cruel King, who clearly has an inherent malignity."*

Sir Simon, as 'Surveyor of the Minster,' had known ever since his appointment to the post that when Beverley Minster had been constructed, the Crypt, consisting of solid stone walls supported by beautifully carved stone ribs, also had built in a thin shell of brickwork cleverly disguising one segment of the Crypt wall, behind which the then Master Mason had secreted a special key-stone. The key-stone could be reached by removing one of the bricks, then by reaching through and pushing it, the entire wall segment would swivel open on its axis revealing three 'secret' stone-flagged passages:

- The first one leading to a closet in the Bishop's Palace.
- The second one leading to a small storage room in Monks Walk.
- A third one leading to the rear of a cupboard in the beer cellar of the Sun Inn.

The well-kept secret of the location of the three passageways had been passed down, by word of mouth, from generations of Minster Surveyors over the years, the only other persons having access to the 'knowledge' being the Bishops.

Sir Simon took a deep breath then slowly and rather unsteadily began edging his way from the bottom of the Crypt steps and over to the far wall. He knew roughly where the removable brick was but would have to fumble around in the gloom to find it. He shuffled slowly across the Crypt without mishap until banging his shin on the war chest, precisely the same shin that he had hit when stumbling into the pew earlier in the day. He thought, *"Curses, that will sting come the morn and I have no doubt that I will have further ripped my hose."* Rubbing his aching leg, he tutted, *"I must make haste, I wonder how comes the hour, T'will surely be twilight outside."*

Once reaching the far wall, he slowly began a careful brick by brick search of it using the palms of his hands, until eventually, he found the all-important brick protruding slightly from the others. Even had there been a light shining directly on it, the cleverly disguised brick could not be seen by the naked eye, the protrusion had to be felt for. *"Aha, success, here we have it!"* he thought. He pushed the brick on its top right-hand corner - and nothing happened. He pressed it again, still nothing. Panicking, he thought for a moment, then tutted, *"What ails thee, nincompoop, 'tis the bottom left corner of the brick to be pressed, not the upper right. Calm thissen!"*

This time he pressed the bottom left corner of the brick and much to his relief it slid backward, until dropping with a clunk onto the flagstones behind it. The hole left by the brick provided him with a solid hand-hold, so grasping hold of it he pushed with all his might. Much to his relief, a door size segment of the wall swung open, groaning as it did so. It had obviously been a long time since the door had been used, but nevertheless, the mechanism still worked efficiently. *"Those lads certainly knew what they were doing when they built this,"* thought Sir Simon.

A little more welcome light seeped into the Crypt, giving Sir Simon a better view of things. Several of his rat companions took the opportunity to make good their escape, scurrying along the dusty and cobweb-ridden passages. Reaching down, Simon picked up the brick and replaced it in its niche. He sighed and thought, *"At least the rats will not be feasting on my remains*," as he stepped through the gap in the wall, "*How clever those builders were. The wall swings with such relative ease, even after all those years*," he thought. "*Now, stir thissen, my lad, time is of the essence.*"

Suddenly remembering the war chest, Sir Simon stepped back into the Crypt and went over to it, thinking, "*I will need funds for my escape. I must look to relieving His Majesty of some of the gold from the chest, if for nothing else as recompense for all of the taxes I have paid to him over the years. I will extract as much as I can carry.*" As he examined the chest he realised that the heavy lock securing it would prevent him from gaining immediate access. "*Buggeration, I have fallen at the first hurdle. I will have to seek out a suitable implement and return to force the lock open before I can raise the lid. I must find a tool and return here in short order.*" he thought.

Simon turned and considered the three options that the passage offered him, then decided that the best choice for him to escape would be the passageway leading to the Sun Inn where he could hopefully slip out unnoticed by the revellers. At this time of the evening, the Inn would surely be filled with customers and he would be able to exit from behind the cupboard door virtually unnoticed. He hoped and prayed that the Sun Inn would be the correct choice for him. After all that had happened, it would not do for him to be seen and recognised, there were too many loose tongues in Beverley eager to cause mischief by courting favour with the authorities.

He needed to find something with which to force the lock of the war chest open, it was no good making his escape without funds. In order for him and his family to make good their escape and survive, he had to gain access to Henry's war chest. He decided to have a mooch around the cellars under the Bishops Palace, being familiar with the layout there. Simon had recently supervised a gang of builders and labourers in the cellars whilst they carried out some repair work to the walls, caused by damp. There would surely be some implement tucked away in a nook or cranny that he could use as a lever, so he decided to head off there to investigate.

Replacing the key-brick in the wall and swinging it closed, thus disguising it from both sides, he strode down the dimly lit passage leading to the cellars of the Bishops Palace. He decided that once he'd got his hands on a decent amount of Henry's gold, he would make his way over to the Sun Inn via the secret passage, perhaps take a room for the night and then formulate a cunning plan for his and his families escape from the area. It would not be wise to be out and about on the streets of Beverley at night. There was the ever-present danger of being apprehended by a military foot patrol. He had his fingers crossed that he would be able to enter the premises of the Sun Inn covertly and without having to answer any awkward questions. In addition, as he wasn't a regular patron of the establishment, he hopefully wouldn't be recognised.

It would be best, he thought, if made his move from the Sun Inn very early the next morning, making his way to his home, opposite Beverley Minster, then rousing his family, collecting what few valuables they could carry and then head off on foot for York before the sun came up. None of that could happen, though, until he'd dipped into Henry's war chest and helped himself to some of the King's gold. *"Surely,"* he thought, *"there'll be a suitable implement in the cellars of the Bishop's Palace that I can use to lever the accursed lock off the chest. Maybe he leaves some of his old mitres down there. He's got plenty of them.*" He crossed his fingers and said a little prayer before setting off to investigate.

Eventually, after a secretive and successful tip-toeing foray around the cellars of the Bishop's Palace, Simon discovered and purloined a suitably strong iron bar then returned with it to the Crypt. He opened the secret door once again and stepped back inside the Crypt. After using the iron bar to lever open the lock on the war chest he heaved the heavy lid open, which he saw to his utter delight was cram-packed with gold coins and other valuables, he stuffed his pockets full of coins, then closed the lid of and replaced the lock so that to anyone giving it a cursory glance it would appear not to have been tampered with. Pockets bulging, he then stepped out of the Crypt, hid the metal bar in a nook then swung the wall closed. Job done.

Walking along to the end of the passage leading to the Sun Inn, and to his delight, Simon spotted the keystone projecting out of the cupboard wall. He eased it out of its position, then carefully swung a segment of the wall open. It creaked and groaned but hopefully didn't make enough noise to alert anyone. At the other side of the wall was the back of a cupboard, which in turn slid open, leading into the beer cellar. The cellar was jam-packed full of wooden beer kegs and various bits of junk. Fortunately, there was no-one else there to witness his arrival.

Sir Simon stepped into the cellar, then eased the key-stone back in place before swinging the wall opening closed then slid the back of the cupboard closed. To all intents and purposes, it would not appear to have been tampered with. He noticed that leaning on the wall in the corner of the cellar was a hefty crow-bar which would come in handy later when he made his way back to the Crypt, much better than the relatively small iron bar that he'd filched from the Bishop's Palace. If nothing else, he could use it to defend himself. After listening very carefully at the door at the top of the cellar steps he lifted the door latch.

Gently easing the door open a few inches, he peered around it then seeing that the way was clear, he stepped out into the passageway leading to the rear of the tap room. There were several people lounging around, drinking ale and conversing noisily. The main topic seemed to be about the King closing the streets off and visiting the Minster because, apparently, he wanted to secrete something inside there without being seen. So much for secrecy.

The Landlord, Billy Elvidge, was sat over by the fireplace, chatting to a customer. Noticing Sir Simon, Billy excused himself from his guest and came over to greet the recent arrival. *"Ho there good sir, hast thou come to sup and dine with us?"* Sir Simon replied, *"Yes, I have, Landlord. I know that the hour is late but I had hoped that you might also have a room to spare for the night?"* Billy grinned, *"Why certainly, sir. We have rooms aplenty. "* he replied. Sir Simon rubbed his hands together, greatly relieved, *"Excellent, then I would like to take a room just for the evening and also wish to dine here if at all possible?"* *"Very good sir, I will inform Mrs. Elvidge and she will set a place for thee with immediacy. In the meantime, may I fetch thee something with which to wet thy whistle?"* Sir Simon smiled, *"A tankard or two of ale would not go amiss, for truly I am parched."* Billy walked over to the bar, *"By your leave, sir, I wouldst draw one for thee now."*

Billy Elvidge had recognised Sir Simon. Sir Simon had not frequented the Sun Inn over much, but Billy knew who he was. Billy thought that if Sir Simon wished to spend a night alone at the Inn then that was his own business. He'd probably crossed swords with his wife and sought solace elsewhere for the evening. These things happened. He pointed to a door across from the tap-room and said, *"Er, the privies are over yonder, sir, if thou feelest the need to relieve thissen."* Simon nodded, then made his way over to the fireplace and sat at the table directly behind Graham who was sipping beer from a tankard and contemplating his navel. Hearing Simon's chair scraping on the floor, Graham turned and nodded, *"Evening."* " *Good Evening sir. Hail and well met,"* replied Sir Simon. Graham didn't recognise him as being the man who had been alongside King Henry in the Minster earlier that day.

The Landlord returned with a tankard of foaming ale and placed in front of Sir Simon, *"There thou art, sir, pour that down thy crop. That'll quench thi thirst - and there's plenty more where that came from."* Billy looked at Sir Simon and said mischievously, *"Forgive me sir, but your face appears familiar. Art thou from around these parts?"* Sir Simon shook his head, *"No, I am travelling to York from Lincoln and just passing through here."* *"You do not have a need for stabling, sir?"* queried Elvidge. Sir Simon, lying through his teeth, replied, *"No, I was fortunate enough to obtain a seat in a friends carriage, but he is overnighting with relatives on the outskirts of Beverly so kindly dropped me off here. He will be calling for me come the morn so that we may resume our journey."* Billy smiled, *"Very well sir. Mrs. Elvidge will give thee a call once thy meal is ready to be served."* Sir Simon nodded, *"My thanks, Landlord."* Billy re-joined Graham and they continued chatting, Billy thinking to himself, *"How strange an explanation. I sense that some sort of mischief is afoot."*

Mrs. Elvidge popped her head around the door and called out to Simon, "*Sir, if thou would'st kindly come this way, I have prepared a table for thy delectation. Unfortunately, because of the lateness of the hour, it consists in the main of bread, cold cuts, pickles and the like.*" Simon replied, "*It matters not, madam, anything is welcome. I am so clemmed that my stomach is beginning to think that my throat has been cut.*" Mrs. Elvidge curtseyed and scuttled off back to her kitchen.

Whilst sat feeding his face, Simon was formulating a plan whereby he would return to the Minster, via the secret passage, and relieve the King of some more of his gold before he went home to collect his wife and daughters. He would need to do that because as things stood, he would not only have to fund his escape but also what would be his new life. Luckily, he had sufficient gold coins about his person to pay for his immediate needs, such as overnight accommodation and food at the Inn. He decided that he would have to seek out a suitable container in which to carry the gold, so would keep an eye open. The gold that he was currently carrying was making an unsightly bulge in his garments. There would, perhaps, be something in the Inn that he could 'borrow' perhaps a pillow-slip or something similar in which to place his stash.

As he tucked into his supper he thought, "*Things could be a lot worse, I suppose, although not much.*" Mrs. Elvidge popped her head around the door, "*Begging thy pardon, sir, is everything is to thy satisfaction?*" she queried. Simon nodded, "*Indeed it is, Mrs. Elvidge. Tis a most memorable repast, the like of which I have not had for many a year. Another flagon of ale to help wash it down would not go amiss!*" Mrs. Elvidge curtseyed, "*I'll get my Billy to pour you one and bring it straight in, sir.*" she replied before scuttling off. "*I'd better make that my last,*" thought Simon, "*I need to keep my wits about me.*" as he speared another slice of the succulent beef

'CHAPTER 13'

'Return to the current Time-Zone'

Much later on that night at the Sun Inn, Graham had cleared his outstanding account and handed over a generous tip before bidding a fond farewell to the Innkeeper and his wife, Billy and Elizabeth Elvidge. The Elvidge's thought that it was a little unusual that their generous and likeable guest would choose to leave the Inn at such an ungodly hour, but after all – he was a Pilgrim and they were known to be a little odd and often behaved very differently from the majority of other people. If their guest chose to travel during the dark of night, then that was entirely up to him.

During the course of the evening, Graham had shared several tankards of foaming ale with Billy Elvidge and they had chatted merrily away about Beverley and the Minster, although Graham had to keep his wits about him and do a bit of ducking and diving so as not to disclose the true reason for his visit there. He didn't want to overplay his hand. As Billy and Graham had conversed, Sir Simon, who had slipped into the bar room without anyone really noticing him, sat directly behind the two, 'ear-wigging' and paying close attention to what they were saying, until annoyingly being called away by Elizabeth Elvidge who had come to inform him that his late evening meal was ready. Simon had been listening to hear if there was any tittle-tattle about what had happened in the Minster that day. There was always someone in an ale-house who ferreted out and took great delight in repeating juicy gossip. Sir Simon had finished his meal, thanked and tipped Mrs. Elvidge then gone to his room to sit and think things through.

The winter's night had well and truly closed in and it was crispy cold and pitch-black outside the confines of the Sun Inn. A nithered Graham made his way out of the Inn. He begrudged having to leave the warmth and welcoming atmosphere behind him but it was time for him to make a move. He'd enjoyed his visit to medieval Beverley and to his delight had found out the information that he needed regarding the hidden war chest.

As he trod carefully around the exterior of the Sun Inn, keeping a wary eye out for military patrols, he thought how strange it was not having street lamps to light the way, something else that modern man took for granted. No wonder the locals were afraid of footpads and blackguards when out after dark. Making his way across the two hundred yards or so of the field at the rear of the Inn, he drew his cloak around him for extra warmth and stood there under a tree waiting for the 'Travellator' to de-materialise, stamping his feet and blowing on his hands to keep the circulation moving.

Graham had made sure that he was there in plenty of time and was stood at exactly the right spot for the arrival of the 'Travellator.' He didn't want to linger in the field for any longer than was absolutely necessary. Apart from being freezing cold, some dutiful citizen might spot him, get suspicious and report him to the authorities. You never knew who was watching - and not only that, the King's men who were off-duty were known to be out and about in the streets of Beverley until all hours, boozing and carousing. They were, he'd been informed, always seeking a bit of sport. Graham didn't want to bump into them and be interrogated. He'd had enough 'brain-strain' that evening trying to avoid answering some of Billy Elvidge's probing questions.

Suddenly, and much to his great relief, there was a loud whooshing noise and the 'Travellator' started to materialise in front of him. "*Dead on time,*" thought an impressed Graham. He walked towards the entrance to the 'T2' then leaned forward to tap in the key-code on the 'Access' indicator at the side of the door, before stepping back a few feet as it slid open with a 'whoosh.' "*I might as well have a quick pee before I go,*" he thought, "*I'm awash with Elvidge's Yorkshire ale. It's very moreish but goes through you like lead through a goose.*"

As he was stood near the door of the 'Travellator', relieving himself, a voice called out from the gloom, "*Ho there, Pilgrim – hold a moment!*" A startled Graham, inadvertently peeing down his leg, thought, "*Now what!*" Turning, and to his surprise, he saw Sir Simon Delaney emerging from the gloom, walking towards him. "*Oh my God, it's the bloke from the Sun Inn, what's he doing here?*" thought Graham, as he quickly tidied himself up. "*Er, how may I help you, sir?*" he called out to Sir Simon.

"*I crave a boon, Pilgrim.*" replied Sir Simon, "*Crave a boon, what on earth does that mean?*" asked Graham. "*I am in dire need of assistance and am begging thee for a favour. You see, I was sat to the rear of thee in the bar of the Sun Inn this very evening when I couldst not but help overhear thee speaking with the Landlord, Elvidge, about you returning to Lincoln. Forgive my impertinence*." came the reply. Graham nodded, "*That's right, I remember you now. And, might I ask, how does my journey to Lincoln concern you*?" Simon replied, "*I heard you make mention of having a mode of transport, albeit somewhat unusual I perceive, with which to achieve your aim of reaching Lincoln.*" Simon pointed at the 'Travellator'. "*If I might be so bold, tis a strange looking carriage, I have never seen its like afore. I presume that thou art waiting for a supply of fresh horses with which to haul it?*" Graham didn't know what to say, he needed time to think, so just nodded.

Sir Simon gestured towards the 'Travellator', "*Am I or am I not correct in my assumption that yonder carriage is the mode of transport to which you referred when conversing with Master Elvidge?*" Graham nodded and replied, "*Yes, yes, it is.*" Sir Simon continued, "*Sir if I might explain my somewhat delicate predicament. I have a dire need to depart Beverley with my wife, Lady Susan and our two daughters, at the very earliest opportunity and pondered if thou might assist me by permitting us to share your transport to Lincoln.*" Sir Simon intended travelling on to York, but he didn't see the need to reveal that information to Graham. He continued, "*You see, if we are discovered here by the King's men then we are almost certainly doomed. Unfortunately, I have fallen foul of His Majesty and need to remove myself and my family from his immediate sphere of influence. As you are no doubt aware, Henry is a hard-hearted soul whose control is absolute.*"

Graham nodded, "*Ah, so you're in the shit then?*" Sir Simon smiled and nodded, "*Aye, crudely put but nevertheless true. So, what sayeth thou to my request?*" he asked. Graham replied, *"Well I don't know that I can help you and your family, you see I'm not really allowed to interfere in events."* The smile vanished from Sir Simon's face, *"Come, sir, let us be frank and open with each other. If it is simply a matter of payment then I am happy to fill thy purse with gold coins if it would help to sway thy decision. Let me assure thee that I am no cut-throat or footpad, it is just that I have trodden on the royal toes and need to remove myself from Beverley forthwith."*

Graham shook his head, *"Listen, er, I didn't catch your name?"* Sir Simon gave a small bow, *"Forgive me, I am Sir Simon Delaney of Molescroft,"* Suddenly everything clicked into place and it all made sense to Graham. Listening to and now recognising his voice, he realised that Sir Simon was the man who had been stood at the King's side in the Minster, the one who had been struck over the head by the huge Army Officer, then had fallen down the stairs leading into the Crypt, where he had been sealed in and left there to rot. Somehow, he had made good his escape and, understandably, wanted to get out of town before being discovered. The urgent need for Sir Simon to get himself and his family away from Beverley suddenly made sense.

Graham continued, *"Well, Sir Simon, it isn't just a matter of gold coins. This might be difficult for you to understand, but I'm what's called a 'Time-Traveller.'"* He patted the T2 with his hand, *"This 'carriage' is called a 'Travellator' and it's arrived here from the future to teleport me back to my own time-zone."* Sir Simon looked puzzled, *"You are speaking in riddles, sir,"* he said, so Graham ploughed on, *"I only told the Landlord of the Sun Inn that I was travelling to Lincoln by coach because, like you, he wouldn't have understood if I'd tried to explain the complexities Time-Travel to him. I'm not going anywhere near Lincoln."*

Sir Simon was agog, *"I know not of that which you speak, Pilgrim, it confuses me. Can you, or can you not assist me to escape from here?"* Graham shook his head, *"Regarding you accompanying me, unfortunately, we 'Time-Travellers' are strictly forbidden to do anything that would alter the course of events in any way. So I'm afraid that much as I would like to help you, the answer has to be no, I can't help you. I'm here purely in an observational capacity and definitely not change anything. Unfortunately, you'll have to make your own way to safety or remain here in Beverley and accept whatever fate awaits you."*

An outraged Sir Simon stamped his foot in frustration, *"What piffle and poppycock, sir,"* he hissed, *"I've never heard the like – 'Time-Travel' and 'Tele' whatever it is you speak of. I know naught of the subject, but it smacks of witchcraft and wizardry to me. I am merely asking, nay begging you, as one human being to another, to help me escape from Beverley with my family. Where is the harm in that*?" Graham shook his head, "*Sorry mate, it can't be done. I've just explained the reason why.*"

Sir Simon reached beneath his cloak and slid out a long, wicked looking carving knife that he'd purloined from the dining table at the Sun Inn. He pointed it at Graham's throat, snarling, *"Very well, Pilgrim, I am not by nature a violent man, but I have a desperate need to protect not only myself but my family. They too will be doomed if I am discovered to have survived. I must allow nothing to stand in the way of their safety. Now, either assist me or by all that is holy, I will slit thy gizzards wide open. The choice is thine alone. Decide quickly or suffer the consequences"*

Sir Simon pointed the wicked looking carving knife at Graham's stomach. Graham gulped, causing his Adam's Apple to shoot up and down like a cork bobbing in a bottle, then said, *"Alright, Sir Simon, don't get your doublet in a twist! Looks like I haven't got any choice in the matter. Come on then, we'd better get inside the 'Travellator' there's not much time left before it de-materialises."* Graham pointed to the carving knife, *"Er, you'd better leave that damned carving knife here."* A relieved Sir Simon smiled, *"I fear not, Pilgrim,"* he said, tucking it away back under his cloak. *"it stays with me. It may well come in useful later on, although let me assure thee that I would only have used it upon thy person as a last resort. If truth be known, I am a man of peace."*

They both stepped inside the 'Travellator' and the door hissed closed behind them. *"You can rest easy, Sir Simon, you're safe enough in here. No-one can get at you now,"* said Graham. *"But what of my family?"* asked Simon. *"Don't worry about them just know, old lad, when I've had time to think we can make a plan and probably come back here yesterday and get them, something like that. You're safe and sound for the moment,"* A puzzled Sir Simon sighed, *"I know not of what you speak, but will trust thee. Thou hast an honest face. However, tis not my safety you should be concerning yourself with, sir, 'tis thine own. Were you to be discovered assisting me, the Kings wrath would know no bounds. I will do thee the courtesy of explaining my situation as we go along."*

As Graham pressed various switches to 'crank' the 'Travellator' up for its departure, Sir Simon gazed around, slack-jawed, astounded by the cabin lights and the strange fixtures and fittings in the T2's cabin, *"Tell me, Pilgrim, how doth thy roof torches burn without producing heat and smoke*

- and where are the horses that will pull this instrument of Beelzebub?" he asked, *"Don't worry, I'll explain everything once we get underway. Just sit back and let me concentrate."* replied Graham.

Graham showed Sir Simon how to clip himself into his seat-harness then, after strapping himself in, he pressed the 'RTB' (Return to Base) switch. *"Here we go then. Now don't worry yourself unduly, Sir Simon, there'll be a bit of noise and there's a small chance that you might lose consciousness momentarily. Whatever you do, don't look out of that porthole over there or you'll make yourself travel-sick."* A petrified Sir Simon asked, *"Do I need to hold my breath?"* Graham smiled and shook his head, *"No, just sit back, close your eyes and try to relax."*

As the noise increased, The red, green and yellow lights on the console began to twinkle, then Graham stiffened as he heard a loud noise, *"What the hell was that?"* he said to himself. Sir Simon coughed politely, *"Forgive me, Pilgrim, t'was but a quantity foul air exiting from my bowels, a slight touch of nervous wind methinks, brought about by these strange circumstances,"* then mumbled, *"Tis my sincere hope that I have not followed through, for I do not currently possess a change of apparel."*

Graham smiled, *"Well, you'd better close your eyes tightly then, Sir Simon because things will be getting even scarier from here on in."* *"Saint John of Beverley preserve us,"* replied Sir Simon, gripping the sides of his seat until his knuckles turned white, *"I welcome thy wise words of warning, but 'tis such strange vernacular that you exercise, Pilgrim. I recognise it to be a bastardised form of the English language, but of a type that I am most unfamiliar with,"* said Sir Simon, through clenched teeth. He squeezed his eyes shut and thought to himself, *"May the Lord give me courage and grant me His protection this night and during the hours and days of my forthcoming trials and tribulations."*

Despite being warned not to, Sir Simon couldn't resist taking a peep through the porthole and in doing so saw the blurred flashing lights whizzing past. Unable to comprehend what he was seeing, he quickly averted his eyes, terrified. *"Alas, I believe that I may be about to fill my breeches up to the brim. This is truly a fearsome machine."* he thought. The noise level inside the 'Travellator' increased and as it did so, the blood drained from Sir Simon's face. He couldn't, however, resist the temptation of taking a further glance through the T2's porthole where, again, all he could see was the same rainbow coloured lights flashing past at tremendous speed. His knuckles were white where they were gripping the sides of his seat.

He asked Graham, *"Pilgrim, I was pondering thus; there may be some truth in what thou sayeth about this 'Time-Travel' business. Although we are travelling to your 'time-zone' as you call it, doth that mean that I may never be allowed to return back to my own time?"* Graham smiled and said, *"No, I can take you back there whenever you wish. As I said, we can go back to yesterday if we wish."*

Sir Simon looked greatly relieved, *"I would like that, but of necessity, I would need to make two of your time-journeys, one to collect my family and the other one for us all to travel on and perhaps arrive after the demise of Henry the Eighth and his ilk. That would guarantee us safe passage."*

Mike smiled and nodded, *"Yes, I can understand that, and anything's possible, but it'll take some organising. I can't imagine what Mike Fraser is going to say about it all when I*

rock up in Hull with you in tow, he's going to go ballistic."
Sir Simon looked puzzled, *"Ballistic? Where is this place, ballistic?"* *"Oh no, here we go again, look I'll explain the term whilst we're on our way home."* said a frustrated Graham. Simon, a little of the colour returning to his cheeks, nodded and asked, *"This man Mike Fraser, he will be displeased when he sees me?"* *"That's a bit of an understatement."* said Graham, *"When he sees that I've got you in tow it'll go down like a fart in a space-suit!"*

The whirring DDI (Digital Date Indicator) on the dashboard of the 'Travellator' started to slow down until finally clicking to a stop. *"Right,"* said Graham*, "here we are then, Sir Simon, back in my time-zone."* *"Praise the Lord for having the good grace to let me survive this truly mortifying experience,"* replied Sir Simon. Graham unclipped his safety harness then leaned across to Sir Simon and undid his. Tapping the buttons on the console he opened the door of the 'Travellator.' *"Come on, Sir Simon,"* said Graham, *"we'd better be off, we've got a bit of explaining to do."*

Sir Simon stood up then gingerly followed Graham out of the 'Travellator.' They were still in the field at the rear of the Sun Inn but the geography of the area had altered substantially. The field was now much smaller and most of it was filled with modern shops, houses, and buildings. As they walked across the field, skirting the Sun Inn they finished up on the pavement directly opposite Beverley Minster.

Utterly gobsmacked, Sir Simon looked around then murmured, *"Ye Gods, what have we here, Pilgrim? Have we descended down into Hades?"*

They were surrounded by buildings, the design and materials of which Simon did not recognise, most of which had strange pieces of metal sticking out of their rooves and large wooden poles with lines strung between them were equally placed into the footpath. There were solid pavements everywhere and the wide pathway in between them was covered with a strange hardened black material with small white dots painted down its centre. He gulped, it was all too much for him to take in.

Chattering pedestrians meandered by, wearing strange, colourful apparel, the like of which Sir Simon had never seen before. He relaxed a little when he saw that none of them wore a uniform. As he looked in the direction of Beverley Beck, he took a pace backward as he saw a frighteningly large vehicle pulling four other carriages, hurtling itself along two metal rails towards what was, unbeknownst to him, a railway crossing. Once again, no horses. Simon nearly fainted with shock when the driver of the train gave a warning blast on his klaxon. Seeing his state of fear and confusion, Graham thought, "*Oh dear, this is all going to be very difficult. Wait until I get him in my car, that'll really scramble his brain*!"

'CHAPTER 14'

'A Royal Visit to Beverley Minster'

"You OK, Simon?" asked Graham. Sir Simon looked at him, gave him a quizzical glance then replied, *"OK, thou sayest? Ho-hum, yet another one of thy unfathomable gobbledy-gook phrases. Speak plainly Graham, what meaneth thou?"* Graham smiled, *"Sorry, I was just wondering if you're feeling alright?"* Sir Simon nodded, *"Well, I am gradually adapting to being in this era, but there is so much for me to see and absorb that I think I could quite easily go mad. What, for instance, are these strange, colourful garments that thou wouldst have me wear?"* he said, pointing to his jeans. *"That's what we call Denim or Jeans, Si, they're a form of casual wear. It's just to help you blend in with everyone else. If you'd wandered around wearing doublet, hose, and curly footwear then we'd be attracting some very strange glances from the populace, although knowing Beverlonians as I do, they probably wouldn't even give blink an eyelid."*

Simon shook his head, *"Huh, Denim or Jeans, you say. Fie, 'tis the devil's cloth if you ask me. Having said that, these 'Doc Marten' boots that thou kindly supplied me with are most comfortable. Wouldst that I could take them back to my own time with me."* he replied. Pointing towards Beverley Minster, where, in the distance crowds were gathering on the pavements, Simon asked, *"What are all those folk gathered there for?"* *"They're probably just tourists,"* replied Graham, *"We get coachloads of them here most days, especially if there's a market on."*

Whilst they were waiting for the team at 'Time-Travellers' to organise the return of Sir Simon to his own era, which would take a few days, Graham had decided to take him around Beverley Minster and explain precisely what had happened on the day that he'd been dumped into the Crypt. Sir Simon had given some of King Henry's gold coins to Mike Fraser, as a 'sweetener' for his help and co-operation with sorting out the time-travel. As a consequence, Mike had agreed to keep the breach of Time-Travel rules between the three of them and organise a 'T2 Travellator' which would then return Sir Simon to a pre-agreed time-zone to collect his family, after which they could be moved on to a date after King Henry had shaken off his mortal coil. It was just a matter of waiting patiently for Mike to get back to them with the details.

Graham and Sir Simon were mooching around Beverley, walking along Highgate, past Monks Walk, towards the Minster when they were halted in their tracks by a burly young policeman. *"Sorry to bother you, guys, but would you mind hanging on here for a moment or two. We're expecting Prince William and Catherine, his wife. We've had orders to keep the public at bay. The Royal couple will be arriving here at any moment, after which you can be about your lawful business.*" Sir Simon looked at Graham and was about to say something when Graham chipped in, "*Yeah, no problem officer, we're not in any rush.*" Graham placed a finger on his lips, urging Sir Simon to be quiet. The Policeman nodded and moved on. "*Who is that in the blue costume and wearing such a strange helmet?*" asked Sir Simon. "*That was one of our Policemen. They're what's known as Coppers, responsible for keeping law and order. I'll tell you all about Sir Robert Peel when we get a spare moment or two,*" said Graham. Simon nodded, "*Not a name with which I am particularly familiar. Is he one of the Yorkshire Peels?*" "*Later,*" replied Graham

Two very highly polished black Land Rover Discoveries drove around the corner of Highgate, escorting a long, gleaming cherry red Bentley, with a colourful Royal Standard fluttering from the roof above the driver's head. The crowds on the pavements waved and cheered at the two occupants sat in the voluminous rear of the Bentley. The small convoy drove slowly along Highgate until drawing to a halt at the entrance to the Minster. "*That's the Royals,*" said Graham. Once the vehicles had passed them, the policeman called out, "*Right gents, you're free to crack on.*" Graham, nodding his thanks to the Policeman said, "*Come on, Si, let's try and get a bit closer to the Minster and you can have a good look at the modern Royals.*"

They walked closer to the Royal vehicle and, just as they reached the edge of the pavement, a security officer reached forward and opened the rear door of the Bentley, then smiled and bowed to a smiling Prince William as he stepped out, followed by a demure Catherine, waving at the enthusiastic crowd who were shouting out welcoming comments like, "*Nice to see you in God's county again, sir!*" "*Thi wife's looking reytd grand today, Wills!*" and "*How's thi Father, lad?*" The Prince, accompanied by a tough-looking member of the Royal Protection Squad, walked across to the roped-off pavement and started chatting to members of the crowd.

Sir Simon said, "*Ye Gods, but she is a fair maiden. Huh, he hath the sweet smell of success about him! You say that he's the Crown Prince?*" Graham shook his head, "*No, his Dad, Prince Charles, is the Crown Prince, well he's not actually the Crown Prince but he's the next best thing. William's next in line for the throne after Prince Charles.*" Simon asked, "*Well who sits on the throne now?*" "*That'll be Queen Elizabeth the Second,*" replied Graham. Sir Simon, noting the cheers, said, "*The common folk appeareth to be fond of him?*" "*Yes, he's very popular at the moment. I'll tell you what though, he's put a lot of weight on since I last saw him has the lad. Must be being married and all that good living.*" replied Graham.

As Prince William was glad-handing the crowd he was joined by his wife, Catherine. "*And yonder beautiful creature, she is also popular?*" queried Sir Simon, "*Oh yes, very much so. Prince William's wife, Catherine, Duchess of Cambridge will be our Queen one day.*" Sir Simon nodded appreciatively, "*Mmm, the lad hath a good eye, the Duchess is exceedingly comely. She hath a fine pair of ankles.*" he continued, "*Doth the Prince Charles have a wife and doth the Queen have a husband?*" he asked. Graham nodded, "*Yes, Prince Philip, Duke of Edinburgh is the Queen's husband and Camilla, Duchess of Cornwall is Prince Charles' wife. Prince William is Prince Charles' first born, but Camilla isn't his mother, that was Diana, Princess of Wales.*" "*Why is not the Prince Philip a King if he is married to the Queen?*" asked Sir Simon. "*Look, I'll explain it all to you later over a pint. It's a bit complicated,*" replied Graham.

As Graham and Sir Simon were chatting, Prince William moved along the front of the crowd shaking hands and joking with some very enthusiastic members of the crowd. *"Forsooth, Graham, His Royal Highness approacheth us. What are we to do?"* whispered Sir Simon. Graham replied, *"It's OK, he's only coming for a quick chat. That's what Royals do for a living."*

The Prince arrived in front of them, and after a slight pause smiled, saying to Sir Simon, *"Hello, have you come far?"* Before either Graham or Simon could answer, the Prince gave Sir Simon a puzzled glance and asked him, *"Er, don't I know you, you look vaguely familiar?"* Before either Graham or Simon could answer, Prince William said, *"Yes, I'm certain that we've met before. Who are you?"* Sir Simon replied, *"Your Highness, I am Sir Simon Delaney of Molescroft,"* then gave a flowery, courtly bow, much to the amusement of those stood around him. A Yorkshire voice said, *"Look at that pillock, he'll be kissing the lads shoes if he bows much lower!"*

As he straightened up, Sir Simon and Prince William's eyes met. Sir Simon stepped back and nearly gasped out loud. He instantly recognised the cruel, forceful eyes gazing back at him as not being those of Prince William, but those of Henry the Eighth. The 'Prince' smiled and turned to his police escort and said, *"Inspector would you have these two gentlemen escorted into the Minster, please. I would like to have a lengthier chat with them once I've finished out here."* The Inspector replied, *"Very good, sir. Please come along with me gentlemen."*

As he was speaking he lifted his jacket to one side, partially revealing a holstered pistol. Graham nudged Sir Simon and said, *"Come on mate, we'd better do as he says."* Graham and Sir Simon, like lambs to the slaughter, stepped past the metal barrier at the side of the pavement and headed towards the main entrance of the Minster, the Inspector following closely on their heels. On arrival at the Minster, they were ushered straight inside, Sir Simon whispered to Graham, *"A pox on King Henry, it strikes me that somehow he hath also managed to avail himself of your Time-Travel methods. Make no mistake, Graham, 'tis the King in the guise of a Prince."* An astounded Graham nodded and whispered, *"I think you could be right, Si, and the Inspector looks like his Captain of the Guard. What's his name?"* Sir Simon nodded in agreement, *"Yes, of course, stap my vitals, tis the slimy toad, Captain Sir David Kiernan who hath shaved off his whiskers, that is why I failed to recognise him in the first instance!"*

'Inspector' Kiernan turned to them both and said *"Now then, let's not be having any fuss from you two gentlemen. Just go over there and park yourselves on one of the pews. You can both wait there quietly until His Majesty arrives. It's a private visit and the Minster has been cleared of all visitors, so there'll only be a few of us present."* Graham asked, *"What does he wish to speak to us about, Sir David?"* Kiernan smiled and replied, *"Ah, not as stupid as you look. You have seen through my disguise. Well, you will find out what His Majesty wants once he gets here, now go and sit down over there!"* *"Before we proceed further, I would have you confirm your name, sir,"* said Sir Simon. Kiernan smiled and replied, *"My name, sir?* He sighed, *"Oh, very well, if I must although your friend has already ascertained that I am here under the guise of Inspector David Kiernan, attached to the Royal Protection Squad, but am in fact, Sir David Kiernan and we have crossed paths afore, now come on, shift yourselves, I don't want to have to get my pistol out!"* he said, pointing ominously at the bulge under his jacket.

As Graham and Sir Simon sat in the Minster they could hear the faint sound of cheering coming from outside. *"Looks like we're in deep cack now,"* whispered Graham. Sir Simon nodded, *"Deep cack indeed, my friend. Did you note that Kiernan said, 'His Majesty' and not 'His Royal Highness!' so I am correct in my surmisal that it is Henry"* A shocked Graham asked, *"Well what the hell's he doing here?"* *"Verily, I feel that the King hath followed us to this moment in time, disguised as a Prince, in order to recover the contents of his war chest, Why he hath tarried and chosen to do so now eludes me – and that man posing as an Inspector, the swine Captain Sir David Kiernan, is the man who struck me on the head and left me to perish in yonder Crypt."* Graham replied, *"Well Henry hasn't really 'tarried' as you so quaintly put it, has he? It's all to do with time-zones. How the hell did he find out about the ''T2 Travellator' and your involvement in all of this malarkey?"* Sir Simon said, *"Harken, someone approacheth. All will soon be revealed to us, methinks."*

The door to the Minster swung open and the sound of cheering from a very enthusiastic crowd increased in volume until fading into the background once the Minster doors were slammed shut. The 'Prince,' followed by the dainty Catherine, walked across to Sir William and Graham, who stood up. A smiling William, without any warning, viciously backhanded Sir William in the face, sending him sprawling back into the pew. A shocked Graham said, *"Now just hang on a minute, mate, there's no need for that! Shame on you!"* Kiernan placed his hand on Graham's shoulder, *"Remember that you are addressing your King and may speak only when you are spoken to, sir."* Prince William said to Sir Simon,

"*On your feet, dolt!*" A dazed Sir Simon stood up. The Prince turned to Catherine and said, "*My darling Catherine, if thou wouldst care to linger in the Vestry, we will join you once we have completed our business here with these two gentlemen.*" Catherine smiled, performed a sweeping curtsey and replied, "*As Your Grace desires,*" then swept off to wait in the Vestry.

Prince William turned to face Sir Simon, "So, we are revealed, Sir Simon. Let us dispense with the 'Prince William' title and revert to being King Henry, it's so much nice, don't you think? The guise was working wonderfully right up until this moment and if truth be known, we were rather enjoying ourselves. We assume that you are wondering how we found out about your 'Time-Travel' carriage? Well, you can put that down to the 'Time-Travel' agent who was ensnared outside the Sun Inn whilst being apprehended for being drunk and disorderly."

Kiernan chipped in, "*Forgive me, Sire, if I might be permitted to continue?*" King Henry nodded, and Kiernan said, "*Aye, the man had partaken of too much of the grape. With a little forceful encouragement from the soldiers, he told them a rather strange tale of mischief and skull-duggery taking place in the field at the rear of the Sun Inn, late one evening. That, tied in with the information supplied by one of our secret agents, the Landlord of the Sun Inn, a Mr. Elvidge, gave us the full tale regarding the whys and wherefores of you making good your escape, Sir Simon.*"

Sir David continued, "*Mr. Elvidge, a loyal servant of the Crown, followed you into the field at the rear of the Sun Inn and noted everything that transpired on the night that you departed. We encouraged the Time-Travel agent to summon the Time-Machine and have it transport us back here to*

Beverley where we knew you to be in hiding." Sir Simon asked the King, *"But why wouldst thou wish to follow a lowly person such as me, my lord?"* The King glared at him, *"Because back in our own time when we despatched Sir David to see how you had fared and check on our war chest in the Crypt of St John, he found it to have been emptied and also discovered that you had managed to escape from the Crypt. Putting those facts together it was as obvious as the nose on thy face that you knew of a way out of the Crypt and had stolen my gold to use for your own nefarious purposes. You are an unprincipled thief, sir! Once Master Elvidge passed on his information to us then everything else fell easily into place."*

Sir Simon snorted, *"Billy Elvidge! That two-faced varlet! I should never have trusted him; his eyes are too close together and tis rumoured that he waters his ale down! A pox on the black-hearted traitorous swine!"* he continued, "*My father always warned me to beware of a man who laughs too easily. I should have paid more heed to him.*"

Henry turned puce and roared, *"How could they be the actions of a traitor when he was protecting his Sovereign's interests! 'Tis you, who is a traitor and an unprincipled thief to boot, Sir Simon of Molescroft – wherever that might be!"* Sir Simon was outraged, *"Me, Sire, a traitor, and unprincipled thief! I will not have it! That is a foul calumny! I am a Knight of the Realm by birth and always have been thy loyal and faithful servant. Might I respectfully remind thee that t'was His Majesty himself that gave the order for yon villain,"* he pointed at Kernan, *"to strike me a cowardly blow on the back of my head and then purposefully leave me to fade away in St John of Beverley's sacred Crypt! Nay, tis you, Sire, who art an unprincipled popinjay!"* King Henry's jaw dropped. He hadn't been spoken to like that for many a year.

Kiernan slid his pistol out of its holster and pointed it at Sir Simon's head, *"Damn you, sir, hold your tongue. Remember to whom you speak!"* Henry smiled, *"Yes, hold your tongue, wretch! We pondered awhile about the riddle of thine escape from the Crypt, then when we saw thee today we knew that we would soon be in a position to discover precisely how you managed to escape, and, more importantly, discover what became of the contents of our war chest!"* Sir Simon smiled, *"I have naught further to add. That Sire is for me to know and for thyself to find out!."*

Henry's hand shot out and he struck Sir Simon in the face again, *"You are not our court jester so cease thy feeble attempts at wit, we have no patience for frippery. The sand drains through the hourglass far too quickly for our liking and we have dallied here in Beverley for too long. We wish to recover the contents of our war chest and return back to our own time where there is much of importance to be done. The Spaniards are up to their foul trickery yet again and we need to build more warships. Our Ministers have proven to be grossly negligent and laggardly by allowing the English fleet to fall into a massive state of disrepair. We would willingly pay for the construction of a new fleet using the gold from my various war chests, but t'will take the contents of them all for us to do so. The negligent Ministers, of course, will also pay, but in their case, with their lives!"*

The King turned to Kiernan, *"Fetch the implement, Sir David, and let us lever open the marble cover from the Crypt entrance. T'would appear that we will have to do this the hard way, as Sir Simon refuses to co-operate and tell us of his secret entrance. It is blindingly obvious to us that he hath hidden the contents of the chest underneath the Minster somewhere other than the Crypt. Let us discover precisely where."* Kiernan reached behind the pews and pulled out a hefty crowbar, *"This will certainly do the job, Your Majesty,"* he said. *"Get on with it then,"* said Henry impatiently. Turning to Graham and Sir Simon he ordered, *"And you two, assist him - and put your backs into it. Time is of the essence!"*

After a fair amount of levering, grunting and groaning, the marble slab covering the entrance to St John of Beverley's Crypt gave up the fight and lifted. The three men then heaved it to one side, whilst Henry stood and watched. *"Fetch a lit candle from the altar, Sir Simon, we will put it to good use lighting our way down into the Crypt and beyond."* ordered Henry. Sir Simon scuttled off and after a short while returned with an altar candle.

The King went to walk down the Crypt steps but was restrained by Kiernan. Henry brushed his hand away, saying, *"Unhand me, sir!"* Kiernan bowed, *"Forgive me, Sire, but wouldst thou permit me to enter the Crypt before thy good self. We know not what dangers may lurk within its confines."* The King, having second thoughts, nodded and said, *"Very well. Take those two oafs with you, Captain. Once the hiding place of my gold coin is revealed by Sir Simon, it can then be put back into the chest with whatever else remain there, then they can assist thee to carry it up here. If Molescroft refuses to reveal the hiding place of the gold once you are down in the Crypt, you have my authority to 'encourage' him to speak! Use the metal bar if you have to!"* Sir David smirked and replied, *"T'would be naught but a pleasure, Your Grace."*

Sir David, Graham and Sir Simon made their way gingerly down the steps leading into the Crypt. After a few minutes the King, now wildly impatient, roared, *"Well, what is it that delayeth thee, Kiernan?"* *"Tis thy chest, Sire, 'tis still here but is now virtually empty, most of the gold coins, the gold plate, the precious jewels, hath all but gone. Tis less than a third full and there are but only a few bags of gold coin left."* Henry grunted, *"Damnation! Box Sir Simon's ears!"* There was a sound of a blow being struck, followed by a groan from Sir Simon. Henry continued, *"Bring what's left of the gold up here – along with those two rogues. I have further plans for them."*

Although relatively empty, the three men struggled to carry the heavy war chest to the top of the steps and place it at the Kings feet. Henry swung the lid open and looked inside, *"Thunderation!"* He glared at Sir Simon, *" We suspect your misbegotten hands in this misdemeanour, Sir Simon! Now, for the last time, we advise you to tell us where lies the rest of our gold and precious artifacts or I will command Sir David to do more than box your ears!"* he roared, *"Tell us or be in no doubt that it will be off to the Tower for both of you where you will be lowered like a squealing pig into vats of boiling oil! We do not make idle threats!"*

A tremulous Sir Simon replied, *"I know nothing of the gold or other precious items to which you refer, Your Majesty, nor does my friend here."* knowingly lying through his teeth, *"The three so-called secret tunnels that lie under the Minster are, alas, known to many. One passage leads to the \Bishops Palace, one to Monks Walk and the other goes right across to the Sun Inn. Mayhap someone else stumbled across the war chest and helped themselves to its contents, but I know not whom."*

The seething King turned to Sir David, "*He speaks arrant nonsense. Trust me, Kiernan, there is more to this than meets the eye! Remove the remainder of the contents from the chest then have it thrown back down into the Crypt where it can keep the bones of Saint John company for all eternity.*" He turned to Sir Simon and Graham and said, "*As for you two blackguards, you will return with us to our time-zone and we will have you reveal the whereabouts of the remainder of the contents of the chest then Sir David will return here once more to collect it. However, for the moment we ought to make our way to Beverley Westwood and prepare to board the 'Time-Machine' which will be there within the hour to return us to Hampton Court. Let us, therefore, make haste!*"

Sir David turned to Sir Simon and Graham, "*You heard His Majesty, help me empty the chest of its contents then we can throw it down the Crypt stairs – and no tricks. Remember, I still have the pistol,*" he said, patting his jacket.

They emptied the remaining contents of the chest onto the Minster floor then slid the heavy chest over to the opening of the Crypt before pushing it over the edge, watching it as it bounced noisily down to the bottom of the steps. "*Now,*" instructed Henry, "*slide the marble slab over the opening. No-one must know what we have been about this day, Place the gold bags into my cloak, then carry it out to my vehicle and let us be away from here sharpish to Beverley Westwood. You can drive us in the horseless carriage!*" ordered Henry, pointing at Graham. Sir David respectfully removed Henry's cloak, laid it on the floor and they began loading the gold into it. The King called out to Catherine, "*Come, my lady, for 'tis time for us to return Hampton Court. We have a date with the 'Time-Machine.'*"

A short while later the King and Queen, both Knights and Graham were stood by the trees in a small copse on Beverley Westwood, waiting for the 'T2 Travellator' to arrive. Suddenly there was the familiar whooshing sound and there it stood. Sir David leaned across and pressed several numbers on the keypad to release the door, which then hissed open. The King followed Catherine into the 'T2' easing himself noisily into a seat, before calling out, "*Come on board, Sir David,* " pointing at Sir Simon and Graham, and adding sarcastically, "*and perhaps Sir Simon and his friend might care to join us? We can arrange for a suitable and searching interrogation for them both once we return to our own time and mayhap ascertain the whereabouts of the remainder of the contents of our severely depleted war chest. You enter first Kiernan, then you two follow him – and no tricks mind you! Make haste now, or we will have Sir David loose off his weapon. Shift thyselves, for we hath pressed the departure button and the countdown hath commenced.*"

As he backed inside the doorway of the 'T2 Travellator' Captain Sir David Kiernan slid the pistol out of his shoulder holster and pointed it directly at Graham and Sir Simon, gesturing forcefully with it for them to follow him inside the T2. As he stepped towards the entrance, Sir Simon momentarily blocked Kiernan's view. Graham, moving swiftly, hit the exterior door control with the palm of his hand and as the door started to close, dragged Sir Simon away from the T2's entrance. Kiernan managed to loose off a shot before the door closed completely. Fortunately, the bullet went wild, completely missing Graham and Sir Simon, who had both rolled onto the ground and leopard-crawled around to the far side of the 'T2 Travellator,' completely out of the line of fire.

Through the walls of the 'T2' Graham could hear King Henry bellowing loud obscenities accompanied by abusive shrieks from Catherine. Just then the 'T2 Time-Transporter' started to materialise - and with a 'whoosh,' it disappeared completely, heading back to the past. All that remained were the several bags of gold coins and the King's cloak laid on the floor of the copse.

Sir Simon rolled around on the grass, laughing so much that his ribs hurt. He said, "*What a waste of time-travel, Henry, thou great bullying oaf. I have most of thy precious gold safely tucked away where no-one will ever find it. This measly pile is not even one-quarter of the quantity. If and by the time you return here, I'll be long gone. There are no flies on Sir Simon Delaney of Molescroft.*" Graham said, "*Come on, Si, snap out of it, let's pick this gold up and get out of here, just in case Henry does decide to come back for us. We can stash it all in my garage at home. Let's use the limo that King Henry left here, then dump it.*" They grabbed a corner of Henry's cloak each and staggered off towards the car.

The following day Graham and Sir Simon were due to visit Mike Fraser at the 'Time-Travellers' offices where Mike would be completing the complex arrangements to have Sir Simon returned to his own time-zone. Simon was desperately missing his family and wanted to return to medieval Beverley to collect them then whiz them off to safety, probably up to Scotland where he had relatives. Some of the contents of the bags of gold that he and Graham had carried back to Molescroft would be used to cover the remaining costs of his Time-Travel, the remainder would go back with Sir Simon to help fund his new life.

Try as he might, Graham couldn't persuade Sir Simon to tell him where he'd hidden the remainder of the gold, jewels, and precious objects, Simon would just tap his nose with his fingers and say, "*Fear not dear boy, they are hidden away somewhere safe in Beverley.*" Not to be beaten, Graham had taken Simon to the Sun Inn and plied him with drink, pestering him to reveal the precise whereabouts of the goodies. A bladdered Sir Simon finally caved in and revealed all.

The treasure had not been hidden away in Monks Walk. Sir Simon told Graham that he had slipped that into the conversation to mislead the King and anyone else that might have overheard the vocal shenanigans that took place inside the Minster. He confessed to Graham that the remainder of the King's gold and jewels, a substantial amount, had actually been stashed away in a deep, dark corner in the cellars of the Bishop's Palace. Precisely where in those voluminous cellars he would not admit to. Sir Simon just tapped his nose and said, "*Seek and thou might find, but I doubt if you will ever winkle it out!*"

Graham had pointed out to Simon that the Bishop's Palace had been demolished a very long time ago and no longer existed. Where it had once proudly stood, in the shadow of the Minster, there was now just a grass field upon which cows grazed peacefully. "*There's nothing left to indicate that there ever was a palace in the area,*" said Graham. Simon had winked and replied, "*Aye, that's above ground, but the Palace and the three secret passageways underneath the Minster, with all of their nooks, crannies, and hidey-holes, will undoubtedly still exist in my time and I have great faith that the Kings treasure, or should I say, 'my treasure,' will still be there where I tucked it away. Tis my 'rainy-day' fund and I will collect it once it is safe for me to do so.*"

He laughed and nudged Graham in the ribs, saying, *"Now then, sither, before you begin your, Techno-something talk,"* Graham smiled, *"Techno-babble,"* *"Aye, that's it, 'Technobabble,' let's sink another pint, old lad. I would know more of this time-travel malarkey. Despite your previous lengthy discourse on the subject, I profess to not really understanding its workings, it is most complex. Now come along , my hearty fellow, you do the chelping whilst I summon the buxom young lady from the bar to fetch us another two pints of foaming 'Sneck Lifter' eh!"* *"Well,"* said Graham, *"Funnily enough, it all started back in 1895 when a chap called H G Wells wrote a book called 'The Time Machine' which popularised the concept of Time-Travel."* Sir Simon's eyes began to glaze over.

'CHAPTER 15'

'A New Adventure Begins'

Several weeks later, after his return from Medieval Beverley, Graham was attending a meeting with Mike Fraser in the 'Time-Travellers' office.

"Well, Graham," said Mike, *"I haven't done as much ducking and diving since the last time I played rugby, but I'm rather pleased that I finally managed to get Sir Simon on his way. I'm afraid that it cost him an arm and a leg, but he didn't seem to be short of a few quid."* Graham smiled, *"He'll be OK financially. He obviously knows where the real treasure is hidden and he had more than a few knicker tucked away here and took most of it back with him so he'll have plenty of money to do whatever he wants to do!"*

Mike continued, *"He seemed to be a very decent chap."* Graham nodded, *"Yes, I miss him in a funny sort of way. He was just getting used to things here and it took me all my time to drag him away from the TV. He loved the Jeremy Kyle Show, said it was much better than watching jousting. He wanted to get back home though, he was very concerned about his family. Who knows,"* said Graham, *"we'll more than likely bump into him again one day. I suppose that we could always go back to pay him a visit and see if he wants to come back here for the rest of the treasure. If we do, let's hope that King Henry and that odious fart Captain Kiernan don't follow him again."*

Mike smiled, *"That's not going to happen, Graham. I've recovered the 'T2' that they misappropriated and I've replaced my Beverley rep from that time-zone, he was getting too fond of the local brew. Our agents only stay in place for six months at a time now – oh, and we've changed all of the Travellator entry codes so that anyone who's unauthorised won't be able to open the door from the outside unless they know it."* *"That's great,"* said Graham,

"By the way, Mike, Simon asked me to apologise on his behalf for all the trouble he'd caused you and wanted me to give you this for helping him to return home." Graham reached into his pocket and pulled out a small leather pouch which he threw across the desk. *"Hello, what have we got here?"* Mike said. *"Go on! Undo the strings and pour the contents onto the desk,"* a grinning Graham replied. Mike undid the pouch and carefully emptied its contents onto his desk, gasping with pleasure when he saw what was laid there in front of him. There, in a little sparkling pile on his desk lay a breathtaking array of jewels and precious stones.

Mike sat back in his chair and said, *"Bloody hell! Where'd all this lot come from?"* A grinning Graham replied, *"They're a gift to you from Simon, provided, albeit unknowingly, by Henry the Eighth, from the contents of his Beverley war chest. The proceeds from the sale of that lot should make up for any drama's that Simon's unexpected*

197

arrival and departure caused you. I got a similar pouch from him as well – along with some gold coins. Happy days eh."

They both started laughing. "*Incidentally*," said Mike, "w*hat happened to Sir Simon once he got back home, do you know?*" Graham nodded, "*Well, as we'd discussed, it was his intention to go back to his own time-zone in Beverley a few days or so before the dramas of Henry's arrival there, just to tie up a few loose ends, then travel with his family forward in time until after the death of Henry the Eighth. Anyway, once he'd got back home he changed his mind. He didn't think that his wife and two girls could handle the Time-Travel aspects, so they all boarded a ship in Hull and sailed away to safe haven in Scotland where he planned to remain until King Henry the Eighth died."*

"And did he do that?" asked Mike. Graham nodded, *" Yes. Once Henry had docked his clogs, the Delaney's returned to England under an assumed name and settled down in Newcastle to live a full and happy life."* "*How did you find all that out*?" asked Mike. Graham said, "*I asked Sir Simon to arrange for a note to be sealed in a pot and have it tucked away in the Sun Inn, just inside the secret passage behind a cupboard in the pub's cellar – and that's exactly what he did. I sneaked down there and got it one night. It's at home in my wall-safe. "*

"*That's all well and good,*" said Mike, "*but if Sir Simon had legged it before the arrival of Henry in Beverley then he wouldn't have been party to the war chest being hidden in the Minster, would he?"* Graham nodded, *"I had thought about that, but I suppose they could have got someone else to open up St John's Crypt. Whoever helped the King is probably still down there guarding the chest!"*

Mike, gazing down at his newly acquired pile of precious stones and jewels, smiled, *"This lot'll come in very handy. I've just got my Council Tax bill in. Thieving swine!"* he said, *"I can't believe it."* *"What, your Council Tax Bill?"* asked Graham. *"No, this stuff! There's enough loot here to ensure that I'll never have to work again if I don't want to. Good old Simon."* Mike gave a deep sigh of satisfaction and then took a slurp of his coffee, *"So, Graham, have you got anything else planned?"*

"Funny you should as. Yes, I have, Mike, and I need your help," said Graham. *"Oh yes, do tell?"* asked Mike. *"I'd like you to arrange another little trip for me,"* said Graham. *"Haven't you had enough Time-Travel this year?"* asked Mike. Graham shook his head and said, *"It's not Time-Travel. I just want your girls to sort out a 'routine' trip to Paris for me. I need to pay a visit to the La Conciergerie in Central Paris and have a shufty around a certain cell there."*

Mike smiled, knowingly, glancing at the file on his desk, *"Aaaah, François III Maximilien de la Woestyne, 3rd Marquess of Becelaere, Grande of Spain and Lord of Walincourt'- and I'm not saying that twice! I'll bet you're going there to try and find the little snuff box that old Franky tucked away in the cell wall, eh?"*

Graham nodded, *"Got it in one! I've been online and checked that they do the usual touristy type of visit around the Conciergerie."* Mike replied, *"No prob. I'll have the girls sort it all out for you. Got any specific requirements?"* *"Yes, I'd like to travel from here to King's Cross by Hull Trains, first class naturally, then I'll walk across to St Pancras, spend an hour or two in the Champagne Bar, just to loosen up, then take the Eurostar to the Gard du Nord in Paris. I've always fancied doing that trip, but I've never been able to afford it. If the girls could book me a suite at the George Cinque for a couple of days, that would be just the job,"* said Graham. *"Not taking the better half?"* asked Mike. Graham shook his head, *"No, she's made her own plans. Shell be heading off up to Glasgow to stay with our daughter Sara for a few days and do a bit of shopping."*

Mike nodded and replied, *"OK. I take it that you've managed to raise a few quid from the sale of the proceeds of your pouch then?"* Graham nodded, *"Well, some of the gold coins I got from Simon I managed to unload on a dealer in Goole, no questions asked. I'd be able to raise more than a few quid though, if I could flog my precious stones, then I'd be pigging loaded. There's some lovely stuff in my pouch!"* Graham looked at Mike, *"Are you listening, Mike? You've gone a bit vacant on me?"*

Mike smiled, *"Sorry Graham, I was just thinking. If you have no objection, I'd like to go with you to Paris for a few days, then I'll hire a car and motor on over to Amsterdam, to the diamond district to be precise. I've got a few days holiday left and I might as well use them up. It'll be much easier for me to 'dispose' of these precious stones in Amsterdam. They're not quite as 'fussy' about that sort of thing there as they are here."* said Mike, *"and anyway I have a good 'contact' in downtown Amsterdam. "Oh,"* said Graham, *"that's brill. It'll be nice to have a bit of company. I'm assuming that I can go with you to Amsterdam and do a bit of the jewellery disposal business there myself - once I've sorted out the Conciergerie thing?"*

"That's precisely what I was thinking," said Mike. *"It shouldn't take too long for me to locate the snuff-box if it's still there. You can give me a hand with that if you like, two heads are better than one,"* replied Graham. Mike smiled,

"Madness not to." Graham said, *"If I can get into the Conciergerie, search the cell where they kept me and François and find that snuff-box- and his treasure map is still inside it, I'll be laughing. Then you and I can then go and have a poke around his Chateau. It's still there, I've looked it up on the internet. It's all a bit of a long shot after so much time has passed, but I'm going to have a crack at it anyway."*

Mike interrupted him, *"That's a fair lot of 'ifs' Graham."* Graham nodded, *"Yes I know, but you've got to speculate to accumulate! If we do find owt hidden away at François' place I'll cut you in for half. Can't say any fairer than that can I?"* Mike nodded and said, *"This is 'Boys Own' stuff but it's right up my street and I'm well up for it. When do you want to leave?"* he asked. *"Let's strike whilst the iron's hot - what about next Saturday,"* said Graham. Mike replied, *"Right Graham, next Saturday it is then. I'll tell my wife that I'm checking out some new holiday venues over there. So, you and I can do the Paris thing, then head off to wherever it is that Franky lived and do a bit of ferreting around there."*

"It's called the Château Walincourt. There's probably nothing to be found after there after all these years, but you never know, we might just strike lucky. The Germans commandeered the Château during the war, but there's no mention anywhere of them finding anything. " said Graham. Mike nodded, *"OK, the Château it is then, after which we can hit the road for Amsterdam. I'll get the girls straight on to it."* *"Don't worry about the overheads,"* said Graham, *"I can cover us for that, thanks to the gold coins I got from Sir Simon. I'll cash a few more of them in."*

"By the way," asked *Mike,* *"whatever happened to your mate François? I take it that he didn't manage to escape*

from the Conciergerie?" Graham shook his head, *"Well, he did get out, in a manner of speaking. He came to a bit of a sticky end though. The revolutionaries topped him. I've read up on it, there's a record penned by an Abbé Boniface testifying that François' execution was horrible, primarily because the Guillotine's blade had chopped off so many heads that day that it was blunted, so they had to pull and reset it three times to finish François off. The people witnessing his execution said that François was still alive and continued crying until the end. Bloody gruesome and it sends shivers down my spine just thinking about it. He was such a nice bloke and he certainly didn't deserve to go like that. The buggers executed his wife as well – on the same day."*

Mike said, *"Rough old time, eh. You mentioned his lads, what happened to them then?"* Graham replied, *"Well, François told me that when everything kicked off in France he'd been warned to get his family out of there and go to Spain where they'd be safe until things quietened down a bit. He sent his three lads away, but for some reason, he remained in France with his wife and we now know what happened to them. A few years later, after things had settled down, his lads returned to the Château Walincourt at Cambrai and got on with their lives."*

"Eventually the family line petered out and the Château fell into total disrepair after World war 2, I think that the Germans nicked most of the contents of the Château, furniture and stuff like that and left the place in a bit of a state. It was bought and fully restored fairly recently, by a couple of Brits actually. They've turned it into a hotel. It's very popular, by all accounts."

"*No mention of any 'treasure' being recovered there before or during the restoration then?*" asked Mike. "*No, not a word. If anyone did find anything they kept it very quiet. I suppose that François lads wouldn't have a had a clue where to look without having the map in the snuff box. It's a huge place.*" said Graham.

Mike continued, "*So, depending upon the slim chance of us finding the snuff-box and map, tucked away in the cell wall at the Conciergerie, we could still be in with a chance of finding out where François stashed his family valuables?*" Graham nodded, "*I know that it's a bit of a long shot after all these years, but – 'nothing ventured, nothing gained.*" Mike nodded, "*One step at a time, Graham, eh. To hell with it, let's head for that Conciergerie place in Paris, blag our way into the cell and see where that leads us. Another coffee?*" he asked. "*Madness not to!*" replied Graham.

'CHAPTER 16'

'Return to La Conciergerie, Paris'

Just a few yards away from the Champs-Elysées, sat in the unabashed splendour of l'Orangerie Restaurant of the Hotel George Cinq, Mike was chatting to Graham on the hotel's internal telephone system, *"Hi Graham, it's Mike. I'm down in the restaurant. I've just finished having a chat with the Concierge, he's got us two tickets for the Conciergerie Palace and sorted out a chauffeur driven limo to take us there and bring us back. There'll there be a professional guide waiting to meet us when we arrive. The limo will be outside the hotel entrance at half ten, so that gives us plenty of time to meet up here and have a coffee before we go. You OK with that?"* Graham replied, *"Yup, I'll just finish getting dressed, pay the Masseuse off and meet you downstairs in about ten minutes."* Mike laughed, *"Dirty boy!"*

In l'Orangerie, the immaculately dressed waiter sauntered over to Graham and Mike, sniffed officiously and, rather ingratiatingly said to Mike, *"Pardon Monsieur, your limousine, a white Citroen, is parked directly outside the Princess Diana entrance, awaiting your pleasure."* Mike replied, *"Merci, Monsieur,"* and slipped the waiter a folded fifty euro note. No expenses spared on this trip, thanks to the generosity of King Henry's gold. The waiter's demeanour immediately changed, he smiled and the euros were was trousered before you could say *"Jacques Robinson."* *"Right, Graham, finish your coffee and let's get cracking then,"* said Mike, *"Off out into the wild blue yonder to see what fate awaits us."* Graham finished off the last few dregs of his coffee and said, *"The adventure begins."*

A few minutes later their classical and beautifully restored Citroen Safari slid to a halt outside the Conciergerie Palace. Graham said, *"It sends shivers down my spine coming back to this place. Apart from the parking meters outside, it's hardly changed at all."* Stood at the entrance, to La Conciergerie was a very pretty and petite Mademoiselle Bernadette Becelaere, *"Ah, Monsieur's St Anier and Fraser, I presume?"* They both nodded. *"Welcome to La Conciergerie. I am Bernadette Becelaere, your tour guide for today."* Graham went to shake hands with Bernadette and was pleasantly surprised when she ignored his proffered hand, held him by the shoulders and gave him a pleasant little peck on each cheek. She smiled at him, *"Oh you Englishmen, you are so formal."* She then leaned across and did the same to Mike. Mike said, *"Oh, I could quite easily get used to this. It's much better than just shaking hands!"* They all laughed.

Mike said, *"As we're being so terribly European, I'm Mike and this is Graham. May we call you Bernadette?"* Bernadette nodded and smiled, *"Certainement. Now, if you would care to follow me, gentlemen, here is a guidebook for each of you, and now we can commence our tour. La Conciergerie would normally be closed to visitors today, but we are making an exception for you two. Your Hotel Concierge is my Uncle and he has asked me to make your visit here as interesting as possible. So, we will, as you say, 'push the boat out' n'est-ce pas. Have either of you been here before?"*

Graham glanced at Mike and replied, "*Er, no.*" "*OK,*" said Bernadette, "*In which case, I'll give you the full works then! It'll take us just over one hour. Perhaps once we have finished we could indulge ourselves in a spot of lunch? I know a perfectly delightful little Bistro just around the corner from here, the Bistro Sainte Marie.*" Graham's jaw dropped as he recognised the name. "*That's just the ticket,*" said Mike. Mistaking his meaning, Bernadette said, "*Oh, not to worry gentlemen, I 'ave your tickets here. Please walk this way, I think we'll begin our tour down in the cells if you're OK with that?*"

As they meandered along, Bernadette said, "*Now, just let me begin by giving you a few facts and figures about La Conciergerie. As you know, having just been driven past there, La Conciergerie is located on the west of the Île de la Cité, literally 'Island of the City' right here on the banks of the Seine. It was formerly used as a prison but is presently used mostly as law courts. It was also part of the former royal palace, the Palais de la Cité, which consisted of La Conciergerie, Palais de Justice, and the Sainte-Chapelle. I'm sure you know that it has something of a dark past. During the French Revolution, many hundreds of prisoners were taken from La Conciergerie to be executed by Guillotine at a number of locations around Paris, the most well-known location being the Place de la Revolution. Indeed, one of my very distant relatives, François III Maximilien de la Woestyne, the 3rd Marquess of Becelaere,*

*Grande of Spain and Lord of Walincourt and his wife were
held prisoner here prior to their execution."*

Once again Graham's jaw dropped. It was beginning to
become a bit of a habit for him. He nudged Mike and
mouthed, *"Unbelievable!"* Mike whispered, *"I should close
your mouth, Graham, you look as if you're trying to catch
flies!"* Bernadette continued, *"A famous VIP prisoner
detained here was our very own Queen Marie Antoinette of
France. If you wish, we can see inside her cell, which has
been preserved in its original state."*

Bernadette continued, "*The buildings which form this prison
still retain the hideous character of feudal times. The inner
courtyard has a gallery that leads to the cells, connected by
stairs to the lower levels. Partially constructed in the
thirteenth century it was partly rebuilt in modern times, and
is ten or twelve feet below the level of the adjacent streets.
The cells, which have not been used for the last thirty or so
years, are quite small and have, how would you say, "not
enough room to swing a cat in? A strange English phrase
that – "Swing a cat."* Graham smiled, *"It's not a cat as in
feline, it's 'Cat of Nine Tails' – the whip. It's an old British
Navy term."* Bernadette tapped him on the shoulder, smiled
and said, *"Ah, you English and your strange habits."*

She continued, *"Back to La Conciergerie. It was
decommissioned in 1914 and was then opened to the public
as a national historical monument. It is a very popular
tourist attraction, although only a relatively small part of the
building is open for public access because much of it is still
used for the Paris law courts. Today we are closed to the
general public as there is an important trial taking place.
Since 1862 it has been listed as a monument historique by
the French Ministry of Culture. Fortunately, despite the*

trial, I am able to take you to see some of the places that the general public would not normally have access to. Everything OK so far?" she asked. Mike and Graham nodded. Graham said, *"It's fascinating. Er, would it be possible for us to have a look inside any of the cells, Bernadette?"*

Bernadette smiled, *"Oui, certainement. I am sure we can do that for you."* Graham said, *"Did you say that one of your distant relatives was incarcerated here?"* Bernadette nodded, *"Oui, that is correct. Both François III Maximilien de la Woestyne, the 3rd Marquess of Becelaere, Grande of Spain and Lord of Walincourt and his wife were detained here, treated most cruelly and then sent to the Guillotine. My family came to France from Spain and that is how we are linked."* *"Is it possible to see his specific cell?"* asked Mike. Bernadette replied, *"Oui, of course, but I could not go into the cell with you. It just would not feel right for me to do so. Too many ghosts from the past."* *"I understand,"* said Graham, nodding sagely, *"er, just one more little request?"* *"Oui?"* Graham continued, *"Would it be possible for me and Mike to be locked in the cell for a few minutes? Just so that we can stand there and absorb the atmosphere and perhaps get a feeling of what it might have felt like in the bad old days. You see, back home Mike here organises tourist trips and holidays to Paris and not only would it broaden his knowledge but he could also add a little local 'colour' to his stories when offering tours to his potential customers."*

Bernadette smiled, *"Ah, you English, you never miss a trick, how is it you say, 'to make a couple of bob!' Tell you what, I'll take you down to the cell and lock you in there for about ten minutes whilst l go and telephone the Bistro Sainte Marie to book us a nice table. Once you are released, we will finish the tour by going to take a look at Marie Antoinette's prison*

cell then pop out for lunch. Will be acceptable to you?"
"That's just the job," said Mike. *"Trés Bien,"* said
Bernadette, *"then follow me please, gentlemen, and I'll take
you down to the cells."*

Mike and Graham stood in the cell and watched as
Bernadette slammed the cell door closed behind her, then
locked it. She smiled through the small barred opening at the
top of the door and said, *"You have been two very naughty
boys and will have to stay in there for at least ten minutes as
punishment!"* She smiled and walked away. Mike turned to
Graham and said, *"You know what Graham, she's a bit of a
cracker is that Bernadette! I wouldn't mind being locked in
here with her for ten minutes instead of you!"* Graham
replied, *"Oh yes, and what would you do for the other eight
minutes? Look, we'd better get a move on, Mike, there isn't
much time."* He gazed around, *"You know what, this place
has hardly changed at all, apart from the electric light and
the lack of pissy straw."*

He walked across to the far cell wall and started running his
hand over the stonework. Suddenly he paused, *"This one's
definitely sticking out a bit, not that you'd notice just from
looking at it straight on."* Mike took a small pen-knife out
of his trouser pocket and passed it to Graham, saying, *"Go
on then, see if you can dislodge it."* Graham began picking
away at the masonry until he was able to slip the pen-knife's
blade in for half of its length. He jiggled it about a bit and
suddenly the stone moved. *"It's shifted,"* said an excited
Graham. He eased the stone out a few more inches, then used
his fingertips to grip it and pull it out completely out of the
wall.

He handed the stone to Mike, saying, *"Hang on to this,
mate."* then shone the small beam of his appropriately named

cell-phone torch into the cavity behind where the stone had been sat in the wall, apparently undisturbed for all those years, and there, to his absolute astonishment, was the snuff-box – the very same one that had been hidden away there by François III Maximilien de la Woestyne, the 3rd Marquess of Becelaere, Grande of Spain and Lord of Walincourt. *"I don't believe it!"* said Graham, *"It's still here after all this time!"* *"Well get it out of there and trouser it before Bernadette comes back and sees what we're up to."* said Mike, *"And let's get that stone back into the wall so that no-one else knows that we've been sniffing around. It's a good job that they haven't installed CCTV down here."*

Graham removed the snuff-box from its hiding place and put it into his trouser pocket, then carefully eased the stone back into position. Pulling out his handkerchief, he spat on it and collected some dirt from off the floor before wiping it around the edges of the stone to cover the scratch marks made by the blade of the pen-knife. After a few moments he said, *"There we are, you'd never know that we'd moved it."* said Graham. Just as he'd finished speaking, there was the sound of the key being turned in the lock of the cell door. Graham looked up and saw a face peering through the grill of wrought iron bars fitted to the small window in the cell door. The door slowly creaked open. Graham very nearly filled his pants when he saw the man standing at the entrance to the cell. The man smiled at them and said, *"Bonjour Gentlemen, permit me to introduce myself, I am Armande Parmentier."*

Mike looked over at Graham, who had turned drip white, and said, *"What's wrong Graham? You look as if you've seen a pigging ghost!"* Armande looked at Graham and said, *"Are you unwell, Monsieur, may I get you a glass of water?"* A stuttering Graham shook his head and replied, *"I, er, I, er, er, no thank you."* Armande smiled and continued, *"Very well. Bernadette has been called away for a few minutes so has asked me to pop down here and collect you then escort you to the front desk. Firstly though, I have been instructed to show you around the cell where Queen Marie Antoinette of France was held, prior to her execution. I am happy to tell you all about it. My family has been connected with La Conciergerie for many, many years, so therefore I am a mine of useless information"* said Armande, throwing his head back and laughing. *"So, if you could kindly follow me, Gentlemen."* then turned and walked away. Mike whispered, *"What's up with you, Graham?"* Graham replied quietly, *"It gave me a funny turn when I saw him stood there saying that his name was Parmentier. I thought that I was going to keel over. It's another strange coincidence. I'll tell you all about it later,. !"*

After they'd had a good look around Queen Marie Antoinette's cell, and then the rest of the court, their tour was completed. Not only had they achieved their prime aim of reclaiming the snuff-box, but they'd also had a very interesting and informative couple of hours looking around La Conciergerie. After thanking Armande, they met up with Bernadette and went on to have a splendid lunch at the Bistro Sainte Marie, which Graham recognised as being the very same Pension Sainte Marie where he'd been captured during his last time-travel visit to Paris. To his surprise, it had hardly changed.

After a very pleasant lunch and expressing their gratitude to Bernadette, Graham and Mike returned to their hotel. The snuff-box was burning a hole in Graham's pocket and he could hardly wait to get back to his room to open the lid and see if the silk cloth had survived the passage of time. *"I can't believe that the snuff box was still there,"* said Graham. *"Are you certain that it's the same one?"* asked Mike. *"Of course it is. I recognise it, it's a very distinct design and it was where François said it would be."*

On the way back to the hotel, Graham explained to Mike all about Citizen Captain Armande Parmentier and how he had been both arrested and ill-treated by him. *"What a coincidence, I mean how strange is it that both Parmentier and Bernadette have historical links with François and the original Armande. You couldn't write it. I'll tell you what though, today's version of Armande is the spitting image of the old Armande, his second cousin twenty-eight times removed, or whatever it is. He looks just like him. It made my skin crawl."* said Graham. *"It really is a small world,"* said Mike. *"I'll bet that he's just like the original Armande, he looks like a nasty piece of work and he guffaws just like him. I was glad to see the back of him,"* said Graham. *"He seemed OK to me,"* said Mike, *"You can't visit the sins of his forefathers on him. And he looked after us very well whilst Bernadette was away."* *"Yes, you're right,"* agreed Graham, *"But he still made my hair stand on end."* *"I can't wait to get back to the hotel and have a look inside the snuff-box, I'm so chuffed that you found it. All this excitement's making me giddy."* said a laughing Mike. Their limousine drew up outside the George Cinq Hotel, Mike thanked their chauffeur, tipped him generously, then both he and Graham legged it as fast as they could up to the privacy of Graham's suite.

Mike poured them both a glass of chilled white wine, which they sipped appreciatively, then Graham took the snuff-box out his pocket and placed it on the writing desk. They both gazed at it for a few seconds then Mike said, *"Well, are you going to open it or what?"* Graham replied, *"What if I do and there's nothing in there?"* Mike shook his head, *"Don't be daft, I'll bet that it hasn't been touched since old François tucked it in the wall cavity all those years ago. Anyway, it's no big deal if it is empty, we've still got the Amsterdam excitement to look forward to haven't we. This is a bonus. Go on, open it and have a look*!" Graham picked up the snuff-box and with great care prised the lid open. "*Well*?" asked an impatient Mike.

There was a slight pause before Graham replied, "*My God, it's still here! The silk map's still here - and it looks as if it's in one piece!*" "*Well, get it out and open the chuffing thing up then, you wee torment*!" said Mike. Very cautiously Graham extracted the piece of silk out of the snuff-box, then gently unfolded it before carefully spread it out on the table. "*It's in great condition, considering its age and where it's been,*" said Graham, "*Look, you can still read everything on it, the writing and the drawing.*" Mike leaned across and took a couple of photos of the silk square with his cell-phone, "*We'll have a couple of piccies just in case anything happens to the silk,*" he said. "*That's a good idea,*" replied Graham.

Graham grabbed a notepad and pencil, kindly supplied by the hotel, and carefully started to copy out what was written on the piece of silk. "*With your smattering of schoolboy French and the help of Google on my tablet, we should be able to translate these instructions,*" he said. Mike replied, "*Oui, I'll give you a hand, je parle un petit peu français. That writing on the silk looks a bit flowery, but I can recognise the words Château de Walincourt already.*" Mike rubbed his hands together, "*Och, this is bloody beyond exciting pal, innit*!" Graham nodded, then they began patiently translating the information from the silk square onto the notepad.

Once they'd finished, Graham said, "*Let me just have another quick browse on Google and see if there's anything else on there about the Château de Walincourt,*" He fiddled around on his tablet and after a few moments said, "*Here we are, there's a full page about it." "What does it say?"* asked Mike. *"That it was built in 1735 and there are some other bits and pieces of information about the area, then it goes on to say that Françoise Maximilien Becelaere, Marquis de la Woestyne, Lord of Walincourt, his wife and some of his Aristocratic friends took refuge there when the French revolution was in full flow. Despite thinking that they were safe there, they were betrayed and arrested as enemies of France then taken to La Conciergerie Prison to await trial. That happened on the 8th of May 1789. His three sons had legged it to Spain in April 1789, a few weeks before their Father's arrest. I know that because he told me all about it. Anyway, their well-appointed Château was sacked by hungry and foraging peasants then left to fall into disrepair, although the three sons did eventually return there after a couple of years and got things up and running again."*

He continued, *"Now, this bit's interesting, Mike. When installing a new sewer at the Château in 1960, a mechanical digger uncovered an until then unknown arched vault leading to a cellar and a series of passages under the building. It doesn't say where they led to, though, or if anything of value was found. As well as being a hotel, the Château contains a small but popular museum containing some expensive paintings, antique furniture, portraits of previous inhabitants, books and other artifacts"* Graham tutted, *"That's torn it." "Why?"* asked Mike, *"There's bound to be some sort of security there, cameras etc keeping a watchful eye on things,"* sighed Graham, *"Is there any mention at all of any treasure or family heirlooms being discovered there?"* asked Mike *"No, not a sausage,"* said Graham, *"so if we go there and have a careful scout around, we stand a reasonable chance of finding something, especially as we've got the precise location described on the square of silk."* Mike nodded, *" I'm getting good vibes about this, Graham."*

'The arched vault discovered at the Château de Walincourt'

Mike continued, *"We can have a crack at that then head off for Amsterdam to get rid of the diamonds and, of course, any other stuff from the Château that we can get our sticky mitts on. Finders keepers!"* Graham nodded in agreement, *"Well it's not as if we're robbing the Château is it. I mean, if we do find anything that's been hidden away they won't know about it, so they won't miss it because they don't know it's there - and the family is long gone, well the French side is."*

Smiling, Mike said, *"There is a wee sort of twisted logic in that, I suppose. What we should really do is Time-Travel forward a few days in the 'T2' and see if we found anything."* Graham looked puzzled, *"But wouldn't we have to find something first before we could do that?"* he asked. Mike replied, *"Oh, don't start all of that techno-babble crap again."* *"I'm just puzzled by it, that's all,"* said Graham.

"So, let's get down to brass tacks. Precisely where is the Château de Walincourt and when are we leaving?" asked Mike. Graham replied, *"Well Mike, we need to finish translating all of the information on the silk square, then try to make some sense of it, after which we'll know where to look. The Château sits on the outskirts of St Quentin, just*

215

outside Paris" Mike nodded, *"I've already asked the Concierge to book us a self-drive car for our trip to Amsterdam. I asked him to get us something roomy but fast. Ever since I crossed his palm with euros he's been my new best friend. Oh, and I'd better get him to book us a couple of rooms at the Château Walincourt as well."*

Graham said, *"Well, there's no ball-breaking rush, so why don't we spend another night here in Paris?"* Mike nodded, *"Great idea. I've always wanted to visit the Moulin Rouge, it's supposed to be brilliant. We can have a nice meal there, sink a few glasses of something fizzy then take in a show before heading back here to hit the sack. After a good kip and a hearty brekkers, we can set off for the Château."*

Nodding, Graham replied, *"Yes, I'm up for that and I like the idea of a leisurely continental breakfast in the morning."* An enthusiastic Mike continued, *"We can book out of here and set off at about tennish, that way we'll miss the early morning traffic. It's hell on wheels first thing in Paris. That Périphérique is a nightmare - it's like driving in the Le Mans Grand Prix."*

Mike reached for the telephone, *"I'll ring the Concierge now and ask him to get us a couple of choice tickets for the Moulin Rouge, so leave that with me. I'll ask him to book us a nice table at the front and, as you said, we can have a meal and some decent champers there as well"* Graham smiled, *"That Concierge is going to think that all his Christmases have come at once with all the tips that he's been getting from us."* *"Aye, he's a canny bloke, a man after my own heart, and he always comes up with the goods. Worth every cent,"* said Mike. *"OK, well you crack on with that and I'll lift the rest of the info from this silk then,"* said Graham.

❋ ❋ ❋ ❋ ❋ ❋

'CHAPTER 17'

'Le Château de Walincourt'

After dinner, Graham and Mike went to have a look at what was now the large exhibition hall in Le Château de Walincourt. It had been restored to perfection and was a fine example of the architecture of the period, with a very impressive Minstrel's Gallery. Much to their relief, the CCTV free exhibition hall was empty, leaving just the two of them to have a good nose around.

Mike was holding the drawing that he'd copied from the piece of silk and examining it closely. Spotting the ornate fireplace at the far end of the hall, Mike said, "*Great, there's the fireplace that your mate refers to. Whilst there's no-one else in here let's crack on with inspecting it and see if we can find anything.*" The walked across the exquisite marble flooring to the impressive marble fireplace and there, top centre, as had been drawn on the square of silk cloth taken from the snuff-box, was a section that had been carved into the marble depicting two guardians protecting a heart with a lion's head beneath it.

Graham could hardly contain his excitement, *"The head of a lion beneath a heraldic shield - that's got to be it! I can't see anything else that looks like that."* "So, what do we do now?" asked Mike. *"Well, according to the instructions kindly provided by François, we just give the lion's head a firm push and then all will be revealed,"* said Graham. *"Surely it can't be that simple?"* asked Mike. *"There's only one way to find out,"* replied Graham.

'The fireplace at the Château De Walincourt'

They looked around to check that no-one else was watching, then Graham leaned forward and pressed the palm of his hand as hard as he could on the lion's head in the centre of the fireplace. Nothing happened. *"Try again,"* said Mike. Graham pressed the centre-piece again. For a moment nothing happened then suddenly there was a quiet rumbling emanating from the behind the soot-stained firewall at the rear of the fireplace - then a large segment of the firewall slid slowly to one-side. *"Bloody hell,"* said Mike, *"look at that!"* Graham pulled his cell-phone out of his back pocket, switched the light on and shone the beam through to the hollow at the back of the fireplace, revealing the entrance of a gloomy stone-flagged passageway. "*Come on then Mike, this is what we came for. Let's go and investigate.*"

Ducking down, Graham, stepped into the fireplace and then across into the passage, closely followed by Mike, who said, "*Good job they haven't got a log fire blazing away there or it would have been our chestnuts roasting by an open fire!*" Graham laughed, "*Yeah, and we might have had to wait until early tomorrow morning when the fire had gone out.*"

A musty smell permeated the air, "*It certainly niffs in here,*" said Mike. "*Well, what do you expect,*" replied Graham, "*it's hundreds of years old. Come on, let's go and have a wander further along this passage.*" As Graham stepped forward onto one of the stone flags, it dipped a few inches, "*Oh, oh!*" he exclaimed, freezing on the spot. There was a grinding sound and suddenly the back of the fireplace slid shut, closely followed by the stone flag at Graham's foot clicking back into place, leaving them both sealed in. "*That's torn it, how are we supposed to get out of here now? There was nothing written on the square of silk about that!*" said Graham. "*Stand on that flagstone again, Graham, that might do it!*" said Mike.

Graham pressed on the flagstone a couple of times with his foot, then when nothing happened he jumped up and down on it with all his might and although it depressed quite easily, nothing else happened. "*Shine your torch around the walls, Graham. There must be something around here that we can press or pull that re-opens the firewall.*" said a despairing Mike.

"*I certainly hope so,*" replied Graham, "*fingers, eyes, and toes crossed.*" Graham and Mike carefully searched the walls and the surrounding nooks and crannies but found nothing to indicate how they could get the fireplace wall to re-open. Graham gave a wan smile and said, "*Nothing doing here mate, it's all just smooth stone. You couldn't get a bus ticket between the cracks.*" "*Come on then, let's go along the passage and find out what's at the other end, there's bound to be some sort of exit somewhere,*" said Mike. "*Good idea,*" replied Graham, "*follow me.*" They strode off along the gloomy passage, the light from the torch in Graham's cell-phone casting grotesque and spooky silhouettes onto the passage walls.

At the end of the passage, there was an old but solid wooden door. "*Knowing our luck, that'll be locked,*" said Graham "*Well, there's only one way to find out, turn the handle and see,*" replied Mike. Graham turned the door handle and pushed the door, which to his great relief, swung open, revealing a cavernous room. The beam from the cell phone's torch shone onto a large wooden chest placed in the centre of the room, across which was draped a bundle of dusty, moth-eaten rags. On closer inspection, Graham saw that the rags, and bits of metal looking like uniform buttons, were draped around a skeleton, presumably that of a military man as there was also a rusty old rapier and dagger laid at the side of the box just beneath a bony claw.

After carefully examining the rags, Graham said, "*This outfit's vaguely familiar. You know, I think it's the street uniform of an officer from the French Revolutionary period. It's held its colours.*" said Graham. "*The poor soul, he must have come in here the same way that we did and then couldn't get back out. That doesn't bode well for us,*" said Mike as he leaned down and picked up an old, battered, empty metal flask on the floor at the side of the skeleton, unscrewing the top and giving it a shake, "*Nothing in there.*"

Looks like he ran out of drinking water. Probably died of a raging thirst. What a way to go." *"Hmmm,"* said Graham, *"I don't know what he was doing in here, but if he couldn't find a way out then, what chance do we stand. No-one's going to hear us shouting through these thick walls!"*

At the side of the skeleton laid, next to the rapier was a dried-out cracked leather pouch. Mike picked it up and examined it. *"Hey Graham, that wee chappie that you mentioned, Citizen Captain Armande Parmentier, you're not going to believe this, but his name's inscribed into the flap of this satchel Have a look, you can just make it out."* *"Give us it here,"* said Graham who then studied the writing for a few moments. *"Bloody hell, it's him all right! What the hell's he doing down here? You don't suppose that he tortured poor old François and made him tell him where he'd hidden the family treasure, do you?"* *"I can't see that happening. It's too much of a stretch,"* said Mike, *"I mean how would Parmentier know about the treasure in the first place?"* *"Perhaps François let something slip whilst he was being tortured by that bloke, Pontonier the 'Fang Farrier. Maybe as some sort of bribe to stop the torture or get out of prison."* said Graham, shaking his head sadly, *"How else could that swine Parmentier have known about this place, and no doubt Parmentier would have been working hand in glove with Pontonier."*

Mike shook his head and said, *"Well it didn't do Parmentier much good, did it! He's been stuck in here ever since – and it looks like we'll be joining him, unfortunately."* replied Mike. *"Huh, it couldn't have happened to a nicer bloke,"* said Graham.

"Anyway," Graham continued, *"might as well have a look in that wooden chest. That's why we're here, after all. Let*

me just move our friend Armande out of the way," he reached across and unceremoniously brushed the rags and skeleton off the top of the box, *"Come on, out of the way, you bag of bones."* He then slid them into a corner of the room with his foot, *"Sod him, he got what he deserved."* After a bit of heaving, grunting and groaning, Graham and Mike managed to heave the screeching lid of the chest open, revealing its magnificent contents.

'The Walincourt Treasure Trove'

Mike gasped, *"Feast your mince-pies on that little lot, Graham! Your pal François was certainly worth a bob or two, eh"* The chest was crammed with gold plate, gold coins, pearls, gold candelabra, sparkling jewellery, and the piece de resistance - a magnificent gold crucifix embedded with huge precious stones. *"This lot'll be worth a chuffing fortune!"* said Mike, letting a handful of gold coins dribble through his fingers. *"Only if we can get it – and us – out of here,"* replied Graham, *"We'll have to start searching for a hidden lever or counter-balance or something. There's got to be one somewhere, otherwise this place would be full of skeletons."* *"Aye well, you ken what happened at the Taj Mahal!"* said

Mike, "*Everyone that helped to build that was topped on the orders of Mumtaz Mahal!*" Graham smiled, "*Mike, you're a mine of useless information. Let's just concentrate our efforts on getting out of here. There must be a way!!*"

Mike suddenly smacked his forehead with the palm of his hand, exclaiming, "*Hang on! What's the matter with me, I've just remembered, I have the authority to summon a 'T2' in an emergency by using a special chip in my moby.*" Graham looked puzzled, "*Your moby?*" "*Yes,*" replied Mike, "*My mobile 'phone. I just tap in the special code and it gives me an instant link with home base. I can then put in an urgent request for the ERP Protocol (Emergency Rescue Package) to be activated. Then the 'T2's' sensors will locate us and de-materialise right here in this room, there's plenty of space for it. We'll load as much of this loot as we can on board the T2, then nip off back to last night to where we parked the car and stash everything in the car boot, ready for when we leg it for Amsterdam. Perfect!*"

Graham said, "*Yes, but won't someone at your Travel Agency wants to know why you're sending for the 'T2'?*" Mike smiled, "*Let me worry about that, my wee friend. I'll just cross a few palms with some of those gold coins when we get back and I can guarantee that nothing else will ever be said about it. And once we've unloaded the 'T2' and sent it back to its holding hangar, no-one will be any the wiser as to what we've really been up to here in La Belle France.*"

Mike opened his mobile 'phone, "*Yup, there's a strong enough signal,*" he said, keying in the code before tapping out a message, "*Let's hope that there's a 'T2' available.*" he said. "*How soon will we know?*" asked Graham. "*Any second now,*" replied Mike. His telephone pinged and Mike smiled, "*There we are. I've had a reply from the Duty Officer* in the Operations Room saying that the 'T2' will be with me *very shortly*." "*Very shortly?*" asked Graham. "*In about five minutes*." replied Mike, "*So let's get ready to start moving the loot.*" "*Will it all fit into the 'T2'?*" asked Graham. Mike nodded, "*Yes, but we'll have to take remove from the chest and spread it around the spare seats and floor of the cabin. That hefty chest definitely won't fit into the 'T2.' If there's anything that we can't fit in, we'll leave it here for that old bag of bones to look after,*" he said, pointing at the skeleton of the late Citizen Captain Armande Parmentier. "*Huh, I'm not leaving anything for him!*" said Graham.

There was a familiar disturbance in the air at the side of Mike and the 'T2 Time-Transporter' suddenly materialised. "*I love it when a good plan comes together*," he said. He tapped the entry code into the keypad at the door to the 'T2' and with a gentle hiss, it swung open. "*Come on, Graham, don't just stand there gawping, let's get the valuables stashed on board. I'll go inside and you pass the stuff through to me. The sooner we start loading, the sooner we can be on our way out of here.*"

After about half an hour, every bit of the treasure had well and truly been transferred into the 'T2.' "*Oh dear, how sad, I'm afraid there's nothing left for the Captain; we've managed to fit it all in,*" said Graham. "*He can keep the treasure chest,*" replied Mike, "*Hey, I've had an idea, why don't we put his skeleton into the chest, he'll fit in there quite easily, and if anyone ever finds him, they'll think that he's supposed to be in there and not the treasure.*" Graham nodded in agreement, "*Good idea,*" so they carefully lifted the remains of Captain Citizen Parmentier into the chest and then closed the lid. Mike said, "*We'll take his leather pouch with us, that way anyone who finds Armande won't be able to identify him. Let's leave them with a bit of a mystery.*"

Graham nodded in agreement, then picked up the pouch, chucking it into the 'T2.'

After Mike had sealed the door of the 'T2' they both eased themselves into their seats and got strapped in. "*Huh, we've only just managed to squeeze in here,*" said Graham, "*Will it cope with all this extra weight?*" Mike nodded, "*Yeah, not a prob. We've had some very portly Time-Travellers using the 'T2's' without any probs. Now then, let me set the TMD (Time Manipulator Digiclock) so that we arrive back at the car park to the rear of the Château last evening, about 1700 hours should do it. It'll be nice and dark by then and no-one will be able to see us when we cross-load the treasure.*"

He turned the TMD to the previous day's date and tapped in 1700 hours, readjusted the graphical locator so that when they arrived they'd be in the car park, then pressed 'GO.' The 'T2' started the process leading to materialisation. "*Here we go then,*" said Mike, "*brace yourself.*" The cabin lights flickered and away they went, hurtling off through time.

After what seemed like only a few moments, the 'T2' de-materialised and the fogged up port-hole on the side of the cabin began to clear, Graham unclipped his seat-belt and stood up. "*I'd better do a quick check of the area to make sure that there's no out there in the car park before you open the door,*" he said. He wiped the port-hole, gave a gasp and recoiled, "*Bloody hell fire!*" "*What's wrong pal?*" asked Mike. "*Look – out there!*" said a white-faced Graham, pointing a trembling finger at the port-hole where a familiar face had suddenly appeared, peering into the 'T2.' It was a leering Captain Armande Parmentier. "*Who on earth is that ugly sod?*" asked Mike. "*It's Citizen Captain Armande Parmentier.*" "*What, the skeleton?*" "*Yes – we must be back in the 1700's!"* said Graham. Parmentier was pounding on the glass and shouting something.

"Just what time-zone did you tap in, Mike?" asked Graham. *"Well I thought I'd input yesterday at 1700 hours,"* replied a puzzled Mike. *"Obviously you've cocked up the input code,*" said Graham, *"We're back in Paris and it's 1793. Look!"* said Graham, pointing at the TMD (Time Manipulator Digiclock), *"What can't speak can't lie – and that sour-faced git at the port-hole looking in at us is the evil Armande Parmentier, the man who slung me in prison!"* Mike said, *"What, the bag of bones that we put in the chest?"* Graham nodded, *"The self-same."* *"Well don't panic, he can't get in here,"* said Mike, *"so all I have to do is re-set the TMD and we can revert back to our original plan and just disappear into the ether."*

A panicky Graham replied, *"You say that he can't get in here Mike, but what if he spots the key-pad by the door, the one that flashes and gives an, 'In an Emergency – Press here to Open' type of clue. Even a numpty like Parmentier can figure that one out!"* *"Bugger, I forgot all about that,"* said Mike, *"in which case I'd better get a move on and input the correct data before he spots the keypad."* Mike quickly started to re-set the Time Manipulator Digiclock."

There was a sudden hissing noise, Mike turned to Graham and said, *"Oh, oh, think I might be too late!"* as the door of the 'T2' swished open. Graham's jaw dropped as Captain Citizen Parmentier's head appeared inside the cabin. Parmentier grinned evilly at them and said to Graham, triumphantly, *"Aaah, Bonjour Monsieur English! I thought that I recognised your miserable features. I see that you have an accomplice with you, a fellow English spy no doubt."* Mike said, *"Less of the English, pal! I'm Scottish!"*

Parmentier looked around the cabin, *"So, this is the carriage in which you plan to make your escape from Paris,"* he laughed, *"Alas, my friends, it does not take the brains of an Archbishop to work out that if you have no horses to pull your fine carriage – then for you there will be no escape!"*

A shocked Graham spluttered, *"You speak English, Monsieur Parmentier?"* Parmentier nodded, *"Oui, not very well I admit, but I do speak your piddling, colourless little language. You see Monsieur, there's quite a lot that you do not know about me – and conversely, there's quite a lot I do not know about you, but that will soon be rectified, let me assure you. It has served me very well playing the buffoon."*

As Parmentier was speaking, his eyes widened when he noticed the mounds of gold plate, gold coins, and sparkling jewellery laid all around the T2's cabin. *"Mmmmm, obviously there is a great deal of explaining to be done here."* He pointed a finger at the treasure, *"Have you anything you wish to tell me?"* Parmentier asked Graham. Graham replied, *"Yes, your fingernails are filthy and your breath stinks of garlic!"* Parmentier glanced malevolently at Graham and replied, *"You have a keen wit, English, but you would be wise to keep your insolent comments to yourself."* He went to strike Graham in the face but Mike leaned forward and gripped his hand, stopping him, *"I wouldn't do that if I were you, pal! You're heading for a Glasgow kiss!"* he said. Shaking his hand free, Parmentier continued, *"Let us wait and see if you are both quite as amusing and disrespectful once you have had the opportunity to spend a little quality time with our friend Monsieur Pontonier, the 'Fang Farrier,' As for your cell-mate, François, my English friend, oh how the information spewed out of his aristocratic maw once the 'Fang Farrier' manipulated the thumb-screws on his poor little fingers. He told us all about the traitorous Jailer, whom we then apprehended. After a little persuasion, he told us about your Agent and the arrangements that had been made to collect you from Paris. We were out searching for you and – zut alors – it is a miracle, here you are, exactly where the Jailer told us you would be."*

Graham shuddered as he recalled the horrendous damage that had been caused to François' fingers. He looked at Mike and gulped. Excited by his response, a delighted Parmentier continued, *"Monsieur Robespierre will be most impressed when I present both of you to him, in addition to all of this gold and those precious stones, although I might keep just a little of it back for myself. I will probably receive a reward and instant promotion!"* then his face darkened and he snarled, *"Now come, we have wasted enough time. Let's have both of your rank English bodies out of there!"*

Mike called out, *"Excuse me, pal, er Captain."* Parmentier turned and looked at him, *"Oui, what is it?"* Mike continued, *"If you could just see your way to stepping back from the doorway, just a couple of feet, and then perhaps the three of us could form a chain and pass the valuables out to your men."* Parmentier gave Mike the evil eye, *"Do you take me for a fool, Monsieur? Perhaps you think that I am a witless imbecile? You are up to some sort of mischief, neh?"* Mike shook his head, *"Certainly not, sir. As you so cleverly pointed out, we have no horses, so we can't go anywhere, can we? I'm just trying to co-operate and make things a little easier for you."* *"Mmmm, very well,"* replied a suspicious Parmentier, *"but do not try to trick me, or hide anything in your carriage. Let me assure you that it will be the worse for you if you do! I want everything out of there, including you two!"* Parmentier then stepped back from the doorway of the 'T2.'

Mike whispered to Graham, "*We'll only get one chance at getting away, so nip back to your seat, try and look busy then get ready to strap yourself in. I think I can get us out of here - I've had an idea.*" Graham replied, "*What's the use of trying to escape. He'll only press the keypad and open the door again.*" Mike smiled, "*I can tap in an emergency temporary over-ride code on the keypad. It'll give me just enough time to close the door and punch in the new time coordinates. We can be on our way well before he gets anywhere near the exterior keypad. Now come on, stop faffing about*!" Mike shouted to Parmentier, "*Be with you in a moment, Citizen Captain!*"

Mike hurriedly readjusted the Time Manipulator Digiclock and then slapped the palm of his sweating hand on the flashing 'GO' button. "*I can't be certain that we'll get back to the right time-zone,*" he said, "*but it doesn't matter. Wherever we finish up, I can move us back to the Château from there.*" As the door of the 'T2' started to close, they could hear Parmentier shouting, "*Merde! You treacherous, lying English dogs….*" then the door clunked shut. They could hear Parmentier shouting and banging furiously on the outer casing of the 'T2,' then much to Mike and Graham's relief the 'T2' materialisation process kicked in.

As it did so, the sound of Parmentier banging on the side of the 'T2' gradually faded away. "*That's settled his hash!* said Mike. "*Phew!*" said a smiling Graham, "*What a relief. I'd like to see Parmentier explain that little lot to his 'Master.'*" Mike reached across to the Time Manipulator Digiclock and said, "*Well, we can always go back and see what happens to him if you want to!*" Graham shook his head, "*I'd rather not if you don't mind, that would be tempting fate. Let's get back to the Château, I'm a nervous wreck.*"

The 'T2' de-materialised in the corner of the car park at the rear of the Château de Walincourt. Night had fallen and the car park was lit by just the one feeble security lamp, which, fortunately, had been placed over in the far corner of the car park, well away from their car and out of sight of the Château. *"OK, here we are."* said Mike, *"Got it right this time. Hadn't you better have a quick peek and see that Parmentier isn't lurking behind the bushes before I open the door, Graham!"* *"Not funny."* replied Graham as he stood up and peered through the window. *"I can see our car over there, so it looks as if we're OK to crack on."*

Mike pressed the button to open the 'T2's' door. Once it had fully opened, some crisp, fresh air wafted into the cabin, *"That's much sweeter than your mate Parmentier's minging breath,"* said Mike. Graham stepped out of the 'T2' and had a quick look around the area, *"All clear, Mike"* he said. Mike replied, *"OK. Bring the car over here, Graham and we can start the cross-loading straight away."* *"Have you got the car keys?"* Graham asked. Mike shook his head, *"Good point, well presented. No, they're up in my room. I'll nip up there and get them and collect my suitcase at the same time. Give me your room card and I'll grab your stuff as well."* Graham handed him his room card, *"My wall-safe number is 1947, can you just check that I haven't left anything in there please."* *"Wilco,"* said Mike, *"You stay here with the 'T2' and guard the treasure. We don't want any cock-ups at this stage of the game."* Graham nodded.

Mike headed off for the Château to collect the car keys and their personal effects. When he eventually returned and brought the car over to the 'T2' Mike said, *"Right, I've put our suitcases behind the front seats of the car. Our passports and other bits and pieces are in the glove compartment, oh and I've paid the bill and booked us out. I told the*

Receptionist that we'd decided to leave earlier than we'd originally planned, just in case anyone asks her. I told her that we wanted a nice early start. So, let's do it then."

He opened the voluminous car boot. *"This looks plenty big enough for the job. OK, Graham, you pass the goodies to me and I'll pack them away. We should get it all in there, there's tons of room. Good job it's a Citroen Safari, we can fiddle around with the suspension to allow for all that extra weight."* They started cross-loading the precious items from the 'T12' into the car.

About half an hour later when they'd finished the cross-loading, Graham said, *"Whew, I'm lathered. I didn't realise that there was so much of it, not that I'm complaining. Still, it's all done now. I could murder for something to eat and a glass of wine to wash it down with. I'm that hungry I could eat a scabby dog."* *"Let's get well away from here first and then we can stop off somewhere along the Autoroute,"* said Mike, *"I'll just tap the ERPRC (Emergency Rescue Package Return Code) into the 'T2's' automatic command pad and send it back to base. I can do all of the explanations and kow-towing once we get back to Hull."*

Mike leaned inside the 'T2 Time-Transporter' tapped several numbers onto the keypad, then jumped out of the way just before the door hissed closed. As they both stood watching, a car drove into the car park, parked up and switched its lights off. A young couple got out, waved at them and then headed for the Château. *"Whew, that was a close call,"* said Graham. *"OK pal,"* said Mike, *"job's done. Let's hit the road and head for Amsterdam. We can sort a route out on the sat nav once we get cracking. I'd better give my Amsterdam contact a bell and let him know we're on our way - and give him our ETA (Estimated Time of Arrival)."*

Graham nodded and pointed at the treasure in the boot, *"And you'd better warn him off that we'll be bringing some 'extras' with us from the Château, eh?"* Mike smiled, *"He'll be dead chuffed about that and I can guarantee that he'll give us a fair deal."*

"How long's the journey likely to take?" asked Graham. *"Well, if we chuck a quick meal break and a refuelling stop into the equation. it'll take us at least five or six hours from here, but the roads should be pretty quiet at this time of night, so we'll be able to get the pedal to the metal, although we mustn't go too fast or we'll be getting pulled up by 'Les Flics!"* A puzzled Graham asked, *"Pulled up by 'Les Flics' That sounds a bit painful. Les Flics? What or who is that?"* *"The French Gendarmerie,"* said Mike.

'CHAPTER 18'

'Amsterdam – City of Diamonds'

As they drove steadily along the Autoroute heading towards the border, Graham said, *"I can't believe how lucky we've been."* *"How do you mean?"* asked Mike. *"Well, you know, finding the map in the snuff box that then lead us to the hidden treasure at the Château de Walincourt, then you being able to send for the 'T2' when we were trapped behind the fireplace, oh, and then managing to escape from Parmentier's evil clutches by the skin of our teeth. I mean, you couldn't write it, could you!"* Mike smiled and nodded in agreement, *"Aye, it's been a wee bit of crazy adventure, but we're not quite out of the woods yet."* *"Aren't we?"* asked Graham *"Well, we've just got one or two more hurdles to jump and then we've cracked it,"* replied Mike.

"One or two last hurdles?" asked Graham. *"Yes,"* said Mike, *"We've got to exchange all of the valuables we've 'acquired' for some hard cash and then somehow we've got to get the proceeds back to England without raising any attention from the Customs and Excise. And then, of course, there are the UK banks."* Graham asked, *"What about them?"* *"They're*

233

very twitchy about large amounts of cash suddenly appearing from nowhere, particularly if they think that it's anything to do with drugs money or some other form of illegal activity." Graham nodded.

Mike continued, "*I think that the best plan is to get the treasure disposed of, sort out the proceeds with my contact, then you and I leg it to Europort and head for home. We can get an overnight P&O ferry back to Hull and sort things out from there. I've got a contact on the Ferries and I think that she can arrange for us to get off the ship pretty sharpish at the other end without too much trouble.*" "*What about the hire car, are we just going to dump it?*" asked Graham. "*Nae bother, we can leave that in Europort and the car hire firm will collect it. Bog standard stuff is that.*"

"*The bloke that we're meeting up with at Amsterdam.*" said Graham, "*What about him?*" Mike asked. "*Do you really trust him?*" said Graham. "*Yes, I think I mentioned to you that I was in the Army for a couple of years when I was a bit younger. I was a 'Sneaky Beaky.'* Graham looked puzzled and asked, "*What's a 'Sneaky Beaky?'* Mike said, "*SAS.*" "*Wow SAS, you've never mentioned that before. What did you get up to with the SAS then?*" said Graham!" "*I can't tell you that – I'd have to kill you. What I will tell you though is that's how I met our Amsterdam contact, Edward, Ed, De Jong. A few years ago I was sent from Hereford on a special operation and was tasked to meet up with the Dutch Defence Force in Djibouti to act in an 'advisory capacity.' That's where I bumped into Ed. It was a very interesting and hairy six months and we'll say no more about that either.*"

Mike continued, "*Ed's a tremendous bloke, the right sort of guy to have at your side when the going gets rough. I've kept in touch with him ever since Djibouti and have had all sorts of dealings with him down the years, since we both left the Forces, not, admittedly, as big as this gig's going to be. He's got a lot of contacts across Europe has Ed, and I'm certain that he'll do the right thing by us. It'll just be a matter of working out what our precious stones and the Walincourt stuff's worth and what his percentage cut is going to be. He won't rip us off though, I'm absolutely certain of that."*

"*Let's hope he can get his hands on plenty of money then,*" said Graham. "*That won't be a problem,*" said Mike, "*He's got a finger in a lot of pies. Speaking of which, I'm peckish, it's high time that we tied on a nose-bag. I'll pull off at the next Autoroute Station. We can get the car juiced up and buy some scoff.*"

As they drove on through the night, Mike yawned, "*We're just passing Hoogstraten, so we'll be crossing over the border quite soon. We can stop there for a coffee if you want?*" Graham nodded, "*That'd be nice, I'm starting to flag and I need a pee.*" "*You know, I was just thinking,*" said Mike, "*it's brill is that Schengen Agreement, you can just cross the border without any fuss and bother. I remember back in the 'good old days' when I had to queue for hours at the Border Posts and everything got closely scrutinised. Sometimes you were sat there for hours on end. It seems strange that you can just drive across borders now without any official interest.*" Graham nodded in agreement, "*I know. Sometimes the only way you can tell you've crossed a border is by the change in vehicle number plates.*"

Mike spotted Service Station lights in the distance, "*Ah, here we are. Let's pull in there, Graham. You go and have your pee then nip into the café and grab some sarnies and a couple of cups of coffee, I'll stop with the car and get her topped up.*" "*OK,*'" said Graham, "*Any particular sandwich?*" "*I think a couple of nice crusty rolls or a hot pasty wouldn't go amiss, whatever you can get your hands on will be fine by me.*"

After they'd finished eating, and had a good slurp of strong, reviving coffee, Mike said, "*OK Graham, I'll do the driving from here on in, if you don't mind. You get your head down. It's a straightforward run in from here, just a matter of following the signs for Amsterdam, via Breda and Utrecht.*" "*OK, give me a nudge if you need to swop back over,*" said Graham, then snuggled down to make himself comfortable. After a couple minutes of listening to the soporific humming of the tyres on the tarmac, he was snoring gently. As Mike had predicted, the motorway was relatively quiet and they were able to make good headway, the comfortable Citroen Safari easily gobbling up the kilometers. Before they knew it, they'd arrived on the outskirts of Amsterdam, so Mike gave Graham a gentle nudge.

"*Wassup?*" asked Graham. "*Amsterdam. Nearly there, mate,*" he said. Graham yawned and stretched, "*That was quick, I don't seem to have been asleep for more than a couple of minutes. Do you want me to take over the driving?*" "*No, it's OK,*" said Mike, "*Better if I stay at the wheel, I know Amsterdam like the back of my hand. Just keep an eye out for the 'De Beers' building. I'll be turning off the E35 Autosnelweg just after that and taking us into what's known as the 'Diamond District.' That's where we'll be meeting up with my old mate Ed. He's got his offices there.*" "*I hope he can lay on some breakfast for us. It seems like ages since we had a 'proper' meal.*" said Graham, his stomach rumbling. "*He'll have something organised, but it'll probably be a Continental Breakfast, sliced meats, boiled eggs, and crusty rolls. That sort of thing.*" "*I don't care what it is, I'm*

236

clemmed," said Graham. Mike laughed, *"Aye, I could murder a full Scottish myself!"*

"So, this mate of yours," said Graham. Mike nodded, *"Ed De Jong. What about him?" "You say that he's a good operator." "Definitely."* replied Mike, *"He's one of the best. I'd trust him with my life – and have done. He's a very convivial bloke is Ed, but it wouldn't pay to underestimate him. He's not as fast on his feet as he once was, a bit of grenade shrapnel in the legs, but he can still look after himself. I'm sure you'll like him, he's a man's man. His business is called 'Van der Ploodens.' It's been in his family for years."* Mike peered at the Motorway signs, *"There we go, the sign for Amsterdam Central. Just a few more kilometres. We've been lucky, I haven't seen one cop car throughout the entire journey."*

"Ed, this is my friend Graham St Anier. Graham this is my friend Ed De Jong." The two shook hands. *"Pleased to meet you, Ed,"* said Graham. Ed nodded and smiled, *"And a pleasure to meet you too, Graham, Mike's told me all about your 'Time-Travel' adventures. We're hoping to get a 'Time-Travel' office here in Holland this year so I might have a crack at it myself. I thought that my life had been shall we say 'colourful' but apparently it's not been a patch on yours!"* They all laughed,

"Now," continued Ed, *"My boys, Diederik and Ludo have emptied the boot of your car of all of your very impressive and, may I say, rather heavy valuables. They're stored away safely in my impregnable strong-room, so you can relax and not worry about them. Now, why don't we go and have some breakfast? There's a nice little café around the corner from here called 'Schnakkers.' The cook's from London, so you'll be able to order a full English, or full Scottish in your case*

Mike. The cook even does that strange thing that you foreigners like so much - fried bread!" Graham grinned and smacked his lips, "*Mmm, I can feel my arteries furring up as we speak.*"   A smiling Ed continued, "*We'll take my sons Diederik and Ludo along with us, they love a 'full English' breakfast, the pair of Philistines. I've got an Uncle of mine stood by to come and assess your stuff this morning. He'll be able to carry out a valuation whilst we, as Mike would say, are filling our faces.*"

After they'd eaten a quality fried breakfast at 'Schnakkers', washed down with gallons of hot sweet tea, which to Graham's surprise and delight was proper 'Yorkshire Tea,' they returned to Ed's offices, replete. Ed, Graham, and Mike sat down, whilst Ludo and Diederik left them to get on with it.

Ed picked up a sheet of paper and after taking a moment or two to read through it, said "*Well guys, time for business. My Uncle has been beavering away in the vault assessing the value of all of the items you brought with you. He's a clever man and can value things down to the last Euro. However, he's only halfway through the stuff and it's going to take him a bit longer than we expected, so why don't you both go and get your heads down? There are fully furnished guest rooms upstairs with all of the facilities that you will need. You can take a shower and get some rest. The lads have hauled your suitcases up there already.*" "*That's a great idea, I'm cream-crackered,*" said Mike, "*Yes, thanks very much Ed,*" said Graham. Ed smiled, "*No prob, my friends. I'll call you when Uncle has finished his evaluation, which will probably be at lunchtime or thereabouts. You OK with that?*" Mike nodded, "*Yes, I'm happy with that. Are you Graham?*" "*Yes, delighted. I could do with a shower and a change of clothes. It's been a manic couple of days.*" replied Graham. Ed pressed the office intercom and said, *"Ludo, come and show our guests to their luxury camp beds please."*

Later that afternoon, a fully refreshed Graham and Mike had bid a fond farewell to Ed. They'd reached a very amicable agreement about the valuation and sale of the precious stones and Walincourt valuables and everyone was happy about the deal. Ed had kindly offered the services of his son Diederik to drive the pair to Europort on the outskirts of Rotterdam, in time to catch the P&O Ferries (North Sea) ship that would be leaving at 2030 hours local time that evening. They settled back into the plush leather seats of Ed's top of the range Bentley Mulsanne, happy to let someone else do the driving. Ed had promised to see to the return of their hired Citroen Safari, so all was well with the world

"Well," said Mike, *"3.5 million Euro's each – that's not to be sniffed at – is it!"* *"I'm over the moon,"* replied Graham, *"I didn't expect anything like as much."* Mike nodded, *"It was the jewelled crucifix that swung it. A very rare and valuable piece apparently. I told you that Ed wasn't a rip-off merchant, he's a damned good bloke."* Graham said, *"Yes, he's one of those guys that you take a liking to straight away, not that I'd like to cross him though,"* then continued, *"I wondered how we were going to get the Euro's through customs and how we'd be able to exchange it for English money. As you said, there are so many safeguards now."*

Mike smiled, *"Ed's got all that sussed. He'll have bankers drafts made out to each of us, then send one of his lads over to Switzerland to open up numbered accounts on our behalf in the Swiss bank where he stashes his own funds. It's 'easy peasy' to a man of his abilities. Have another glass of whiskey, Graham, we can afford to indulge ourselves now."* Graham nodded and reached for the crystal whiskey decanter, "*I'm very impressed with this Bentley. Look at the walnut facia on the bar. Might even buy one myself, once the money's sorted.*" Mike and Graham were both carrying an impressively large wad of Euro's just to 'tide them over' until Ed had sorted out an account for each of them with his Swiss Bank.

Once they'd reached Europort and were dropped off by Diederik, they made their way to the P&O Information Desk where they eventually managed to secure themselves a couple of cabins on that evening's P&O Ferry for Hull, without any problems. Fortunately, it was not particularly busy at that time of year and so they'd both managed to book themselves a top grade cabin each. They had some money and were determined to enjoy themselves.

Later that evening as the ship battled its way across the North Sea, and they were tucking into a splendid dinner in the ship's restaurant, Mike said, "*You're very quiet tonight, Graham. Penny for your thoughts.*" Graham said, "*Well Mike, I've got another money-raising idea buzzing around inside my bonce, if you're interested?*" Mike smiled, "*Ye Gods, there's no stopping you once you've got the gold bit between your teeth, is there! Haven't you got enough loot stashed away with that three-plus mill that you've just scooped?*" Graham grinned back at him, "*It's not really the money, is it, although that's not to be sniffed at.*" A puzzled Mike asked him, "*Well, what is it then?*" "*It's the excitement of the challenge and the sense of adventure. I can't remember when I've enjoyed myself as much. I never had as much fun as this when I was in the police-force..*" Mike nodded, "*That's very true, I must admit, I lapped it up myself.*" They sat quietly for a moment or two whilst sipping their champagne and pondering on their good fortune.

Go on," said Mike, *"let's hear what you've got in mind then."* Graham pulled his chair forward and said, lowering his voice, *"Have you ever heard of a place called Lake Toplitz?"* Mike nodded, *"Yes, of course I've heard of it, I'm a travel agent in case you'd forgotten! Lake Toplitz, isn't it in Bavaria, er no, Austria somewhere?"* *"Yes, that's right, Austria."* replied Graham, *"I'll bet what you don't know is that when the Third Reich was collapsing in 1945, it was rumoured that 35 billion quids worth of bullion, belonging to Adolf Hitler himself, was packed into crates and hidden somewhere at the bottom of the lake by his Nazi henchmen and there's a high probability that it's still there waiting to be lifted."*

Mike poured himself another glass of champagne, *"I'm beginning to like what I hear."* he said.

'Hitler's Gold'

Graham continued, *"If we did have a crack at recovering the gold, it wouldn't be easy. The lake's in dense mountainous forest up in the Austrian Alps, 61 miles from Salzburg, Western Austria, so it would be hard to reach and we'd have to keep a very low profile. Raising the gold, if there is any, would be difficult."* *"How do you mean 'difficult?"* asked Mike. *"Apparently it's very dangerous for*

241

diving is Lake Toplitz. It's very deep and very cold and there's a layer of sunken tangled logs and branches hovering near the bottom of the lake, making full exploration very dangerous. That's why not many people have tried; of those that have tried, several have died." Mike nodded, *"Mmmm, it sounds like it's worth having a crack at though, particularly as we've got plenty of cash available now to fund a well-equipped expedition. We can buy the best and safest diving equipment available."* Mike laid his knife and fork down, *"You've definitely got me interested, Graham,* so *what else have you found out?"* he asked.

*** THE END ***

STORY TWO

'FIND THE FÜHRER'S GOLD!'

CHAPTERS

Introduction

Background

CHAPTER 1
'Here And Now'

CHAPTER 2
'The Führerbunker, Berlin 1945'

CHAPTER 3
'The 'T3' To Lake Toplitz'

CHAPTER 4
'Lake Toplitz'

CHAPTER 5
'And So It Begins'

CHAPTER 6
'Captured'

CHAPTER 7
'A Reversal Of Fortunes'

CHAPTER 8
'Hell On Earth'

CHAPTER 9
'Escape From Berlin'

CHAPTER 10
'Guardian Of The Führer's Gold'

CHAPTER 11
'The Evils'

CHAPTER 12
'The Recovery Phase'

CHAPTER 13
'Heading For Home'

CHAPTER 14
'What Comes Next?'

'Introduction'

'Lake Toplitz - 'Toplitzsee'

Lake Toplitz is situated in a dense mountainous forest, some 2000 feet high up in the Austrian Alps, 98 km (61 miles) from Salzburg in Western Austria. It is surrounded by cliffs and forests in the Salzkammergut lake district, within the Totes Gebirge (*dead mountains*) and is notoriously difficult to reach. The water in Lake Toplitz contains no oxygen below a depth of 20 m. Fish can survive only in the top 18 m, as the water below 20 m is salty, although bacteria and worms that can live without oxygen have been found below 20 metres. The depth of the Lake is 103 Metres (338 feet). During a 1959 diving expedition, a sunken aircraft was spotted on the bed of the lake. There's a layer of sunken logs floating halfway to the bottom of the lake, making diving beyond it hazardous and near impossible. The area is now only accessible on foot, via a private mile-long track that serves the Fischerhütte (*Fisherman's Hut*) Restaurant at the western end.

In 1943 and 1944, the shore of Lake Toplitz served as a Nazi Naval Testing Station. Using copper diaphragms, scientists experimented with different explosives, detonating up to 4,000 kg charges at various depths. They also fired torpedoes from a launching pad in the lake into the Tote Mountains, making vast holes in the canyon walls. Crates containing over £100 million of counterfeit pound sterling notes were dumped in the lake after 'OPERATION BERNHARD,' designed to be used to seriously damage the British economy. Fortunately, 'OPERATION BERNHARD' was not activated.

It has long been the subject of rumours about hidden Nazi gold, which is said to have been sunk in the lake as World War 2 drew to a close. Reports of a convoy of SS vehicles taking crates to the lake in early May 1945 began to emerge soon after Germany surrendered. With US troops closing in and Germany on the brink of collapse, they were supposed to have transported the crates to the edge of the lake, first by military vehicle and then by horse-drawn wagon, and 'deep-sixed' them. No-one knows what was inside the crates. Some believe that they contained gold looted by German troops as they swept through Europe, carrying it back to Germany. Others claimed that the crates contain documents showing where assets stolen from Jewish victims were hidden in Swiss bank accounts.

There is speculation that there might be other valuables to be recovered from the bottom of Lake Toplitz. In 1959, a diving team salvaged several crates and discovered inside them forged British banknotes with a face value of seven hundred million pounds. The notes had been produced in the concentration camp at Sachsenhausen, near Berlin, and were part of a plan devised by Hitler himself.

A medal that once belonged to SS-Obergruppenführer Ernst Kaltenbrunner was found purely by chance in 2001 by a Dutch tourist diver in a second lake in the region - Lake Altausee. It was believed to have been thrown into the water by Kaltenbrunner as he moved through the area trying to evade capture. Ernst Kaltenbrunner was eventually found hiding in a hut about twenty miles just over a mountain range from Lake Toplitz and Altausee and was arrested by US soldiers. He was hanged in 1946 after being tried at Nuremberg. Adolf Hitler and Heinrich Himmler both escaped the hangman's rope by committing suicide. Himmler on the 29th of April 1945, and Hitler the following day on the 30th of April 1945.

Equivalent Ranks in Germany during World War 2
(used in the story)

FÜHRER
The Leader of the German Third Reich

REICHSMARSCHALL
Nominated Deputy & Successor
to the Führer
(and the highest rank in the Wehrmacht)

REICHSFÜHRER-SS
The Leader of the Schutzstaffel

SS-OBERSTGRUPPENFÜHRER
Lieutenant General

SS-STANDARTENFÜHRER
Colonel

KAPITÄN ZUR SEE
Naval Captain

SS-OBERSTURMBANNFÜHRER
Lieutenant Colonel

SS-UNTERSCHARFÜHRER
Sergeant

SS-STURM MANN
Lance Corporal

SS-SCHÜTZE
Private

'FIND THE FÜHRER'S GOLD!'

'Background'

The state of the art 'Time-Travellers' office, situated in Kingswood just outside Kingston-Upon-Hull, had been shut down for the day for Staff Training. There was a great deal of excitement in the office because after the briefing the staff were being taken to Humberside Airport, where the 'Time-Travellers' organisation owned and operated from a huge hangar where their 'Time-Travellers' were sent off on their holidays back through time, until returning, safe and sound, many having enjoyed the experience so much that they immediately booked another journey.

The very select 'Time-Travellers' outfit had recently taken delivery of the 'New and Improved' time-machine, the 'T3

Travellator' which was bigger, faster and had a larger passenger capacity than its predecessor, the 'T2 Travellator.' Mike Fraser, the recently appointed 'Director and Part Owner of 'Time-Travellers' had just finished briefing his six office staff about the benefits and increased capabilities of the new and improved 'T3' and was about to take them across the magnificent Humber Bridge over to Humberside Airport where they would then be shown around a 'T3' - after which Mike was going to surprise them by taking them all back in time to the summer of 1963 in the 'T3.'

He then planned to take them for a walk around Carnaby Street for a 'Swinging 60's' experience before going for an upmarket lunch at the Ritz Hotel, followed by front seats at a Beatle's Concert, before returning them all to the current time-zone.'

Mike Fraser had only just returned from a 'Time-Travel' adventure himself, one that had been very profitable, so profitable in fact that he had been able to become a majority shareholder in 'Time-Travellers.' What the office staff didn't know was that Mike had recently made plans with his good friend, Graham St Anier, to travel back in time to 1945 and hopefully discover precisely where the German Dictator, Adolf Hitler, had ordered that a large amount of gold bullion was to be hidden in the Lake Toplitz area of the Austrian Alps.

Hitler had concluded that the war was drawing to a close and that his beloved 'Third Reich' was tottering on the brink of disaster and would not be able to last for very much longer. He had made plans for what would follow the final collapse of the 'Third Reich' and needed the gold to fund what was planned to be the 'Fourth Reich' (Empire).

251

Scotsman Mike Fraser and his friends, adventurer Graham St Anier and retired soldier of fortune, Dutchman Edward De Jong and his two sons Ludo and Diederik, had formed a small but effective group dedicated to recovering the 'Führer's Gold' from Lake Toplitz. A dangerous but potentially lucrative exercise which, if they were successful, would make them all very rich men.

They'd decided that to discover more about the whereabouts of the gold meant them travelling back in time to 1945 to Lake Toplitz in Austria. What they couldn't have foreseen was that they would also be travelling on to war-torn Berlin, where they would meet up with some very unsavoury characters.

'CHAPTER 1'

'Here and Now'

Late one evening in the surprisingly pleasant ship's restaurant of the P & O Ferry sailing from Europort near Rotterdam to Kingston-Upon-Hull, Graham St Anier, and Mike Fraser, were sat tucking into a splendid dinner, Mike laid down his knife and fork and said, *"You're unusually quiet tonight, Graham. Penny for your thoughts."* Graham St Anier replied, *"Well Mike, I'll get straight to the point, I've come up with another money-raising idea if you're interested?"* Mike smiled, *"Ye Gods, there's no stopping you once you've got the bit between your teeth, is there! Haven't you got enough brass in the bank with the three-plus mill pay-out from our last little haul?"*

Graham grinned back at him, *"It's not really all about the money for me, Mike, although the princely amount that we got isn't to be sniffed at."* A puzzled Mike asked him, *"Come on, what is it all about then?"* *"It's the challenge and the sense of adventure. I mean, searching for a treasure hidden by Henry the Eighth in Beverley Minster and then actually finding it, and then topping that all off by finding the treasure chest that was hidden in the Château de Walincourt was just the icing on the cake. I can't remember when I've enjoyed myself as much. I never had this much fun when I was a Copper.*" Mike nodded in agreement, *"Yeah, me too. It's been exciting."* Graham continued, *" OK, we had a few close calls, but I've never felt so, so alive."* Mike sighed, *"You're right. It was a bloody good laugh, but now that we're gentlemen of leisure we don't have to work again, or put ourselves in harm's way - if we don't want to, so why bother?"*

Mike took a sip of his champagne then, after smacking his lips, said, *"Bloody nectar of the Gods! Come on then, don't drag it out, let's hear what you've got in mind!"* Graham slid forwards in his chair and said, dropping his voice, *"Have you ever heard of Lake Toplitz?"* Mike nodded, *"Yes, of course I've heard of it, I'm a travel agent in case you'd forgotten! Now let me think, Lake Toplitz, isn't it in Austria somewhere?"* *"Yes, that's right,"* replied Graham, *"but I'll bet you don't know that when Germany's 'Third Reich' was collapsing in 1945, some 35 billion quids worth of gold bullion, that's billion, belonging to Adolf Hitler himself apparently, was supposed to have been packed into crates by his SS Nazi henchmen and hidden somewhere at the bottom of Lake Toplitz - and there's a high probability that most of it's still there waiting to be brought back to the surface."*

Mike poured himself another glass of champagne, *"I'm beginning to like what I hear. What's the catch though, there's got to be one, there always is?"* he asked. Graham shrugged his shoulders and continued, *"No particular catch, it's just that raising the gold won't be easy. You see, the lake's in dense mountainous forest up in the Austrian Alps, 61 miles from Salzburg and apparently, it's difficult to reach. The other thing is that anyone raising the gold would have to keep a very low profile and stay out of the public eye throughout the entire recovery operation, otherwise, if anyone from the Austrian government found out what they were up to, they'd want a hefty slice of the action. So raising Hitler's gold, if there is any, without anyone latching onto what was going on would be a bit of a challenge."*

"How do you mean a 'challenge? Couldn't we just sneak out there and lift the gold over a couple of nights?" asked Mike. *"It wouldn't be as easy as that, amigo. First of all, you're supposed to get authority from the Austrian government to dive in the Lake and they're a bit reluctant to give it!" "Reluctant? Why's that?"* said Mike. *" Well, not too long ago a diver drowned whilst searching the bottom of the lake. He was only one of several other divers who'd got into difficulty down there since the end of the World War Two. The Austrians have refused permission for anyone to dive there ever since the last fatality."*

Mike smiled, *"The Austrian government won't be a problem. We can always cross a few of the local pen-pusher's palms with some dosh. We've done it before."* Graham nodded and continued, *"I've been reading up on the area. Apparently, it's extremely dangerous to dive in the lake. It's very deep and freezing cold and there's a layer of sunken tangled logs and branches near the bottom of the lake where the gold is supposed to have been sunk, which makes full exploration very dodgy. Plenty tried to find the gold and as I said, quite a few of them died making the effort!"*

Mike nodded, *"That aside, it sounds like it's worth having a crack at it, particularly as we've got money coming out of the ying-yang now with which to fund an expedition. We can buy the best and safest equipment available, that alone should make it a lot easier, surely?"* Graham smiled, *"Ah, so despite the difficulties, your appetite is well and truly whetted then?"* Mike nodded. *" I thought it might be," said a smiling Graham.*

Mike put his knife and fork down on the side of his plate, *"Yes, you've definitely got me interested, old chum. So, what else have you discovered?"* he asked. Graham continued, *"There's a definite air of mystery surrounding the gold. It's as if someone doesn't want the gold to be recovered. So, as you say, we'd more than likely have to cross a few palms to get diving permission!"* Mike nodded, looking thoughtful, *"Either that or we don't ask for permission at all, we just sneak in there below the radar and covertly lift the gold. By the time anyone discovers what's been going on, we'll be long gone and the loot will be tucked away in our Swiss piggy-bank. Better to ask for forgiveness after the even than to ask permission before!"*

Mike continued, *"You know what, I think I watched a programme about Lake Toplitz on the Sky History channel not so long ago. Wasn't there something to do with some counterfeit English twenty-pound notes as well as the gold?"* Graham nodded, *"Yes, apparently there was about £100 million quid's worth of forged twenty-pound notes that were also sunk into the lake, although that won't be of much use now. It's the gold bullion I'm interested in."*

Graham took a sip of his champagne and continued, *"You see, Mike, right at the side of Lake Toplitz there was a German Navy 'Kriegsmarine' Testing Station, and apparently all the scheming and plotting to hide the gold was done from there, under direct orders from Berlin."* *"Wow,"* said Mike, *"this all sounds very interesting. So how do you propose getting your sticky mitts on the gold bullion, if it actually exists that is, 'cos we can't really be sure can we?"* Graham said, *"I managed to dig up some key information on the Bundesarchiv Internet, the German Federal Archives, in Koblenz. It took some ferreting around, but I found it eventually. It was tucked away at the back of a very boring and lengthy document. The gold's down there in the lake alright, you can see that just by reading in between the lines."* Mike nodded, *"Mmm, this gets better and better."* Graham continued, *"It'd be a bit of a challenge getting at it though. Broadly speaking, we'd have to carefully plan and fund a small, tightly-knit diving and recovery expedition. I've given it some thought, but everything's been on the back-burner until we got the Paris thing sorted."*

Mike asked, *"So how would you propose getting this show off the ground then?"* *"Well,"* said Graham, *"For starters, we could travel back in time to 1945 in a 'Travellator' and monitor what went on there at the side of the lake and see precisely where they dumped the gold. There was a written record in the Bundesarchiv about an armed convoy leaving Berlin in 1945 and travelling to Toplitz, although it didn't mention what they were carrying. You know what the Germans were like for keeping things under their hats. I can have another look at the Bundesarchiv website for more details or I might even nip across to Germany and do a search, it's only in Koblenz. I enjoy doing that sort of stuff."* *"Won't they be a bit suspicious?"* asked Mike. *"No, I'll tell them that I'm studying the Kriegsmarine Base at Lake Toplitz, something like that. I can think of a good cover story. I'm sure that we can pull this off."*

Graham continued, *" I keep saying 'we' – I'm assuming that you don't have any objection to being a part of it?"* Mike nodded, *"Wild horses couldn't drag me away from this one. I'd have been offended if you hadn't asked me! We'd need to take some back-up with us though, a couple of hard-men,"* said Mike, *"Just in case we bump into any nasty Nazi's or 'difficult' locals. That would be Phase 1 of the recovery process."*

Graham grinned, *"I knew that you wouldn't be able to resist it and that's why I was waiting for the right time to raise the subject with you. It's not going to be easy. For instance, we'll be surrounded by war-like Germans for the first part of the gig - and they won't just be fighting for sun-beds, they'll be dedicated Nazis wanting to take us out! The area in and around the Naval Base will undoubtedly be well guarded and patrolled, so we'll have to tread very carefully. As for the Lake itself, apparently, it's a hellish place. It's very deep and there's no oxygen below 20 metres, so once you get down there it's dark, freezing cold and muddy, although, as you said, we'll be able to mount a proper search using the latest diving equipment. That'll be Phase 2 of the operation. I thought it would be better for us to go back to 1945 in the first instance to see if we can spot precisely where the Nazis hid the gold. It'll save us having to carry out a prolonged search of the area."*

Mike nodded, *"Yeah, see what you mean. If we were there for any length of time in 1945 we'd have every man and his dog spying on us." "I agree, but that'd all be part of the fun,"* said Graham, *"We'd have to play this very close to our chests at the planning stages though. The fewer people who know what we're up to the better. It'd need a small, tightly-knit team, just like the one we used in Amsterdam."* Mike grinned, *No prob there. As you know, I'm an experienced Diver, it's my hobby, and so is our Dutch friend, Ed de Jong. If you like, I can contact Ed and ask him if he and his two sons would like to sign on the dotted line and come along with us, We'd be safe and sound with them on our team. They wouldn't take any prisoners if you know what I mean. We'd have to cut them in on the deal though."*

Graham smiled, *"I've got absolutely no problem with that. That'd be really great, I was rather hoping you'd say something like that - and if we do find anything I'm sure that there'll be more than enough gold to go around."* *"OK then, I'll give Ed a call when we get back home and run this by him. You happy with that?"* Graham nodded his approval, *"Happy! That's an understatement, I'm as loose as a chuffing goose!"*

Graham continued, *"As I said, for Phase 1 we'd have to travel back in time towards the end of World War Two, then carry out a covert recce to see if we can spot what and where things were going on. I'll do the research to see if I can find a specific date for when the gold was moved to Toplitz by the Germans. Then, once we've been back there for a good scout around, we can return to our time-zone and draw up a suitable recovery plan for Phase 2."*

Mike nodded, *"OK, then we'll get Ed to buy the equipment and go and seek then head off to Austria to find whatever it was the Nazi's hid down there – if anything at all."* Graham nodded, *"Well, very broadly speaking, that's about it. I don't think that we should let the Austrians know what we're up to in the first instance though, they'd probably deny us permission. Anyway, those were just my initial thoughts. When we get back to Hull I'll need to sit down, give the idea some serious thought and sketch out a proper plan of action. So, do you fancy having a crack at it then?"*

Mike nodded, *"Yes - count me in! You mentioned several 'mysterious' deaths,"* he said. Graham replied, *"Well, apparently there's been dirty deeds afoot in the area over the past few years, the deaths weren't all 'accidental' so to speak, so we'll have to keep a watchful eye on things and tread very carefully. I would imagine that there are some Nazis supporters still lurking out there, even though most of 'em will be knocking on a bit – but they'll have a lot of influence, even now. I never trust blokes that wear lederhosen. Too much thigh slapping for my liking!"*

An enthusiastic Mike said. *"Well, you can definitely count me in. I was intending to 'retire' from the 'Time-Travellers' outfit in a year or two and then perhaps sail around the world enjoying the fruits of my ill-gotten gains, but I think I'll hang on until this next little adventure's sorted. I've realised that I'm not quite ready to be put out to grass just yet. This 'Hitler's Gold' business has fired my retro's!"*

Graham said, *"I've got lots of ideas buzzing around my brain already." "Such as?"* asked Mike, *"Well, we'll definitely need unfettered access to a 'Travellator' and we'll both need a German language transplant, so 'Time-Travellers' could provide that for us."* Mike nodded in agreement, *"That'll be my department. I know that Ed and his lads can speak the lingo fluently, but my German's a bit rusty, as is yours no doubt." "My German's not just rusty, it's non-existent, although I can still order a beer and some pomfrets without too much difficulty,"* said Graham, laughing. *"That's not a problem,"* replied Mike, *"as I said, the Time-Travellers language transplants will resolve that issue."*

Mike grinned, *" Huh, one thing I haven't quite got my head around yet though is the amount of gold that could be there, lurking at the bottom of the lake - increasing in value every day - just think, 35 billion quids worth! We'll need a convoy of bloody armoured trucks to carry that lot, never mind vans."* Graham scratched his head, *"There's a shedful of information about it on the internet and I'll bet a pound to a pinch of you know what that there'll be some serious competition - particularly if anyone gets wind that we're showing an interest. Still, you've got to be in it to win it. "*

Mike nodded in agreement, *"And don't forget, Graham, they haven't got easy access to a 'Travellator' as we have. 'Time-Travellers' is the only licensed operator for Time-Travel in Europe and I'll put the mockers on anyone else trying to get to Austria in one. My people will see to that!"*

Graham continued, *"Great. It'll take some time to organise suitable clothing, diving equipment, weapons, transport, travel documentation and disposal of the gold - if and when we find any."* Mike smiled, *"Oh, if it's there we'll certainly find it!"* Graham rambled on, *"Then there'd be the problem of avoiding getting anyone in the Austrian government interested in our search. That'll be the first difficulty, the clunking wheels of Austrian beaurocracy; I'd imagine that if they did find out about us, they'd want to know the far end of a fart, so that's why I think that you're right, it's better that we should just ignore them. If we are found out then we'll just have to cough."* Mike nodded in agreement.

Graham continued, *"We'll need to buy a couple of hefty trucks to move the bullion, 'cos like you say, Mike, I have every faith that we could find it! 'Who Dares Wins!'"* *"I'll drink to that!"* said Mike. *"I think that this calls for more champagne. All this excitement's given me a raging thirst."* Mike winked at Graham and reached across the table to shake hands with him, *"It's Champers all the way for us from here on in, mate!"*

"There's just one baby elephant in the room though, well two actually," said Graham, *"We've got to tell our wives about all of this. We can't just leg it off to Amsterdam and Austria for a few days and not say anything to them. They'll know that we're up to mischief."* Mike sighed, *"Oh yes, I'd forgotten about the girls in all of the excitement. Well, we'll just have to trust them and explain everything , after all,*

they'll have to keep schtum, especially as they'll be helping us to spend the profits from any ill-gotten gains!" Graham laughed, *"Anyway if things go tits up and we do get caught, wives can't give evidence against their husbands, can they!"* Mike said, *"It won't get to that. We're going on a treasure hunt, not robbing the Bank of England. Once we've got this properly organised it'll all go like a well-oiled machine. And speaking of well-oiled!"* Mike lifted the champagne bottle out of the ice-bucket to refill their glasses and saw, to his disgust, that it was empty.

Summoning a hovering waiter, Mike asked him to bring another couple of bottles of iced champagne to their table, *"The decent stuff, cocker,"* he said, pointing to an exclusive brand name at the top of the extensive drinks list, *"That Armand de Brignac Brut Gold will do, not that German Sekt that we've just been drinking!"* When he returned, the waiter opened one of the bottle's with a great flourish, then poured them both a glass of chilled, sparkling champagne. Mike crossed the man's palm with a fifty euro note and after quickly trousering the generous tip the man withdrew, leaving them to it. Mike tapped Graham's champagne flute with his own and said, *"Well, Graham St Anier, here we go again! Here's to the 'Führer's Gold' sat waiting for us in Lake Toplitz – Adolf Hitler's lads will never know what's hit them!"* Graham smiled as they clinked flutes and said to Mike, *"Cheers mate!"*

At the mention of the 'Führer's Gold' and Adolf Hitler, a portly middle-aged German and his wife sat at a nearby table glanced at each other. The man leaned across to his wife and whispered, *"Did you hear what those two Englanders were talking about, Renate?"* She shook her head, *"No, I wasn't really paying attention, Hartmut, I was too busy demolishing the last of the delicious pork schnitzel."* Hartmut continued,

"They were saying something about the 'Führer's Gold' in Lake Toplitz!" The woman smiled, *"Ach, not that alte kastanie (old chestnut) again. I should ignore them, Hartmut, have you seen the amount of champagne they have put away? Typical loud-mouthed English football hooligans. They are, of course, talking complete sheisse, liebchen!"* The man stood up, *"Where are you going now, schatzie? We haven't had our apple strudel yet!"* asked Renate in a whiney voice. *"You must excuse me for just a moment, I just need to make a quick 'phone call to a colleague of mine in Salzburg,"* he replied, before waddling off.

As he walked past Graham and Mike, he smiled at them both and said *"Chentlemen, you are having a pleasant evening, Ja?"* Graham nodded back and smiled, *"Aye, we're doing reyt grand thanks."* The German smiled and as he walked on he was thinking, *"Huh, after the 'Fuhrers Gold' neh. Englander Schweinhunds! Well, we'll soon put a stop to that."*

Hartmut's wife called out, *"Hartmut, another bottle of wine please!"*

'CHAPTER 2'

'The Führerbunker, Berlin – 1945'

In the Führerbunker, deep underground and not too far away from the totally devastated Reich Chancellery, in a relatively small badly furnished ante-room, immediately adjacent to the Führer's office sat Hitler's Secretary, an impatient Martin Bormann. He was awaiting the arrival of the Reichsführer-SS, Heinrich Himmler, who had been summoned to the bunker by Hitler.

To Bormann's annoyance, the Führer had not told him why Himmler's presence was required at the bunker. Bormann hated being kept out of the loop, he liked to keep his finger on the pulse. Knowledge was power.

'External view of the Führerbunker, Berlin'

These days the Führer always seemed to be distracted by seemingly trivial problems and in Bormann's opinion, he thought that 'Dolfie' was, metaphorically, just fiddling whilst Berlin fell about his ears. No longer could Bormann work out what the Führer was thinking, Hitler's twisted logic defied all reason. It didn't take the brains of an Archbishop to work out that the 'Third Reich' was on the verge of total collapse and that in his, Bormann's opinion, what remained of the Nazi hierarchy should be concentrating on commencing the carefully constructed escape plans for getting out of Berlin and then continuing the fight from safer ground. Perhaps that's why the Führer wanted to see Himmler? The clock was ticking.

After a difficult and time-consuming journey through the devastated and dangerous streets of central Berlin, the Reichsführer-SS, Heinrich Himmler, eventually arrived at the Führerbunker. Even at that late stage of the war, Himmler dare not ignore the Führer's summons, although Himmler thought that anyone with an iota of intelligence could easily work out that the 'Third Reich' was tumbling down around the Führer's ears and his insistence that he was still commanding and directing thousands of fighting soldiers was laughable. None of his generals that remained dare tell him otherwise.

"Why doesn't the Führer just get out of Berlin and hand the leadership to someone else, like me?" he thought. The hand to hand fighting in the streets was brutal, both sides incurring heavy losses. The Russian Army drew ever closer to the Führerbunker, the Germans defenders being completely overwhelmed and decimated by the rapidly advancing Red Army. Himmler knew that it would be foolhardy for him to linger in the Führerbunker for any longer than was strictly necessary. He knew precisely what would happen to him if he fell into Russian hands - shades of Mussolini – and it wouldn't be a pretty sight.

Once Himmler had passed through all of the intensive security checks and finally gained access to Bormann's office, the portly, inelegant and faux-obsequious Martin Bormann, stood up, clicked the heels of his highly polished jackboots together, saluted and called out, *"Heil Hitler!"* Although always appearing to treat Himmler with great respect, Bormann actually despised the odious and secretive little creature, often describing him as being, in what was common German military parlance, a *"Scheissehausfliege"* (a shit-house fly). Himmler's gimlet eyes were always watching, ears always listening and he was always appraising opportunities for self-aggrandisement. Himmler, like Bormann, never missed a trick. They were two of a kind.

Himmler nodded somewhat off-handedly at Bormann and, waving his hand in the air, languidly returned Bormann's salute, saying somewhat dismissively, *"Heil Hitler. Now, can we dispense with the fripperies, Bormann? I do not have a lot of time and there is much left to be done."* Inwardly seething, Bormann nodded and smiled, *"The Führer is eagerly awaiting your arrival, Herr Reichsführer."* Lowering his voice he continued, *" He is with his physician, Doctor Morell, at the moment who is administering the*

266

Führer's daily booster injection. I don't think that the Führer would appreciate you seeing him with his trousers around his ankles and the pimply Führer-arsche on display, eh?" Himmler nodded, *"I very much doubt it,"* he replied, appalled at Bormann's crudity.

'The Führer, Adolf Hitler
and
The Reichsführer-SS, Heinrich Himmler'

'Martin Bormann'　　　**'Theodor Morell'**
'Head of the Nazi Party　**'Hitler's Physician'**
Chancellery and the
Führer's Personal Secretary'

It was well known in the very upper echelons of the Nazi hierarchy that Hitler received a daily injection of the drug Pervitin, a methamphetamine stimulant. The Führer had been lied to and informed that the injection was merely a vitamin booster and honestly believed that the shots did him the world of good. Unlike everyone else, Hitler hadn't realised that for virtually 24 hours a day he was smacked off his tits.

Shaking his head, Bormann said, *"As you know, the Führer's health is not good and you will undoubtedly notice that the trembling in his hands has greatly increased. I'm afraid that he will not listen to my advice to get rid of that fat bungling oaf, Doctor Morell, who I'm certain doesn't know his own arse from his elbow, never mind the Führer's! There are so many other highly qualified medical experts here in Berlin that I could send for, but the Führer will not hear of it. I can see him physically and mentally deteriorating on a daily basis, despite all of the crap that's being pumped into him."* Himmler nodded, *"Perhaps it would be better if the Führer left Berlin for somewhere much safer?"* *"I totally agree,"* said Bormann, *"the Führer would much rather be back in his beloved Berchtesgarten with his wife Eva than be here in Berlin with its inherent risks. It is heart-breaking to see him suffering."*

Himmler nodded, trying his best to look sympathetic, but failing miserably. He knew full well that Hitler was on his last legs and was secretly pleased that that was the case. For many months Himmler had been making highly secretive plans to replace Adolf as Führer. From what Himmler was now hearing from Bormann, that possibility could be sooner rather than later. Once that had happened and once he had claimed the 'Third Reich' throne as his rightful inheritance, one of Himmler's very first priorities would be that the intensely annoying Martin Bormann would be moved to the very top of his list of those to be swiftly disposed of.

Apart from anything else, Bormann knew far too much about the inner workings of the Nazi Party for his own good, particularly the 'Final Solution.' Bormann knew where all of the skeletons were hidden. The manner of Bormann's despatch had yet to be decided by Himmler, but it would be something very special and guaranteed to be lingering and torturous. Himmler smiled to himself as he thought, "*I might even have it filmed. It would make excellent after-dinner entertainment.*"

An impatient Himmler pointedly glanced down at the face of his wrist-watch, tapped it and sniffed airily. Taking the hint, Bormann said, "*If you will just wait here for a moment, Herr Reichsführer, I will check that the Führer is ready to see you.*" He paused, then said, "*Oh, and Reichsführer, with respect, if the Führer invites you to have a cup of coffee, might I suggest that you decline. He will feel duty bound to join you and, as you will notice, he has great difficulty holding a cup and saucer for long without spilling the contents everywhere. He has already changed his uniform jacket twice today.*" Himmler smiled graciously and nodded as Bormann left the ante-room.

In reality, Himmler was displeased, he was unaccustomed to being kept waiting - he was the Reichsführer-SS. He thought, "*Huh, I am like some little schoolboy kept waiting to see the Headmaster! I have plans for you, my dear Bormann and I will be there to watch you squirm when it happens.*" Outside his office, Bormann thought, "*Huh, I don't know what your game is, you two-faced little chicken farmer, but I will make it my business to discover what it is you are up to! Whatever it is, it will end up in tears for someone - it always has does when he's involved."*

Bormann had always found it difficult hiding the malice and loathing he felt for Himmler, whom he regarded as being an odious, creepy and talentless creature. Nevertheless, he still had to tread very carefully, despite his own current exalted position as the Führer's right-hand man. Although a paper warrior, Himmler was still a man who wielded a lot of power, surrounded as he was by his beloved SS. If the Führer succumbed to ill-health, Bormann's top-cover would be blown and he knew that Himmler was waiting in the wings, plotting and scheming to fill the Führer's highly polished boots.

Bormann tapped on the Führer's office door. A familiar gruff voice from inside the office, the Führer's, called out – *"Enter!"* Bormann stepped smartly into the office and saw Hitler slumped in his desk chair, hands trembling, gazing up at the portrait of his hero, Frederick the Second, hung on the wall opposite his cluttered desk. *"With your permission, my Führer!"* *"Yes, what is it, Martin?"* the Führer asked him. *"The Reichsführer-SS has arrived and is outside, waiting to see you, as ordered, my Führer."* Hitler nodded, *"Excellent, ask him to come in, please."*

'Hitler's office deep inside the Führerbunker'

The grandly titled Reichsführer-SS strutted into the Führerbunker, the metal heels on his gleaming jack-boots noisily ringing out on the concrete floor. He halted, clicked his heels together, then saluted - crying out enthusiastically, *"Heil Hitler!"* Hitler nodded, *"Take a seat, Heinrich. Would you care for a cup of coffee?"* he asked. Remembering Bormann's advice, Himmler shook his head, *"No thank you, my Führer."* Himmler could see that the trembling in the Führer's hands had significantly worsened. Adolf's voice, though, was still clear and his cold, piercing pale blue eyes were as hypnotic as ever.

Before sitting down, Himmler reached across the Führer's desk and shook hands with him. The Führer's handshake was weak and clammy. *"You are looking well, my Führer,"* he lied. *"My faithful Heinrich,"* replied the Führer, *"in truth I am utterly exhausted. Every day the news gets worse and the Bolsheviks draw ever closer. Bormann informs me that the Russian Army Assault Troops have been seen in the Charlottenburg area! Huh, Jews and Russians will be the death of me! What can I do? I am surrounded by a coterie of cowardly, spineless Generals, half of whom are traitors, plotting and scheming behind my back, the other half are witless quivering, cowardly buffoons who I should have put out to grass many years ago. They do nothing but whine about conditional surrender. That will never happen!!"*

Himmler replied, *"My Führer, let me assure you that the SS, my own people, are doing their utmost to root those cowardly traitors out,"* adding icily, *"then they, and their families, are dealt with most severely as a lesson to the others, as per your directive."* Hitler nodded, sighed then slumped back in his chair, *"It needs to be done, Heini. There are too many vipers in the nest."* If Hitler only knew that Himmler was the 'Viper-in-Chief' and had recently been in touch with the Allies to discuss the terms of German surrender then it would be Heinrich himself who would be dangling from a length of piano wire at the Plötzensee prison, alongside the Generals.

Hitler smiled at Himmler, *"Now then, you'd better update me on the state of play regarding 'OPERATION GOLDGRÄBER,'"* he said. Himmler returned Hitler's smile, and said smugly, *"Everything is going swimmingly, my Führer. The last of the gold bullion has been crated and removed from the Reichsbank by the SS under the strictest conditions of secrecy. It will leave Berlin very shortly by road and be taken to the Naval Testing Station at Lake Toplitz in Austria, scheduled to reach there late tomorrow afternoon. The vehicles are disguised as ambulances. At your direction, I have placed SS-Obergruppenführer Kaltenbrunner in charge of the convoy. He and his men will stick like glue to the gold until it reaches its final destination. You need have no concerns for its safety, I give you my word."*

'SS-Obergruppenführer Ernst Kaltenbrunner'
'Chef der Sicherheitspolizei und des SD'
(Chief of the Reich Main Security Office)

The Führer smiled and said, *"A good man is Kaltenbrunner. If I had fifty more like him under command we would not be where we are today. I have every confidence in him and in you, of course. You have been one of my staunchest friends."*

Himmler nodded, saying, *"Thank you, my Führer,"* whilst thinking, *"My dear Adolf, you wouldn't be quite so confident if you knew that my man SS-Standartenführer Albrecht Krancher will be arresting and disposing of Kaltenbrunner and his guards the instant they arrive at Lake Toplitz."* Himmler had made his own post-war plans for the 'Führer's Gold' and he didn't intend that it would be hidden in Lake Toplitz. If everything went to plan, the gold bullion would be heading straight for Switzerland and to a bank where Himmler had lots of other valuables stashed away. He did not intend being a chicken farmer again.

Hitler gazed at Himmler, *"On a slightly different issue, Heini, and whilst I have you here, have you dealt with the problem of the traitor Göring yet?"* he asked. *"It is proving to be a little difficult under the present circumstances, my Führer,"* replied Himmler. Hitler, now impatiently drumming his fingers on the desk, stared unblinkingly at

Himmler, making him wriggle and feel very uncomfortable, *"Difficult? Why so?"* he asked icily. Himmler blustered, *"Well, my Führer, the Reichschmarschall,"* Hitler jumped out of his chair and shouted, *"He is no longer the Reichschmarschall! He is no longer my nominated successor and deputy! He is guilty of treason and is a relic of the Third Reich. I gave implicit orders that he is to be disposed of!"* A fearful Himmler gulped, then continued, *"Forgive me, my Führer, old habits die hard. The, er, traitor Göring has hidden away inside his country estate in Carinhall at Schorfheide and has surrounded himself with a large, well-armed bodyguard."*

The Führer slammed his fist onto the desk, his face contorted and puce – a sure sign that he was about to 'go off on one.' *"So what! He is a useless drug-taking blob of lard WHO HAS TRIPPED AT EVERY HURDLE! The idiot promised to eat his hat if ever Berlin was ever bombed by the Allies – no wonder he is so gross, he must spend all day eating hats!"* Beads of spittle ran down Hitler's chin as, incandescent with rage, he bellowed, *"I gave you a direct order that Göring was to be arrested. Must I do everything myself? If you are unable to arrange for his removal with all of the resources at your disposal, Himmler, then I will find someone who can! Maybe Kaltenbrunner! Do I make myself clear?"*

Himmler shot out of his chair and stood rigidly to attention, the cheeks of his arse cracking walnuts, *"Jawhoul meine Führer! I can certainly have Göring arrested, my Führer, it is just at what cost. The manpower alone...."* Hitler stamped his foot and slammed his fist down on the desk again, *"Just see to it! The butcher's bill is irrelevant! I have given you a Führer-directive. See that it is carried out!!"* shouted Hitler, *"If the 'Third Reich' is going to go down in flames then Göring, for one, will be accompanying it!"*

Hitler was starting to calm down, *"You also have my authority to arrest his immediate family! Have him shot and announce that he fell in battle or has had a heart attack or something similar. I leave the method of his disposal up to you! The same with his family!"* Himmler nodded, *"It will be done, my Führer!"* *"It had better be, or this will all end in tears!"* said Hitler, as they both resumed their seats. *"Oh, and one other thing,"* said Hitler, *"When I promoted Göring to Reichsmarschall I presented him with a gold signet ring with the initials S.L. inscribed on it (Sein Lieber – Dear Friend). It is a rare and very personal gift from me given to demonstrate the high esteem that I held him in. You will recognise it quite easily. It has a blue enamelled seal, combining our national emblem and Göring's personal eagle. I want it back. He is no longer deserving of it!"* The Führer's voice rose several decibels, *"Find it and bring it to me. Chop it off his fat finger if you have to!"*

"God in Heaven," though Himmler, *"that was very nearly a carpet chewing moment. Well, Göring will have to wait, there are more important issues bubbling under. Huh, the Führer sits here at his desk, fiddling whilst Berlin burns."* He could feel a bead of sweat rolling down between his shoulder blades; this meeting wasn't going exactly as he had planned. *"One thing's for definite,"* he thought, *"I'll be kicking arse once I've left the Führer's office."*

Unusually for Himmler, he had let his eye slip off the ball by not seeing to the arrest of the ex-Reichsmarschall, but Göring's days in the sun were definitely numbered. *"Now, Heini, sit. Enough unpleasantness."* said the Führer, calming down, *"I do not wish to waste any more of my valuable time and effort on that useless swine Göring."* Himmler nodded in agreement, *"Let us get back to the all-important 'OPERATION GOLDGRÄBER.' Explain to me precisely what arrangements have been made for the gold once the convoy has reached Lake Toplitz."*

Outside the bunker door, Bormann was listening closely to Hitler's ranting and at Himmler's cringing, subservient replies. Bormann sniggered malevolently to himself. *"Old Heini is sailing very close to the wind today."* he thought, *"Herr Himmler may think that he has his spidery little finger on the pulse, but what he doesn't know is that I have sent for the Führer's personal pilot, Hans Bauer and that arrangements are well in hand to have him fly the Führer and his wife out of Berlin very shortly - and I won't be too far behind them."*

What Himmler also didn't know was that Hitler's spookily realistic doppelganger, Gustav Weler, was tucked away out of sight in a different room of the Führerbunker, having been fully briefed, and ready and willing to take the Führer's place once Adolf finally scuttled out of Berlin. Despite the obvious consequences to him, Gustav Weler was more than willing to forfeit his life for his beloved Führer; to him, Adolf Hitler was some sort of deity. Inexplicably, Gustav had informed his masters that he would happily take a bullet for the Führer. Unknown to the unfortunate Gustav, it was an ambition that was soon to be achieved.

Despite his protestations to the contrary, the Führer knew in his heart of hearts that he was teetering on the precipice of total disaster as the brutal and savage hand-to-hand final battle for Berlin was being fought out just streets away. He knew that now was time to draw stumps and leave for somewhere safer. Not for him the fate of the Italian dictator, Benito Mussolini and his mistress Clara Petacci, who had been executed by Italian partisans, then their blood-stained corpses strung up in a town square, left hanging grotesquely by their heels, swinging upside down for all to see. For Hitler, it was the stuff of nightmares and he would not let that happen to either him or his beloved wife, Eva.

Hitler mumbled, *"Those Allied swine, they will come to regret that they wish to deny the German nation the right to exist,"* then his eyes suddenly ablaze, he shouted, *"Make no mistake, Himmler, Germany will rise again from the ashes! It is not over, not by a long chalk. We have one last throw of the dice available to us! The ultimate weapon!"* Himmler smiled inwardly at the Führer's latest fatuous utterance, knowing that the deluded and self-centred Hitler would leave Berlin without so much as a backward glance. The whole 'Battle for Berlin' thing was a débâcle from start to finish and as for the alleged ultimate weapon – the scientists had been promising him that for years. It was all too little, too late.

Despite Hitler's desperate efforts, the 'Third Reich' was tumbling down around his ears, and despite his many well-publicised announcements that he would die fighting valiantly at the head of his troops in Berlin, Adolf Hitler knew full well that he wouldn't be there in the shattered city, alongside the ragged and brave remnants of his army, to witness the grand finalé. The fall of Berlin was of little consequence to him. He considered that the soldiers and citizens who were fighting to the bitter end had failed him and was utterly convinced that the fight would continue from elsewhere and that it was the 'Fuhrer's Gold' - his gold - that would be funding it. Not only was gold being stashed away in Lake Toplitz but many tons of it had also been secreted away in several other safe areas.

"Now, Heinrich," said the Führer, *"Despite the traitorous nay-sayers, all is not lost. There is something else that I wish*

to discuss with you. The one last throw of the cards!" pointing with a trembling finger at a classified file on his desk marked '**Streng Geheim – Uranverein**.' (*Top Secret – Uranium Club*), he smiled and said, *"Let me update you on this gift from God."*

'CHAPTER 3'

'The 'T3' to Lake Toplitz'

Graham and the team were sat chatting in the ultra-plush 'Time-Travellers' VIP Transit Lounge at Humberside Travelport. "*So, just how did you get the weapons and ammunition through customs at the Hull Ferry Terminal, Ed?*" asked Graham. Ed smiled, "*Simply a matter of who you know and what you know, oh, and the right amounts of money changing hands, my dear friend. Greed and avarice know no bounds. I can reveal no more, otherwise, I would have to kill you.*" Graham smiled but was unsure if Ed was pulling his leg or not. He decided to give him the benefit of the doubt and not broach the subject any further. It was obviously a 'Need to Know' matter. Having been 'Special Forces,' Ed would certainly have the right sort of contacts throughout Europe to be able to both obtain and move illegal items.

Mike Fraser stood up, yawned, stretched then looked at his watch, "*Well, now that we've all got changed into suitable clothing for the mid to late 1940's era, we'd better get the weapons and ammo stashed on board the 'Travellator.'*" Ed nodded at his two sons, Diederik and Ludo, "*Boys, see to that will you, please.*" They both nodded. Graham said, "*Whew, I'm lathered in this heavy weather clothing, but I suppose it'll come into its own once we get up there into the chilly Austrian mountains.*"

Diederik and Ludo picked up the several ominous looking black cases containing weapons and ammunition and began loading them inside the 'Travellator.' Looking at the cases, Graham exclaimed, *"You've got enough stuff there to start World War 3, Ed!"* *"We might need it all, Graham,"* replied Ed, *"Don't forget that where we're going there's still a war on. The Krauts won't fanny about if they discover us snooping around their base at Toplitz,"* he smiled, *"and that's when you'll appreciate all those hours you spent doing weapon handling at the gun club."* Mike called out, *"Right chaps, let's get a wee shift on then. Speaking of 'wee' - this is your last chance to use the 'facilities' before we leave here for 1945 so I suggest that you go and pay a visit."*

Once they'd had a final pee, they returned to the 'Travellator' and began strapping themselves into the large, comfortable seats of the 'T3 Travellator' and got ready for the off. *"Here we go then, lads, brace yourselves."* said Mike pressing the button to close and seal the 'T'3's' door. As it clamped shut, Ed grimaced, *"This 'Time-Travel' business is a first for me, my friend!"* Mike smiled and looked across at Ed, *"Don't worry yourself, Ed, it's just like a fairground ride."* he said, pressing several buttons, *" So, watch out 1945, 'cos here we come!"*

The lights inside the cabin of the 'T3' flickered and dimmed, then a gentle whirring noise began. The digital clock on the main console started to roll backward in time towards the year 1945. Ed's hands gripped the arms of his seats tightly as he wondered just what it was he was he'd gotten himself and his two lads into. Still, he loved the excitement and adrenaline rush of it and to him, that's what it was all about. One of Ed's favourite sayings was *"Live for today! You're a long time dead!"* he glanced across at his two sons and winked. They smiled back at him, having not a care in the world. For all intents and purposes, they could have been flying off somewhere on their holidays. *"Oh to be that young and carefree again."* thought Ed.

'CHAPTER 4'

'Lake Toplitz'

The slimy SS-Standartenführer Albrecht Krancher sat back in an expensive leather armchair, one of several in the Base Commandant's personal dining room, beckoning imperiously and clicking his fingers loudly at the ancient and apprehensive Officers' Mess Steward, Ludi Spitzenberger, who was stood in the corner of the room doing his utmost to fade into the background. Everyone was nervous when Krancher was around. He was a mean machine.

Hearing Krancher summoning him, the Steward walked across the plush carpet, clicked his heels and bowed his head, *"Herr Standartenführer?"* *"Refill my wine glass!"* *"Jawhoul, Herr Standartenführer."* He refilled Krancher's wine glass with sparkling white wine. *"Leave the carafe there!"* ordered Krancher. The Steward nodded, then turned to the Base Commandant, Kapitän zur See Manfred Von Mülheim, *"Herr Kapitän?"* Von Mülheim smiled and placed his hand on top of his wine glass, *"Not for me Ludi, I need to keep my wits about me."* The Steward nodded, clicked his heels again then returned to lurk the corner of the room. Krancher turned and called across to Ludi, saying, *"You may leave us now – and close the door behind you!"*

More clicking of heels, *"As you wish, Herr Standartenführer."* said Ludi giving a half-bow before leaving the room and closing the door quietly behind him.

As the door closed, Krancher smiled at Von Mülheim, raised his glass and took a sip of wine then said, *"What is those infernal British say, "Walls have ears!"* The Kapitän smiled, *"I think that we are perfectly safe with old Ludi. He was a Stabsbootsmann (Senior Boatswain) in the Kriegsmarine during the first World War. That's where he lost a leg."* Krancher nodded, *"Mmmm, that was careless of him. I thought that he had a rather curious, mincing gait,"* he said. On the defensive, Von Mülheim continued, *"He is a loyal and proud German, always has been. I have known him for many years!"* *"It goes without saying that we are all loyal and proud Germans, Herr Kapitän, nevertheless, we will both have much to lose if word of 'OPERATION GOLDGRÄBER' leaks out,"* replied Krancher, tapping the finely tooled leather briefcase at the side of his chair.

Krancher and Von Mülheim, both of whom detested each other, were closeted in the select Commandant's Dining Room of the Officers' Mess at the Toplitz Naval Base. Krancher, who considered himself to be the senior of the two, continued speaking, *"As I was explaining, the 'Fuhrer's Gold' will be arriving here at approximately 1800 hours tomorrow evening in military truck disguised as ambulances, with an armed escort of course. All reception arrangements must have been made by then. Speed is of the essence if we are to be successful.* Von Mülheim started to speak, *"I can assure you, Herr Standartenführer..."* but was silenced by Krancher rudely interrupting, *"Let me finish, Von Mülheim! I wish to reiterate, the Drivers and Escorts of the gold bullion vehicles, once they have unloaded their trucks, are to be transported immediately to the Luftwaffe Feldflugplatz in*

Bierbaum where there is an aircraft stood by to fly them all straight back to Berlin. They are not to converse with any of your chaps, is that understood?" Krancher took a perverse delight in browbeating people. Von Mülheim nodded. Krancher continued, *"Let us say that 'other arrangements' have been made to ensure their silence and leave it at that, shall we."*

"May I speak?" asked Von Mülheim. *"Yes, of course."* said a nodding Krancher. *"And what, may I ask, am I to do with my men once the task is completed?"* Krancher smiled, *"It will be in all our interests if they are similarly, shall we say, disposed of. It is regrettable, but there must be no leaks!"*

A furious Von Mülheim leaped to his feet, raising his voice he said, *"But that is quite outrageous! They are good and loyal Germans!"* Krancher replied, *"Do sit down, and stop shouting, Herr Kapitän, you are not on board ship now. Must I remind you that this operation is being carried out at the express order of Reichsführer-SS Himmler himself, who is acting directly on behalf of the Führer, both of from whom all blessings flow. I hope that I make myself clear?"* Von Mülheim sighed and sat down, *"Yes, of course, Her Standartenführer."*

Krancher reached down and opened the flap of the leather briefcase at the side of his chair, then pulled out a beige folder, on the cover of which, top and bottom, was stencilled in bold red letters, '**Streng Geheim'** (*Top Secret*) and on the centre of the cover was written, '*OPERATION GOLDGRÄBER.*' '*Nur für Offizier*' (*Officers Only*)

Krancher opened the folder and read from the first page, *"You also need to know that the Reichsführer-SS sought and received permission from the Führer for SS-*

Obergruppenführer Ernst Kaltenbrunner to accompany the gold bullion here and also witness it's 'disposal.'" Von Mülheim was impressed, and gasped, *"What, 'the' Ernst Kaltenbrunner?"* Krancher nodded. *"Yes, the very same. And let me assure you that with him at the helm, nothing must go wrong. He will be accompanied by his swinish Adjutant, Arthur Scheidler, and a detachment of some thirty finely-honed SS Guards who will be armed to the teeth."*

"Mein Gott!" thought Von Mülheim and made a mental note that his men would have to be extremely well briefed as to their duties and responsibilities, Kaltenbrunner was definitely a man not to be tampered with and it would not do to tread on his toes. He had been known to shoot people on the spot for very minor disciplinary infractions and seemed to be accountable to no-one for his actions. Anyone with admirers like the two Adolfs, Adolf Hitler, and SS-Obersturmbannführer Adolf Eichmann, was to be avoided like the plague. It was very bad news that he would be coming to Toplitz.

Krancher placed the classified file on the table and said quietly, *"Just a moment."* He then, rather comically, tip-toed over to the door and quickly pulled it open, looking to check that no-one was outside eavesdropping. He then shut the door, returned to his chair and sat down, *"You can never be too sure,"* he said. Von Mülheim suppressed a smile at the ridiculousness of Krancher's theatrical gesture.

Krancher said, *"Now, Von Mülheim, where was I? Ah yes, there will be at least our vehicles carrying the gold, with escort vehicles front and rear. The Obergruppenführer and his Adjutant will, of course, be free-running in his staff car and will probably arrive here first."* *"May I make a few notes?"* asked Von Mulheim, reaching for a notepad.

"*Certainly not! You must retain this information in your head! It is highly sensitive. We cannot afford for any of this material to leak!*" he said tapping the classified file, "*I have told you all that you need to know for the moment.*" said Krancher, closing the file and placing it back inside his briefcase before locking it. "*More wine*?" he asked Von Mülheim.

'CHAPTER 5'

'And so it begins'

The 'T3 Travellator' slowly de-materialised, its door hissing open and the team gingerly stepping out into a heavily wooded area at the side of Lake Toplitz. After having a quick look around and checking that the area was secure, they quickly emptied the 'T3' of the weapons and ammunition cases, before programming the Travellator to return to base. The weather was miserable and it was freezing cold, so it was a good job that they were all well wrapped up.

After a few minutes, Mike and the others they were rubbing their hands and stamping their feet to try and keep warm. '*This bloody weather reminds me of bonny Scotland! Damned good job we're wearing this heavy duty clothing!*" said Mike, "*And I'm glad I'm no wearing ma kilt − this weather would freeze the balls off a brass monkey!*" As Ed distributed the weapons and ammunition, Graham leaned across to Mike and said, "*Mike, can I have a quick word?*" A puzzled Mike said, "*Of course you can, what's up?*"

"*I didn't go to the bogs before we left but I need to go now!*" said Graham. "*No big deal, just nip over there behind that tree,*" said Mike. "*I can't, I don't need a Number One - I need a Number Two. I'm touching cloth!"* Mike sighed, and looked around, *"Well go behind those bushes over there - and don't be too long mate, we need to get moving, and keep an eye out for the Krauts. Leave your weapon here with me. You don't want to lose it in the bushes."*

Graham passed his gun over to Mike then nipped across towards a large bush, intending to go behind it. Unfortunately, he tripped over a root sticking out from the undergrowth, stumbled then slithered down into a small ditch, finishing up in an ungainly heap at the bottom, landing in a tangle of arms and legs and finishing up sat pool of freezing cold water. *"Bugger it,"* he thought. Still desperate to 'ease springs' he stood up then clambered out of the ditch, hurrying across to another bush, unbuttoned his trousers then squatted down to do the business, or 'opening the bomb doors.' as he referred to it. The icy wind whistled around his exposed nether regions as he let nature take its course. Graham had a thought, *"I wish I had some of those forged twenty-pound notes, I could put them to good use just now."* A job was never finished until the paperwork was done.

"OK guys, that's everything we need," said Mike, *"I've programmed the 'T3' to return to base so let's send it on its merry way."* He leaned inside the 'Travellator' and pressed a button before quickly stepping back. The door of the 'T3' hissed to a close and after a few seconds, it materialised, totally disappearing. *"It seems fairly* quiet around here, my friend, No sign of any German patrols," said Ed. Mike nodded, *"Yes, that's good. No 'Nosey Parkers!' We'll just wait a few more minutes for Graham to sort himself out then we can crack on with the recce, as planned."*

Meanwhile, out in the woods, a thoroughly bored SS-Sturm Mann Erhard Schrenk and the five SS-Schütze members of his foot-patrol froze as they heard the sound of someone breaking ferocious wind. *"Mein Gott, what was that!"* asked Schrenk, *" Wait here boys, I'll go and check it out. Sounds like a Warthog to me!"* he whispered. He trod carefully over the path of dead leaves leading towards where he thought the sound had emanated from and spotted Graham, trousers down, squatting behind a bush relieving himself. Schrenk beckoned his mates over and pointed at Graham.

Schrenk grinned and shouted, *"Hands up!"* Graham, mid-strain, froze. Schrenk repeated, *"Hands up or I will order my men to open fire!"* Graham glanced across at them and called out, *"Give me a break, I've got my hands full at the moment!"* The soldiers burst out laughing, *"At least they've got a sense of humour."* thought Graham. *"Well you'd better be quick or I will get Karl here to have a pop at you – and I warn you, he's good at hitting small targets!"* shouted Schrenk. The soldiers roared with laughter.

An embarrassed Graham quickly finished what he was doing then stood to hitch up his trousers. He knew that he was in big trouble and hoped that Mike and the others had seen what had happened. *"Put your hands in the air and come over here!"* ordered Schrenk.

'The SS Foot-patrol'

As Graham walked across to the patrol and stood in front of them, he raised both of his hands in the air. SS-Sturm Mann Schrenk nodded his head and, voice oozing sarcasm, said, "*You'll excuse me if I don't shake hands!*" then turned to SS-Schütze Karl Hanke and ordered, "*Search him!*" Hanke searched Graham, roughly and thoroughly, finding nothing. Luckily for Graham he'd handed his weapon over to Mike for safekeeping, "*He's clean, Erhard, no weapons.*" "*Danke, Karl,*" he turned to Graham, *Now my friend, perhaps you could explain just what you are doing wandering around in a restricted military area?*" said Schrenk.

Graham, thinking on his feet, blustered, "*I'm doing a bit of hill walking that's all. I got lost.*" Schrenk nodded thoughtfully then held his hand out, "*Your papers, please?*" he demanded. "*Er, I left them in my hotel. I, I didn't want to get them wet,*" replied Graham lamely. Schrenk glanced at him disdainfully, "*That is not a satisfactory explanation. You must know that you are required to carry your identity papers at all times! I think that you'd better come with me to the Headquarters and explain yourself to the Duty Officer. I warn you – you'd better have your story in order when you speak to him. If he is not happy with your answers he will send for SS-Standartenführer Krancher – and you wouldn't like him, would he boys!*" The group of guards laughed.

A sniggering SS-Schütze, Karl Hanke, prodded Graham with the snout of his evil looking MP40 9mm machine pistol and said, "*Finish fastening your trouser buttons and then get moving!*" pointing towards the gravel path.

Hiding in the trees, Mike Fraser and the team had witnessed Graham's capture. Mike turned to Ed and whispered, "*That's *buggered things up a bit, they've arrested him." "I thought that this was a Naval Base?" said Ed. "It is," replied Mike, "they must use the SS to guard the place." "Should we go and sort them out?" asked Diederik, "There's only six of them." "No, we'd better just follow them from a distance and see what happens. It'll give us time to work out a rescue plan. If anything kicks off now there's a risk that Graham'll cop it in the cross-fire. The crafty Krauts have put him right in the middle of the patrol. Let's keep our distance, follow them to wherever it is they're taking him and then see what the score is. Agreed?"* said Mike. Ed, Diederik, and Ludo all nodded in agreement. *"Not a very good start though, is it, we've only been here for a few minutes!"* said a disgruntled Ed. Mike nodded, replying, *"No it's not, but have a bit of sympathy for Graham, Ed, when you've got to go, you've got to go. Now come on, let's not lose sight of them."*

As the German patrol walked towards the Headquarters, SS-Schütze Karl Hanke turned to SS-Sturm Mann Schrenk and said, *"Hey, we'll get a commendation for capturing this bloke. I'll bet he's a spy!"* *"Well he's obviously up to no good and, he looks very shifty to me,"* replied Schrenk, *"and how did he get past the electric fence eh, we didn't spot any holes. Hill walking my arse!"* Hanke nodded, *"Well, let's hear what he has to say to the Duty Officer. There might be a simple explanation for all of this."*

Schrenk shook his head, *"Nah, there's something going on here. I smell a rat!"* *"Are you sure you haven't trodden in anything? What's that on your boot?'* asked Hanke. Schrenk turned, bent his knee and raised his boot to examine the sole, Hanke called out gaily, *"Oooooh, 'Hello Sailor!'"* The rest of the guards all laughed heartily. Graham, with his hands in the air, looked exceedingly glum.

'CHAPTER 6'

'Captured'

The prisoner, a dejected Graham St Anier, sat on the hard wooden chair, shoulders slumped, he was at the end of his tether, the past few hours had been something of a trial for him. He'd rather carelessly become separated from Mike Fraser and the others then had been discovered by a German SS foot-patrol who'd arrested him on the spot and taken him to their Headquarters for questioning. They'd treated him roughly and kept him without food or water.

It hadn't been an easy day for Graham. Sat in a small windowless room in the Naval Base Headquarters, he was drained, shoulders drooping and head lolling forward. If truth be known, he was more than a bit on edge, although he knew that Mike, Ed, and the boys would be lurking somewhere close by and that eventually, they'd turn up to rescue him.

Despite asking nicely, Graham hadn't been given anything to drink and was very thirsty. The German guarding him was brutish SS-Unterscharführer, Rudolf Gribnitz, who made a point of standing immediately behind Graham and out of his line of sight. He was so close though that Graham could feel the man's fetid breath on his neck. The Unterscharführer's breath stank of garlic, probably from a partly consumed knackwurst sausage laid on a nearby desk. Without warning, Gribnitz leaned forward and gave Graham a fierce slap on the back of the head, *"Stay awake, and sit up straight you slovenly schweinehunde!"* he shouted.

'SS-Unterscharführer Rudolf Gribnitz'

Graham sat up straight, rubbing the back of his head on the spot where the stinging blow had landed. He thought, *"Why is it always me that gets the shitty end of the stick? This never happens to Mike!"* The room door suddenly swung open and in strolled the Base Commandant, a dapper and dashing Kapitän zur See Manfred Von Mülheim.

The Unterscharführer hit Graham a sharp, stinging blow in between his shoulder blades with the butt of his rifle and shouted, *"Aufstehen – Schnell, Englander! Up off your arse!"* A weary Graham struggled to his feet, head and now shoulder aching from the harsh punishment meted out to him by Gribnitz. Graham thought, *"That's torn it, they know that I'm English."* The Unterscharführer shouted, *"Heil Hitler!"* and saluted. Von Mülheim smiled, waved his hand languidly and said, *"Er, Heil Hitler! Please, do not let us not stand on ceremony, Gribnitz, the prisoner may resume his seat."*

293

Gribnitz pushed heavily on Graham's shoulders, forcing him to sit down. *"Now what happens? "* thought Graham.

Von Mülheim stood directly in front of Graham, and said, *"Permit me to introduce myself. I am Kapitän zur See Manfred Von Mülheim, the Base Commandant. Now, perhaps you'd better explain yourself?"* Graham nodded and began telling Von Mülheim that he had been out doing a bit of hill walking and had simply got lost in the woods. Von Mülheim looked at him and smiled, then held up his hand, and started speaking in English, *"Let me stop you right there, my friend."* he said. *"You will note that I am now conversing with you in English. You are English, are you not?"* Graham nodded. The Commandant continued, *"I thought so. Your German is so lumpy that it is obvious that only an Englishman could speak it so badly. Let us continue to converse in English so that the imbecile guarding you, Unterscharführer Gribnitz, an uneducated and brutish fellow, does not understand us. It might just be better for both of us if he doesn't know what we are talking about."*

Graham nodded then Von Mülheim continued, *"You must excuse the brutality of the Unterscharführer, he is not a member of the elite Kriegsmarine. I doubt if he's ever seen any proper fighting, he was an SS Guard in a concentration camp in Poland before being sent here. He has quite an appalling record of which, for some strange reason, he is inordinately proud. A rather common fellow, he was a butcher before the war, who does not understand the meaning of your Marquess of Queensberry Rules."* Graham replied, *"I think, sir, that you mean the Geneva Convention."* Von Mülheim smiled, *"I know that my friend, it was just my little joke. We Germans are not without a sense of humour you know."*

The Kapitän reached into the breast pocket of his immaculate uniform and extracted a slim, finely tooled gold cigarette case, the logo of the German Navy, the Kriegsmarine, etched on the outer casing. Flipping it open, he slid a cigarette out, lit it then asked Graham. *"These are really quite excellent, much better than the horseshit sweepings that we are normally issued with. These were taken from one of your well-stocked Red Cross parcels. I thought it highly appropriate that they are 'Senior Service.' Highly out of order to misuse the Red Cross parcels, I know, but needs must and so forth. Would you care for one?"* Graham shook his head, *"No thank you, sir, I don't smoke,"*

Gribnitz looked hopefully at Von Mülheim, hoping that he might be unusually generous, for an officer, and also offer him a cigarette. Totally ignoring the Unterscharführer, the German naval officer snapped the cigarette case closed and slipped it back inside his breast pocket. before lighting the cigarette, breathing in a lungful of smoke, then exhaling, deliberately blowing the smoke tormentingly towards Gribnitz, then had a good cough before sitting down in a chair placed directly in front of Graham.

Removing his headdress, Von Mülheim said, *"Ach, these damned Senior Service cigarettes, they will be the death of me. At least the American cigarettes we get occasionally have filter tips. Now then, my English friend, let us get down to the business of the day, eh!"* *"Here we go,"* thought Graham, *"interrogation time. The gloves will come off now. Where's that bloody Mike Fraser and the lads when I need them. They should have been here to rescue me by now."*

Von Mülheim dropped his cigarette onto the floor and stubbed it out with the sole of his highly polished shoe, then continued, *"So, I have ascertained that you are an*

Englishman, which, as I said, was highly apparent from your use of very badly accented German language when trying to bluff your way out of trouble with some ill-conceived fairy tale – and, of course, your lack of identity papers didn't help." He shook his head, *"We Germans are not complete idiots you know,"* then glancing over at Gribnitz said, *"Of course we do seem to have more than our fair share of half-wits. I'm informed that there is no evidence of the perimeter fence being breached. So, you were obviously parachuted into here for some reason, possibly sabotage or merely to have a look at our latest explosive trials?"* asked Von Mülheim.

Graham wasn't paying attention, *"When I get back to my time-zone I'll be having a word with those people at 'Time-Travellers.' They need to get the quality of their bloody language microchip voice implants sorted out".* he thought. When he failed to answer Von Mülheim's question, he received another fierce blow on the back of his head administered by SS-Unterscharführer Gribnitz. *"I wish he'd stop doing that,"* thought Graham

Von Mülheim smiled and continued, *"Now, there isn't much time, we will only get one shot at this. I should warn you that SS-Standartenführer Albrecht Krancher is on his way here as we speak. He has been summoned by the Duty Officer. Krancher is not a man to be tampered with. He's a very close confidant of that ghoul Heinrich Himmler and has immense delegated powers, such as overall control of the activities on this base. He knows all of the goings on here from the SS imbeciles, like the one standing behind you. So listen very carefully. If you tell me everything about yourself and why you're here, I will do my best to protect you from Krancher, a fearsome, creepy man. He even puts the shits up dear old*

August Eigruber, the all-powerful Gauleiter of Upper Austria. Now, who would believe that?"

Graham didn't have a clue of who or what a Gauleiter was, (*Gauleiter - party leader of a regional branch of the Nazi Party*). Von Mülheim continued, *"Krancher will undoubtedly accuse you of being a spy, particularly as you were captured wearing civilian clothing and did not have any military identification on your person. He will, therefore, either have you shot or hanged for being a spy – after a few severe beatings, naturally, to see what useful information can be extracted from you. I can assure you that it won't be a pleasant experience."*

Graham replied wearily, *"Sir, let me assure you that I am not a spy,"* Von Mülheim smirked, *"Ah, the old 'I am not a spy' routine. Then precisely who or what are you then, eh? You are obviously on some sort of mission here?"* Graham took a deep breath and replied, *"You're not going to believe what I'm about to tell you, but I'm a Time-Traveller."* Von Mulheim stared at Graham for a moment then burst out laughing, saying, *"Ach so, you are a 'Time-Traveller.'"* he snorted with laughter, *"Well, there's another rib gone! Thank you – I haven't laughed so much since Rudolph Hess jumped into a Messerschmitt and flew to Scotland on a peace mission!"* Graham replied, *"I'm sorry if you don't believe me, but it's true. I'm a Time-Traveller. I'm from the future."*

Von Mülheim looked at Graham and thought, *"He's not joking. This chap is not the full schilling,"* then threw his head back and guffawed again, *"A 'Time-Traveller' neh! Ach so, that explains everything to my complete satisfaction! Well, I'm sure that Herr Krancher will be delighted to hear your explanation, Such an affable chap is Krancher; his* 'claim to fame' is that he came top of his class at the Gestapo's Prince Albrecht Strasse Interrogation Unit in Berlin for achieving the swiftest confession from an unfortunate prisoner, using dental instruments without the benefit of anaesthetics, or so I'm led to believe. I would advise you not to try his patience with any of your ridiculous 'Time-Traveller' fairy tales, neh!" Graham, his face now as white as a sheet, said, "Listen, sir, I'm happy to tell you everything you want to know. It's difficult for you to believe what I've just told you, but it's true, I genuinely am a 'Time-Traveller!"

As Graham was speaking he waved his hand expressively in the air. Thinking that he was about to strike Von Mülheim, Unterscharführer Gribnitz leaned forward and struck Graham between his shoulder blades with the heavy metal-lined butt of his rifle. Graham gasped with shock. "Whoops," said Von Mülheim, "there he goes again. He's very enthusiastic is Unterscharführer Gribnitz, particularly with unarmed civilians!"

Graham was in absolute agony. Gribnitz had perfected the art of hitting his victims in exactly the same spot each time, in order to ensure maximum pain; it was much more fun for him that way. Gribnitz was hoping that Graham would step out of line again so that he could deliver a few more similarly cruel blows.

Von Mülheim sighed and said, "I will ask you one more time, Englishman. Incidentally, what is your name?" "My name, sir, is Graham St Anier." "Well, Herr St Anier, What precisely are you doing in this God-forsaken place, eh? Why are you here risking your life, when realistically this war is, thank God, is rapidly drawing to a close?" Graham sighed, thinking, "I might as well tell him now, that swine Krancher *will only have it beaten out of me."* He said, resignedly, *"I'm here to try and locate the Führer's Gold."*

The cigarette he was smoking fell out of Von Mülheim's mouth and his face reddened. He shot to his feet, knocking his chair over, *"Do not say another word!"* he commanded. He turned to the Unterscharführer and said, *"Wait outside, Gribnitz and close the door behind you!"* The Unterscharführer clicked his heels together, saluted and said, *"Jawhoul, Herr Kapitän!"* then strode swiftly out of the cell, pulling the cell door closed behind him as ordered.

"Are you insane, Englander?" Von Mülheim asked Graham, *"That simple statement alone could cost you your life"* then added suspiciously, *"What do you know about the Führer's Gold, eh? And keep your voice down!"* Graham slumped back in his seat, *"Where would you like me to start?"* *"From the beginning, that is usually the best place."*

There was a knock on the cell door. *"Ja, was ist los?"* called out Von Mülheim, the cell door was pushed open by an apprehensive Unterscharführer Gribnitz. Irritated at the interruption, Von Mülheim snapped, *"What is it, Gribnitz?"* *"Excuse me, Herr Kapitän, I have just been informed that SS-Standartenführer Krancher will be arriving at the base in approximately thirty minutes. He would like to see both you and the prisoner immediately upon his arrival."* Von Mülheim nodded, *"Thank you, Unterscharführer. Noted. Now leave us!"* Gribnitz stood rigidly to attention, saluted, then shrieked, *"Heil Hitler"* before scuttling away, thrilled at the prospect of meeting his hero, the disreputable SS-Standartenführer Krancher.

Von Mülheim turned to Graham, *"You heard what the Sergeant said, Herr St Anier, we have thirty minutes before that spawn of the devil arrives here. Let me assure you that I am not one of his sort. There are bad apples in every barrel. Now, you must come with me if you wish to live!*" Graham was puzzled, "*But, but?*" Von Mülheim grabbed hold of Graham, "*Come, up on your feet, man! There is no time for questions, just follow me!*" "*Where are we going?*" queried Graham. "*You will see, my friend. I have certain information that may be of great value to you and from which it appears we may both benefit. I will reveal all once we are on a safer footing.*" As they left the cell Graham asked, "*What about that man Krancher?*" Von Mülheim smiled, "*My Kriegsmarine lads will be giving him a taste of his own medicine shortly after he gets here. After which they will be leaving for their homes. For them, as for me, the war is nearly over.*"

As they stepped out of the cell they bumped into Gribnitz who was stood lounging at the side of the door, faithfully guarding the entrance, as ordered. As Gribnitz sprang to attention, a puzzled look on his porcine features, he asked, "*Herr Kapitän, you are going somewhere?*" "*Ah, Gribnitz,*" replied a smiling Von Mülheim, "*Yes, but before I do, I have here a little gift for you.*" surreptitiously easing his pistol out of its shiny leather holster. Not noticing the pistol, Gribnitz smiled, thinking that perhaps he was going to be offered an English cigarette. Von Mülheim swiftly cocked the pistol then shot Gribnitz straight between the eyes.

Gribnitz slumped to the floor, mouth gaping, blood dripping from the small wound in his forehead. Von Mülheim sighed, "*A headshot – huh, unfortunately he won't have felt a thing, the dummkopf!*" he said, stooping to scoop up the weapon dropped by the now late SS-Unterscharführer Gribnitz, He handed it to Graham, "*Here, take this, it may come in very handy. Now, follow me and do exactly as I say.*" he commanded. Graham looked at the unfortunate Gribnitz then at Von Mülheim and thought, "*Hell fire, these lads don't fart about.*"

'CHAPTER 7'

'A Reversal of Fortunes'

Kapitän Zur See Manfred Von Mülheim was puzzled, he said to Graham, *"I can't really get my head around what sort of SS mischief is going on here. What I do know is that Krancher is definitely up to something. Not only is he coming here to interrogate you, but he is coming here to meet SS-Obergruppenführer Kaltenbrunner, who will also be arriving here very shortly, with the 'Fuhrer's Gold.'* "Ah," said Mike, *"So the gold's not actually here yet then?"* Von Mülheim shook his head, *"Not yet, but it will be very shortly."*

He continued, *"We should get out of this base before the SS contingent from Berlin arrives, or we will all be in big trouble, particularly as they'll be accompanied by that swine SS-Obergrüppenfuhrer Ernst Kaltenbrunner and his slimy Adjutant. Kaltenbrunner is well known for his nasty little habit of leaving a trail of dead bodies behind him wherever he goes – and make no mistake about it, he won't want any witnesses left alive here to reveal the whereabouts of the 'Führer's Gold,' I can guarantee that. These are very dark days, you have no idea"* said Von Mülheim.

302

"And just how are we going to escape from here then?" asked Graham. *"There is a back gate and I hold a key. So, we need to get out of here and then hot-foot it over to the Altensee Salt Mines, which is not too far from Lake Toplitz, where I have a vehicle, weapons, civilian clothing and so forth, hidden away and ready to be used in the event of something like this happening."* said Von Mülheim *"OK, and then what?"* asked Graham. *"Look, I will explain my escape plan to you later."* he looked at his watch, *"There isn't time to discuss it now. Come, we must make a start. Incidentally, I am assuming that you didn't come to Toplitz alone. Presumably, you have friends who accompanied you here?"* Graham nodded, *"Four actually,"* *"Then we'd better find them and tell them to come with us. Where are they?"* asked Von Mülheim.

"Right behind you!" said a voice.

The surprised Kapitän turned around and there in the doorway of the hut stood Mike and Ed. Ed pointed his 9mm Sterling sub-machine gun at the Kapitän, *"Hands up, you Krout bastard!"* Von Mülheim sighed, tutted then raised his hands in the air. Mike grinned and said, *"Graham – where've you been? We can't leave you alone for more than two minutes without you getting into some sort of trouble!"* *"Lower your weapons, guys,"* said Graham, nodding towards Von Mülheim, *"He's one of the good guys, he's on our side."*

Graham, greatly relieved to see his friends, rushed across to shake Mike and Ed's hands. *"About bloody time too. I was beginning to think that you'd forgotten me!"* he said. *"As if we would! So, what's been happening to you then, pal?"* asked Mike. *"Well, the SS Patrol caught me with my trousers down, literally, and I got hauled away to be interrogated.*

This is Kapitän Von Mülheim, he's the Base Commander. He very kindly despatched the SS guard who'd been knocking seven bells out of me, and was just offering me a chance to escape from here before a large group of SS 'meanies' arrive from Berlin with the 'Führer's Gold.' Oh, and if that's not bad enough, there's some other SS big-wig coming here with them. so the shit's about to hit the fan. The Kapitän's OK though, I've been having a good chat with him." said Graham.

Ed stepped forward, *"Graham, my friend, this man is a Nazi! They're not to be trusted."* A red-faced and outraged Von Mülheim turned to Ed and snapped, *"Let me assure you, sir, I am no Nazi! I am an officer of the Kriegsmarine - there is more than a subtle difference between the two."* *"Huh, I'll believe that when I see it. You lot are all the same!"* snorted Ed.

"Easy does it, Ed. So what's the score, then Graham?" asked Mike. *"Well, basically, the Kapitän was telling me that once the gold arrives here, plans have been made to ferry it out onto the lake and then sink it until it's needed. They've got a Kriegsmarine launch and crew stood by to help do it."* Ed nodded, *"Yes, we watched some of them preparing the launch. I've left my two boys at the side of the Lake, keeping an eye on things."*

"Well, you'd better warn them about the convoy of SS Guards arriving here from Berlin very shortly with the gold. When they find out that the Kapitän here has done a runner, there'll be hell to pay. Incidentally, there's a bloke coming with the SS called Kaltenbrunner. Apparently, he's a mean machine." said Graham. *"OK,"* said Ed, *"come on Mike, let's go and warn my two lads off then."* Mike nodded, *"Graham, you hang on here with your new friend, and we'll*

come back for you," said Mike. Things were starting to get rather complicated.

After Ed and Mike had gone, Von Mülheim asked Graham, *"Well, my friend, what will happen to me now?"* *"We'll just have to leave you to it, mate. As you were just saying, you've made your plans to escape from the asylum so I suggest that you just get on with it. The war won't last for very much longer."* *"You can guarantee that?"* asked Von Mülheim. Graham nodded. Von Mülheim smiled, *"Anyone with any sense has made plans for when this ridiculous war is over. I myself will return to ….."*

Lay down your weapon then raise your hands!" a harsh commanding voice called out. *"What the …..?"* said Graham, *"Do it now or I will order my men to open fire!"* Von Mülheim carefully replaced his pistol in his belt holster and Graham laid his weapon on the desk. The same voice ordered them to, *"Step a little closer so that I can have a proper look at you – and I warn you, no tricks!"* The two of them moved slowly across to face the tall SS Officer who had stood behind him a dozen or so very fierce looking SS troops who'd encircled the entrance to the building. *"Mein Gott!"* gasped Von Mülheim, springing to attention and clicking his heels together, *"It's SS-Obergruppenführer Kaltenbrunner!"* Kaltenbrunner smiled and replied, *"Got it in one, Herr Kapitän!"*

The six foot four inches tall steel-helmeted Kaltenbrunner was a powerfully built and fearsome figure. He had deep scars on both sides of his swarthy, glowering face and had the type of face much seen on Nazi propaganda posters. He was known to have a volatile temper – which would surface at the slightest provocation. *"Do not make any suspicious moves or I will order my men to open fire. I will not warn you again! And you,"* he snarled, pointing at Von Mülheim, *"you are?"* Manfred answered, *"I am the Base Commander, Herr Obergruppenführer."* *"Perhaps you would care to explain to me precisely what is going on here!"*

Thinking quickly, Von Mülheim said, *"Herr Obergruppenführer, I am Kapitän Manfred Von Mülheim and this man is my prisoner, a Partisan. Somehow, and I have yet to discover how, the Partisans have found out about the 'Führer's Gold' and he and his comrades have been lurking in the nearby woods at the side of the lake, watching to see when the gold would arrive here, presumably with the intention of stealing it."* He pointed at Graham, *" This man, who is one of their group, was arrested by one of my foot patrols and brought here for interrogation."*

Kaltenbrunner glared at Graham, *"And how, precisely, did you find out about the 'Führer's Gold, eh?'"* Von Mülheim turned towards Graham and winked, then continued, *"If I might interject, Herr Obergruppenführer, it would appear that these Partisan swine are working hand in glove with the traitor SS-Standartenführer Krancher."*

Kaltenbrunner, who knew of Krancher, said, *"Krancher you say?"* Von Mülheim nodded, *"That is correct. I was disarmed and arrested by Krancher and his men, who then placed me in close arrest. Rather disgracefully I was held in here with this wretch until thankfully, you arrived, Herr Obergruppenführer. I do not know what plans Krancher had made for me, but I can well imagine. I was about to make good my escape so that I could at least warn someone in the chain of command what was going on."*

"If you were placed in close arrest, why have you still got your weapon, Kapitän?" asked a suspicious Kaltenbrunner.

"Oh that, it was smuggled in here to me by one of my loyal guards, Herr Obergruppenführer. I was about to fight my way out of here when thankfully you arrived and saved me the trouble."

Kaltenbrunner relaxed and smiled, *"Good man. At least there are one or two loyal Germans left here. Well, you do not have to concern yourself with Standartenführer Krancher who has been disarmed and placed in close arrest. The impertinent swine tried to have me arrested when I arrived here. He thought that I was here by myself, with only my Adjutant escorting me. can you imagine that! His face was something of a picture when my SS escort rolled into view."*

He continued, *"Krancher will be accompanying me back to Berlin where he can explain his actions to the Reichsführer-SS. I realised that something unusual was going on when some of your men made a somewhat pathetic attempt to arrest us when we arrived here at the main gate."* *"It would not have been my men, Herr Obergruppenführer, they would have been Standartenführer Krancher's,"* said Von Mülheim. Gesturing with his machine-pistol, Kaltenbrunner said, *"Well, most of the men who attacked us are dead, but we found Krancher cowering under the desk in your office. He gave in without a fight. Huh, such a chicken shit!"*

Kaltenbrunner turned to his Adjutant, SS-Ober Sturmbannführer Scheidler, and said, pointing at Graham, *"Arthur, keep an eye on this Partisan will you."* Scheidler nodded. *"Oh, forgive me, Von Mülheim, may I introduce you to my Adjutant, Ober Sturmbannführer Arthur Scheidler."* Scheidler clicked his heels and nodded at Von Mülheim, who smiled and said, *"Delighted to meet you, old chap."* As they shook hands. Von Mülheim was unimpressed by the slender built, balding and long-faced Scheidler, whom he noticed wore no campaign medals on his uniform. "*A pen-pusher.*" he thought, "*and what a wet handshake he has.*"

Kaltenbrunner drew Scheidler to one side and said quietly, "*Arthur, there is something very fishy going on here. Better keep a watchful eye on them both.*" Scheidler nodded, "*Jawhoul, Herr Obergruppenführer.*" Kaltenbrunner continued, "*Better send some of the lads to carry out a thorough search around the base to find the rest of these so-called Partisans. You know what to do with them once they are found!*" Scheidler nodded, "*Jawhoul, Herr Obergruppenführer.*"

Scheidler waved his machine-pistol at Graham, ordering him to, "*Come with me – and no nonsense or I will not hesitate to shoot you!*" A smiling Von Mülheim, making polite small-talk, said to Kaltenbrunner, "*Did you have a good journey here from Berlin, Herr Obergruppenführer?*" Kaltenbrunner nodded, "*Ja, it was quite pleasant once we reached the outer limits of the city. We were buzzed by an enemy aircraft, but that was of no consequence.*" He smiled and continued, "*Well, Von Mülheim, you will be delighted to know that my men are in the process of ensuring that the 'Fuhrer's Gold' is being safely deposited at the bottom of Lake Toplitz, being assisted by your Kriegsmarine fellows. Arthur's boys will try to find any other Partisan that might be lurking in this area. If found they will be disposed of. Once their search has been completed and I have been assured that the 'Fuhrer's Gold' is in place, we will be returning to Berlin.*"

Von Mülheim asked, "*You are going straight back to Berlin, Herr Obergruppenführer?*" "*That is correct,*" said Kaltenbrunner, adding, "*and I have a pleasant little surprise for you. I will be taking you with me to meet the Reichsführer-SS so that you can explain to him precisely what Krancher has been up to here. I have no doubt that the Reichsführer-SS will wish to thank you personally for your assistance with 'OPERATION GOLDGRÄBER.' We will take Krancher and this Partisan you captured back with us for further interrogation. The rest of his fellow Partisans are of no consequence and will be eliminated. No-one, other than we privileged few, must know of the whereabouts of the 'Führer's Gold.'"*

Suddenly, in the distance, came the crackle of machine-gun fire. Von Mülheim leaped to his feet, *"What in heaven's name…" "Relax!"* snapped Kaltenbrunner, *"That's just my chaps disposing of any unnecessary witnesses."* *"Witnesses?"* said a mortified Von Mülheim. Kaltenbrunner smiled and nodded, *"Yes, anyone involved with hiding the 'Führer's Gold.'"* Von Mülheim was aghast, *"You mean that my men have been executed?"* Kaltenbrunner nodded and shrugged his shoulders, *"Afraid so, old chap. Fortunes of war. Think yourself lucky that you are not joining them at the bottom of the lake! Now, we'd better be making tracks. You can join me and my Adjutant in my staff car for the journey back to Berlin. The Partisan can travel in the rear of one of the trucks with ex-Standartenführer Krancher. Follow me."*

Kaltenbrunner had decided that it would be safer to return to Berlin accompanied by his SS escort and their vehicles. They could all be disposed of very easily once he had returned there safely. He would order his Adjutant to have the aircraft at the nearby base to be stood down.

Von Mülheim reached into his breast pocket and with a trembling hand pulled out his cigarette case, *"Would you care for a cigarette, Herr Obergruppenführer?"* he asked politely. *"Certainly not, it is a filthy habit. Put them away, they will be the death of you!*" said Kaltenbrunner as he strode off,

'CHAPTER 8'

'Hell on Earth'

Niederkirchnerstraße, Berlin, Germany. The thoroughfare was known as Prinz-Albrecht Strasse up until 1951 then the post-war German government changed the name due to its association with Nazi Germany. The street was the location of the feared and detested SS Reich Main Security Office, the Headquarters of the Sicherheitspolizei, the SD, Einsatzgruppen, and Gestapo. The nerve-centre of a totalitarian police state.

The aura of evil surrounding the Gestapo instilled such a level of fear and trepidation in the mass of ordinary Germans that, understandably, they failed to engage in serious resistance to the Nazi dictatorship, an inevitable consequence of the Gestapo's unfettered and limitless power. Everyone but the favoured few feared hearing the sound of the bone-chilling rap on the door first thing in the morning, signifying imminent arrest and God knows what would follow.

'The imposing Reich Main Security Office,
Prinz-Albrecht-Strasse, Berlin'

The small convoy, consisting of the Army trucks and Kaltenbrunner's staff car, drove carefully through central Berlin, picking their way past the craters and wreckage strewn streets. A handcuffed Graham and ex-SS Standartenführer Krancher sat bouncing around on the floor of the lead truck, surrounded by watchful SS Guards. Kaltenbrunner's Mercedes Benz staff car, lead the way through the streets leading towards Gestapo Headquarters at Prinz-Albrecht Strasse. The staff car, a large black Mercedes, arrogantly displayed its rigid swastika and SS Runes attached to silver pennants proudly displayed on the vehicles front wing, notifying lesser beings that the vehicle contained someone powerful and important and that they'd better get out of its way. To delay it would be asking for trouble.

Miraculously the little convoy had not come under either ground or air attack, even when entering Berlin. The drive from Lake Toplitz to the German capital had dragged on interminably, the convoy had to keep pulling off the road and seek cover as marauding enemy aircraft were spotted in the distance. The Luftwaffe, who were supposed to be providing some sort of top cover, was nowhere to be seen.

Every bone in Graham's body ached from being buffeted around on the hard floor of the truck, and whenever his head drooped and he'd started to drift off he was cuffed brutally by one of the guffawing, brutal SS guards, one of whom said to him, "*You should stay awake my friend, you'll get plenty of sleep where you're going - eventually*!" Krancher was given some of the same treatment although toned down. He was still accorded a slight degree of deference because the guards recognised that he had recently held a position of importance within their organisation. The SS guards were long enough in the tooth to recognise that in their crazy world circumstances could change rapidly and the SS-Standartenführer might just be reinstated and come seeking revenge on his captors. Theirs not to reason why!

Those grey-faced and exhausted Berliners who were out and about, wandering the streets seeking food and water, recognised the rigid pennant on the staff car and kept their heads well down as they hurried about their foraging. They knew full well that it was inadvisable for them to meet eyes with those travelling in such vehicles which were usually filled to the brim with raving lunatics who would use any excuse either to exercise their power of arrest or simply shoot them at the slightest opportunity.

Kaltenbrunner's Adjutant, SS-Obersturmbannführer Arthur Scheidler, was driving the Mercedes, whilst Kaltenbrunner and Von Mülheim lounged on the large and comfortable back seat. Kaltenbrunner had been sat next to his Adjutant for the majority of the journey but had decided to move to the rear with Von Mülheim when they had stopped for a pee call on the outskirts of Berlin. Kaltenbrunner was noisily expounding various theories about the Third Reich and other than him, no-one else spoke. Von Mülheim, desperately trying to look interested, just nodded in agreement at the appropriate moments. S

Scheidler was used to fading into the background when out and about with his master but always listened closely to what was being said, noting and jealously guarding Kaltenbrunner's many secrets. Scheidler had often been criticised by Himmler for being far too easy going for a man in his relatively elevated position, but he knew his job thoroughly and did precisely what was expected of him, which was to devote 100% of his life catering to Kaltenbrunner's every whim. It wasn't an easy job, Kaltenbrunner was a hard and demanding task-master, but the rewards made it well worth it.

'SS-Obergruppenführer Ernst Kaltenbrunner's staff car'

As the staff car drew to a halt outside Reich Main Security Office, an SS Guard ran out from the entrance of the Headquarters building, halting smartly at the edge of the curb, then reaching out to open the door of the Mercedes. As Kaltenbrunner stepped out of the vehicle the guard saluted and shouted, *"Heil Hitler!"* Kaltenbrunner nodded peremptorily, not bothering returning the man's salute, and strutted arrogantly into the building, closely followed by his Adjutant and Kapitän Von Mülheim. Although not strictly classed as being a prisoner, Von Mülheim was unarmed, having had his side-arm removed, "*purely as a precautionary gesture*," Kaltenbrunner had assured him.

All the way back to Berlin, Von Mülheim had been constructing a story to use in his defence when his interview with Himmler began. He would only get one chance to get it right. Himmler didn't miss a trick and would carefully pick his way through Von Mülheim's explanation. If he caught Von Mülheim out in his fabrication then he dreaded to think what the outcome would be. Luckily it appeared that he was going be being interviewed before Krancher, so it gave him an ideal opportunity to inflict the maximum amount of damage.

The canvas on the rear of the front truck was rolled up, the SS Guards jumped out and encircled the rear of the vehicle as Graham, and Krancher were ordered to get out. No sooner had their feet touched the pavement than they were jostled into the impressive looking building which, for some inexplicable reason, had suffered a great deal less bomb damage than those immediately adjacent to it. Unfortunately, the Allied bombs had failed to score a direct hit on it. It was, however, pitted with deep gouges and shrapnel marks from both cannon and rocket rounds, and many of the windows were boarded over, but that was about all. It still looked rather imposing and business-like.

Inside the main entrance, stood by the reception desk, Krancher looked a very sorry picture, his badges of rank and medals had been ripped off his uniform jacket and now he was, to all intents and purposes, 'Prisoner Krancher.' Kaltenbrunner turned to his Adjutant and ordered, "*Have those two taken down to the cellars. They are to be placed in adjacent cells – but I don't want them having little chats with each other. Understand?*" The Adjutant, Scheidler, nodded,

"*Jawhoul, Herr Obergruppenführer.*" "*The Reichsführer-SS will more than likely want to speak to them himself. Oh, and finally, could you also arrange for a room and an escort for the Kapitän. The Reichsführer-SS will also want to have a chat with him later. In the meantime, I will just freshen up then go and give my report to the Reichsführer.*" said Kaltenbrunner as he headed off towards the very impressive staircase leading to both his and Himmler's suites of offices.

At the foot of the marble stairs, Kaltenbrunner paused, turned and said to his Adjutant, "*Oh, and Arthur, I would like Herr Krancher to receive a little gentle persuasion before the Reichsführer speaks to him. Just enough to help loosen his tongue - not literally I hasten to add!*" then laughed loudly as he climbed the stairs. On hearing that comment, Krancher had turned as white as a sheet. He knew what was coming, having visited the self-same cells himself on many occasions whilst in Berlin. Still, he was glad that he would have the opportunity to talk to Himmler and could then explain to him why he had failed to execute Kaltenbrunner, as ordered, and perhaps wheedle his way out of trouble.

Scheidler nodded to the four fearsome looking SS guards stood by the reception desk, "*Take those two down to the cells and make sure that they are placed next door to each other. There is to be absolutely no communication between them!*" he ordered. The two unfortunates were hustled off to the cells.

The vivacious Gräfin Gisele Von Westarp, a sexy, lively and very intelligent 22 years old aristocrat who worked in an office adjacent to Heinrich Himmler's, had been Kaltenbrunner's mistress for some time and worshipped the ground he walked on. She was a beautiful woman and a dedicated Nazi who basked in the reflected glory of Kaltenbrunner.

'Gräfin (Countess) Gisela Von Westarp'

Gisela was waiting for her beloved Ernst in his office suite and threw her arms around him when he stomped in, *"Ernst, my love, at last, you have returned. Welcome back to the mad-house!"* Kaltenbrunner smiled, *"Gisele, what are you still doing here, my little sparrow?"* She replied, *"I had intended to leave, but I stumbled upon some information that I felt you should know and decided to remain here and tell you myself."* *"Oh,"* said Kaltenbrunner, *"That sounds most intriguing."* Gisela looked concerned, *"I wanted to warn you that Standartenführer Albrecht Krancher, whom you have brought here under close arrest, was only obeying orders when he attempted to have you and your men shot when you arrived at Lake Toplitz"*

A furious looking Kaltenbrunner recoiled as if he had been struck, *"Ordered? Ordered by whom?"* he asked. *"By Heinrich Himmler himself, I'm afraid!"* said Gisele. *"I don't believe you!"* he said. *"Oh trust me my darling,"* she continued, *"I've read the file and it has Himmler's personal signature on it."* Kaltenbrunner was thunderstruck by

317

Gisela's startling revelation. He reached for the 'phone and asked to be connected to his Adjutant. After a few seconds, Scheidler replied and Kaltenbrunner said, *"Arthur, the punishment for Krancher must wait, he is to remain unharmed, for the moment. Call the lads off will you and have him taken out of the cells and placed into a guest suite. Oh, and you'd better sort out a decent uniform jacket for him."* Kaltenbrunner listened for a moment, *"Nevertheless, he is to be released from the cells but is to remain guarded at all times. I will explain everything to you shortly. Something of interest has come to light."* he said, before slamming the 'phone down.

Kaltenbrunner was spitting feathers, he turned to Gisela and said, *"So that devious little turd Himmler is double-dealing again. I should have seen this coming. I'll bet my last Reichsmark that the Führer doesn't know about any of this. Mind you, I'm told that the Führer doesn't know his arse from his elbow these days because his idiot doctor is pumping him full of unnecessary drugs."*

Gisela placed a warning finger on Kaltenbrunner's lips and whispered, *"Lower your voice my darling, you never know who's listening. This is Gestapo Headquarters after all!"* Kaltenbrunner nodded, *"Of course, I forget myself. Now, schatzie, let me get changed into a fresh uniform and then I must go and have a little chat with 'Hitler's favourite,' Herr Himmler. Once I have got that task out of the way you and I can perhaps have a little something to eat, I'm starving, then we really must leave here as planned. Sadly, the time has come for us to abandon ship."*

Gisela nodded and smiled, *"Please tread very carefully, my darling, Himmler is a cunning devil and will have all of the angles covered. He may know that I have read the file."*

Kaltenbrunner nodded, "*Ja, I am well aware of the way he operates - and make no bones about it, if I had my way he'd get what's coming to him sooner rather than later and it would not be very pleasant, I can assure you!*"

Gisela said, "*Just remember, my darling, that he keeps a loaded pistol tucked away in the top drawer of his office desk. I've seen it.*" Kaltenbrunner nodded, "*Huh, thank you for reminding me, my sweet, but he'll have to get up early in the morning to catch Ernst Kaltenbrunner out. I'd have his scrawny neck broken before he could get the desk drawer open.*" Gisela nodded and smiled. She knew that Kaltenbrunner could do that as easily as blinking and the knowledge thrilled her to bits. She wasn't averse to a spot of violence herself and got off on a bit of slapping, enjoying the vicarious thrill of the rough treatment she often received at the hands of Kaltenbrunner. Kaltenbrunner kissed her passionately then went to off to change into a clean uniform.

Deep down in the ghastly cellars of Gestapo Headquarters, a cell door swung open. An apprehensive Krancher, who had been gazing with horror at the dried blood-stains on the white tiles, his febrile imagination going into overdrive, hauled himself onto his feet, legs trembling. Stood at the cell door was Kaltenbrunner's Adjutant, Scheidler, who said to him, "*Would you please come with me, Herr Standartenführer.*" "*Why, where are you taking me?*" asked a suspicious Krancher, not realising that his previous rank and title had been restored.

"*I have had a more suitable room prepared for you. My apologies for keeping you waiting down here, accommodation is at a premium these days. Now, this way, if you please.*" A nervous Krancher said, "*Is this some sort of trick?*" "*Certainly not, Herr Standartenführer. My orders are to have you escorted to a comfortable room where there will be a change of clothing and a light meal provided for you."* *"And what then?"* asked Krancher. *"I do not know, Herr Standartenführer. I was instructed to do this by Obergruppenführer Kaltenbrunner himself. I am only obeying orders. Although I am his Adjutant, he does not deem it necessary to explain his every action to me."* A little of his old confidence and pomposity returning, Krancher replied, *"Very well, let us proceed then."* before stepping out of the cell with unseemly haste.

As he walked away from the cell, Krancher wondered if this was some sort of cunning ploy to lull him into a false sense of security before taking him into a torture chamber and knocking seven bells out of him, just for the fun of it. It was the sort of psychological trickery that the Gestapo regularly employed to help soften their victims up. Only time would tell, so he would just have to go with the flow. Anything was better than being left in the horrific cell, his imagination running riot as he listened to the sound of the beatings and screaming echoing around the cellar passages as other prisoners were being interrogated.

As he stepped past the door of the cell next to his, he glanced through the open panel in its centre and saw a defiant Graham St Anier gazing back at him. Graham winked at Krancher then gave him a two-fingered salute, mouthing, *"Wanker!"* which Krancher pointedly ignored. If he had his way, the man St Anier would be taken outside and shot, once every bit of information had been squeezed out of him.

The Reichsführer-SS, Heinrich Himmler looked up at Kaltenbrunner, who towered above him, and tried not to let the flicker of fear that he felt show on his face. Himmler was actually frightened of Kaltenbrunner, whom he recognised as being someone who always seemed to hover on the verge of bursting into unremitting violence. Himmler smiled and gesticulated towards a chair, but Kaltenbrunner remained standing, *"I would prefer to stand, Herr Reichsfuhrer."* he said. Himmler replied icily, *"And I would prefer that you sit down. You are making my neck ache!"* Kaltenbrunner smiled grimly as he thought to himself, *"Not as much as your scrawny neck will ache when the hangman's noose tightens around it, Herr Reichsführer."* Kaltenbrunner sat down. *"Now, my dear Ernst, welcome back to Berlin. I trust that everything went well at Lake Toplitz?"* Kaltenbrunner thought, *"The little swine, he doesn't seem at all surprised to see me, or if he is, he is hiding it well."* He replied, *"If you mean, Herr Reichsführer, is the 'Führer's Gold' secured as per your instructions, then yes, it certainly is. Everything went to plan."* *"Good, good,"* said Himmler,

Himmler, not wanting to meet Kaltenbrunner's eyes, gave a very slippery smile then asked him, *"Would you like a cup of coffee or would you care for something a little stronger. I have a nice bottle of French cognac here if you prefer?"* Kaltenbrunner nodded, shooting Himmler a brooding look, *"A coffee would be most welcome, Herr Reichsführer. I will give the cognac a miss, thank you. I need to keep my wits about me."*

Himmler stood up and walked over to a side table where he poured both Kaltenbrunner and himself a coffee. *"Very sensible, Ernst. You never know what is waiting for you around the corner these days, do you? You take your coffee black I believe?"* Kaltenbrunner nodded. *"So do I, it helps to keep me alert,"* said Himmler as he carried the two cups of steaming coffee over to his desk, placing one in front of Kaltenbrunner. *"unfortunately I can't offer you a biscuit or a cake, my wife Marga forbids me to eat them and hides them*

321

away from me." Kaltenbrunner nodded, "*And how is Frau Himmler?*" he asked. "*She is well, thank you. I have sent her and our daughter Gudrun away from Berlin. Regrettably, it is no longer safe for them here.*"

The red light on Himmler's desk telephone suddenly began flashing. "*Excuse me a moment, Ernst,*" he said as he picked it up. After a few moments he said, "*Yes, of course, Martin, please put the Führer through.*" he said grandly, then swivelled his chair around so that he could look up at the portrait of Adolf Hitler hanging on his office wall. Once his conversation with Hitler began, Himmler rather comically hurtled up out of his chair and stood rigidly to attention in front of the Führer's portrait. Kaltenbrunner had to fight not to smirk, "*How ridiculous!*" he thought.

Whilst Himmler's back was turned, Kaltenbrunner reached across the desk and quietly swopped the two coffee cups around. "*If there is anything nasty swimming around in the cup that is intended for me, let that little scheisse drink it,*" he thought. An obsequious sounding Himmler said, "*Yes, my Führer, Kaltenbrunner is here, sat right in front of me. He has just confirmed that 'OPERATION GOLDGRÄBER' was successful. I am about to receive his no doubt comprehensive report shortly then, if I may, will come and brief you about Phase Two of the operation,*" Himmler paused to listen to his hero, then continued, "*Ja, Ja, very well, my Führer, I will arrange that with Bormann. Thank you. Auf wiederhören. Heil Hitler!*"

Himmler turned around so that he was facing Kaltenbrunner and gently replaced the telephone handset in its cradle before resuming his seat, "*The Führer is very pleased that things have gone so well and would like to see you in his office this afternoon at 1400 hours to pass on his personal thanks,*" he sighed, "*and pin another trinket on your chest, presumably.*" Kaltenbrunner nodded and smiled, thinking, "*Let's hope I get to the Führerbunker before the Russians do then.*"

"*Now,*" Himmler continued, "*have a sip of your coffee before it gets cold, then you'd better let me have your report.*" Kaltenbrunner nodded, "*Of course, Herr Reichsführer. If I may, I will give you a short verbal briefing now. My Adjutant, Scheidler, is preparing a typewritten report for your perusal, which will follow shortly?*" Himmler nodded in agreement.

Kaltenbrunner strode across to a map pinned on the Reichsführer's office wall and, pointing at Lake Toplitz, began his briefing. Whilst Kaltenbrunner had his back turned to him, Himmler quickly swopped the coffee cups back over. Himmler had been in the game long enough to know that no-one was to be trusted, not even his beloved Führer.

Kaltenbrunner turned and said, "*Before I speak about 'OPERATION GOLDGRÄBER', Herr Reichsführer, I really need to speak to you about Standartenführer Albrecht Krancher.*" "*Krancher?*" said Himmler, lifting the coffee cup up to his thin lips and trying to look as if butter wouldn't melt in his mouth. He took a sip of his coffee, grimaced, then asked, "*What about him?*"

Himmler listened closely at what Kaltenbrunner had to say about Krancher's attempts to have himself, his Adjutant and their military escort shot, presumably to stop the gold being hidden and then misappropriate it. "*The man is a disgrace to his uniform and, if I may say so, is as thick as two short planks. Someone must have given him the authorisation to proceed. I doubt very much if the word initiative exists in his vocabulary. There is something going on and I mean to get to the bottom of it.*" said Kaltenbrunner. Himmler was nodding as if agreeing with Kaltenbrunner.

His brain racing, Himmler thought, "*Kaltenbrunner wishes to implicate me in Krancher's attempt to assassinate him. He has no evidence or he would have produced it, so there has obviously been a leak. Someone will swing for this.*" As Kaltenbrunner waited for a reply, Himmler said, "*My dear Ernst, I'm sure that someone has got their wires crossed and that this is all a complete misunderstanding. Either that or some devious swine is trying to cause mischief. When I find out who it is, they will pay a heavy price, I can guarantee that. One just does not know whom to trust these days. I suspect the dead hand of Martin Bormann in all of this.*"

Kaltenbrunner, smiling inwardly at Himmler's attempt to deflect responsibility, replied, "*I hear what you are saying, Herr Reichsführer, but I still believe that someone in Krancher's SS chain of command is behind this mischief. I know for a fact that he leads a very expensive lifestyle and has several mistresses. I firmly believe that he was under orders to kill both me and my Adjutant and the SS Guards before misappropriating the 'Führer's Gold.' I personally placed him under arrest and ordered that his badges of rank and decorations be removed from his uniform. He is a disgrace.*"

Himmler nodded, "*Really? The swine. I will interview him personally and get to the bottom of all this, Ernst. Leave that with me.*" Kaltenbrunner nodded and said, "*Of course, Herr Reichsführer.*" Himmler continued, "*Now, I hear that you have brought Krancher back to Berlin with you and that he has been taken down to the cellars and placed in a cell?*" Kaltenbrunner nodded, "*That is correct, Herr Reichsführer.*" Himmler smirked, "*Well, let's keep him on the back foot, shall we? Have him taken from the cells and placed in one of our better guest suites, oh and have his badges of rank and medals returned to him. I want to give him a false sense of security."* Kaltenbrunner nodded, *"Very well, Herr Reichsführer."* *"Now Ernst, you go and prepare for your meeting with the Führer, whilst I sort this whole sordid business out – and well done with 'OPERATION GOLDGRÄBER'."*

Himmler leaned forward and shook hands with him. Kaltenbrunner jumped out of his chair, gave the standard *"Heil Hitler!"* response, clicked his heels together and left the office, waiting until the door had closed behind him before wiping his hand with a clean handkerchief. He'd had to fight to not shiver with disgust as he'd gripped Himmler's clammy little hand. He knew that the Reichsführer-SS was a conniving little double-dealer and that Krancher had only been obeying his master's instructions. It was quite obvious that Himmler wanted any opposition out of the way and wanted to get his clammy little hands on the gold. Kaltenbrunner shook his head, everything that he'd believed in was rapidly going down the pan.

Kaltenbrunner knew full well that Himmler had no intention of interrogating Krancher, nor would he be punished – unless he was going to be slapped for failing in his mission to have him killed and get his hands on the gold. He decided there and then that it was time for him to get out of Berlin accompanied by his faithful Adjutant and his beloved Gisele. The place was a nest of writhing vipers and the smell of defeat and disaster hung in the air. Even so, he decided to delay his departure and pay the Führer one final visit before putting his own 'escape and evasion' plan into action. He stomped off down the passage, heading for his own office.

❊ ❊ ❊ ❊ ❊ ❊

'CHAPTER 9'

'Escape from Berlin'

Reichsführer-SS Heinrich Himmler looked Graham up and down with great distaste, his watery blue/grey reptilian eyes gazing spookily from behind his glinting spectacle lenses. After a few seconds, he turned his head and glanced across at an apprehensive Standartenführer Krancher. There was a long silence before Himmler pointed at a chair and said, *"Please, take a seat."*

A confused Graham moved towards the chair and Himmler snapped at him, *"Not you, you imbecile. You stand there and do not move until I tell you to do so!"* Graham froze as Himmler continued staring at him. Krancher quickly slid into the seat. Himmler waved his hand at Graham and continued, *"Now, I am reliably informed that you are some sort of Partisan, is that correct?"* Graham replied, *"No sir, it certainly is not."* Himmler raised an eyebrow, *"Oh, then who or what are you then?"* Graham grimaced, then replied, *"Well, you're not going to believe me when I tell you."* Himmler smiled, *"Try me but do not attempt to waste my time or you will suffer the consequences. Both my time and patience are limited commodities - your time is just limited."*

'The detestable Reichsfuhrer-SS Heinrich Himmler'

Himmler sighed then nodded at the seat next to Krancher's, *"You may sit down."* A relieved Graham sat down next to Krancher. Himmler gave a very false and deathly smile, *"There, that's better. Now, let me hear what you have to say."* *"Well sir,"* Graham took a deep breath, *"I am what is known as a Time-Traveller. I have travelled back here from England."*

Krancher, who was sat at the side of Graham, hooted with laughter. Himmler glanced at Krancher, who immediately stopped laughing. Himmler continued, *"So, you are a Time-Traveller eh?"* totally unfazed by Graham's unusual reply, *"Have you travelled here from the future or the past?"* Graham said, *"I'm from the future, your future."* Himmler nodded, *"Ach so, and I suppose you are able to tell me what happens here in Berlin in 1945 and afterward?"* *"Well not really, you see the Time-Travel rules strictly forbid....."* Himmler interrupted him, saying icily, *"I shall ask you once more and then if I feel that we are wasting our time, I will have you taken outside and shot. Do you understand me?"* Graham nodded, *"Yes I do sir."*

Himmler turned to Krancher, smiled and said casually, *"Hit him!"* Krancher leaned forward and struck Graham on the face with the palm of his hand. Himmler smiled, *"And again!*" Krancher hit Graham on the other side of his face. "*Good. Now that I have your full attention, tell me what lies ahead for the Third Reich and, if I might be so bold, what awaits me?*" said Himmler.

Krancher could hardly believe his ears. Everyone knew that Himmler took an unhealthy interest in the occult and because of that he now seemed to be falling for the Partisan's web of lies about Time-Travel. He decided that it would be safer for him to sit tight and keep his mouth shut, knowing that he was already in bad odour with Himmler for failing to kill Kaltenbrunner and also for not getting his hands on the 'Führer's Gold.' Himmler had ordered Krancher to stop the gold from being sunk in the lake and bring it back to his Headquarters, but after the failed assassination attempt, and before leaving Lake Toplitz, Kaltenbrunner had foiled Himmler be ensuring that every last bar of the 'Führer's Gold.' had been sunk in the Lake, precisely as per the instructions contained in '***OP GOLDGRÄBER***.'

Krancher sat back in his chair feeling a little bit better after striking the defenceless Graham, but he was still very twitchy because as yet he still didn't know what plans Himmler had made for him. It could be anything from a demotion in rank to simply being dragged off to Berlin's notorious Plötzensee Prison for a date with the hangman. It all depended on Himmler's frame of mind.

Graham continued, "*Well sir, I'm afraid to tell that it all ends rather badly for Germany. The Third Reich is defeated and the Allies are victorious. Germany surrenders unconditionally, followed not too long afterward by Japan's unconditional surrender.*" Krancher snorted, "*Huh, defeatist nonsense!*" Himmler held up his hand, "*Let him continue, Krancher, this is most interesting.*" Graham said, "*Your*

Führer, Adolf Hitler, commits suicide in his bunker. Hermann Göering also commits suicide whilst he is awaiting execution – and as for you...." Himmler stopped him, "*Stop! I have decided that I do not need to know what happens to me. Just tell me about the others.*" Graham continued, "*All of the Nazi hierarchy were captured and placed on trial by the Allies at Nuremberg. Most of them were hung for war crimes and crimes against humanity, the remainder received heavy jail sentences.*" "*And what happens to Germany in the long term?*" asked Himmler. "*Germany eventually gets back on its feet, but it takes many years and becomes more powerful than ever – but as a Democracy,*" said Graham

"*Quite fascinating and almost believable.*" said Himmler, "*And you say that you have travelled back in time to be here?*" "*Yes sir,*" replied Graham. "*To do precisely what, may I ask?*" said Himmler. Krancher interrupted, "*He's talking complete nonsense, Herr Reichsführer, he's a Partisan and he went to Toplitz in order to steal the 'Führer's Gold!' All of his Time-Travel talk is cock and bull!*" Himmler turned to Krancher and said, "*Do not interrupt! I will not tell you again! Now,*" he said turning to Graham, "*are you able to tell me anything that could provide me with solid evidence that you are a Time-Traveller?*" A frustrated Krancher couldn't believe that he was hearing such arrant nonsense, but had the sense to keep his mouth closed.

Graham thought for a moment then said, "*Yes, I suppose I can.*" pausing for a few moments to marshal his thoughts before replying, "*You are currently entering into secret negotiations with the Allies, via the Swiss, to both remove and then take over from Adolf Hitler as Führer – oh, and you have a small glass phial containing poison implanted in your tooth, to be used in the event of your capture by the*

Allies." Himmler turned as white as a sheet and leaped to his feet, slamming his fist on the desk. He shouted, "*How do you know … I mean, that is absolute nonsense. I will support the Führer until my dying day.*" Graham smiled and said, "*No you won't. You'll be off out of here like a rat up a drain-pipe before very much longer, as will Kaltenbrunner and your man Krancher here, along with the rest of the Nazi hierarchy, but it won't do any of you the slightest bit of good. You're all for the high-jump I'm afraid!*"

"*So, who will replace the Führer then?*" asked Himmler icily. "*Grand Admiral Karl Dőenitz will be appointed Head of State,*" replied Graham. Himmler was outraged, "*Dőenitz – he is an old woman! So then, what happens to me?*" Graham replied, "*Do you really want to know?*" "*Yes, of course I do!*" shouted Himmler, sitting back down. Krancher couldn't believe his ears. Himmler had fallen hook, line, and sinker for the Englishman's Time-Travel nonsense. Graham continued, "*Well, Herr Reichsführer….*"

Suddenly the Reichsführer's office door crashed open and there stood Ed and his son Ludo, both dressed as senior SS officers and both armed to the teeth. Himmler and Krancher leaped to their feet. Trembling with rage, Himmler shouted, "*What is this nonsense*!?" Ed snarled, "*Shut up four-eyes, and get your hands above your head - now!*" Ludo and Ed stepped into the office, swiftly closing the door behind them. Krancher shouted, "*How dare you! I will have you both arrested.*" Ed stepped across the office and pistol-whipped Krancher, who fell back into his chair clutching his jaw and whimpering, "*You have broken my tooth!*"

Himmler asked, "*What is this all about, what are you doing here?*" Ed smiled, "*We've come to rescue our friend Graham and get him out of this hell-hole. Now, Herr*

330

Himmler, you may lower your hands and resume your seat. Don't try and do anything stupid because I'm just itching to shoot you!" A seething Himmler sat down, his hands on his desk.

"Now, Heinrich, er, Heini," said Ed, *"I want you to do something for me. I want you to write out a little note on your personal headed notepaper, lots of swastikas and rubber stamps, stuff like that, explaining that I am authorised to take the prisoner, Graham, and Kapitän Von Mülheim away from here to Plötzensee Prison, oh and you can also authorise the use of Kaltenbrunner's staff car as well; the Kübelwagen that we drove here in was very uncomfortable. Now get writing. No-one will dare to question your orders."* Himmler smiled, *"Very well, if you insist."*

He slid his desk drawer open and reached inside, pulling out his pistol and pointing it at Ed, *"Drop your weapon or I will shoot you!"* said Himmler, Ed laughed, *"You won't be shooting anyone – not with the safety catch on!"* Himmler glanced down at his pistol and as he did so, Ludo leaned forward, knocked it out of his hand and onto the floor. Ed laughed, *"You'll have to do much better than that, Herr Reichsführer!"* He turned to Graham, *"Get Herr Himmler's pistol, Graham, we'll take it with us when we leave. It might come in handy later on."* Graham picked up the pistol and examined it, *"Mmm, that'll make a nice little keepsake."*

Himmler sat down and reached back into his desk, *"No funny business this time, Herr Himmler, or you will also be chewing on the barrel of my pistol, Reichsführer-SS or not!"* Himmler snarled, *"I am getting a piece of paper and a pen to write your note, little good it will do you!"* In the background, Krancher mumbled, *"You swine, you have broken two of my teeth, not one!"* Ludo turned to Krancher and said, "*I'd advise you to keep your trap shut or you'll be losing a few more of your fangs!*"   Ed nodded towards Krancher and said, "*Tie him to a chair and gag him, Ludo. He's getting on my tits with his whining!*"

Ludo walked over to the window and ripped a silken sash from the curtaining. He then used it to tie Krancher into his chair before stuffing a handkerchief, none too gently, into his bleeding mouth, making him mumble something about his broken teeth.

Ed turned to Himmler, "*Better start writing, Herr Reichsführer, we don't have much time left!*"   Himmler said, "*Do you fondly imagine that you will escape from this building in one piece, my friend?*" Ed replied, "*I'm not your friend! Just get on with the note, you little toe-rag. Let me worry about everything else.*" Himmler picked up an expensive gold fountain pen and started writing, "*And what do you intend doing with me, once this is written. I suppose that you are going to shoot me?*" Ed laughed, "*Well, I was going to take you with us and hand you over to the Russians for them to have a bit of sport with you, but I don't want to do anything that might change the course of history.*" Himmler looked at him and he smiled, "*Ah, let me guess, you are also Time-Travellers?*" Ed nodded, "*Got it in one!*" Himmler shook his head, "*I don't know quite who or what to believe. Either way, I have nothing to fear. You will not get very far then you will have much to answer for.*" he said.

Graham stepped forward and said, "*We've got lots to answer for! You must be joking! What about you, eh?*" "*What do you mean,*" asked Himmler, "*I have done nothing wrong!*" "*Let me give you a few pointers, Herr Reichsführer! Belsen, Auswichtz, Treblinka! The Warsaw Ghetto. Ring any bells?*" said Graham. Himmler's jaw dropped, "*How do you know about that? Anyway, it was nothing to do with me!" "Just shut up!*" said Graham, *"There isn't time to explain how I know about it right now, but I'll just say that it won't be too long before everyone finds out what evil you and your fellow Nazis have been up to and the unspeakable atrocities that have been carried out on the Jews and others in the name of your Führer!"* Himmler snorted, *"I don't know what you are talking about! I have done nothing to no-one!"* Ed said, *"You mightn't have done anything yourself, but your guiding hand was firmly on the tiller!"*

His hands now trembling, Himmler finished the note, blotted it and passed it over to Ed, who read it carefully, *"Don't want any snarlies, do we!"* he said. A delighted Graham grabbed hold of Ed's hand and shook it enthusiastically, *"It's really great to see you mate, I thought you'd forgotten all about me. Where's Mike Fraser?" "Downstairs with Diederik, waiting for us. I'm getting a bit worried about Mike." "Why?"* asked Graham, *"Because he's wearing an SS uniform and shouting at people. I think he's starting to enjoy it!"*

"I've got lots of questions to ask you," said Graham, *"Like how you got here from Austria," "In the 'Travellator' of course. I'll tell you all about that once we get out of here, "* replied Ed, *"In the meantime, tie that obnoxious little swine Himmler to his chair and shove a gag in his mouth as well."* *"With pleasure,"* said Graham. Using another curtain sash, Graham tied a furious looking Himmler to his chair. Looking around for something to gag him with, Graham ripped off Krancher's neck-tie and stuffed it none too gently into Himmler's mouth. *"Check that he's able to breathe, Graham. I want to make sure that he stays alive."* said Ed, *"We don't want to harm him, he needs to get what's coming to him."* Himmler was furious, his eyes bulging.

333

"*Right, this is the sketch,*" said Ed. "*You, Graham, and Von Mülheim are my prisoners and I'm taking you both to Plötzensee Prison for execution.*" Turning to Himmler, Ed said, "*And you my friend, will pick up that telephone in a moment and order your staff to have a certain Kapitan Von Mülheim taken from wherever you're keeping him and to the front desk - where he is to be handed over to my two men. Do you understand?*" Himmler nodded.

Ed stepped forward and removed the gag from Himmler's mouth. Picking up the phone Ed asked him, "*What number do I dial?*" Himmler replied "*887.*" "*OK,*" said Ed "*I dial – you speak,*" and placed the barrel of his pistol against Himmler's temple, "*And no tricks or I'll be letting a bit of daylight into that scheming brain of yours.*"

Himmler cleared his throat then spoke into the telephone, "*This is the Reichsführer speaking. Listen carefully. The recent arrival, Kapitan Von Mülheim, is to be taken from his accommodation and handed over to the two SS officers who are waiting at the front desk. They will assume responsibility for him.*" there was a slight pause, then Himmler answered, "*What's that? Yes, of course, Heil Hitler.*"

Ed smiled, "*Well done Heinrich, that wasn't too difficult, was it!*" as Himmler started to reply, Ed stuffed the rolled up tie forcefully back into his mouth, making him gag. Ed turned to Ludo and Graham and said, "*Right guys, time to go. Any questions?*" Graham said, "*Why are we taking Von Mülheim with us?*" "*Because he is a professional officer and a decent bloke. He doesn't deserve to be left here with this shower of crap. Plus which, he can tell is a bit more about the 'Führer's Gold.'*" replied Ed. At the mention of the 'Führer's Gold,' Himmler stiffened. Ed smiled, "*Yes, my friend, we know all about it – and guess what, we're going to raise it from the bed of Lake Toplitz and then have a great deal of fun spending the proceeds when we sell it on! Don't look so disappointed, Heini, you won't be needing any money where you're going."*

As he was speaking, Ed dragged Himmler's chair across the carpet to the far side of his office and placed it next to the whimpering Krancher. *"Now just sit here quietly like two good little boys whilst we make good our escape. It'll take you a while to wriggle free, by which time we'll be well on our way out of this hell-hole."* As he was speaking, Ed leaned forward and removed Himmler's spectacles, dropping them on the carpet before stamping on them and shattering the lenses *"Whoops! Childish, I know, but they didn't really suit you, Heini. You're more of a pince-nez sort of guy!"* Himmler stared at Ed with a look of pure hatred

Ed turned to Ludo and pointed at Krancher, *"Ludo, remove this cowardly swine's trousers and boots, whilst I do the same to Herr Himmler, then stuff them in that cupboard over there. It will delay them for a few important minutes should they manage to escape and try to come chasing after us. I can't see the Reichsführer-SS legging around the building with his Nazi arse hanging out of his underpants."*
It didn't take them long to remove the boots and trousers, leaving both captives sat there looking faintly ridiculous. Himmler was so outraged that his face had turned puce and if he'd been wearing spectacles they would have steamed over. Graham laughed, pointing at Himmler's skinny legs and his black stockings, held up by garters, *"The last time I saw a pair of legs like that they were hanging out of a nest!"* he said. Whilst Ludo had been tying Krancher to the chair he'd spotted a very expensive gold watch on Krancher's wrist, so he removed it and put it on his own wrist. *"My need*

is greater than yours!" he said. Krancher glared at him hatefully and tried to mumble something.

"*OK Graham*," said Ed, "*Just mess your hair up a bit and when you walk out of here, walk in front of me with your hands behind your back. Act like you're my prisoner.*" Graham nodded and messed his hair up. Ed then turned to Himmler and Krancher, saying, "*Now you two, be good little boys, play quietly and think yourselves lucky that I haven't got a pistol with a silencer fitted to it – or 'Time-Traveller' rules or not - you'd be on your way to hell!*"

Himmler's beady eyes glinted evilly. He mumbled an obscenity and was clearly furious. Krancher was white-faced and sweating, dreading the repercussions once the Reichsführer-SS was freed. Himmler had a Titanic ego and would want revenge exacting for the way he had been treated, particularly in front of a subordinate.

"*Right chaps, let's see if we can blag our way out of here as easily as we did when we came in,*" said Ed. Turning to Himmler, he clicked his heels together and said, "*Heil Hitler!*" then blew a very fruity raspberry. He opened the office door and shouted, "*Achtung!*" The two SS guards outside the door sprang to the attention and presented arms as the party left, Exiting last and closing the office door behind him. Ed, in his impressive General's uniform, swaggered past the two guards, saying a languid, "*Heil Hitler!*" The party then headed for the top of the stairs, Graham with his head down, stumbling and mumbling, completely over-acting in his role as a beaten down prisoner.

A puzzled Von Mülheim was stood waiting at the front desk with Mike and Diederik. He had started to ask them questions but was silenced when Mike held a warning finger to his lips. Von Mülheim had recognised Mike from Lake

Toplitz and quickly figured out that something rather unusual was going on. Hearing the sound of approaching footsteps, Von Mülheim turned and saw Graham, Ed, and Ludo coming down the stairs. To Von Mülheim's amusement, he noted that both Ed and Ludo were wearing the uniforms of high ranking SS officers and had to fight not to grin at their brass-neck and impertinence.

The two SS Guards standing at each side of the main door sprang to attention. Ed paused in front of them, examined one of the guards and said, "*You there, you are improperly dressed! Fasten that button, immediately! You are a disgrace to your uniform!*" The red-faced guard glanced down at his jacket and saw to his horror that his breast pocket was undone. He quickly fastened it, clumsily dropping his rifle with a loud clatter onto the marble tiled floor in the process. He picked it up then fumbled with his jacket button. Ed turned to the SS-Unterscharführer stood behind the reception desk and said, "*Unterscharführer! Take this imbecile's name and get him out of here! Let us see if a stint out on the streets will sharpen his reflexes, eh!*" The trembling SS-Unterscharführer replied, "*Jawhoul, Herr General!*"

Ed beckoned the others, "*Follow me!*" he commanded, then strode out of the door, where Kaltenbrunner's staff car was parked up at the side of the pavement. Out of the side of his mouth Mike said, "*I hope you've got the ignition keys!*" to Diederik. Diederik smiled and dangled the car's ignition keys in front of Mike's face. Ed stood by the staff car door and Mike opened it for him. They had to make it look good as there were people watching out of the building's windows. As they clambered on board, Graham asked, "*Where are we going, Ed?*" "*I've got a 'T3 Travellator' booked to arrive at a quiet spot near the Berlin Zoo. It will take us all out of here and back home.*" replied Ed. "*What about him,*" asked

Graham, pointing to Kapitän Von Mülheim. *"We'll drop him off at the Berlin Zoo, after which I'm afraid that he's on his own."* The Kapitän smiled and nodded, *"Thank you. Thank you for getting me out of that lunatic asylum. I was never part of that you know!"* Graham said, *"We know that. You're a proper fighting man and not one of those SS louts. Here, I'll leave you with Himmler's pistol if that will help?"* Von Mulheim nodded, *"That is very decent of you, my thanks."* *"Why don't you take the staff car as well, we won't be needing it?"* asked Graham, *"It's fully juiced up and it'll get you well out of Berlin."*

Von Mülheim shook his head, *"Thank you, but no, I will make other arrangements. The vehicle is too well known around here and not only that, they will be out searching for it before too long. If I am caught there will be no second chance for me, I would soon be swinging from a lamp-post!"* *"Hold tight then, here we go!"* said Diederik, starting the car up. The car's powerful engine roared into life, Diederik slammed it into gear and they shot off, heading off towards Berlin Zoo.

Upstairs in his office suite, Kaltenbrunner said to Gisela, *"Schatzie, the time is very nearly here when we will have to make our move."* Gisela was shocked. *"It's no good you looking so surprised my dear, we have discussed this many times."* Gisela held his hand, *"I know, but I didn't expect it to happen quite so soon, my darling, although the sound of the fighting just a few streets away does rather frighten me. It sounds as if the Russians are just around the corner!"* Kaltenbrunner replied, *"They very nearly are but don't worry your pretty little head about it, we'll be long gone by the time they reach this building. Now, I am ordered to meet the Führer very shortly. It will be our final meeting here in Berlin, although he obviously doesn't know that yet. Once I* have returned here from the Führerbunker, I will empty my office safe then we can jump into my staff car and escape from this hell-hole."

Gisela threw her arms around him, "*I can't begin to tell you how relieved I am, my darling.*" she said. He smiled, "*Whilst I am away at the Führerbunker, your job is to double-check those two suitcases that we have tucked away in the cupboard over there. They contain everything we need for the moment, civilian clothes, money, false identity papers etc. I have made other arrangements for when we reach our destination.*"   "*Where are we going, Ernst?*" she asked. "*Now don't worry about that, Gisela. The less you know at the moment, the better. Right. I'd better send for my staff car. The clock is ticking and I don't want to be late for my appointment with the Führer.*"

Kaltenbrunner picked up his telephone and dialled the number connecting him to the SS-Unterscharführer at the front desk. "*Kaltenbrunner here!*" he barked, "*I want my car and driver waiting outside the front door in five minutes. Inform him that he is required to take me to the Führerbunker!*"   Kaltenbrunner paused and listened for a moment then shouted, "*Which SS-General?*" he paused, "*What, in my personal staff car!*" He listened for a moment, "*With a prisoner and Kapitän Von Mülheim?*" He slammed a meaty paw onto his desk, and shouted, "*The General's name, quickly!*"   He waited for the reply, "*There is no such SS-General, you imbecile, you have been bamboozled! Have them arrested immediately, do you hear me!*" He paused and listened, then with a voice cold as ice said, "*So the General left here five minutes ago with two prisoners and another SS officer did he, Unterscharführer! Well, it would be wise of you to send someone after them immediately, idiot – and then find my Adjutant. Tell him to come up to my office straight away!"*

He slammed the 'phone down, *"Idiot. Under normal circumstances, I would have him shot, but there isn't time at the moment!"* A concerned Gisela asked him, *"What's wrong, darling?"* *"There is mischief afoot. I'll bet that cunning little swine Himmler is at the back of all this."* said Kaltenbrunner as he stood up, furiously kicking his chair out of the way, *" Wait here whilst I go and speak to the Reichsführer! Oh, and when he arrives, please ask my Adjutant to organise some suitable transport for us. My staff car has been misappropriated and will be well away from here by now, oh and then ring the Führerbunker to inform Bormann that I will be a few minutes late arriving."* Kaltenbrunner fastened his belt, checked that his side-arm was loaded, rammed his hat on his head then stomped out of the room, slamming the door behind him. Gisela smiled and sighed, *"He's so handsome when he's in a temper,"* she thought.

When Kaltenbrunner reached Himmler's office door, the two SS guards sprang to attention and presented arms. Kaltenbrunner, ignoring them, rapped on the door, waited and getting no reply, he boldly threw it open. Stepping inside, he paused when he saw Himmler and Krancher tied to the two chairs. They looked so ridiculous and pathetic, sat there without their trousers and in stocking feet that Kaltenbrunner burst out laughing. Closing the door behind him he said, *"Having a private party, Herr Reichsführer?"* as he crossed the office and started to undo the sash cord fastening Himmler's wrists. Once he had been freed, Himmler stood up and stamped his feet to get the blood moving, then went to retrieve his boots and trousers. It was plainly obvious that he was absolutely seething. Pulling his trousers and boots on, he sat down behind his desk his hands trembling. There was steam coming out of his ears and he was bordering on being speechless with embarrassment and rage.

Kaltenbrunner pulled the gag from Krancher's mouth, then undid the ropes tying him to the chair. A grateful Krancher said, "*Danke, Herr General. I'm outraged that this should happen here, of all places!*" "*Ach, think yourself lucky, old chap,*" replied Kaltenbrunner, "*You only lost your trousers and what looks like a few teeth – the bandits that did this to you could quite easily have shot you or cut your throat!*" Krancher looked as if he was about to burst into tears, "*One of them stole my gold party wrist-watch, Herr General. It was presented to me by the Führer himself, it is irreplaceable!*" Kaltenbrunner said, "*Oh, I'm sure that we can get you another one, the Führerbunker is full of such ridiculous trinkets. Better put some trousers on, Krancher, you'll catch your death of cold!*" Krancher nodded and began to get dressed. "*Oh, and Krancher!*" "*Ja, Herr General?*" "*You need a change of underwear! The ones you are wearing are, shall we say, a little soiled.* Turning bright red with shame and embarrassment, a mortified Krancher said, "*Ja, Herr General! Forgive me but it's all been a little difficult.*"

Turning to Himmler, Kaltenbrunner said, "*Something is going on here that I do not understand, Herr Reichsführer.*" "*What do you mean?*" asked Himmler. "*Well, let us put aside what has happened to you and to Krancher, but some men have boldly walked into your Headquarters dressed in SS uniforms, taken you both prisoner without so much as a shot being fired and then removed two miscreants, one of them being Von Mülheim, the Base Commander from the Lake Toplitz Naval Station and the other, the Partisan. Not*

341

only that, they have had the impertinence to make good their escape using my personal staff car!"

Himmler snatched up his telephone and began inelegantly ranting at the Duty Officer, explaining to him, in outline, what had happened, but of course, failing to mention the loss of his boots and trousers. He ordered that all roads leading out of central Berlin were to be sealed off immediately and that the missing staff car was to be stopped and its occupants arrested - or heads would roll. The passengers were then to be brought back, unharmed, to his Headquarters. Himmler slammed the 'phone back into in its cradle so fiercely that chunks of Bakelite flew everywhere. He was like a cornered snake, hissing, "*It will be very unpleasant for them once they are returned here, I can assure you of that, Ernst.*"

Downstairs in the duty bunker, the Orderly Officer smiled to himself, knowing that, just like Hitler, the Reichsführer-SS was living in cloud-cuckoo land. There was no-one left to seal off the roads. Himmler obviously failed to realise that every able-bodied man he had at his disposal was out fighting a rear-guard action against the Russians. The remaining few soldiers left guarding the Reich Main Security Offices were the old, bold and badly wounded. It was, the Orderly Officer decided, time for him to 'fold his tent,' slip quietly out of Berlin and return to his beloved Nienburg an der Weser. The Third Reich was well and truly finished and the lunatics that remained were running the asylum. He would be glad to be out of it and would surrender himself to either the Americans or the British if needs be. Were the Russians to capture him, he knew that he'd either be topped on the spot or be heading for a Gulag somewhere in deepest Siberia to be worked to death in a mine or something similar.

About half an hour later Kaltenbrunner arrived at the pockmarked Führerbunker. Before he'd left the Reich Main Security Building, Himmler had begged him not to reveal what had happened in his office. Kaltenbrunner gave Himmler his word that his lips were sealed, although he was tempted to tell the Führer. Martin Bormann was waiting to meet Kaltenbrunner and take him straight in to see the Führer. *"Please leave your side-arm on my desk, Herr General. You know the routine,"* said Bormann. Kaltenbrunner removed his pistol and threw it carelessly onto the desk. He would collect it on the way out. *"Huh, as if I would harm a hair the beloved Führer's head*! *I am not Himmler!"* he thought.

The Führer invited Kaltenbrunner to take a seat, then said, *"Herr General, I called you here to give you my personal thanks for ensuring that the gold bullion reached Lake Toplitz safe and sound. It is of great importance to my future plans that it should have done so."* As the Führer was speaking there was a tap on the door, Hitler bellowed, *"Herein!"* Bormann popped his head around the door and said, *"Excuse, my Führer, the armoured car has arrived at the front entrance and is waiting to take you to your aircraft. Frau Hitler is already on board."* Hitler asked, *"And my dog Blondi?"* *"Blondi has been put to sleep in accordance with your instructions, my Führer,"* replied Bormann. Hitler smiled, *"Thank you, Martin. I will be out in a moment. Oh, and Martin?"* *"My Führer?"* *"Who is piloting the aircraft today?"* *"Hannah Reich, my Führer."* *"Excellent,"* replied Hitler, before waving him away.

Adolf turned to Kaltenbrunner and said, *"Now, where was I? Ah yes, I wanted to thank you personally, Herr General, for the carrying out* **'OPERATION GOLDGRÄBER'** *so efficiently. So much hinges on the success of the operation."*

He opened his desk drawer and reached inside, *"I would like you to accept this small gift as a token of my personal appreciation."* The Führer removed a plush red velvet covered box from the drawer. *"I know that medals and awards are no longer of use, but nevertheless I thought that would like you to have this little memento."* He passed the box over to Kaltenbrunner. *"Go on then, General, open it!"* he commanded.

Kaltenbrunner opened the box and there laid on the plush red velvet inner was a beautifully crafted, slim solid gold wrist-watch with a swastika of diamonds inlaid on its champagne coloured face. Kaltenbrunner smiled, *"My Führer, this is a wonderful gift, I am deeply touched."* Hitler waved his hand dismissively, *"Ach, it's nothing, just a token of my appreciation. I will see that you are properly rewarded in due course. The watch is made out of solid gold and the diamonds are real, of course. Himmler seems to be able to get his hands on an endless supply of such things. Now, if you'll forgive me, you must return to your duties and I must take my leave."*

"You are getting out of Berlin, my Führer?" asked Kaltenbrunner. Hitler nodded, *"Regrettably, yes. I must conduct the fight from elsewhere. The people of Berlin have failed me and most of my Generals and Soldiers have failed me, present company excepted."* *"May I ask where you are going, my Führer?"* *"No, I'm afraid you may not, General."* replied a smiling Hitler, *"For now that remains a State Secret, but you will soon find out. Now, off you go."*

Kaltenbrunner shot to his feet, saluted and said, *"Then may I wish you and Frau Hitler a speedy and safe journey, my Führer. Heil Hitler!"* Hitler stood up smiled and shook Kaltenbrunner's hand, *"We will meet again before too long,*

General Kaltenbrunner." A highly emotional Hitler continued, *"Thank you for all that you have done for the Third Reich. You have been a true and loyal servant. No one could have asked for more.*" The door opened and Bormann came into the Führers room, *"You are ready, my Führer?*" he enquired. Hitler nodded, *"Yes, just see the General off the premises first will you and then I am ready to leave.*" A tearful Kaltenbrunner saluted and said, *"Auf Wiedersehen, meine Führer.*" then left.

Outside the Fuhrer's office, Bormann turned to Kaltenbrunner and grasped his hand, *"I will establish contact with you from the Fuhrer's new location. I have just got to get Reich Minister Goebbels and his family on their way and my duties here are completed.*" Kaltenbrunner nodded, then asked, *"Presumably you will also be leaving here shortly?*" Bormann nodded, *"Yes, but I will be leaving on foot. Once the Führer has departed, the one remaining armoured vehicle will be used to transport the Goebbels family. It won't be easy, but I have every confidence in my plans. Now, you'd better be on your way. Heil Hitler and good luck!*" Kaltenbrunner nodded, *"Heil Hitler indeed!*" thinking to himself, *"Like rats leaving a sinking ship.*"

Outside the Führerbunker, Kaltenbrunner strode manfully across to the Kübelwagen waiting to take him back to the Reich Main Security Building. In the distance, he could hear shells exploding and guns blasting away. It was obvious to him that it wouldn't be too long before the Russians reached the Führerbunker. He smiled, thinking, *"And when they got there, the cupboard was bare!*" before jumping into the vehicle and instructing the driver to get his foot down. It was time to collect Gisela and head for the hills himself. As he was being driven off he passed the two armoured vehicles and a well-armed escort that had come to collect the Führer and his wife and the Goebbels family.

Once Kaltenbrunner reached the Reich Main Security Office, he noted, to his surprise, that unusually the front entrance was left unguarded. Ordering his Adjutant to remain in the Kübelwagen and wait other for him, Kaltenbrunner slid his pistol out of its holster, cocked it then strode into the building. With the exception of the SS-Unterscharführer manning the front desk, the reception area was quiet and totally empty. Even the telephones had stopped ringing. "*Where is everyone Unterscharführer?*" demanded Kaltenbrunner. The SS-Unterscharführer leaped to his feet, "*They have all gone, Herr General, including the Reichsführer-SS and his entourage!*"

Kaltenbrunner raised an eyebrow, "*Gone? The Reichsführer-SS has left the building you say?*" The Unterscharführer nodded, "*Over an hour ago, Herr General, just after you'd left for the Führerbunker.*" Kaltenbrunner tutted and replaced his pistol in its holster, "*Very well. I have a few things to collect from my office and will return in a few minutes. I am also leaving here. You may accompany me if you wish to do so.*" said Kaltenbrunner. The Unterscharführer shook his head, "*Thank you, but no, Herr General. I will remain here at my post.*"

Kaltenbrunner said, "*You know what will happen to you once the Russians hordes arrive here, don't you?*" The man nodded, "*Yes, Herr General, I can imagine, but I prefer to go down fighting for my beloved Führer and for Deutschland. I have plenty of ammunition here and will take as many of those bloody Russians with me as I can. I have a few scores to settle with them from my time on the Russian front.*"

For the first time, Kaltenbrunner noticed that the man was missing his left arm and had an empty folded sleeve pinned to his uniform jacket. He reached across and gripped his shoulder, *"Good man! That is very brave of you, Unterscharführer. I want you to know that, unlike our beloved Reichsführer-SS, I am not fleeing from here with my tail between my legs. I am going to continue the fight from elsewhere."* *"I did not doubt that for one moment, Herr General."* replied the smiling Unterscharführer, clicking his boot heels together.

Kaltenbrunner ran up the stairs to collect his precious Gisela and the two all-important suitcases, containing civilian clothing, and a large quantity of money, gold and diamonds and some false identification papers from his safe. As Kaltenbrunner disappeared out of sight up the stairs, the Unterscharführer reached under his desk and pulled out a half-empty bottle of schnapps, unscrewed the top and took a hefty swig. He smiled, *"Continuing the fight from elsewhere my arse!"* he thought, *"Does he think that I'm a duck-egg. He's as bad as all the rest of them. I should have invited him to stay here and fight alongside me. Huh, pigs might fly!"* There was a message left on the notepad on Kaltenbrunner's desk informing him that his staff car had been found abandoned on a side road, near the Berlin Zoo, its occupants nowhere to be seen. The car was being returned to the front of the Main Reich Security Offices and would be delivered there very shortly, accompanied by a small armed escort.

Kaltenbrunner's Adjutant, Arthur Scheidler, had followed the General into his office and collected both his and Gisela's suitcases to take them down to the main entrance, along with a suitcase that he himself had prepared. He would be driving the staff car out of Berlin himself.

Purely by coincidence, a truck, followed by the all-important Kaltenbrunner staff car, drew to a halt at the front of the building. Kaltenbrunner, looking out of his office window, saw the vehicles arrive and instructed Scheidler, *"Arthur, the staff car is here, go and get the ignition keys – make sure that the fuel tank is full and that we have a few spare cans, enough to get us well on our way. Have those soldiers transfer some fuel cans from their truck, then instruct them that they are to escort us to the city limits, after which we will have no further use for them. They can do what they wish, the game is over."* Scheidler nodded and left the building to carry out his master's instructions. Kaltenbrunner gazed around his office thinking, *"So, this is how it all ends. What times we have had here."* He shook his head then called out for Gisela and they left, Kaltenbrunner pulling the door closed behind him for the final time.

As they reached the reception area opposite the front desk, the Unterscharführer leaped to attention. Kaltenbrunner drew his pistol and shot the brave Unterscharführer in the chest, killing him instantly. The man fell backward onto the floor behind his desk, the sound of his schnapps bottle noisily rolling across the marble floor echoing around the entrance hall. *"Sorry my friend, unfortunately, there can be no witnesses to my departure,"* said Kaltenbrunner as he re-holstered his pistol. He turned to Gisela and said, *"Come along my dear, time for us to go."*

Gisela smiled and followed Kaltenbrunner out of the building. As they stood outside on the pavement, the sound of explosions and heavy firing could be heard from a few streets away. *"And not a moment too soon I think,"* said Kaltenbrunner. *"Darling,"* said Gisela, *"You haven't told me where we are going?"* Kaltenbrunner held the staff car door open for Gisela, telling her, *"I am taking you to Lake Toplitz in Austria, my dear. They tell me that it is quite lovely there at this time of year,"* slammed the car door shut then jumped into the passenger seat alongside Scheidler.

Scheidler turned to Kaltenbrunner, *"The car is fully fuelled, Herr General, and there are spare fuel cans in the boot. I have instructed the Feldwebel in charge of the soldiers that he is to escort us until we reach the city limits and then is free to do whatever he thinks fit with his men."* Kaltenbrunner nodded, *"Excellent. Well, let's be on our way then."*

Kaltenbrunner turned to Gisela and said, *"Make yourself comfortable my dear, we have a long journey ahead of us. You will see that there is a blanket to cover your legs and keep you warm. I will travel here in the front of the vehicle, alongside Arthur, then if we come under fire I can protect you both."* he said, smiling. Scheidler put the car in gear and revved the large, powerful and growling engine, then the small convoy set off, the staff car in the lead. They did a swift 'u' turn, tyres screaming, then hurtled off in a cloud of exhaust fumes, heading for the outer city limits and away from the dangers posed by the rapidly advancing Russian Red Army.

The large, impressive and now undefended Reich Main Security Building stood silently waiting for the arrival of the Russian hordes, many of its secrets having been destroyed in the last few hours, but not all of them. Mountains of sensitive documents lay waiting in otherwise empty offices, their contents waiting to be pored over by the Russians and there were several prisoners still locked away in the bloodstained cells, remaining as evidence of the Gestapo's inhumane activities.

349

'CHAPTER 10'

'Guardian of the Führer's Gold'

A greatly relieved Krancher had been fully reinstated as a fully-fledged SS-Standartenführer by Himmler and was now even more pompous and bombastic than ever. He'd been instructed personally by his beloved Reichsführer-SS to fly back to Lake Toplitz and ensure that the 'Führer's Gold' had been hidden away precisely as per the *'OPERATION GOLDGRÄBER'* instruction and that any evidence relating to the gold had been removed and destroyed, including human witnesses. The complete SS escort that had accompanied the convoy to Lake Toplitz had been sent out onto the streets of Berlin when they returned there. Not one of them survived more than 24 hours.

The cunning Himmler, of course, had recognised that the Third Reich was on its knees but didn't see that as a reason for not slipping his hand into the Reichsbank 'till.' He felt that he more than deserved a slice of the golden pie. Himmler had been absolutely furious that the *'OPERATION GOLDGRÄBER'* plan had been compromised and that 'enemy forces' as he termed it, were on the trail of the 'Führer's Gold.' Krancher had been ordered to stop any filching of the gold at all costs, using whatever manpower he could raise in the Toplitz area.

Herr Himmler, meanwhile, had left Berlin, slinking off to an alternative location well away from the fighting and from where he would be directing future SS operations as he saw fit. He had secret ambitions to become the new 'Führer' once Hitler had shrugged off his mortal coil, which he fervently hoped would be sooner rather than later. Heini liked the sound of "*Heil Himmler*!" it had a certain ring to it and he would be putting all of his efforts towards achieving his leadership aims.

He was certain that it would take many years for Adolf Hitler to be forgiven by the German people for fleeing Berlin with his tail between his legs and leaving Germany in ruins. As a result Hitler, he believed, would fade into obscurity, finishing what was left of his life in splendid isolation in somewhere like Argentina or Bolivia. Either that or he would just do the decent thing and die. It didn't occur to him that he, Himmler, bore a similar amount of responsibility for the misfortunes that had landed on the heads of the German people and that he had also left Berlin to its fate when the going got tough. Still, he wasn't concerned about that; his greed and ambition overrode all other considerations.

In truth, Krancher was greatly relieved to have scuttled out of Berlin when he did. Although a fervent and fanatical Nazi, even he could see that the end had finally arrived. The all-encompassing fear that he'd experienced whilst sat in the cells as a prisoner in the Gestapo cellars would stay with him forever, although that hadn't troubled him one iota when he'd been down there dishing cruel and unjust punishment out to other unfortunates whilst they were being interrogated.

He greatly feared the Russians and wanted to be as far away from them as possible.

Fortunately for Krancher, he was still regarded as being a valuable and key member of Himmler's staff and was pleased beyond measure that he had been handed the task of checking on the safety of the 'Führer's Gold.' Himmler had even promised him another gold watch to replace the one that had been taken from him by the thieving 'Partisan.' As far as Krancher was concerned, he was living the dream. He was such a fanatical Nazi that he was unable to accept the fact that the war was at an end and that his days in the sun were virtually over. He was convinced that the 'Fourth Reich' would rise above all else and he would be a key figure in the organisation.

One of the very last small Fieseler Storch aircraft had been commandeered from the Luftwaffe by Himmler and the pilot had been given orders to fly Krancher back to Lake Toplitz. The very brave pilot had managed to coax the little aircraft off the temporary pitted runway along a stretch of Berlin's Unter den Linden that had been cleared of dead bodies, debris, and burning vehicles, by an exhausted work party. The little aircraft had lurched up into the skies, soaring over the Brandenburg Gate and up out of Berlin, fortunately without coming under heavy enemy fire. They had been extremely fortunate not to be shot down though, as the curtain of Russian ack-ack fire was normally horrendous and virtually impassable. It had been likened to an iron curtain by one wag.

The pilot smiled at Krancher and whistled away tunelessly, pleased as punch to be leaving a doomed Berlin. "*I doubt if we'll be coming back here for the next few years, Herr Standartenführer*," he said. Krancher nodded in agreement, although in truth he couldn't have cared less. The pilot continued, *"My orders from the Reichsführer-SS are that I am to remain at Lake Toplitz with you until receiving further instructions from Berlin."* Krancher replied sneeringly, *"Huh, the only instructions you'll be getting from that hell-hole will be from the Russians!"*

Krancher couldn't believe his good fortune. One minute he'd been a despised prisoner, languishing in the cells underneath the Reich Main Security Office, surrounded by the lingering stench of fear and death and stripped of his rank, medals and authority, waiting to be interrogated, beaten then executed by the ever-present Gestapo torturers. Then, unbelievably, he'd been saved by the direct intervention of his beloved Reichsführer-SS, Heinrich Himmler. Krancher knew full well that if the fearsome SS-Obergruppenführer Kaltenbrunner had had his way then he would have been dragged unceremoniously out to the killing yard at the rear of the Headquarters, tied to a post and then shot. It had been a very close call and just thinking about it turned his bowels to ice.

So, all in all, Krancher was now a happy little bunny and was smiling smugly as he looked out of the aircraft's canopy and down at Berlin, a city in flames and covered in thick black smoke emanating from the many thousands of bombed-out burning buildings. The palls of smoke reached up into the sky, filling the air with the stench of death. Krancher couldn't wait to get back to the peace and tranquillity of Lake Toplitz, where secretly he had arranged for himself and his family to flee to Switzerland and safety. Once he reached Toplitz, he would ensure that there would be no evidence left there to give any clue as to the whereabouts of the 'Führer's Gold.' As he'd been instructed, everything at the Lake Toplitz base would be disposed of including, unfortunately, any remaining witnesses. After that task was completed, he would be well on his way to Switzerland. He had received the approval of the Reichsführer-SS and was told by him to wait in Switzerland until receiving further instructions.

Himmler had promised Krancher that there would be '*life after death*' - the death of the Third Reich and that he, Krancher, would have a vital role to play in the Fourth Reich. Krancher's heart swelled with pride at the thought of it. Undoubtedly there would be a promotion in it for him.

'*The Fieseler Storch used for Krancher's escape from Berlin*'

As the tiny aircraft approached Lake Toplitz, the pilot turned to Krancher and said, "*Herr Standartenführer, if you look down to your left, just there at the side of the lake, you will see a small temporary clearing. That is where we will land.*" "*God in Heaven!*" said Krancher, "*It looks so tiny. Are you sure that we can make it safely?*" The pilot smiled, "*Yes, I can land this delightful little machine on the back of a postage stamp if I have to, absolutely guaranteed. You'd better make sure that you are strapped in nice and tightly though, just in case anything does go wrong.*"

As Krancher looked down he could see a small military reception committee stood at the side of the landing strip, waiting to welcome him. He checked his safety harness, pulling it as tight as he could, then sat back and smiled. It had been an excellent flight and they hadn't been seen or troubled by any other aircraft. "*Nothing can go wrong now*," he thought.

No sooner had he thought that when suddenly the peace was rudely shattered when out of the clouds roared a huge, fearsome American aircraft which immediately opened fire on them. The pilot of the Fieseler Storch took immediate evasive action. "*Hold on tight*," he shouted, throwing the Storch into a steep dive. "*Is it one of ours*?" asked a panic-stricken Krancher. "*No, it's an American B-24L Liberator and they've spotted us!*"

'USAF B-24L Liberator'

The cheerful 22 years old pilot of the mighty B-24L Liberator had been heading back to his home base after a successful mission, bombing and strafing a German troop train. As a result of that, he had hardly any ammunition left, so every remaining round counted. "*Sheeit Tex!*" the American said to his co-pilot, "*Lookee what we've got here, that's probably one of them there Nazi General's hightailing it in that little Krout aircraft. Well, your luck just ran out, buddy! Eat some American lead!*" He instructed Hank, his nose-gunner, to open fire and strafe the Fieseler Storch from

355

stem to stern. Hank opened fire, his guns blazing for only a few seconds before spluttering to a halt, *"That's it, boss, I'm out of ammo, no lead left!"* he shouted. *"Never mind Hank, I think you finished him off!! OK, we'd better make our way back to base, Tex."*

They watched the burning Fieseler Storch as it started to spiral out of the sky, heading down towards the surface of the lake, spinning uncontrollably. *"Enjoy your swim, you Nazi bastards!"* shouted the pilot, then with a quick, *"Yeeeeehah!"* waggled his aircraft's wings and headed off for home, very pleased with his unexpected kill.

Krancher shouted at the pilot, *"For God's sake do something can't you!"* then to his horror saw that the Pilot, head sagging forward, was bleeding badly from several bullet holes across the front of his flying jacket. He was obviously very badly injured, *"I will try and get us down in one piece, Herr Standartenführer"* he mumbled. Like a leaf falling off a tree branch, the aircraft fluttered untidily towards the lake's surface. Miraculously the aircraft's engine was still working, although most of its controls had been shot to bits. The pilot fought to stop the engine from stalling and miraculously the Storch belly-flopped onto the surface near to the edge of the lake, causing a huge splash. As the 'plane slowly settled on the water, Krancher heaved a huge sigh of relief.

The pilot's head dropped, his chin resting on his chest, he was either unconscious or dead. Krancher couldn't have cared less about him, now that he had landed the aircraft he was of no consequence. All Krancher wanted to do was get out of the sinking aircraft and swim to the safety of the lakeside. As Krancher struggled to release his seat harness, pounding on it as hard as he could, to his horror he noticed that the metal buckle at its centre had been clipped by a bullet fired from the American aircraft, causing the release mechanism to jam.

Try as he might, he was unable to free it. No matter how hard he tugged, it refused to open. He was well and truly trapped. As he desperately continued to pound on the release button he saw the cabin of the aircraft starting to fill up with freezing cold water from the lake and could feel it creeping towards his feet. He knew that he had very little time left to get out of the aircraft if he was to survive. The aircraft's badly damaged engine finally spluttered to a halt and, apart from the sound of gurgling water and Krancher thrashing the release mechanism with his bloodied fists, silence descended.

A panic-stricken and sobbing Krancher watched as the lake's icy water crept up the inside of the cabin until it was lapping around his ankles. He realised that there was no escape, he was trapped and was going to drown. The Fieseler Storch began to sink slowly beneath the surface of the lake. Screaming with panic Krancher heaved and pulled on the straps with all of his might, but it was no good. The water inched upwards past his waist, then reached his chest, until reaching his firmly clenched mouth. He desperately beat the release button on his harness with his freezing hands, but to no avail, it refused to budge.

After a few agonising seconds, the water reached his nostrils. He strained to keep his head above the water but it was no good, he was going to drown. Struggling manically, Krancher heaved desperately on the harness straps, cursing roundly, but the release button refused to depress. As the water-filled aircraft slipped beneath the surface of the lake, Krancher, fighting to hold his breath, thought, rather illogically, *"Scheisse, I will now become the Guardian of the Führer's Gold!"*

The little aircraft gently pirouetted down into the gloomy waters, heading for the murky bottom of the lake, like some nightmarish fairground ride. Krancher gave one final scream of fear, inadvertently using up the last of his air, the little silver bubbles of oxygen from his mouth collecting under the canopy of the Fieseler Storch. As the little aircraft finally settled on the bed of the lake, through his rapidly fading eyesight, Krancher could see the crates of sunken gold lain higgledy-piggledy in the mud, the very last thing that he would ever see. As the last few precious bubbles of oxygen vanished from his lungs, darkness descended.

Onshore, the small welcoming party, all that remained of the local SS, stood and watched helplessly as the badly damaged aircraft sank out of sight. They had seen the passenger struggling to free himself but there was nothing they could do to help him. Even if they'd had a boat, they wouldn't have been able to reach him in time. After a few seconds, apart from a small patch of oil, there was no sign of the aircraft and its occupants ever having been there.

One of the soldier's said to the NCO in charge, SS-Sturm Man Schrenk, *"Poor sods. who was on board the aircraft then, Erhard?"* Schrenk replied, *"The pilot, obviously, and SS-Standartenführer Krancher, who was returning here from Berlin."* The first soldier nodded, then turned and whispered to another of the guards, *"Ah, Krancher. I thought that we'd seen the last of that turd; no great loss there then! That Yankee pilot has done us all a great favour."* Schrenk smiled and said, *"Come on lads, let's get out of here, there's nothing we can do now. Let's go and tell the Duty Officer what's happened. He might want to radio the information through to Berlin – if he's able to make contact. I wonder if he can speak Russian?*" They all laughed as they tramped back to the Headquarters.

'CHAPTER 11'

'The Evils'

SS-Obergruppenführer Kaltenbrunner stepped out of his staff car, stretched and then strode purposefully towards the Guardroom at the entrance to the Nazi Naval Testing Station, Lake Toplitz. It was unguarded and strangely quiet. He turned to his Adjutant, *"Keep the engine running, Arthur, I'll be back in a moment."* Thinking it strange that there wasn't an armed guard on the main gate, Kaltenbrunner unholstered his pistol and stepped gingerly into the Guardroom.

SS-Sturm Mann Erhard Schreck and his two mates, SS-Schütze Karl Hanke, and Freddie Handörf were sat around a table, playing cards and glugging champagne from fine crystal glasses, several empty bottles of champagne littering the floor. Their drink stained uniforms were in a state of disarray and they were all obviously the worse for wear. Handörf had even removed his boots and socks, the rank smell of his cheesy feet permeating the atmosphere. Schreck threw his head back and gave a hearty belch. *"This is the life lads, eh!"*

An enraged Kaltenbrunner roared, *"On your feet!"* The surprised soldiers turned and looked him up and down.

Handörf mumbled, *"Whoops!"* *"And who is this chocolate soldier, lads?"* said Hanke, sniggering drunkenly. *"This 'chocolate soldier' is SS-Obergruppenführer Kaltenbrunner. Now, on your feet!"* replied Kaltenbrunner icily. Hanke cocked his leg, farted then said, *"Oy mate, give it a rest, eh! Come and share a glass of champers with us. We're celebrating! Haven't you heard, our beloved Führer has fought and died valiantly in the grounds of the Reichschancellery! The 'Battle of Berlin' is lost and the Russkies are in control there – so it's all over. Peace has broken out and we're all free to go."*

"Ja, that is correct, Herr General, " said Schreck, *"The war is lost, Germany has surrendered unconditionally and so we're all equals now."* Hanke nodded, *"Ja, we're all citizens again and we're all in deep shit. Come and join us in a glass of bubbly, Herr General. Nothing but the best – it's from the Officers' Mess!"* The three soldiers laughed. "So, you have been *looting!"* said Kaltenbrunner. *"That is correct Herr General - and what are you going to do about it, eh? Nothing I suspect,"* said Hanke, pouring himself another drink. Because they were three sheets to the wind, the soldiers failed to notice that Kaltenbrunner's face had paled with anger. They didn't realise that they were treading on very thin ice.

Hanke continued, pointing at the champagne bottles, *"You see, there was a party laid on at the Officers' Mess to welcome the delightful Standartenführer Krancher back here from Berlin, but unfortunately his plane crashed into the middle of the lake and sank, taking him with it. So, the only drink he'll be getting is a gob full of lake water."* *"The Standartenführer 's aircraft crashed, you say?"* said Kaltenbrunner. Schreck nodded, *"Yes, it was shot down by a passing American aircraft, Herr General. For Krancher it was the wrong time and the wrong place. Pure bad luck I'd say, but it couldn't have happened to a nicer bloke."* said Schreck, laughing uproariously. *"And where are your officers?"* asked Kaltenbrunner. *"Oh that shower of shit, they all legged it once they'd heard the news about Adolf!"* said Schrek. *"Which is just what we'll be doing once this last bottle of plonk is finished,"* slurred Handörf.

There was the loud crack of a pistol shot as, without warning, Kaltenbrunner shot Schrek in the face. Schreck hurtled backward across the room, hitting the wall then slid lifelessly onto the floor, blood pouring from the gaping wound in the socket where his left eye had once been, a gormless look on his face. Kaltenbrunner snarled at the remaining two soldiers, *"Wrong time, wrong place for him! Now, you two - get up off your arses!"* The remaining two soldiers leaped out of their chairs and stood to attention, swaying in front of Kaltenbrunner, a look of sullen resignation on their faces.

Indicating the dead Schreck, Kaltenbrunner sneered, *"The war is definitely over for your comrade! Now, what is going on here and where is your Station Commander, Kapitän Zur See Von Mülheim?"* Handörf replied, *"Herr General, our Station Commander has left here for good. He told us that the war is over and that we should lay down our weapons and return to our homes. We are the only three, er, two left here."* *"So why are you still hanging around like a bad smell then?"* asked Kaltenbrunner, *"Herr General, I am from Mülheim an der Ruhr and my friend Karl here is from Münster. We thought that we'd better wait here for a few days until things had calmed down a little, get rid of our uniforms then try to make our way back home to our families."* Kaltenbrunner nodded, *"I see, so you are deserting your posts! Well, we can't have that, can we!"* and without even blinking, shot them both. *"That will save you both a difficult journey,"* he sneered, putting his still smoking pistol back into its holster.

Kaltenbrunner's Adjutant, Scheidler, came running into the Guardroom, *"I heard shots, Herr General?"* *"It's OK, Arthur. I was just doing a bit of housekeeping. It would appear that the Station Commander, the bold Kapitän Zur See Von Mülheim, has abandoned ship and instructed his men to desert their posts and return from whence they came. Apparently, in the relatively short time it took us to get here, the Führer has died, the war is over and we lost."* Scheidler shrugged, *"The Führer dead, that is almost unbelievable! So now what do we do now, Herr General?"* he asked, *"We revert to 'Plan B' I suppose and head for the hills ourselves."* replied Kaltenbrunner, sighing, *"It would appear that the battle for Berlin is finally over and our valiant Führer has met his fate in the grounds of the Reichschancellery whilst fending off the Russian hordes. How very heroic of him."* They both laughed, and Kaltenbrunner winked, *"But we know different, eh, Arthur!"* Scheidler nodded and smiled.

Kaltenbrunner continued, *"Anyway, we'd better get out of here, my old friend. As I said, time for Plan B."* Scheidler nodded, *"Very good, Herr General, er, what about Krancher?"* he asked. *"I'll tell you all about that later, but he is no longer a concern of ours. Just bring the suitcases in here from the car and we'll get changed into civilian clothing."* *"Straight away, Herr General,"* said Scheidler. *"And Arthur,"* *"Herr General?"* *"You can cut all that 'Herr General' crap out now. It's no longer needed."* Scheidler clicked his heels, *"Forgive me, sir. Old habits die hard,"* he said as he turned to leave.

Kaltenbrunner called out to him, *"And could you kindly ask Gisela to step inside the Guardroom. She might as well get changed out of her uniform as well.*" Scheidler nodded, "*And the 'Führer's Gold,' Herr General?*" forgetting Kaltenbrunner's previous suggestion about dropping rank titles, "*That is safe enough where it is, for now, Arthur. We can make the necessary arrangements for its recovery in due course. Now go and get the suitcases, there's a good chap.*" Scheidler saluted and left the Guardroom.

Kaltenbrunner smiled to himself, "*I can just picture Himmler, Dőenitz and that buffoon Göering scrambling for position at the top of a very greasy pole now that they think the Führer is dead and gone. It will be like three bald men fighting over a comb. A lost cause.*" It gave Kaltenbrunner more than a hint of malicious pleasure thinking about it and he laughed out loud.

He reached over to the table where the three dead guards had been playing cards a few minutes earlier, picked up the half-empty bottle of champagne, wiped its greasy neck, took a hearty swig, then sneered, "*A shame to waste this. So our beloved Führer has managed to escape from Berlin. Sounds like his stand-in, good old Gustav Weler has done his bounden duty then.*" He looked at his gold wrist-watch, yawned then threw the empty champagne bottle against the guardroom wall, the shattered glass falling over the bodies.

Gisela and Scheidler hurried into the room carrying the suitcases. Gisela glanced dismissively at the three dead soldiers and said, "*I'll just go into the other room and get changed, Ernst.*" Kaltenbrunner smiled and nodded, "*Quick as you can my dear, it's better that we don't linger here for too long, there are Americans lurking nearby.*" He turned to Scheidler, "*Arthur, is there sufficient benzine left in the car to get us to the mountain hut?*" Scheidler nodded, "*Plenty, Herr General, er sir.*" "*Good, so let's get changed into civilian clothing and then we can be on our way. We'll abandon the staff car somewhere near to the hut and continue the rest of our journey on foot. Not too far away though, Arthur, my leg is playing up and to be honest I'm quite tired. It's been a long and trying day."*

'CHAPTER 12'

'The Recovery Phase'

After a long and seemingly endless journey by road from Amsterdam, most of it in fierce, freezing rain, the 'Gold Recovery Crew,' as Graham had named it, arrived at the edge of Lake Toplitz and parked their three vehicles and trailers under the trees near the edge of the lake. They'd deliberately planned their journey so that they would arrive under cover of darkness, most of the final leg of their journey having been completed 'off-road.'

Lake Toplitz itself had proven difficult to reach, decent metalled roads were few and far between. Their little convoy had deliberately driven quietly and slowly along a small track through the woods leading down to the side of the lake, guiding their way on side-lights only, to reduce the chances of being spotted.

After arriving at a suitable location, they'd quickly covered their Mercedes-Benz 4x4 Off-Roaders with military-style camouflage netting and then underneath the netting set up a small catering area, where Ludo and Diederik de Jong were preparing a much needed European style breakfast of crusty rolls and various sliced meats, whilst their Father, Ed de Jong, Mike Fraser, and Graham St Anier were unloading various pieces of diving equipment and checking out the inflatable rubber dinghy in preparation for the first dive into the lake. They were moving quickly, as they wanted to get cracking. The kettle was bubbling away and the smell of coffee permeated the area. It wasn't cordon bleu standard but would see them adequately through until their next hot meal.

Ed, Ludo, and Diederik had agreed to do the diving, Mike was Commander-in-Chief of the RIB (*Rubber Inflatable Boat*), whilst Graham would be dealing with administrative matters and site security. They'd allowed themselves a 'window' of three full days to complete the covert operation but were hoping to do it in two. Knowing the coordinates of precisely where the gold bullion had been dropped off into the lake at the end of World War 2 had given them a head start.

"Right guys," said Ed, *"not teaching you to suck eggs but I just want to refresh you on a few key points. As we discussed at the various planning meetings, I'll be doing the diving with Ludo and Diederik. We've got the latest 'rebreathers' so we can spend a bit more time at the bottom of the lake than we would be if using conventional gear, so that's good. Now remember what I told you, there is to be no off-gassing whilst we're descending, the only time for off-gassing is when we're coming back up. That's very important. We'll be using Aquacom throughout to talk to each other and will be connected topside to Mike so that's good also. Ludo and*

Diederik, you pass your comments via me and I'll let Mike know anything that he needs to."

He turned to Mike, *"Mike – you'll be looking after the RIB and Graham will be our man on the ground watching our backs. Also, Graham has very kindly volunteered to be chief cook and bottle-washer throughout the dive, which is a bit of a relief as my sons have been known to scorch water!"* They all laughed. *"I'll make sure that there's a good hot meal waiting for you when each dive's completed. I've got all sorts of catering tricks up my sleeve. I loaded plenty of supplies."* said Graham.

Ed continued, *"Great, look forward to that, Graham. We've got plenty of tanks filled with Nitrox, certainly enough for us to do what we need to do at the bottom of the Lake and we've also got sufficient tanks filled with oxygen to pump into the IFB's (Inflatable Flotation Bags) that we'll need to raise the gold to the surface – if we find it. There'll be no give-away bubbles from our Nitrox tanks and the bubbles from the Oxygen tanks will be negligible, so in the unlikely event that someone is watching us, they won't know precisely where we are."*

Mike laughed and said, *"Don't you mean 'when' we find the gold!"* *"When we find it then,"* replied Ed, then continued, *"As I explained before, both me and the lads will be wearing rebreathers so we're not going to be too pushed for time whilst we're underwater, although we will be watching the dive depth and clock very carefully. It'll be very dodgy territory down there and I don't want anything to go wrong. I'm acting as 'Dive Master' throughout and I'll be keeping a close eye on everything. There have been enough fatalities in this Lake and we don't want our names adding to the list. We've all been through the diving and resurfacing procedures a thousand times, so there shouldn't be any problems. It's all a matter of careful timing and monitoring – and that's my responsibility."*

Ed continued, *"Then Mike, any gold we do find you'll be ferrying ashore in the RIB to be unloaded by Graham, who'll use the sack barrow to shift it to the trailers. If you just stash it at the side of the trailers, Graham, then we'll give you a hand to load it onto the trailers once we're all back on to dry land. Now, we're all carrying torches with masked lenses, and I suggest that you do a final check to make sure that you've got the green lens fitted. If there are any dramas, we switch the lenses to red so that we can all be alerted. You know the routine, we rehearsed it enough times. So, any questions before we get started?"* *"Well, I haven't got any. I've got the easy bit,"* said Graham, as the others shook their heads. Ed grinned, *"OK, let's finish our coffee off then. We all know what we've got to do, so let's get on with what we came here for."* He looked at his wristwatch, *" We've got five hours before it's daylight and we've got to be back here under cover."*

Although the RIB was fitted with a new quiet running 10 horsepower outboard motor, the team had decided that it would better to use paddles both to reach the drop-off point on the lake and for the several journeys back and forth to the lakeside. They'd agreed that the powerful outboard motor clamped to the rear of the dinghy would only be used in the event of an emergency. Mike would have to use 'paddle-power.'

Ed, Ludo, and Diederik, all experienced divers, had changed into their diving gear and were eagerly anticipating the dive. After having a quick look around through their night-sights to make sure that no-one was around, they lifted the dinghy into the freezing cold water and the four men climbed on board. Ed nodded, *"Full steam ahead, Mike!"* Mike started to paddle, assisted by Diederik.

"OK," said Mike, looking at his sat nav, *"This is the precise spot where we saw the Germans dropping the gold bullion over the side, so let the fun begin."* Ed and his lads checked and secured their diving masks then quietly slipped over the side of the RIB into the water, did a quick communications check then gave a 'thumbs up' sign to Mike before sinking out of sight.

Mike sat back in the dinghy and started to sweep the shore with his night-sight, looking for signs of unexpected movement. So far it had been as quiet as the grave. Mike double-checked the area where the vehicles had been hidden and couldn't see anything. His and Ed's military training had come in handy for that particular aspect. Other than that, he'd just have to sit there and wait.

To Ed, Ludo and Diederik's astonishment, when they eventually reached the murky bottom of the lake and their eyes had adjusted to the surroundings, lit up by the beams thrown out by their torches, the first thing they spotted was the downed Fieseler Storch aircraft with its two bodies still trapped inside the cockpit. The little aircraft looked as if it had been parked there just the day before.

It appeared to be in reasonably good condition considering the amount of time that it had lain underwater, it's Luftwaffe markings still clearly visible, although it had a broken port-side wing and its propeller was bent back and twisted at a crazy angle. The canopy covering the cockpit was, miraculously, still in one complete piece but was peppered with large holes caused by the American aircraft's cannon shells. Two skeletal bodies sat next to each other on the seats inside the aircraft, gently swaying gently in ghostly concert as the water filtering through the shell holes was disturbed by the diver's movements. It was decidedly spooky.

Ed tapped Diederik and Ludo on the shoulder and pointed to the far side of the aircraft's broken wing where he'd spotted a pile of wooden crates. They swam over to the crates then Ed gave them a thumbs up. He pointed at the lids of the crates which were clearly marked 'Reichsbank.' "*This looks like it lads! I love it when a good plan comes together*!" he said. They'd struck lucky. Diederik slid out his diving knife and levered the lid off the first crate, revealing several gold bars shining brightly in the light emitted by his torch. Their journey back through time to see where the gold had been dumped had not been a waste of time.

Giving another 'thumbs up.' Ed released a small buoy so that Mike would know precisely where they were, securing its long chord to one of the crates, then began fastening an IFB floatation device to the first crate. Opening the tap to fill the IFB with oxygen, they gently eased the first crate out of the mud and off the bed of the lake, watching anxiously to see if the wooden crate would be OK as it slowly made its way up to the surface to Mike.

Ed called Mike and warned him that the first crate was on its way up to the surface. Once it arrived on the surface, Mike would then ease the crate onto the dinghy then release the oxygen from the IFB before sending it back down to the bottom of the lake to be attached to another crate - and so it would go on. They'd practiced the routine many times in a lake near Amsterdam until the procedure was slick and efficient. Their rehearsals had been well worth the effort, the actual recovery operation was working like a dream. Each of the old crates held up well, considering their age and where they'd been stashed. Mike had to be careful that the sharp edges on the boxes didn't damage the fabric of the RIB, so took his time sliding them onboard. They'd allowed for that by bringing along some thick rubber matting that hung over the side of the RIB. The last thing they wanted was for it to spring a leak.

Down at the bottom of the lake, Ed pointed to another small pile of crates sat just a few feet away from the originals, then to several more just a short distance away. They'd hit the jackpot. There, in all its glory, lay 'Hitler's Gold.' Ed looked at the others and tapped his watch, *"Let's get moving lads, the clock's ticking."* then they continued with the recovery procedures.

Before attaching any of the crates to the IFB's, Diederik removed each crate lid and checked the contents. To the three's obvious delight, each of the crates was filled to the brim with shiny gold bars. It was even possible to read the 'Reichsbank' markings stamped into each of the bars. During their remaining allocated time, they managed to send ten of the crates up to the dinghy and would try to send up just a few more up before they had to make the slow ascent to the surface themselves. It was exhausting work, but they knew that each crate they raised was worth a fortune.

It was planned that they'd continue very early the following morning to raise the remainder of the gold, but not until they'd had something substantial to eat, had a good rest and then thoroughly checked out their diving equipment for their second dive. There was very little margin for error, particularly when they were working at those depths and in such dangerous conditions.

Back up on the surface, Mike Fraser had paddled the dinghy back to the side of the lake with the first lot of gold bullion, where Graham was eagerly awaiting his arrival. When Mike arrived with the first few crates, Graham asked him, *"Is it the gold bullion then?"* Mike nodded *"It sure is. Let's get this lot unloaded and I'll get back out there a.s.a.p. to see what else they've sent up. I don't want to leave them out there for too long without any surface contact."* Graham nodded, *"How many crates do you think there'll be down there in total, Mike?"* he asked Graham. *"Don't really know mate, but don't forget we saw the Germans drop at least twenty-five of them over the side of their launch,"* replied Mike as they heaved the last crate from the RIB. *"Right, see you shortly with even more pay dirt,"* said Mike as he started to paddle away from the shore. A cheerful Graham waved him off, *"Not only is it raining,"* he thought, *"it's raining gold bullion."*

Easing the first crate onto the sack barrow, Graham hauled it across to where the vehicles and trailers were hidden under the camouflage nets, then stashed it at the side of the first trailer. He couldn't resist using a claw hammer to raise the lid of the first crate just so that he could have a sneaky peep at what was inside. Shining his torch on the contents he saw to his delight that the crate was jam-packed full of shiny gold bars, glinting in the torchlight. He rubbed his hands together, smiling gleefully. *"Every one a winner!"* he thought.

Lifting a gold bar out of the first crate just to feel the weight of it, he was surprised at just how heavy it felt. There was something about gold that made his blood race. Replacing the bar and refastening the lid of the crate he returned to the lakeside to move the rest of the crates and get them under cover. It was hard, sweaty work dragging the sack-barrow across the uneven surface, but Graham wasn't worried about that, he was too busy thinking about how much each crate of gold was worth. He was humming the song, "*Happy Days are here again*!"

Down at the murky bottom of Lake Toplitz, Ed and his lads had managed to send just four more crates up to Mike before informing him that they were calling it a day and starting their slow ascent back to the surface. The remainder of the crates would just have to wait until the following day. Well within the safety margins that they'd allowed themselves, they'd managed to raise more crates of gold bullion than expected and had floated them up to Mike without any problems.

It had been cold, hard and dangerous work but the excitement, adrenaline and excellent diving equipment they'd brought had got them through it with relative ease. It had been difficult for Mike to heave the crates onto the dinghy, but he was a big lad and had managed it very well, although he was absolutely exhausted by the time the last crate had risen to the surface of the lake.

As the three divers resurfaced at the side of the dinghy, Ed lifted up his mask and said, "*Hi Mike, if you head for the shore we'll stay at the side of the dinghy and give you a push! Flipper power!*" Mike smiled, nodded and then started paddling for the shore. It worked out well and they reached the shore of the lake just before dawn. Once at the side of the lake they all mucked in to get the dinghy unloaded and the crates out of sight before dragging the RIB over to their campsite and tucking it away under the camouflage netting. Then, finally, they stacked the crates onto the trailers, covering them up, away from prying eyes. After they'd done that, Graham put the kettle on to make a much-needed brew to warm them up and help raise their energy levels.

To celebrate their successful dive, Graham had cooked them all a very simple meaty and filling stew which they washed down with hot, sweet Yorkshire tea. They'd brought along a crate of their favourite German Beer but that would remain untouched until after the diving had been completed. As he tucked into the stew, Mike said, "*It's gone much better and quicker than I expected.*" They all nodded in agreement, "*There's so much that can go wrong, especially at that depth and in those conditions,*" replied Ed, "*and those sunken logs are a damned nuisance. Anyway, better get our heads down and get some kip. We'll need to repeat exactly the same procedure tomorrow morning,*" Mike said, "*Graham, you'd better take the first watch, and I'll take the second one. Ed and the lads will need all the shut-eye they can get. The way things are going, with a bit of luck and a fair wind we should be able to finish the job before sunrise tomorrow morning.*" "*I'll drink to that!*" said Graham.

The following night, after having had a decent amount of sleep, Ed, Diederik and Ludo suited up and helped Mike to relaunch the dinghy, accompanying him out to the middle of the lake where they resumed the second dive and continued raising the gold until eventually there was a total of twenty crates stashed away in the trailers. After they'd surfaced at the end of the second dive, Ed said, "*Mike, there's a few more crates down there, five more to be precise. We've reached the limit of our dive time today, so it'll need one last quick dive tomorrow morning and then I think we'll have got the lot,*" Mike nodded, "*OK lads, let's get this lot over to Graham and get them unloaded then. Same procedure as yesterday.*"

Come very early morning on day three, to everyone's delight, the last five crates had been raised to the surface and heaved on board the RIB. Ed and the boys had had a good scout around the bottom of the lake near the sunken aircraft just to make sure that they hadn't left anything behind before making their way back up to the dinghy. There was an annoying delay whilst Ed returned to the bottom of the lake to cut the small marker buoy free and chuck it and it's support rope into the RIB. They didn't want to leave any traceable evidence behind them at the diving site or evidence of recent activity. All that was left at the bottom of the lake now was the undisturbed little Fieseler Storch aircraft and it's two skeletal occupants, gazing into infinity.

They escorted the dinghy back to shore where it was unloaded, lifted out of the water and then dragged away to be deflated before being packed away in the back of a 4x4. Just as dawn broke, the last five crates were placed inside trailer number three and then covered with a tarpaulin. Job done!

"That's it then troops. Definitely no more crates then?" Graham asked. Ed grinned and replied, *"No, I think we got the lot. Twenty Five crates in all."* *"Come on then,"* said Mike, *"Let's see what culinary delights Graham's prepared for us. I'll bet that it's another one of his rib-clinging stews!"* *"Got it in one,"* said Graham, *"but I've put some curry powder in this one. That stew will put hairs on your chest – oh, and now that you've finished diving we can break open the crate of German hooch and celebrate a job well done,"* said Graham. *"Come on then, let's tie on a nose-bag, have a wet then get our heads down,"* said Ed, *"We can surface at lunchtime, strike camp and get out of this miserable bloody place. It's hardly stopped raining since we arrived."*

It continued raining throughout the morning and everything remained thoroughly soaked. Mike and the divers couldn't have cared less. They were tucked into their sleeping bags in the 4 x 4's catching up on some sleep, *"stacking some 'Zed's'"* as Mike called it. Then, just before lunchtime, the team members surfaced from their slumbers and had a simple meal of soup and sandwiches before carrying out a final check of the area to ensure that absolutely everything had been loaded onto the 4 x 4's and that nothing had been left to indicate that anyone had ever been there.

"OK guys, let's leg it out of here and head back to Amsterdam, whilst our luck holds," said Mike. Ed nodded, *"Yes, we've been very fortunate my friends. The dives went much better than I expected and more importantly, no-one spotted what we were up to."* Mike nodded, *"I don't know about you lot, but I'll be glad to see the back of this sodding place. It has the kiss of death about it."* he said. *"OK then, mount up and start your engines!"* called out a cheerful Graham, *"I'll be the lead elephant."*

'CHAPTER 13'

'Heading for Home'

"*Well lads,*" said Graham, "*I could bloody well kick myself. We didn't factor cloying mud into our plans, did we?*" Because it had been raining solidly all night, the ground around them had turned into a slimy clinging swamp. Under normal circumstances the Mercedes 4 x 4's would have had no trouble at all dealing with that type of terrain, the problem lay with the trailers they were towing. The weight of 'Hitler's Gold' had caused the trailers to sink down to their axles and they refused to move. "*The clock's ticking – we need to get out of here. What the hell do we do now?*" asked Graham. "*I suppose we could run one of the trailers backwards and forwards down to the bottom of the mountain with smaller loads and then repack the trailers once we get onto hard standing, but that will be a bit of a faff and it'll take ages,*" said Mike. Ed nodded in agreement, "*Not only that, my friends, it's quite some distance and we risk the chance of being spotted. It only needs once telephone call to the Bundespolizei and we'll be in big trouble.*"

"*Well we can't linger here.*" said Mike, "*We've pushed our luck so far. If someone does see us and decide to reports our activities to the Austrian authorities we'll be in deep cack.*

Ideas anyone?" he asked. Ludo and Diederik shook their heads. They were the 'persuaders', not the planners. "*What about if I send for a 'T3' and we transport the gold back to Amsterdam in partial loads. That would work, although it all depends if there's a 'T3' going begging. I can always give the office a quick bell and find out?*" said Mike. "*That's a great idea,*" said Ed, "*We should have thought about doing that that in the first place I suppose. Let me call them and see what's what.*" said Mike, wandering off to the side of the vehicles to send make a call. "*Back in a minute, chaps,*" he said cheerfully.

"*Hang on a second, Mike,*" said Ed. Ed turned to Ludo, "*What's the matter son, you look a bit concerned?*" Ludo replied, "*Dunno Pops, I just get a feeling that we're being watched.*" Ed nodded, "*Well why don't you and Diederik have a bit of a scout around the immediate area and see if there's anyone lurking out there in the woods, eh? Probably be just an animal.*" The lads nodded and sidled off to investigate. "*And be careful!*" Ed called after them as they vanished into the trees. Mike moved off to make his call.

When Mike returned he said, "*Good news, I got through to the office and I've organised the loan of a T3.*" he said. Just as Ed started to reply, a small group of men stepped out from behind the trees. Ludo's sixth sense hadn't let him down. One of the arrivals was white-haired and frail, and resting heavily on a shooting stick. "*Good morning, gentlemen,*" he called out in a surprisingly commanding voice for a man of his obviously advanced years.

"*Permit me to introduce myself,*" he said, "*I am Manfred Von Mülheim and these two chaps with me are my sons.*" As he was speaking, Ludo and Diederik returned. They had both eased pistols out of their jackets and were pointing them at the visitors.

Manfred smiled and held up his hand, *"There's no need for any of that, gentlemen. We mean you no harm."* *"What do you want?"* asked Ed. Manfred walked carefully across to Ed and held out his hand, *"I come in peace, my friend. Do you not remember me?"* Ed was puzzled for a moment, *"Remember you? Can't say that I do."* then paused, *"Wait a minute, why yes, of course!"* said Mike, *"Manfred Von Mülheim, you're that German Naval Captain from the war aren't you? You were the Commandant of the Toplitz Naval Base."* Manfred nodded, *"Correct."* then smiled, *"That was a very long time ago and although much has changed since then I can certainly remember your faces."*

Ed turned to his lads, *"Put your guns away boys. It's OK."* Manfred nodded, *"Danke! Do you recall what fun we had with those appalling Nazi's? Such times, eh! Do you mind if I lean against your trailer for a few moments, we have been tramping through these woods for what seems like hours and my legs are no longer what they once were. I even need this damned shooting stick to help me get around. There is no dignity in old age, neh?"*

Mike nodded, *"Yes, now that you mention it I do remember us ducking and diving around Berlin escaping from the Nazis – and remember it hasn't been that long for us."* Manfred nodded, *"Ja, of course, the 'Time-Travel' machine thing. I recall you saying that you'd be back for the gold, but you didn't say when. I couldn't get my head around it all at the time and thought that it was all flimflammery."*

Manfred leaned heavily on the tailboard of one of the trailers and patted the tarpaulin covering the gold bullion containers,

"*So, it appears that you have succeeded where so many others failed. That's quite a lot of the 'Führer's Gold' that you have in your three trailers,*" he said. Mike smiled, "*Aye, we got it all – and it's not the 'Fuhrer's Gold' anymore, it's ours. Finders Keepers. I think we've managed to raise it all – and let me tell you that it hasn't been easy. It's very dodgy at the bottom of that lake. The SS couldn't have chosen a better spot to hide the gold.*" Mike smiled, "*Oh, and there's even an aircraft and two of your chaps down there guarding it.*"

Manfred nodded, "*Ah, that will be the remains of the odious SS-Standartenführer Albrecht Krancher and his unfortunate pilot, I suppose. They were shot down by an Americans aircraft right at the end of the war. There was nothing that could be done to save them. They were seen struggling, but couldn't escape from their damaged Storch which had crash-landed on the surface of the lake. A shame for the poor pilot, but a jolly fine ending for creepy Krancher. It was no less than he deserved, the vile creature. He had a much easier death than many of his innocent victims.*"

Graham gasped, "*Krancher! Wasn't that the nasty little Nazi turd that came to Berlin with us?*" Von Mülheim nodded, "*Yes, the very same.*" Graham asked, "*But I thought that he'd been arrested like us and was due to be topped? I saw him being escorted out of his cell.*" Manfred nodded, "*That is correct, my friend. He was arrested by SS-Obergruppenführer Kaltenbrunner after he made a failed attempt to have Kaltenbrunner assassinated here at Toplitz, but it came out later that Krancher was working covertly for Himmler. General Kaltenbrunner was most displeased when Krancher was reinstated as a Standartenführer by Himmler but was powerless to do anything. Himmler explained it all away as being confusion brought about by the fighting and lack of good communications.*" said Manfred, "*Kaltenbrunner wanted Krancher to be taken outside and put in front of a firing squad, but Himmler ordered Kaltenbrunner to, how do you say it, 'wind his neck in.'*"

Manfred turned to Ed and laughed, "*Yes, I remember you telling me how you removed Himmler and Krancher's trousers and boots before tying the swine to their chairs. I'd have paid good money to have seen them wriggling!*" Ed grinned, "*They were lucky that I didn't top them both there and then! If I'd have had a silencer on my pistol, I would have done - and to hell with the 'Time-Traveller' rules!*" "*You would have done the world a favour had you done so, my friend.*" said Manfred, "*Still, it was all a matter of timing. Himmler escaped the hangman's noose by chewing on a poisoned capsule. He didn't even have the courage to face his enemies – and we all know what happened to Krancher and Kaltenbrunner. They all got their just desserts!*"

As they stood there at the side of the trailer, Manfred said, "*Would you mind if I had a quick look at one of the crates? I'd like to see what all of the fuss has been about.*" Mike replied, "*Feel free.*" Manfred lifted a corner of one of the tarpaulins and examined one of the crates, "*Ach, you can still read the Reichsbank Logo stamped onto the lids. I'm amazed that the crates have held together after all this time. German built you see, made to last. You know, the closest anyone got to finding the 'Führer's Gold' was way back in 1959 when a diving team found the boxes with the counterfeit twenty-pound notes in them that had been hidden at the same time. Twenty-pound notes, huh, totally useless now other than for use as bum paper. A different matter altogether if it had been American dollars.*" He replaced the tarpaulin.

Ed said, "*Listen, we were just about to have a brew, would you and your lads care to step out of the rain and join us?*" Manfred nodded, "*That is very kind of you.*" Ed turned to Ludo and Diederik and said, "*Come on you two, get a brew on then!*" he turned to Manfred, "*Why don't you come and sit in one of the 4 x 4's with me, Graham and Mike and discuss why you're here?*" "*OK,*" replied Manfred patting the crates, "*but I think that you can guess why.*"

Manfred, Mike, Graham, and Ed sat in the Mercedes sipping the hot coffee, whilst Ludo, Diederik and Manfred's two sons, Otto and Karl, remained outside, keeping a wary eye on the gold and each other. "*So, how did you latch on to us then?*" Mike asked Manfred. Manfred smiled, "*Well it wasn't particularly difficult really. We have a little restaurant further along the lake and I keep a very close look at what's happening around here. I knew that eventually someone would come along and try to raise the 'Führer's Gold' despite the previous disastrous failures. I never expected it to be you chaps though, that was a very pleasant surprise.*"

"*How long have you been watching us for then?*" asked Graham. "*Ever since you arrived,*" said Manfred, "*You were spotted when you first set up camp. My son Karl often goes out fishing in the early hours and spotted your vehicles in the woods.*" Ed shook his head, "*I'll have to work on improving my camouflage skills. I've obviously gotten rusty.*"

"*So where do we go from here then?*" asked Ed. "*Well, my friends,*" replied Manfred, "*I thought that perhaps you could see your way to sharing some of the gold with me and my lads. We are not greedy, I would like just enough of the gold to help secure their futures. We don't get many tourists up here now and it's a bit of a struggle keeping our restaurant going if I'm honest."* Mike looked at Graham and Ed, *"What do you reckon, guys?"* They nodded in agreement. *"Fair enough,"* said Mike, *"we're OK with that and I'm sure that Ed's two lads won't mind. Fair's fair, the gold came from Germany so I suppose you've got a bit of a claim on it."* Manfred smiled, *"Well that's a bit of a tenuous link, but it will do for me. Thank you!"*

After a short discussion, the men had reached a 'Gentleman's Agreement' and decided to hand over five of the crates of the 'Führer's Gold' to Manfred and his sons, after all, they'd agreed, there was plenty of gold for everyone, so they shook hands on the deal. Ed wiped the mist off the vehicle's window and said, *"See Manfred, things are looking up. It's even stopped raining!"*

"Incidentally, Manfred, I was wondering, what happened to you after we dropped you off in central Berlin in 1945?" asked Graham. *"What, after we'd escaped from the Reich Main Security Office?"* replied Manfred. Graham nodded, *"Yes, remember, we nicked Kaltenbrunner's staff car. A cracking vehicle that, wish I had it now, it'd be worth a packet."* Mike smiled, *"You can make that your next project, Graham – 'Find Kaltenbrunner's staff car!' It's probably either in Russia or America. That's where most of the good stuff went to at the end of the war."*

Manfred smiled, *"After you very kindly dropped me off near the Berlin Zoo, for which I am eternally grateful, I eventually managed to make my way through the confusion of war-torn Germany and got back here to Toplitz. It wasn't easy though. There were many SS Death Squads roaming around Berlin that day, hanging innocents from lamp-posts, even though it was blindingly obvious that Germany had lost the war and the Third Reich was collapsing about our ears. I had plenty of Kriegsmarine friends and contacts who were happy to help to provide me with food and clothing and help me make my way back home. I was just one of many thousands of 'refugees.' As you may or may not know, Herr Hitler had made contingency plans to continue the fight from elsewhere and despite what history tells us, had slipped off into the shadows. The gold bullion that was deposited in Lake Toplitz was a key part of his funding for future plans. I was determined that neither he nor any of his cohorts would get their hands on it, so I've been watching the site ever since. Only a very few of us knew of the gold and its precise whereabouts, but rather surprisingly no-one came seeking it until well after the war. Luckily they didn't get anywhere near to locating it."*

"You see, unfortunately, Krancher and Kaltenbrunner had virtually everyone on the base involved with hiding the gold arrested, executed or in the case of the SS escorts sent off out into the streets of Berlin to fight the Russians. Not a single one of them was ever heard from again. I'll leave it to your imagination to figure out what happened to them. It was tragic, there were some good and brave men here. Anyway, we received a call from a contact in Berlin saying that Krancher was flying into the base as an emissary from Himmler, so I had a small party of the few loyal guards that remained, waiting at the lakeside to detain him. I really wanted to shoot him myself. Fortunately, an American pilot resolved that little issue for me by shooting his aircraft down. A fitting end for the schweinehunde! Kaltenbrunner and his girlfriend also hot-footed it here, but fortunately he had no time to do anything as the Americans were snapping at his heels. He ran off with his paramour and hid in the mountains."

Mike said, "*Yes, I read up on that. Kaltenbrunner had slid off to a mountain hut and was in hiding there until he was denounced and got arrested. Apparently, he tried to claim that he was a Doctor, of all things.*" Manfred nodded, "*That is correct, my friend. 'Doctor Death!' The Assistant Burgermeister of nearby Alt Aussee, Johann Brandauer, a jolly fine chap and dear friend of mine, had heard that Kaltenbrunner was hiding out in the hut and informed the relevant Allied authorities who then went up there and captured him. The brave Kaltenbrunner surrendered without a fight. He eventually received his just desserts at the Nuremberg Trials when they stretched his neck- and of course once Herr Himmler had chomped on his suicide capsule, the gold, and its precise whereabouts was forgotten – or at least that's what I thought, There were only two other key personnel that knew about the gold bullion, Martin Bormann and Kaltenbrunner's Adjutant, Arthur Scheidler, both of whom vanished without trace and have not surfaced since.*" "*What about Hitler,*" asked Mike, "*he knew?*" Manfred smiled, "*As you know, he was never seen again, but I have my suspicions.*"

"*Whatever happened to Kaltenbrunner's flash girlfriend, the blonde with the big title?*" asked Graham. Manfred smiled, "*You mean Gräfin, or as you would say, Countess, Gisela Von Westarp?*" Graham nodded. "*Well, apparently she bore Kaltenbrunner twins and then faded into well-earned obscurity. I believe that she died in Munich in 1983 or thereabouts.*" "*You'd have thought that she'd try and get her hands on the gold, She knew that it was here in Lake Toplitz,*" said Graham. Manfred nodded, "*Well perhaps with the help of her son or daughter she might have wanted to organise some sort of recovery programme, although she may well have not passed the information on to them and was just waiting to receive further instructions herself. We'll never know now."*

"*So,* why *didn't you try to raise the gold yourself?"* asked Ed. "*It would have been too difficult and expensive for me to do that, my friend. I knew roughly where the gold was but not its precise location. I couldn't afford to mount a search – you must know the cost of ROV's! (Remote Operated Vehicles) and support diving equipment! Not only that, unlike you, we didn't have access to any diving expertise in my family and we would have had to involve too many people. The information would inevitably have leaked to the Austrian authorities and they would have inevitably tried to raise and keep the gold bullion for themselves."*

"*Many other groups tried to locate the gold and as you know, some of them died. Krancher, who had originally selected the hiding place for the gold, was very clever. He knew that Lake Toplitz was deep and dangerous and therefore the gold would be safe down there. Also, as you can imagine, there are many eyes and ears around here and still many Nazi sympathisers who would love to get their hands on the gold to help fund and further their ambitions. My two boys knew all about the gold and hoped eventually to retrieve it. We just don't have the funds or expertise available to do it.*"

"*Well, we've saved you the trouble now, Manfred, we found it and lifted it all."* said Ed, "*There is one little problem, though. We're having difficulty moving the gold out of here because of the weight versus the boggy ground. The trucks are OK, it's the bloody trailers that won't budge.*" Manfred nodded, "*Presumably you have made or are making alternative arrangements to get the gold out of here. I can't see you falling at the last hurdle?"*

Mike smiled, *"We've decided to use our 'T3 Travellator' to move the stuff to Amsterdam."* Manfred looked puzzled, *"A 'T3 Travellator'? I do not understand."* Mike grinned, *"All will be revealed shortly,"* said Mike, continuing, *" It'll take a couple of journeys in the 'T3' and we'll have to unload the gold out of the wooden containers first, but we can manage that OK."* *"My lads can give you a hand with the cross-loading if you wish?"* said Manfred. *"Great. The more hands the merrier."* replied Mike, *"And we'd better burn the wooden crates once we've finished. Don't want to leave any evidence behind."*

Manfred smiled and said, *"You know, Mike, it's funny, I read an article recently in the 'Toplitz Zeitung' about this strange 'Time-Travel' business and now that I think back, I recall hearing you discuss it when we were on the run in Berlin. I confess I didn't have a clue what you were talking about back then, and I'm not really sure that I do so now!"* Mike laughed, *"Well, the latest 'T3 Travellator' will be arriving here very shortly, so you'll be able to see one in action for yourself."* Manfred nodded, *"I can't wait!'* he said.

"The principle of Time-Travel is very interesting, Mike. Does it mean therefore that I could travel back in time and say, for instance, meet up with my younger self?" asked Manfred. Mike shook his head, *"Fraid not, that's against all of the rules. I mean, you'd be able to see yourself from a distance, but you're absolutely forbidden to make any form of contact."* Manfred said, *"What a damn shame, I would have liked to have met up with my younger self and perhaps given myself a few share tips, something like that!"* Mike laughed, *"That's precisely why it's forbidden. It's so that you can't change anything that would affect the course of history in any way, you're not even supposed to swat flies!"* Manfred sighed, *"Ah well, it was just a thought. Back to reality."*

Manfred looked at his watch, *"Time flies like an arrow. I'll send one of my sons back to the restaurant for a Quad bike and trailer to help move our share of the gold back there if that's OK with you?"* Mike nodded in agreement. As they were speaking there was a disturbance in the air at the side of the vehicles and a 'T3' started to de-materialise. "*Here we go then,*' said Mike. *"the Seventh Cavalry has arrived*! *OK, let's do it!*" he shouted to the others, "*Come on troops, let's get stuck in,*" said Graham, heaving the tarpaulin off the first trailer.

'CHAPTER 14'

'What Comes Next?'

The transfer of the gold to Amsterdam via the 'T3' had gone extremely well and the few bars that remained were now resting securely in the Swiss bank's vaults, tucked away as a 'rainy day' fund. The main body of the gold had been melted down and sold on to dealers in the Channel Islands, the profit from the sale being shared out equally amongst the 'Gold Recovery Crew' – minus the expenses for the expedition, which were minimal by comparison. The 'Gold Recovery Crew' had all done extremely well out of the deal and not one of them would ever have to work again unless they really wanted to. The vast profits they had made sat safely in their secret numbered accounts in the Swiss bank.

Ed had tipped a grateful Manfred Von Mülheim off about the Swiss bank that he used for his transactions and had also put him in touch with his contact there, so Manfred and his sons were able to resolve their own financial issues and could live happily ever after running their family restaurant on the side of Lake Toplitz, watching knowingly as various treasure hunters came searching for the 'Fuhrer's Gold.' Of course, Manfred and his lads remained silent about the whereabouts of the gold and their involvement in its recovery. Why spoil a good story by revealing the truth - after all, Manfred said, *"Look how the' Loch Ness Monster' continues to attract tourists from all over the world*!"

A few weeks later, when everything had quietened down, Mike and Graham were sat chatting over a cup of coffee in Mike's Hull-based office. *"So, Mike,"* said Graham, *"how does it feel to be the sole owner of 'Time-Travellers' then*?" Mike grinned, *"It feels very nice, thank you. Once the government licensing approval comes through I'll be much happier though. Everything's ground to a halt at the moment. I've even sent the office girls off on paid holiday until the licensing comes through. It's costing me a bomb."* *"You don't need to worry about that, you've got plenty of money you tight Scottish git!"* said Graham. Mike laughed, *"I, we, have now that Ed's had notification that the sale of the gold has finally been cleared through our Swiss Bank."* *"Yes, I expected a few problems there, what with it being Reichsbank Gold, covered in swastikas. I mean, in reality, I suppose that it should have gone back to Germany,"* said Graham.

"The Swiss bankers won't be too fussy about handling Reichsbank Gold," said Mike, *"their vaults will be full of stuff like that. The value of our loot will be chicken feed compared to what they'll have stashed away in their vaults – and I don't agree with you that the gold should have gone back to the Germans. They'll have nicked it from someone else in the first place. Anyway, now that it's been melted down it's untraceable."* *"Suppose you're right,"* said Graham.

Graham continued, *"Now Mike, I want to discuss something else with you. Brace yourself because I've had another idea."* *"You never stop do you, Graham. Louis the Sixteenth, Henry the Eighth, François the Marquess of whatever it was, and last but not least, 'Hitler's Gold.' Haven't you got enough loot stashed away in the bank, you old Yorkshire nipscrew? You've nearly got as much money in the bank as the Queen!"* Graham shook his head, *"I've told you before, Mike, it's not the money, it's the excitement and challenge of the chase."* Mike smiled, *"Go on then, let's hear it. what've you got up your sleeve this time?"*

"Have you ever heard of Colonel Blood?" asked Graham. Mike nodded, *"Yes, it's a film starring the actor Errol Flynn. A good old rollicking pirate movie. Ha Har!"* *"No,"* said Graham, *"not Errol Flynn! I mean the real Colonel Blood, the Irish guy that tried to steal the English Crown Jewels."* *"Well I can remember vaguely that someone once tried to nick the Crown Jewels, but that's about all I do know, to be honest,"* said Mike.

"Colonel Thomas Blood was an Irish adventurer. He was a Parliamentarian during the Civil War and because he chose the wrong side to fight with was punished by being deprived of his estates at the Restoration. He was left on the bones of his arse. I've been reading up on it at the library and making some notes," said Graham, pulling out a small notebook, *"Interested?"* he asked Mike. Mike sighed, *"Go on then."*

"Well, briefly, and I'm paraphrasing here, on the 9th of May 1671," said Graham, *"Thomas Blood and three of his mates, names not known interestingly, somehow blagged their way into the Tower of London, captured the 'Keeper of the Jewels' and gave him a thoroughly good seeing to before stealing a State Crown and the Sceptered Orb from the Crown Jewels. To cut a long story short, they very nearly got away with both items, but got captured."*

"*Hang on a minute, mate!*" said Mike, "*You're not seriously suggesting that we go after the English Crown Jewels are you?*" Graham nodded and smiled, "*I am – and there's more! On the very same subject, did you know that someone also tried to lift the French Crown Jewels?*" "*I didn't know that the French had any!*" said Mike.

Graham flipped over a couple of pages in his notebook, "*Oh – oui - certainement! They've got some right crackers, they're on display in Paris at the moment - but some of them were stolen during the French Revolution in 1792 when the French Royal Treasury was stormed and sacked by rioters. Also, their Queen, Marie Antoinette, had some of her jewels sent to Italy when things started to get difficult. Most, though not all, of the French Crown Jewels, were eventually recovered, and that's the interesting bit, 'most – though not all were recovered.' I'm intrigued. I want to find out what happened to those jewels that weren't recovered. I think that they're still somewhere, probably in Italy.*"

Mike laughed, "*Right, so you're not content with getting involved with Colonel Blood and the English Crown Jewels, you want us to have a crack at the French ones as well?*" Graham nodded, "*Well, we've got plenty of money available to fund two new expeditions and once you get the 'Time-Travellers' license back we'll be able to trot all over the shop using the new 'T3 Travellator' Are you up for it?*" he asked. "*Well I admit, it all sounds very interesting, Graham. Incidentally, who were those three 'mysterious' blokes that accompanied Colonel Blood?*" Mike asked. "*Ah, well, thereby hangs a tale,*" said Graham.

*** THE END ***

Final Notes:

Adolf Hitler, the Führer – is purported to have shot his wife Eva and then committed suicide inside his private quarters in the Führerbunker on the 30th of April 1945 -   but did that really happen? There are many stories intimating that Adolf and Eva escaped from Berlin when the fighting was at its fiercest. Hitler's place in the Führerbunker could easily have been taken by his lookalike, Gustav Weler. (*See 'Three Tall Tales' - 'Does the Führer Live?' by this author*).

Heinrich Himmler, Reichsführer-SS. When the Third Reich collapsed in chaos and defeat, Himmler slinked off into hiding under the alias of Sergeant Heinrich Hitzinger. He was stopped and detained at an Allied checkpoint and then moved around to several prison camps until eventually being taken to the British 31st Civilian Interrogation Camp near Lüneburg, Germany on the 23rd of May 1945, after which he was taken to the Headquarters of the 2nd British Army in Lüneburg, where a Doctor attempted to conduct a medical examination on him. When the Doctor began looking inside Himmler's mouth, Himmler jerked his head away and bit into a potassium cyanide pill that had been hidden in his tooth. The ex-Reichsführer-SS died shortly afterward. His body is buried in an unmarked grave near

Lüneburg, a fitting end for an evil 'Henchenbauer' (*Chicken Farmer*).

Martin Bormann, SS-Obergruppenführer, Head of Nazi Party Chancellery, Hitler's Private Secretary and Party Minister of the National Socialist German Worker's Party – was allegedly killed by enemy shelling in central Berlin whilst attempting to escape on the 2nd of May 1945, but was thought by some to have escaped. Over the coming years, the CIA and the West German Government tried unsuccessfully to locate Bormann. Sightings were reported at points all over the world, including Australia, Denmark, Italy, and South America. Nazi intelligence officer Reinhard Gehlen even claimed that Bormann had been a Soviet spy and that he had escaped to Moscow. 'Nazi Hunter' Simon Wiesenthal firmly believed that Bormann was living in South America. In 1963, a retired postal worker named Albert Krumnow told police that around 8 May 1945 the Soviets had ordered him and his colleagues to bury two bodies found near the railway bridge at Lehrter Station, West Berlin. On the 7th of December 1972, construction workers uncovered human remains near the station, a few feet from the spot where Krumnow claimed to have buried them. When an autopsy was conducted, fragments of glass were found in the jaws of both skeletons, suggesting that the men had committed suicide by biting cyanide capsules. Dental records identified one of the skeletons as being Bormann's. Forensic examiners determined that the size of the skeleton and the shape of the skull were identical to Bormann's. Soon afterward, the West German government declared Bormann dead. The remains were finally identified as being Bormann's in 1998 when German authorities ordered genetic testing on fragments of the skull. Bormann's remains were then cremated and his ashes scattered in the Baltic Sea on the 16th of August 1999.

Ernst Kaltenbrunner, SS-Obergruppenführer and Chief of the Reich Main Security Office - was discovered hiding out in the Austrian mountains in a cabin near Alt Autensee. After a short standoff, Kaltenbrunner surrendered without a shot being fired. Kaltenbrunner claimed to be a Doctor and offered up a false name. However, upon his arrival under escort back at the nearby local town, his mistress, Gräfin Gisela Von Westarp, spotted him as he was being led away, called out his name and rushed to hug him. Her action resulted in Kaltenbrunner's positive identification. He was eventually taken to Nuremberg where he was tried and found guilty of war crimes at the Nuremberg Tribunals and was executed by hanging on the 16th of October 1946. He was cremated, and his ashes scattered in a tributary of the River Isar.

Gräfin Gisela Von Westarp - Her only 'crime' was that of being Kaltenbrunner's long-term Mistress. Gisela died, at the relatively early age of 62, in München (Munich), on the 2nd of June 1983.

Also by Terry Cavender
(*Available on Amazon Books/Amazon Kindle*)

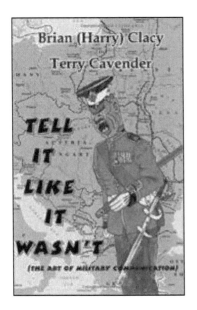